Tom McNab has experienced success as Olympic coach, prize winning novelist and Technical Director of the Oscar-winning film *Chariots of Fire*. He has coached international athletes, the British Olympic Bobsleigh team and England's silver medal-winning squad in Rugby's 1992 World Cup. In the same year, he was awarded the British Coach of the Year. In Tom's early days of teaching he was instantly recognised for his outstanding ability in being able to bring the best out of young athletes. As National Athletics Coach, Tom created several programmes, including the national decathlon programme, which produced Daley Thompson.

Tom has written several bestselling novels, including his worldwide best-seller, *Flanagan's Run*, which has been republished by Sandstone Press. The volume, *The Fast Men*, his unique marriage of Western and Athletics novels followed with similar success. In 1982 he won the Scottish Novelist of the Year award and his repertoire of sporting films includes his work as script consultant and technical advisor for *Chariots of Fire*.

Also published by Sandstone Press

Flanagan's Run

THE FAST MEN

Tom McNab

SANDSTONEPRESS
HIGHLAND | SCOTLAND

This edition published in Great Britain by
Sandstone Press Ltd
Dochcarty Road
Dingwall
Ross-shire
IV15 9UG
Scotland.

www.sandstonepress.com

Commissioning Editor: Robert Davidson
Technical Assistance: David Ritchie

First published in the United States of America in 1986 by Simon and Schuster
First published Great Britain in 1987 by Arrow

The publisher acknowledges support from
Creative Scotland towards publication of this volume.

ISBN: 978-1-910124-63-5
ISBNe: 978-1-910124-64-2

Cover design by Two Associates, London
Typeset by Iolaire Typesetting, Newtonmore
Printed and bound by CPI Group (UK) Ltd, Croydon CR0 4YY

CONTENTS

PROLOGUE

1876 was the year of the Little Big Horn. It was also the first
season of the National Baseball League, the pennant going to
the Chicago White Stockings. 'Vagrant' won the Kentucky
Derby and 'Shirley' the Preakness. At Covington, Kentucky,
the Englishman Joe Goss took the heavyweight bare-knuckle
championship of the world, beating the American, Tom Allen.
The first national intercollegiate track and field meet was won
by Princeton in July, while a month later the America's Cup
was won by the United States boat *Madeleine*.

For generations of filmgoers, the Wild West has been the
world of Buffalo Bill, Billy the Kid and Wyatt Earp, a place
where speed of draw was paramount. But, as they trekked
west across the Great Plains, European immigrants brought
with them a complete culture, one ranging from theatre to
sport.

Thus each cow-town or mining camp had, alongside its
troupe of visiting actors, its best fist-fighter, horseshoe pitcher,
wrestler or horseman. And if they were truly fortunate they
had a Fast Man: a sprinter on whom they could lay their
money, a man who could show his heels to any visitor who
fancied his fleetness of foot.

This is the story of two such men, footracers separated only
by inches on the running-path; of their rivalry and their
comradeship.

1

1

THE MADMEN IN THE VALLEY

White Wolf would always remember the day the madmen came to the valley.

He had long dreamed of such a moment — when the white man would come with all the warriors gone and only he, White Wolf, there able to save the tribe. Then his father Swift Dog would return and White Wolf would point to what he had done, show the scalps, limp and blood-red, dangling by Swift Dog's tepee.

But it had not been as he had dreamed. His father had that morning posted him on the bluff above the valley and he had spent the hours peering down its broken slopes to the winding path leading through it, the only way east to the white man's village, a day's ride away. But no one had come, and he had laid at noon on his back on a flat rock above the canyon, dozily enjoying the warmth of the spring sun on his stocky brown body.

After a while he had taken to practising with his bow, aiming at a twisted yucca twenty paces away. He had loosed a hundred shots, only sixteen on target, before his arms began to tire, and at noon he had dawdled his way home down the slopes, kicking at stones, towards the lazy, vertical smokes of the camp a hundred yards away, on the banks of a turgid stream. He had idled through the village, swiping at the camp dogs with a branch, and stopping for a moment to watch his friends poking at three tethered sparrows.

3

He walked on to the tent of his sister, Morning Star, at the edge of the village, near the stream. It was for her feast that the warriors hunted, the feast that would mark her time of readiness. Five days of celebration, not a glimpse of which she would be allowed, after which her eyebrows would be plucked and she would be available to suitors. White Wolf knew that it would be a great occasion, a time of tall tales from gnarled warriors of battles with the Spaniards, of days past when a Sioux on horseback with a quiver of arrows was more than a match for the White Eye with his slow-loading rifle. Though he had never understood the feast's significance, for him it would be a time of a full belly, of venison, honeycakes and perhaps even an illicit swig of the potent *twili-kah-yee*.

The thought of the feast made him more aware of his present hunger. As he approached her tepee Morning Star was absorbed in her work. She squatted in the midday sun, sewing tinsel and bells on to the skirts of her brown buckskin robe, smiling to herself. He stood above her, shifting from foot to foot, eager for her attention. Without indicating her knowledge of his presence she abruptly stopped her work and crawled back into the tepee.

It seemed like hours to him before she emerged, her hands behind her back, her wide black eyes sparkling.

'Shut your eyes and put out your hands,' she said. This he had obediently done, to feel something soft in one hand, something hard and leathery in the other.

'Open them.

When he had done so it was to see two cornflour cakes in his right hand and some brown pemmican in his left. As he rushed off to resume his vigil she shouted after him, 'That must last till sundown.' But he did not hear her.

The food had lasted barely twenty minutes and then, drowsy, he had experienced difficulty in keeping his eyes open as he lay back on the rock and gazed down into the mouth of the valley in the still heat of the early afternoon. Then he

4

remembered his spear, standing vertical since morning in the soft earth beside the rock.

He picked it up and laid it flat along his palm, doing as Swift Dog had told him, placing index and third finger behind the binding to give him a strong ledge on which to pull. He was taking aim at the arrow-scarred yucca when he heard the whinny of horses below. At once he dropped his spear, scampered to the flat overhang and looked down into the shadowy depths.

A covered wagon, drawn by two horses, had trundled into the mouth of the valley and had stopped in the shadow of the slope above, furthest from him, about two hundred yards away to his left. Its driver, a tall, lean, slightly stooped man in black trousers and boots, white collarless shirt and Mexican sombrero, jumped down from the wagon and walked round to the back where he was momentarily hidden from sight. When the man reappeared he was naked from the waist up, his trunk stark white in the shadows. He was wearing red long-johns and what appeared to be black moccasins. White Wolf scrutinised the white man as he walked to the front of the wagon and watered his horses. The man was clearly not young, about the same age as his father, but strangely his walk had the spring and bounce of youth.

The man stood for a moment at the base of the hill, then began to run quickly up its rough, rocky slope. All the way up the white man's rhythm was unbroken, until he finally reached the summit and leant forward, chest heaving, hands on knees. White Wolf would always remember him as he stretched and stood to his full height, the marvel of his whiteness in the sun. Then the man jogged slowly back down to the base of the hill.

For a moment, White Wolf considered running back to the village to bring the other boys. No, he thought: this is *my* moment. I am the one who was asked to guard the camp, who has spent all day boiling here in the hot sun. This is mine.

When the man reached the base of the hill he turned and immediately started on his way up again, at the same inexorable pace as the first time. But as he attained the mid-point of the hill there was another visitor to the canyon. It was a younger man, dressed in buckskins and riding a brown pinto. The rider looked up at the older man, who was now struggling, only a few yards away from the hill's crest. As the runner reached it and turned to look down into the canyon the newcomer shouted to him and waved. The runner, leaning forward, chest heaving, raised an arm in recognition. He then jogged down the zig-zag path to the base of the hill, pebbles and dust spurring before him.

The men shook hands, the rider dismounted and both went to the back of the wagon, out of sight. When they reappeared a few moments later all had changed. For the runner was fully dressed and it was the rider who was stripped to the waist, clad in white long-johns and black leather moccasins.

The younger man walked away from the wagon and out into the depths of the canyon, taking strange, stretched paces, his arms stiff and straight. He walked over a hundred paces into the gloom of an overhang on the other side, scratched the ground with his right foot in front of him, stopped, then pawed the earth, first with one foot then the other. Finally he turned to face the wagon and stood quite still.

The older man shouted and raised his right arm high. The other raised his in response. White Wolf ignored the roughness of the rock as he stretched full length, straining his eyes to pick out the young man now standing in shadow on his right.

The man at the wagon suddenly dropped his right hand and the young man rushed towards him down the valley. White Wolf had never seen anyone run at such speed, his legs a white blur. Stranger still, up from the valley came a staccato scratching noise with each stride. The man surged past the wagon, then eased off to a lope, next a jog, before turning to walk back to the wagon, where he stood, circling his arms and talking with the man in black. Even from the hill White Wolf could see the gleam of sweat on the runner's milk-white torso.

A few minutes later the whole process was repeated, with

6

the young man in white long-johns again bounding up the valley like some wild and wonderful animal chased by eager hunters. So engrossed was White Wolf that he pressed forward, causing a tiny cascade of pebbles to tumble down towards the valley floor. But neither of the white men noticed. They were too involved in studying something which gleamed in the older man's right hand.

Then came the strangest thing of all. The runner took off his long-johns and shoes, and for the first time in his life White Wolf saw a naked white man, the hairy blackness at the base of his trunk in stark contrast to the white of his body and legs. The older man went to the back of the wagon and returned with a bucket of water, which he proceeded to splash over the naked runner, who whooped and shouted as the cold water hit his skin.

The sun was fading fast as the runner made his way to the back of the wagon and returned fully clothed in his brown buckskins. The men shook hands and the rider re-mounted his pinto and trotted slowly east, down the valley. A few moments later the older man again took his place at the reins of his horses, turned his wagon and made west, into the setting sun.

White Wolf stood up cautiously then scampered down the hill back into the village, his head buzzing with the strange tale; but it was hours before the warriors were due to return, and his story trembled on the tip of his tongue as he sat waiting beside Morning Star, who continued to work quietly and assiduously on her robe.

When the warriors returned, three hours later, heavy with deer, White Wolf rushed to his father, the words tumbling from him. Swift Dog had listened with patience, for he knew that his son was as conscientious in his duties as any boy of ten was likely to be. Then, summoning the medicine man, Dark Cloud, and four warriors, Swift Dog made his way down to the valley floor.

At the mouth of the valley the warriors found what they sought. Yes, a lightly-laden wagon had been there, with two horses, both well-shod. So, too, had a horse and rider. The slope

7

where White Wolf had first seen the older man run was pored over, yard by yard. It was agreed that someone had indeed passed that way, the depth of the indentations clearly indicating that he had run, rather than walked, upon its surface.

Swift Dog and Dark Cloud together followed the path of the second man up the canyon, checking every foot of its rough, dusty surface. It was clear to see that someone had indeed run upon the canyon floor, but not with moccasins, nor with white man's shoes. The marks were unknown to them, and this disturbed Dark Cloud.

Most troubling of all was the point at which White Wolf had seen the White Eye start his run. For there, beside a scrape on the ground, similar to that made by a knife or a pawing dog, were two shallow holes, about a foot-length apart. It was then that Dark Cloud asked if either man had made any sign, and if so, had it been towards the sun? White Wolf recalled the raising of the hand and Dark Cloud shook his head. But the medicine man appeared most troubled when White Wolf spoke of the naked man and his cleansing with water, and he began to shuffle, shake his prayer-bones and mutter to himself.

From all of this Swift Dog kept himself aloof, pressing his lips together with thumb and index finger and looking up to the mouth of the valley, then bending to place his fingers in the two indentations. The warriors crowded round Swift Dog, jabbering, then fell silent as they saw that he was at last ready to make his opinion known.

Finally Swift Dog rose, and Dark Cloud, White Wolf and the others waited in silence for his judgement. He looked up the canyon and pointed to its mouth, then placed his hand back to his lips. Swift Dog took a deep breath and put his finger to his right temple in a screwing motion.

'Madmen,' he said. 'Madmen.'

Buck Miller had passed through Custer's Camp just three miles outside Canyon City. The 7th Cavalry were based on the banks of Sun River, a skeleton force being left to guard the camp while the majority of the soldiers had ridden into town for the festivities. As he trotted through the camp which straddled the road Buck exchanged badinage with the guards who squatted by their tents rolling cigarettes or playing cards and dice. Buck wondered if he might catch a glimpse of Custer's woman, the fabulous Indian girl Monah Seetah. She was Custer's personal interpreter, though he'd heard tell she understood not a word of English. Buck often wondered how well she had interpreted the general.

As he rode, Buck thought of what was to come in Canyon City and of what lay directly behind him, packed in his saddle bag, sharp, supple and new, and his pulse quickened. When they had arrived back in Culver City he had spent all morning greasing them, flexing them, caressing them. Now both they and he were ready.

He felt the sweat again begin to gather on his upper lip, hanging for a moment on the shadow of a past black moustache. In a reflex action he wiped his mouth and forehead with the back of his hand.

He came upon the first banner on the outskirts of town, in the Chinese quarter, a hundred-yard straggle of laundries, eating houses and shops lying at right angles to Main Street. It was strung across the dusty street about six feet above him, a twenty-foot by four-foot banner made of rough white canvas, declaring, 'GRAND FOUNDER'S DAY SPORTS GALA', with a confetti of Chinese writing underneath it, probably saying the same thing.

But none of the Chinese showed much of a sporting inclination, he noted. Ancient, withered men sat in the boardwalk sun serenely playing chess or a game involving pebbles which he could not fathom. Others practised strange, slow-motion shadow-boxing in the street, oblivious to the screaming half-naked children who scampered past and round them. Buck reflected that he had never seen no Chinee worth a lick at no sport, and never likely would.

9

But even before he directed his pinto into Main Street he could hear the noise, a mixture of music, shouting and babble, spilling out from the town's centre of gravity, the three hundred yards of Main Street itself.

As he turned right at Conlon's Hostelry he was engulfed in a mass of men on foot and horseback — farmers, mountain men, soldiers, miners. To his left was a tight circle of men, knees bent, eyes fixed on a flutter of fighting cocks who screeched below them on the street. As he passed, one of the cocks dropped limp on the dust of an improvised cockpit and the winner's owner grabbed his crowing bird in both hands and kissed its bloody neck. Meanwhile his winnings were collected by a friend — a negro in blood-stained dungarees — from the circle around the cockpit.

The man, burly and bearded, his face spattered with his bird's blood, raised the cock above his head in triumph. 'I've got me a dandy fighting bird!' he roared, spitting the cock's blood on to the road. 'I got me a real dandy!'

Buck was soon swamped by the crowds — and the noise of a brass band, pumping out a blare of military marches about a hundred yards down the street, in front of the Last Chance Hotel. For a moment he was forced to stop, because of the mass of people pressing around him. Several drunks were weaving across the street like corks on a choppy sea.

Buck's mount, distressed by the pressure of the crowds, became restless, whinnying and twisting. Buck removed his hat, leaned forward and cupped his hat to his horse's ear, then whispered into it. The effect was immediate. The animal calmed and steadied. Buck smiled and replaced his hat, tightening its face thong at the chin as he did so.

Across the road, to his right, on an improvised stage, stood a large bearded man, stripped to the waist, his white belly flopping over his trouser belt. He was wrestling with a black bear, which seemed to have little heart for the battle. It was not much of a bear, a scraggy creature with rheumy eyes and

10

mangy coat; but then, Buck observed, it was not much of a man either. A space opened in front of him and he moved into it, observing below him a row of steaming brown puddings of horse droppings. He wrinkled his nose as the rich smell reached his nostrils, then leaned forward to check the surface of the street below him. It was good. And flat. And he had coped with horse-shit before.

He edged slowly up Main Street, only to be stopped once more, this time by a crowd which stood transfixed round a card-sharp who had placed a green baize table at the edge of the sidewalk. There were three cards face down on the table and the sharp, a lean, wiry little man with a waxed snuff-coloured moustache and impeccable white ruffled shirt and black bow-tie, lifted the middle card and held it aloft, facing his audience.

'Here you are, gentlemen,' he shouted, in a thin, wheedling voice. 'The ace of hearts is the winning card. Follow it with your eyes as I shuffle.'

He shuffled and reshuffled the three cards on the table surface, then stopped and looked at his audience.

'Here it is, you see. And here again. The ace of hearts, gentlemen, is the winning card. Please note that Carl Medina takes no bets from paupers, cripples or orphan children.'

The man continued to move the cards back and forward on the table. Buck felt certain he had located the ace. But when the sharp picked it up from the table Buck knew that he had been wrong.

The ace of hearts. It is my regular trade, gentlemen, to move my hands quicker than your eyes. Remember, you always have two chances to my one. The ace of hearts. If your sight is good enough, you beat me and I pay; if not, I beat you and take your money. The ace of hearts. You will go me twenty? My hands against your eyes!' He reshuffled the cards on the table and there was a rush to place bets.

Buck smiled and pushed slowly on along the seething street. There was a sudden roar from the crowd on his right, just beyond

11

the wrestling stage, as a cowboy, stripped to the waist, reeled back, spitting blood and teeth on the raised platform of a crude boxing ring. The would-be boxer, bellowing in pain, bounced off the ropes, to be felled in one blow by a gnarled prizefighter with a face like the shape of Ireland. The cowboy lay face down, blood spurring from his nose, while friends stood above him, sloshing water from a bucket over his head. Above the ring, leaning from the windows of a house that proclaimed itself 'The Golden Nugget Saloon', grotesquely rouged girls from the local sporting house waved at the men below.

A sure and certain path to pain, embarrassment and mercury ointment, thought Buck, nudging his way towards the Last Chance, now only fifty yards away on his left. Just before the hotel, in direct competition with a medicine show across the street, stood a gaudily-coloured wooden wagon, and in front of it a small stage. Behind them on a tiny stage was propped an even more garish canvas backdrop, depicting the drawing-room of a mansion, and having at its top the words, 'Paris, France'. On the side of the wagon was emblazoned the legend 'MORIARTY'S THEATRE OF THE WEST' while on the stage stood a man and a woman, facing each other, waiting for the laughter of the crowd below them to subside.

The woman, red-haired, in her early thirties, was dressed in a magnificent green silk gown, and strikingly handsome. The man, slightly older, lean and aristocratic, wore a black 'Sunday-go-to-meeting' suit and shining patent leather shoes; but his most significant feature was a mop of curly black hair.

'Do you believe in clubs for women?' asked the woman, in a clear, bell-like voice.

'Only if all else fails,' replied the man, winking as the audience roared.

'Look at my clothes, Moriarty,' said the woman. 'If someone came to visit me they would think I was your cook.'

'Not if they stayed to dinner,' replied the man, holding his stomach, as the laughter erupted again.

12

'And what about your drinking?' she said, hands on hips. 'If you hadn't drunk so much last night, you wouldn't be feeling so horrible.'

'The drink had nothing to do with it,' replied the man. 'I went to bed feeling wonderful and woke up feeling horrible. It was the sleeping that did the damage.'

He surveyed her critically. 'Anyhow, look at you,' he said. 'Five years and you still look the same as you did at our wedding.'

She grimaced, arms akimbo. 'I should,' she said. 'I'm still wearing the same dress.'

Unlike those around him Buck did not laugh. Instead, his clear blue eyes narrowed and he shook his head before dismounting and tying his pinto to the hitching-rail in front of the Last Chance. He climbed up on to the boardwalk, then up the steps to the saloon.

The foyer of the Last Chance buzzed with activity. On the right, at the curved reception counter, a sweating clerk struggled desperately to cope with a babble of enquiries from guests. On the central staircase, three ladies from the sporting house negotiated on the hoof as they led their clients upstairs. To the left of the staircase, on three sofas amongst the potted plants, a dozen of Custer's young soldiers, none more than nineteen years old, sat drinking beer and eyeing the ladies.

Buck looked about him and found what he sought. It was an owlish, bespectacled little man sitting at a desk to which was pinned a white card on which was printed in black ink '$200 Street Dash'. The man did not raise his eyes as Buck came to a halt in front of him but continued to scribble on a piece of paper.

Buck took off his hat and cleared his throat. The little man looked up, blinking at him over his glasses.

'Yes, cowboy, what can I do for you?'

'The Dash,' said Buck, pushing back a shock of lank black hair. 'Entries still open?'

'If you got your ten bucks,' said the man, dipping his quill into a pot of ink on his desk. 'But I got to warn you, young feller. This here's a scratch race, one-thirty yards straight up, English style. That means no starts for no one. That's the way it's always been, leastways ever since I been here.'

Buck reached up into the pocket of his waistcoat and withdrew a leather purse. 'Ten dollars, you said, sir?'

'Yup. Sonnie, you know we got some of the fastest men in the territory here?'

'I still want to enter, sir,' replied Buck, handing over the ten coins.

The little man took off his spectacles, laid them on the table and looked up at Buck, squinting. 'Paul Ledoux, you've heard tell of him?'

'He the feller they calls the Flying Frenchman?'

'The very one. He's Canyon City's Fast Man. Picked us up a parcel of dollars, has Paul Ledoux.' The little official scrutinised a sheet in front of him. 'And there's young Sam Withers — they say he ran two yards outside even time back in St. Louis. Then we got the breed McCluskey and the feller fro Silver City . . .'

'That the one they calls "The Savannah Stag"?' volunteered Buck.

'That's the very feller,' said the official. 'Now don't get me wrong, son. If you want to run, then that's surely your right and privilege. Just that I don't want to see no young cowboy throw away ten silver dollars.'

Buck's expression was serious. 'I still want to run, sir.'

'You done some sprinting Mr —?'

'Miller, Buck Miller. Yup. I won me a few picnic races back in Pennsylvania when I was a boy. I reckon I still got some starch left in these legs.'

The man shook his head. 'You're a-going to need it, Mr. Miller. You running in spiked shoes, or moccasins?'

Buck did not reply but turned and made his way quickly from the table, weaving his way through the crowded foyer

14

and out of the swing doors. The little man blinked, shook his head and returned to his writing. In a matter of seconds Buck had returned, spurs jingling, carrying a pair of shiny new patent leather running-shoes. He put them on the table, then turned them over to show the pristine yellow leather, the six needle-sharp spikes in each sole.

The little man picked up the shoes and surveyed them. 'Them's mighty fancy running shoes,' he said. 'I ain't never seen none to match them.'

'That ole Sears Roebuck catalogue says these are even time shoes,' replied Buck proudly.

'Only if'n you got even time legs, sonnie,' came a deep voice from behind him.

Buck looked over his shoulder at a tall, middle-aged man with black droopy moustache, in black bowler hat, with jacket, waistcoat and boots to match. On his left breast was pinned a tin star.

'This here's Marshal Boone, Buck. Mr. Boone, he's a gentleman of a considerable sporting disposition,' said the official.

'How many boys we got entered for this here dash?' asked Boone, ignoring Buck and taking a wet, dying stump of cigar from his lips before fumbling in his waistcoat pocket for matches.

'Nineteen, Marshal, at the last reckoning. This Yankee boy here, Buck Miller, he makes it up to a round twenty.'

Boone struck a match on the heel of his boot and relit his cigar. He drew on it and exhaled into Buck's face. 'Then give it all you got, son. No man can ask more.' The Marshal turned and made his way slowly through the crowds parting before him at the door.

The little man watched him go and looked at Buck's six-shooter, nestling snugly on his right hip.

'I suggest you rest your gun here, Mr. Miller. And when you leave call for your pistol. But don't ride out shooting; omit that. Most cowboys think it's an infringement on their rights to give up shootin in town. But if it is, it stands, least here in Canyon City. Your six-shooters are no match for the Marshal's Winchester. And Boone's officers are as game a set of men as ever faced danger.'

Buck nodded and withdrew his pistol. He laid it carefully on the table.

'I ain't looking for no trouble,' he said. 'When are the heats?'

'Three o'clock,' said the little man. Buck turned away and walked back through the crowds towards the swing doors.

'Finals, five o'clock,' the official shouted after him. Then, under his breath, he added, 'but I don't reckon that'll be your concern, cowboy.'

It was four o'clock. Professor Moriarty and Marshal Boone sat side by side in Lung Chow's barber's shop, both laid back at an angle, their faces swathed in wet towels, from which steam rose, misting the mirrors in front of them. From Boone's mouth projected a cigar, its smoke mixing with the steam above him. The actor spoke first, his voice deep and resonant.

'Marshal, if there's anything more pleasurable than a good, clean shave, then I swear I've yet to hear of it.'

'There is,' growled Boone through his cigar. 'But I am not disposed to think of such things, not when I have one hundred silver dollars laid upon that Frenchman's back in the final.'

'You bet your money on Ledoux?' said Moriarty with interest, as the barber removed the hot towels and began to replace them with cooler ones.

'Picked up one hundred bucks on him in his heat,' replied Boone.

'Cross-tie,' corrected Moriarty. 'In pedestrian circles we call it "cross-tie", Marshal.'

'Heat, cross-tie, call it what you will,' growled Boone. 'I bow to your superior knowledge. You've won a few big ones

16

in your time, or so I've heard tell. But that Frenchie, our Fast Man, he ran five yards outside even time for one hundred and thirty yards, looking round. So I give him two yards better in the final, perhaps three.'

'But the Frenchman, can he run with money on his back?' pressed Moriarty, as Boone's towels were carefully replaced by Lung Chow so as not to disturb his cigar.

'No question of it, Moriarty. Ledoux is the Fast Man hereabouts.' The thin, hard voice came from the door. It was Carl Medina, the card-sharp, who had that morning relieved the citizenry of Canyon City of nearly three hundred dollars of hard-earned cash. Lean and dapper, he stood poised at the door of the shop and withdrew from the pocket of his yellow-flowered waistcoat a gold watch. 'Fifty minutes from now, gentlemen,' he said, pocketing the watch again and seating himself on the third seat, nearest the window. 'And l will pick me up five hundred dollars, courtesy of Mr. Ledoux.'

He withdrew a sheet of paper from an inside pocket and surveyed it. 'Lookee here,' he said. 'The stop-watch says it all. Ledoux thirteen point five seconds, singing the Marseillaise. McCluskey and Withers thirteen six, eyeballs out. This cowboy — '

'Buck Miller,' offered Moriarty.

'Yes, Miller, that's the feller,' said Medina, lying back as the Chinaman lathered his face with thick white soap. 'I never seen him before but he ran thirteen point seven, all screwed up tight as a crab's ass. So I don't reckon much on him.'

Moriarty stood up and took the towel from his face, wiping his jowl clear of traces of soap as he did so. He surveyed himself for a moment in the mirror, and smiled. The skin of Moriarty's tanned face had the quality of fine papyrus. And though his nose was sharp, almost hawk-like, when he smiled in Lung Chow's mirror he was smiling at himself, at his own vanity. He drew his hands through his shock of black hair, pulled down on his lapels and tightened his bow-tie.

'My money's on young Miller,' he said. 'One hundred bucks at four to one.'

'Down the privy,' grunted Boone, still somehow retaining his cigar.

The Chinaman began to scrape the left side of Medina's face. The card-sharp's eyes hardened. 'What's your reasoning, Professor?'

Moriarty reached forward to the shelf in front of the mirror and took from it a square green bottle of perfume. He poured a little on to both palms and patted his cheeks, wincing as the astringent bit into his skin.

'Gentlemen, let's just call it instinct,' he said, flexing and relaxing his face muscles. 'Twenty years of pedestrianism.'

Boone rose and divested himself of his face-cloths, handing them to Lung Chow. 'But the cowboy will have to find four, maybe five yards,' he said, looking into the mirror, both hands on the shelf before it. He withdrew his cigar stump, wiped a fleck of lather from it, replaced it in his mouth and stood erect, surveying himself. 'No man ever ran that fast here, not even the Indian himself.'

'He'll have to be slicker than greased ice,' said Medina, as the Chinaman stood poised above him with the open blade. 'A hundred dollars — that's a lot to put on instinct.'

Moriarty flipped a dollar to Lung Chow, who caught it, smiling all over his moon-face, and placed one hand on the door, looking back into the shop. He put his index finger to his left nostril and winked.

'See you all at five,' he said.

From the moment that Mayor Halsey fired the pistol it was clearly Ledoux's race. The handsome Frenchman, who had been offered free services at Dolly Brown's for a win, surged into an immediate lead over the first thirty yards, heading Sam Withers by half a yard, with the other two runners a further half yard behind.

18

The four men surged up the narrow canyon created by the crowd, swamped in their cheers, while spectators marvelled at Ledoux's pace. For the Frenchie fairly ate up the ground with long, devouring strides, and at fifty yards had a lead of at least a full three feet. Medina, watching with Boone and Moriarty from the balcony of the Last Chance, wished that he had put a grand on the Frenchman. For this was not a race; it was an exhibition.

At seventy yards, Sam Withers seemed to gain a few inches, edging away from Buck Miller and McCluskey, though as yet no menace to Ledoux. But at ninety yards he had gained a foot, and at a hundred yards he was only a few inches short of the Frenchman, who was beginning to tighten up.

With only thirty yards to go, and the crowd in a frenzy, young Withers was level, locked with Ledoux. Then, from nowhere, like some avenging angel, came Buck Miller, cutting through the field in the final twenty yards like a scythe. With fifteen yards to go, he gave the kiss of death to a fading Ledoux and ten yards further on he cut down an already smiling Withers, to take the tape a clear yard ahead.

The band struck up 'Hail the Conquering Hero' and there was pandemonium as Buck was engulfed by the crowd. He was lifted aloft, holding his shiny, new leather Sears Roebuck shoes to his chest, grinning all over his dark, swarthy face. Above him, on the balcony of the Last Chance, Medina scowled and Boone stomped his cigar on to the floor. Beside them, Moriarty's face was radiant.

'Let me buy you boys a drink,' he said. 'Looks to me as if Canyon City's got itself a new Fast Man.'

2

THE ENGLISH METHOD

The town had never had it so good. In the months of May and June there were six challenges to Buck Miller, Canyon City's new Fast Man. From Culver City came Carl Pepper, said to have run ten seconds for one hundred yards – though Moriarty had hinted that it had more than likely been downhill with his mother's finger on the stopwatch. Buck had put more than two thousand dollars into the town's economy by his whupping of Pepper by a clear two yards.

Then General Custer had put up one of his soldier boys, an Irishman called Sean Riordan. Custer claimed two yards start on Buck, and laid $500 on his man. Medina, fearing a 'ringer', had checked back on Riordan's record and, reassured, advised the town to put their shirts on Buck. The race had been over a hundred yards and the Fast Man had toyed with Riordan till ten yards from the finish before taking him on the line.

Then Buck had creamed a Yankee boy, come by train all the way from Connecticut, name of Plunkett. It had been close, but Buck had got his nose in front in 13.4 seconds over one hundred and thirty yards, thus equalling the time which he had first recorded in the Founder's Day Dash, then gave Plunkett a yard start for another hundred bucks and this time beat him by a full stride.

But the Fast Man had declined to take on Professor Moriarty (who himself had already thrashed the citizenry of Canyon

City over half a mile on Founder's Day before going on to play Tamburlaine that same evening) over the distance of a mile.

'Short and sharp, for me, Professor,' he had said, politely tipping his hat. 'I knows my distance.'

Moriarty had shrugged and accepted gracefully; after all, he was already two thousand dollars ahead on Buck. He had, however, missed the Fast Man's next three winning runs, being absent in Culver City with his wife Eleanor playing his *Selections from Shakespeare* and *Davy Crockett* to packed houses.

By the time Moriarty had returned to Canyon City in late June to play in his own version of *Oliver Twist* Buck had achieved his greatest feat. It was the day that the St Louis Orioles had come to town to play exhibition ball against the Seattle Comets, beating them 9-3, the same day as Canyon City's pride, 'Boy' McGraw, had his nose broken in two places by a forty-year-old pug from Chicago by name of Mickey Malone. The town had lost a parcel of money on McGraw and was licking its wounds.

Buck had agreed to take on the fastest men of the Comets over their favourite distance, fifty yards, in three races, within an hour of each other, all against fresh men. In addition, he agreed to give each player a remarkable advantage: the ball players would start straight up, English style, with Buck lying on his front, his head facing away from the finish.

There were those, Mayor Halsey among them, who thought that this time the Fast Man had bitten off more than he could chew, but Boone and Medina, flush with a month's money from Buck's running, put everything they had on the Fast Man, both getting odds of six to one against his winning all three encounters.

The first race had been no contest. Turning swiftly on all fours, like a cat, to face forward, Buck had picked up his man at thirty yards and won strolling. The Comets then put in two of their best men for the second race, cursing and swearing at them as they followed them towards the start.

This time it was real close. Buck only picked the two Comets up on the final five yards, throwing himself in on the tape, and finishing spitting dust and appearing to hurt his shoulder as he landed on the gritty surface of Main Street. Medina and Boone together picked Buck up, wiping the blood from a deep scrape on his cheek, fearful that their six-to-one shot had gone down the privy. But the Fast Man had winked and whispered to Medina to put his family jewels on the final run against the Comets' fastest man. The gambler had taken him at his word: he had sold both his watch and his cuff-links for a hundred and fifty bucks and had got odds of eight to one against the now bruised and bloody Buck Miller.

Marshal Obadiah Boone was not a man of many words but it was he who was to say that in the final race Buck Miller 'burned the earth like a canned dog'. At thirty yards Buck had trapped his man, and the Comets went on to San Francisco five thousand dollars lighter than they had arrived.

Buck took well to his success, bearing it lightly on his broad young shoulders. Every Sunday he would be in the front row of the little Baptist church at the end of Main Street, his strong tenor voice rising above the congregation. He was always respectful to the matrons of the town and never a drop of liquor was seen to touch his lips. Indeed, his taste for sarsa-parilla might have occasioned remarks by some of the coarser denizens of Mulligan's Bar, had the Fast Man not been such a stimulus to the economy of the entire town.

The citizenry could set their watches by Buck Miller's regime. Nine o'clock, it was steak and eggs at the Last Chance, the steak always rare, the eggs done easy over. A couple of hours' snoozing in a rocking chair in the shadow of the sidewalk outside Macy's hardware store, then it was off to Macy's livery stable. There Buck pursued rigorous training routines which no one was allowed to witness, deep in the gloom of Macy's, engulfed in the sweet smell of horse manure. It was said that the eight-year-old Ally Broughton had once sneaked a view of the Fast Man's rituals and been whupped good for it by his paw, but folks reckoned that was probably all talk. Ally had whispered to the other kids of Buck, half-naked, running on the spot, knees to chin, sweat spraying from him in showers for more than half an hour, of a hundred push-ups before he had lost count, and other such fancies, but no one paid much heed. Anyhow, it was not deemed wise to probe too far into the mysteries of a man's private training.

At noon, Buck would be down at Lung Chow's for a bath and rub-down, then it was back to the Last Chance for a modest lunch: two lamb chops, grilled light, and a glass of luke-warm water. For the afternoon, Buck was back to his bed for three hours' further shut-eye, before his evening two-mile constitutional walk round town and a dinner which invariably consisted of Irish Stew and a wedge of Pennsylvania Dutch apple pie, washed down with two cups of coffee, no more, no less.

The people of the town soon grew accustomed to Buck Miller's inexorable rhythms. The only exception was on Wednesday afternoon, when Buck gave up his time to the doing of good works for widow women in outlying farms, chopping wood, picking up strays, digging potatoes — anything that could be of service.

Had it been known that many of these ladies were satisfied not only with Buck's labours in the field but also with his less publicised activities upon their counterpanes then it is doubtful that many hands, Baptist matrons' apart, would have been raised against him in Canyon City. Was it reasonable, after all, the argument would have run, that the energies developed in the gloom of Macy's should be focused entirely upon the running-path? Better, surely, that the Fast Man should avoid the risks of disease with Dolly Brown's girls and keep his manhood pure by assisting ladies of undeniable virtue whose only misfortune was to have lost a husband.

But in early July the matches and with them the money

dropped to a trickle, and though Buck still walked the streets lean and trim folks began to remark that the Fast Man had begun to look a little stale — 'peaky', the womenfolk called it.

A flush of prospectors, hot-footing towards the Black Hills, hoping to steer an illegal path 'twixt 7th Cavalry and Sioux, brought a slight return to boom times when Buck, carrying a 56 lb grain bag on his back, beat the fastest miner over fifty yards; but the prospectors were low in cash, and it was all small beer compared with the palmy days following his Founder's Day victory over Ledoux. But no one blamed Buck. It was only natural that few would be willing to take the trail to Canyon City to challenge a man of such pace. But, no question of it, Buck *was* beginning to look a little peaky; though none of the recipients of his Wednesday afternoon services was ever heard to voice a complaint.

Meanwhile the Theatre of the West, now based at Budd's Saw Mill, had become an established feature of Canyon City life. The Theatre of the West travelled light, carrying only a handful of 'sets', confining itself to the most basic and symbolic of materials. This meant a single half-pillar for the senate scene in *Julius Caesar* or a bare strip of tapestry for the court scene in *Hamlet*. This simplicity worked well in the primitive circumstances within which they usually had to work, and Moriarty, who had an excellent feel for form and texture, used his limited resources to the full. In this he was complemented by Eleanor, who created all the company's costumes. She, like her husband, kept things simple, for experience had shown that expensive, complicated costumes did not travel well and would, in any case, be 'lost' in the shadowy 'theatres' within which she and Moriarty usually had to play.

Moriarty's Theatre of the West was unique in its mixture of professional and amateur performances. The professional 'theatre' amounted to just Moriarty and Eleanor, and their own performances consisted of excerpts from Shakespeare, such as the balcony scene from *Romeo and Juliet* or Othello's murder of Desdemona. Alternatively, there were soliloquies from *Hamlet*, *Macbeth* or *The Merchant of Venice* and verse-readings from Shakespeare's sonnets or the works of Byron, Shelley and Keats. At the other end of the scale, to leaven the mix, Moriarty and Eleanor presented farces, popular comic sketches and knockabout husband-and-wife banter.

But the presentation of full plays (or even Moriarty's 'individually edited' condensed versions of the classics) required larger casts, and here he turned the longings of the men and women in the street to his advantage. From the best products of their daily classes in Scientific Speech Production (for which they charged 50 cents a lesson) Moriarty and Eleanor drew the supporting casts for their big productions. They were good teachers, Eleanor calm and supportive, Moriarty the demon-coach, the inspirer. 'Don't *sell* the word, don't colour it, ladies,' he would implore them. 'Don't push it down their throats. *Think* it.'

Eleanor and Moriarty made each of their classes a form of play, and although their early groups were almost exclusively women, word of the good times to be had in the Scientific Speech Production Programme travelled fast and soon shopkeepers and blacksmiths were filling out the male parts. Dolly Brown's girls, accustomed as they were to acting (albeit generally horizontally) begged to be included, though to humour the God-fearing ladies of the town they always had to be accommodated in separate sessions and productions. Moriarty found some of his best actresses in the ladies of the Sporting House. He also discovered that he could let his hair down with them, for these were ladies with few inhibitions, no false modesty.

'It's a plumbing job, acting,' he would roar to the berouged belles. 'Unblocking the pipes which carry the impulses from the inner to the outer world, to express the character in you. So prepare to unblock your pipes, ladies!'

But it was not Dolly Brown's ladies who were to produce the star of Canyon City, for Amanda Boone, the daughter of the widowed Marshal Obadiah Boone, was proving to be the best natural actress of whom Eleanor and Moriarty had had experience. Miss Boone, though her stage-movement was still stilted, possessed two rare qualities — a natural feel for verse and the gift of presence. After a fortnight, when she had improved her voice-control through hours of rigorous diaphragm exercises under Eleanor's tutelage, Moriarty took a chance and used her as Desdemona in the death scene from *Othello*. Mandy Boone had given an excellent performance for an amateur, winning the pleasure not only of the populace but even of a grudging father who had previously shown little interest in or patience with his daughter's play-acting. But the after-glow of *Othello* resulted in no softening of Obadiah Boone's opposition to his daughter's desire to become an actress rather than to continue as a teacher of children in Canyon City. In the Marshal's view, actresses were only a cut above whores, whatever Mrs Moriarty's airs and graces, and he was not going to see his only daughter end up in a cathouse, however much she detested teaching. Moriarty and Eleanor avoided any part in the debate. Obadiah Boone had a lot of pull in Canyon City, and they had no wish to court unpopularity.

It was Judge Halsey who was first to call Moriarty 'Renaissance Man', though no one was willing to admit that he did not know what that meant. Halsey had heard the phrase used of President Lincoln, back in the palmy days when the Mayor had stumped for Lincoln in his bid for the presidency. For Lincoln had been a fancy rassler back in his youth and no mean foot-racer, and Halsey recollected that your Leonardo da Vinci had been able to bend coins with his fingers and that George Washington himself had leapt twenty-two feet in the long jump, a hundred years or so back. Thus Moriarty, with his mixture of Thespian and foot-racing abilities, had become something of an idealised figure to Halsey, and the tubby little Mayor had been stumbling his way through history, extolling Henry VIII's hammer-throwing abilities and Plato's wrestling skills at the rail of Mulligan's Bar on the day when the Great Dash first took shape

It was just on noon, and outside the July sun was hard as a hammer on the silent street. Moriarty, Boone, the card-sharp Medina and Buck were on their third drink of the day, the flies buzzing around them in the heavy heat as Halsey prattled on interminably about his 'Renaissance Man'

Then Moriarty, seizing on Halsey's theme, put in his own two bits. Acting and sport were much the same, he declared. When you were at your best, on the boards or on the running-path, there was a feeling of power, energy flowing unforced through body and mind. You were above the performance — *it* was performing *you*.

Medina, desperate to change the subject to one with which he had at least a passing acquaintance, then brought up the news of Bat Wilson's recent killing of two men in Dodge City. Halsey promptly asked Boone if he would be willing to stand against Wilson, should the need ever arise.

It was an uneasy moment, for the roly-poly little Halsey was questioning the Marshal's mettle. But Boone, leaning on his left elbow, his bottle by his side, was in his cups, and seemed to ignore the implications of the remark.

'Courage, gentlemen,' he said, 'is a mighty peculiar thing.' He uncorked his bottle with his teeth and slowly poured himself another large slug. He lifted his glass and surveyed it before downing its contents in a single gulp.

Boone looked behind him for Mulligan, the barman, who had been hovering on the edge of the conversation, and beckoned for another bottle.

'Nobody's got it, at least not all the time. Take me on a summer day, full of good grub and a couple of drinks under

27

my belt, I'd stand up to a regiment and take my chance.'

Mulligan placed a fresh bottle at Boone's right elbow. He poured himself out another long hit, but this time sipped it, teasing out the expectation of his listeners. 'But take me before daybreak, in the rain, hungry and cold, and I'd run from one greaser, if'n he was hunting me.'

There was a pause. This was not what they had expected to hear.

'But surely, Marshal,' said Moriarty, 'there's some difference between a top gunman and the man in the street?'

'Willing,' said Boone enigmatically, sipping his whiskey. 'Willing.' Boone stopped, as if the single word was sufficient explanation.

'I don't quite follow your drift, Marshal,' said Carl Medina.

'Your ornery cowpoke ain't willing, Medina. Sure, they might hate a guy right enough but they ain't willing to shoot a hole in a man. They'll draw, but there's just that split second when they're not willing.'

'To take the consequences? To kill?' pursued Medina.

Boone nodded. 'And that moment, if they're up against a halfways good man they're on their way to Boot Hill.'

'And what about speed?' asked Moriarty.

'Speed of draw?' said Boone.

Moriarty nodded. Boone shook his head and again inspected his glass. 'Only makes a difference if a man's willing.'

For a moment the conversation seemed about to die and the four men could hear only the buzz of bar-flies and the snoring of several drunks slumped behind them at the tables in a shadowy corner of the bar.

'Buck here has speed, at least in foot-racing,' said Moriarty. 'How do you think he would rate with a six-shooter?'

Boone's reply was immediate. 'Only one way of telling,' he said. 'Mulligan,' he roared, and the barman, his face white as melted lard, responded with a shout from the far end of the semi-circular bar. 'Seek out Buck's shooting irons.'

28

In moments Buck's six-shooter was slid along the bar. Boone picked it up and scrutinised it.

'Don't look to me as if it's been used much, Buck,' he said.

'Never had much occasion in my line of business, Marshal. When I hear the sound of gunfire I usually have to get my legs moving.'

Boone nodded and smiled sourly through his drooping walrus moustache. He pushed open the gun, took out its five cartridges and laid them on the table. Then he closed the weapon and laid it beside the cartridges.

'Stand back, gentlemen,' he said, reaching into his pocket to withdraw a silver dollar. He placed the dollar on the back of his left hand and held his arm out horizontally. He then cleared his jacket coat-rails from his right-hand holster.

'I will drop the dollar, gentlemen, and draw and cock before it hits the floor.'

'Ten says no,' whispered Medina to Halsey.

'Taken,' hissed Halsey.

The men moved clear of Boone, who seemed to have gained a coolness, a poise which had been lacking only moments before. The marshal seemed to be in some still and distant world, but one in which he was perfectly clear-headed.

It was over before anyone could draw breath. The dollar dropped from Boone's hand, but only inches before it touched the sawdust floor Boone faced them, bent-kneed, his six-shooter cocked and pointed.

'That was worth the ten dollars, just for the seeing, Marshal,' said Medina admiringly.

'How d'you mean?' said Boone, replacing his gun as if he had returned from a deep sleep.

'Worth a *hundred* dollars,' said Moriarty, sparing Medina embarrassment. 'What d'you think, Buck?'

Buck pulled his right hand through his glossy hair, his blue eyes assuming the strange, piercing quality the other men had often observed, but only before the races.

'Never saw the like,' he said, reaching forward to take his pistol from the bar and put it in his holster. He lifted the silver dollar from the floor and surveyed it, shaking his head. Then he placed it on the back of his hand, let it drop and, turning his hand, caught it three times, his brows slightly furrowed. He placed his six-shooter in his holster and slowly cleared it, cocking and pointing it in slow motion. Medina looked at Halsey and shook his head. Then Buck made three more attempts at progressively higher speeds, before finally he nodded.

'I'm ready, Marshal.'

'Fifty says he can't clear and cock before the second bounce,' said Medina.

'Taken,' said Boone.

'Two hundred says he'll take it before it hits the sawdust,' said Moriarty.

'You got it,' responded Halsey.

'Let's give Buck here some space,' said Moriarty, and the three men backed off.

Buck wiped his mouth with the back of his right hand, and wrinkled his nose. He slowly put the dollar on the back of his left hand and raised his arm to the horizontal. For a moment he was fixed and frozen.

Then came the strangest thing. Buck turned his left hand to release the coin and appeared to draw and cock simultaneously. But the strangest thing of all was that he dropped like a cat and caught the coin in his left hand when it was only inches from the floor. For a moment, even the flies seemed to stop buzzing. The three men looked at Buck, cool and still as he straightened up. He showed no emotion but the look had now gone from his eyes.

'Jesus Christ!' exclaimed Medina.

'Darndest thing I ever did see,' said Halsey, abstractedly reaching to the bar for Boone's whiskey bottle.

'That'll be two hundred bucks, Mr Mayor,' prompted Moriarty.

Buck returned his gun to Mulligan and the dollar to Boone, whose dour expression had remained set since Buck's feat. The older man looked at the coin for a moment then replaced it in a side pocket of his waistcoat.

'Doesn't mean he's willing,' he said curtly.

'Of course not, Marshal,' said Moriarty. 'Buck's forte is sprinting, just as yours is defending the peace, and Medina here is skilled at cards. Just shows what any man can do with athletic training.' He accepted a bottle slid along the surface of the bar by Mulligan and filled the three men's glasses. 'I've done the same with several athletes over the past ten years.' He lifted his glass. 'Your health, gentlemen.'

Mayor Halsey drew out his money-clip from an inside pocket and withdrew a wad of notes. He thumbed through them and handed Moriarty two hundred dollars.

'You mean to say you reckon you can train *anybody* to be a Fast Man?'

'If he's young enough, has no major disabilities and has a good set of teeth,' said Moriarty.

'How fast?' pressed Medina.

'Fast enough,' said Moriarty. 'Using the English Method.'

Medina frowned. 'Now what the hell is the English Method?'

Moriarty sipped his drink slowly, stretching the moment. 'You've heard of the Cribb versus Molyneux fight?'

'That up New York way?' said Halsey.

'No, Mr Mayor,' said Moriarty patiently. 'It was in England, way back in 1810. Tom Molyneux was a nigger, a fine upright figure of a man. Came all the way from Virginia to fight Tom Cribb, the Champion of All England.'

'And he used this English Method, this feller Cribb?' asked Medina.

Moriarty nodded. 'Paradoxically, it was the invention of a Scot, Captain Barclay Allardice, a gentleman. When Cribb came to Scotland to stay with Barclay he was in poor shape. Two hundred and sixty pounds of bone and blubber. Then he was put on an eight-week preparation of training and medication.'

'Like what?' asked Medina.

Moriarty looked around him and fumbled in an inside jacket pocket. He withdrew a small black notebook and thumbed through it, then took from his waistcoat pocket a pair of pince-nez, which he placed on his nose. He began to read slowly, the notebook held close to his face.

'The skilful trainer attends to the state of the bowels, the lungs and the skin and uses such means as will reduce the fat and at the same time invigorate the muscles. The athlete is purged by drastic measures, he is sweated by walking under a load of clothes and by lying 'twixt feather beds. His limbs are roughly rubbed. His diet is beef or mutton. His drink, strong ale.'

'Strong ale? That's the best thing your captain has said so far,' said Boone, reaching back for his bottle again.

'Sounds like hell on earth to me,' said Halsey.

'A man's got to die before he can live, Mayor,' said Moriarty, lowering the notebook for a moment and taking off his spectacles. 'And then of course there's "Black Jack".'

'Where's this feller come in?' said Medina.

Moriarty replaced his spectacles and thumbed through the little black notebook till he came to the paragraph he sought. He cleared his throat, then began.

'The pedestrian must begin with a regular course of physic, called Black Jack. It consists of one ounce of caraway seed; half an ounce of coriander seed; one ounce of root liquorice, and half an ounce of sugar candy, mixed with two bottles of cider and boiled down to one half.'

'That would go straight through a man and end up in his boots," growled Boone.

'But what about the training?' persisted Medina. 'The exercises?'

Moriarty took off his pince-nez once again, closed his

notebook and replaced both in his inside pocket. 'I'm afraid I've said far too much already, gentlemen. Secrets of pedestrianism.'

Buck spoke for the first time, a little smile on his lips. 'And what about the ladies, Professor?'

Moriarty shook his head. 'Poison to the athlete, Buck. You must know that. Vital bodily fluids. Ladies sap a man's strength. A man has to retain his essential juices.'

'And did this fighter feller . . .' Medina paused.

'Cribb?'

'Yes.'

'Did he win his fight?'

Moriarty nodded. 'They carried the negro out in the thirty-third round. Molyneux, he had a lot of sand, though. And as for Cribb, he said he could face the fight again, but not the training.'

Boone pointed over to the drunks snoring in the corner of the saloon.

'You telling me you can train one of them, using your English Method, to be a Fast Man?'

'A *faster* man,' said Moriarty, defensively.

'Come on, Moriarty, stand your ground,' said Medina, for the first time in the conversation going on the offensive. He walked over into the shadows of the saloon and stood above a grey-haired man who slumped face down at a table, the spittle oozing from bleeding lips.

'Not him, Medina,' said Mayor Halsey. 'That's Sam Bunce. A horse stomped his foot in the livery stable two years back.'

Medina moved to his right, to the next table, at which a man sat nose to table, his arms straight in front of him. He lifted the man's head for Moriarty's scrutiny. The drunk was bloated, pock-marked, and at least forty-five years of age.

Moriarty raised his right hand, palm forward. 'I said I could train men, not raise the dead.'

Medina shrugged and moved to the next table. Beneath it

33

a young man was curled, in foetal position. Medina knelt and put his face close, scrutinising him.

'He looks young enough,' he said. 'Someone fetch me a jug of water.'

Boone walked over to the table and surveyed the man while Buck went for the water. The Marshal lifted the man's head. He was young, blonde and baby-faced and dressed in brown buckskins.

'I know him,' said Boone. 'From Texas. A drummer, sells patent-leather shoes. Been booze-blind for a fortnight.'

'I saw him open his shirt collar just to have a piss,' said Halsey, handing Medina a pitcher.

Medina slowly poured the water over the young man's face. 'This looks like the very man, Professor,' he said. 'To run against Buck Miller.'

'What's your name, son?'

The young man spat out the water which had got into his mouth, struggled to his feet and sat up on the table.

'Speed, sir,' he said. 'Billy Joe Speed.'

3

BUCK VERSUS BILLY JOE

It had taken a further day's protracted wrangling for the terms to be agreed for the match-race between Billy Joe Speed and Buck Miller, for Speed had shown no great inclination to subject himself to the rigours of the English Method, or indeed any other. In the end, it was economics that had the final say. For the Texan, though unquestionably an excellent salesman of Benjamin's patent leather shoes, had, in the previous fortnight, drunk and gambled away every cent of his commissions. Aside from the rumpled clothes he stood in and six pairs of size 13 black patent leather shoes (for which Boone assured him the citizens of Canyon City would have little use) Billy Joe Speed was in a state of bustitude.

But the big problem had been Moriarty. First, he had demanded a ten-yard start for Billy Joe. Of course, he protested, he could make Billy Joe *faster*; that was not in question. But to get him anywhere close to Buck Miller would test the abilities of Captain Barclay himself, God rest his soul. No, if Billy Joe were expected to race in a match on scratch terms against Buck Miller it would require some fancy odds, plus a month's free food and lodging and complete freedom from surveillance or interference by any interested parties.

He had asked for odds of ten to one. That Billy Joe, one night in a drunken stupor, had claimed an unbeaten record as a sprinter was, reasoned Moriarty, of no great account.

Sixty-yard dashes, three-legged competitions and sack races back in Texas at the age of twelve were, he argued, no great record of pedestrian achievement. Buck, after all, was probably the swiftest man in Arizona, perhaps only a couple of whiskers off the Indian himself. Ten to one was therefore only just.

Medina, however, had been adamant. If Billy Joe had been a one-legged man then ten to one was fair odds, but the Texas boy had two good legs and was a well-set young fellow, with all his teeth in good order. Five to one was all he could stretch to, and Halsey and Boone agreed. At that point Moriarty would not budge, and the bet looked set to fall through when Medina, tongue in cheek, suggested a side bet at ten to one if Billy Joe could beat the record time for the street dash of 13.4 seconds for the 130 yards, win or lose, and Mayor Halsey took five hundred bucks from Moriarty at those odds.

It all ended with Moriarty putting in a thousand at five to one with both Medina and Boone, and five hundred with Buck himself, and another thousand in the winning time with Halsey. The Last Chance Hotel put up the month's room and Mulligan's the vittles, while Macy's agreed to allow Buck and Billy Joe to have free training facilities at different times during the day.

Billy Joe's preparation began on 1 July 1875, with a 6.30 a.m. visit to Lung Chow's. There he was weighed and the result inscribed in the little black notebook which lodged in Moriarty's wallet by day and in the Last Chance's safe by night.

Then, a day later, came Billy Joe's first 'sweat'. It also marked the initiation of the Chinaman's brand new sweat-box, which had arrived from St Louis only a week before. At 7.30 a.m., after a vigorous massage by Lung Chow, Billy Joe was placed in the box, naked, and seated on a wooden bench. The box was then closed and hot vapour injected into it. Billy's screams as the jets of vapour burned his thighs prompted even the stern

36

heart of Moriarty to pity. The box was opened and Billy Joe provided with thick towels to protect his legs.

Moriarty decided that half an hour would be ample for the first 'sweat' and Billy Joe, the moisture pouring in streams down his body, was duly released, dried off, weighed and the results noted in Moriarty's black book. Then Billy Joe, roaring, was doused by Lung Chow for ten minutes in icy water and again massaged vigorously. By 8.30 a.m. Billy was seated in Mulligan's, eating stale bread and half-raw mutton chops and drinking ale.

Then Moriarty took his charge back to the Last Chance for an hour's sleep, sitting outside his locked door to discourage intruders. Sixty minutes later the pair were off in a two-horse buggy to Blanco Canyon, an hour's ride away, for Billy Joe's first time-trial.

No one would ever know how fast Billy Joe had run on that first day in July; indeed, it was unlikely that even the Lord God Almighty was permitted a peek at Moriarty's stop-watch. Whatever the time, (and even Obadiah Boone himself did not venture to enquire) Moriarty's visage had been gloomy when he returned and he drank more than usual that night. When asked about Billy Joe's condition he had made only one remark, 'Out of snow, you can't make cheesecake', and Carl Medina had spent a fair part of the evening trying to figure that one out.

After the first day the training became a ritual, similar to that of Buck, albeit without the Wednesday afternoon gymnastic diversions. 6.30–8.30 a.m. Lung Chow's for sweats and massage; 8.30–9.30 a.m. breakfast; 9.30–10.30 a.m. snooze; 10.30–12.30 p.m. running training; 12.30–1.30 p.m. lunch; 1.30–3.0 p.m. snooze; 3.0–5.0 p.m. exercises at Macy's livery; 5.0–6.0 p.m. bath and massage; 6.0–7.0 p.m. dinner; 7.0–9.0 p.m. cards with Moriarty and his wife Eleanor, or attendance at *Oliver Twist*; *Shakespearean Selections*; *Mose in New York*; *The Bells*, or *Dramatic Recitations*.

For Eleanor, her husband's involvement in Billy Joe's preparations meant that the day-to-day running of the Theatre of the West bore more heavily upon her. The business side of the enterprise had always been her responsibility, but now practical matters such as clearing up the theatre, the issue of playbills and the repair of sets also fell upon her, as the bulk of her husband's day was being spent with his charge. Here Mandy Boone was a tower of strength, and her father, only too aware that she was his main link with Billy Joe Speed, was content to allow her her hobby.

But Obadiah Boone's none too subtle probing on Billy Joe's state of health elicited little useful information from his daughter, intent as she was in learning the basics of theatre life. Moriarty, occupied with preparations for the match, had cut down on his number of productions and Eleanor had taken the opportunity to repair sets and patch up costumes. Thus Mandy Boone was heavily employed in these mundane but necessary tasks. But Boone did discover that Billy Joe had lost ten pounds in his first two weeks of preparation, most of it in Lung Chow's sweat-box, a piece of information casually thrown Mandy's way by the Texan one day at lunch. This was not much use for the likes of Boone and his crony Medina, but it was better than nothing.

But Billy Joe's appearance in *Julius Caesar* after a fortnight's training gave Boone and the sporting fraternity of Canyon City their best picture of the contender's condition. Billy Joe, appearing in a toga as Casca in Moriarty's half-hour version of Shakespeare's play, provided Boone and his cronies a clear glimpse of what they longed to see — his legs. The general opinion was that they looked good: thick calves and heavy, muscular thighs. Not that there was much time to get a good view, for in the assassination of Caesar scene a Navajo, seeing the daggers and the blood, ran a-whooping and screaming from the saw-mill, raving that the White Eyes were murdering each other. In the general confusion, other Indians rioted and

38

several of the ladies present fainted. When order was finally restored Moriarty decided to discontinue *Julius Caesar* and go on to the less controversial *Mose in New York*. But Boone had got his money's-worth; a sixteen-inch calf and a twenty-three-inch thigh — that was the general opinion, and odds against the Texan dropped.

Mandy Boone, waiting in the wings to play Portia, viewed Billy Joe's limbs from an entirely different perspective, as had several other ladies in the audience. The Texan, whatever his history of debauchery, was a strapping young fellow, and perhaps worthy of attention.

Billy Joe, after a fortnight of 'sweats' and Black Jack, seemed anyway to have dried out and appeared to the citizenry to be a quiet, personable young man, less outgoing than Buck perhaps, but then that was perhaps not surprising, considering the amount of time he spent in the john. Halsey had checked him out and concluded that in the first fortnight Billy Joe had spent an average of three hours a day in the privy.

Medina had enquired of Moriarty how he had kept his man from boredom during these long hours of excretion. The actor's reply had been prompt. Billy Joe, it seemed, did not waste his time, and devoured the works of William Shakespeare, though he was occasionally allowed some light relief in the form of the Canyon City *Enquirer*.

By the end of the first fortnight the Black Jack regime appeared to have done its work and Billy Joe's bowels were allowed to pursue their normal rhythms. During this period Medina, Halsey and Boone continued to keep close watch on Moriarty and his charge, but the actor's security was impeccable, and even during his dramatic shows, in which the Texas boy had played several minor parts in Moriarty's *Merchant of Venice*, Billy Joe was never out of his sight. Indeed the talk of the town had been Mandy Boone's fine Portia. The trio also kept a close watch on their own investment, but Buck's behaviour was

39

beyond criticism; indeed, his step seemed to have acquired a fresh spring, as if in anticipation of the big race.

Even when the odds rose to four to one on Buck, hardly fancy odds, money kept coming in on the Fast Man's back, with Halsey, Boone and Medina becoming the town's unofficial bookmakers. Dolly Brown's ladies, though they had never had an opportunity to inspect their investment at close hand, laid three thousand dollars on the Fast Man's legs, while, at the other end of the social spectrum, whey-faced Baptist ladies were venturing a cautious ten bucks on the Chapel's best tenor. By contrast, in Chinatown, the population, reckoning that at least a tenth of Billy Joe's bodyweight had been poured into their part of town via Lung Chow's sweat-box, bet heavily on the Texas boy at high odds.

Thus, for the first time, the whole town, rich and poor alike, was involved in a foot-race; but they were betting blind, and the pressure on Medina, Boone and Halsey to check out their gamble became painfully acute. Access to Macy's had been denied them, but the judicious use of children as spies brought one notable, if curious, piece of information. It appeared that Billy Joe was using a speed-ball, daily executing thousands of blows in the gloom of Macy's, under Moriarty's stern gaze.

This was established on 13 July by two of the older boys, who had enlarged a knot-hole sufficiently to confirm what some of the younger lads had only deduced from the sound of Billy Joe's endless, rhythmic pummelling. Halsey and his colleagues discussed this report in serious conference, but could come to no useful conclusion.

It was the day after this information had been gleaned that the first break in protocol occurred, when Boone and Medina decided to break their solemn agreement and look in on Moriarty and Billy Joe's daily visits to Blanco Canyon. Accordingly, on 14 July at 8.0 a.m., Boone and Halsey trotted discreetly through town, past Lung Chow's, on their way to the canyon. There, an hour later, perched high on a bluff, they sat chewing jerky and drinking bourbon under the blistering summer sun, anxiously awaiting the arrival of Moriarty and his charge.

At 11.30 a.m. precisely Moriarty and Billy Joe arrived and immediately got down to business. First, Billy Joe's trainer scraped a starting-line and slowly paced one hundred and thirty steps up the flat surface of the canyon, removing all stray stones and branches as he did so. Meantime, Billy Joe pranced up and down on the spot like a fractious filly, stripped to the waist, dressed in white long-johns and black spiked shoes.

Finally, all was ready, and Moriarty stood, gun aloft, with Billy Joe coiled like a spring at the mouth of the canyon. The explosion of the gun released Billy Joe and, high above them the flickering hand of Medina's 1/100 second stopwatch fluttered on its circular path. The angle was bad but Medina reckoned that he had the time accurate to within a couple of tenths. Boone peered over his shoulder.

'What did you get?'

'Fourteen point six five seconds,' said Medina. 'Give or take a tenth.'

'Not bad,' said Boone. 'Moriarty's done a good job.'

'Good?' hissed Medina. 'He's over ten yards out. It's money in the bank.'

'More like money down the privy,' observed Boone, smiling. 'It'll take Billy Joe one helluva lot of shitting to take off another whole second.

Though they were both bent upon the same task, neither Billy Joe Speed nor Buck Miller showed the slightest sign that he was aware of the other's existence. Indeed no one could recollect either man having passed words with the other since that first day in the saloon — and Billy Joe, had he been asked, could hardly have remembered those. Both men lived in the same town, breathed the same air; but for practical purposes they lived on different planets.

41

Naturally, it was Billy Joe's fitness which still occasioned most discussion. It had been clear, after only a week that he had lost considerable weight — some said as much as six pounds, but Lung Chow's lips remained sealed. It was clear, too, half-way through the preparation, that he was walking tall, that there was a new spring in his step. But Moriarty would say nothing about the condition of his precious charge, and the knot-hole at Macy's Livery was bunged up, thus ending all possibility of further intelligence from that quarter.

The town was split down the middle, father against son, husband against wife. True, the Fast Man had brought a few bucks into Canyon City; but the odds against Billy Joe were too tasty to ignore — anything from five to eight to one, depending on the brightness of Billy Joe's eyes that day, or the vigour with which Buck attacked Ma Mulligan's stew. Not a nuance of either man's behaviour was ignored, from the length of his sleeping hours to the amount of liquid he consumed. There was too much at stake — not only the dollars placed on each man's back, but each investor's pride in his ability to assess a man's condition, a matter of art as much as science, and one in which elderly Methodist matrons felt they possessed at least as much skill as any butcher or bartender

Meanwhile Moriarty's thrice-weekly dramatic performances maintained their quality, revealing none of the tension that his onerous athletic responsibilities might well have produced. Buck looked hard and fit as ever, but so now did the quiet Texas boy — the living embodiment of the English Method. No one knew if Billy Joe could run a lick, but sure as hell he was beginning to *look* like a runner. The odds against him began to drop.

They only began to rise again after 21 July, when Moriarty took Billy Joe Speed out to Blanco Canyon for his next trial. At precisely 10.30 a.m. their buggy trotted slowly out on the hour-long drive and there was not a man in town that did not know their purpose. Certainly Medina, Boone and Halsey did, for since 8.30 a.m. they had been perched on the bluff above the canyon, awaiting the two men's arrival.

At 11.30 a.m., almost to the minute, Moriarty and Billy Joe made their appearance. Halsey, who had never before seen Billy Joe stripped off, remarked on the leanness of the Texan boy. Moriarty ritually paced out the necessary one hundred and thirty yards; Billy Joe performed his setting-up exercises, and there, as had occurred over a month before, was Moriarty, gun aloft, poised at the mouth of the canyon, with Billy Joe Speed frozen in his starting position, arms high, ready for the signal.

The gun exploded and Billy Joe rushed towards Moriarty, showing a balance and rhythm that had not been evident on Boone and Medina's first illicit surveillance. It took him fully thirty yards to slow up and return to his trainer. As the two men walked together away down the canyon for the last time Moriarty consulted his watch.

'What did you get?" said Halsey, peering over Medina's shoulder. His companion took out a magnifying glass and consulted his stopwatch. He shook his head.

'Mighty good!'

'Good be damned!' expostulated Halsey, his face red as meat. 'What was the time, man?'

Medina smiled and showed his watch to Halsey. 'Fourteen dead.'

'That's 'bout what 1 got,' said Boone, from behind, handing Medina his own watch. 'Fourteen and one-sixteenth of a second.'

'Then we got 'em cold,' said Halsey. 'That's still six-tenths of a second out.'

'Six yards', agreed Medina. 'A lifetime.'

'There's more,' said Boone, pointing down into the valley as below them Moriarty's buggy made its way back to Canyon City. 'Look at the wind.'

Down in the valley, tumbleweed was rolling down into the canyon mouth.

'Billy Joe had a wind behind him. A back-wind.'

'How much is that worth?' said Halsey.

'Two-tenths of a second, perhaps a tenth more,' said Boone.

Medina stood and dusted himself down. 'Marshal, you are one helluva man,' he said. 'I bet you wipe your ass before you shit.'

Boone also got to his feet, withdrew a white handkerchief from his top pocket and wiped the sweat from his brow. 'Now however did you know that?'

The day after that particular trial, the odds against Billy Joe mysteriously rose.

Nothing like it had ever happened in Canyon City, nor would it again. It was quite unlike Founder's Day, with its clanjamfry of fighting cocks, fist-fighting and drunken carousal. This was not merely a race, rather a contest between the forces of modern science, personified by Professor Moriarty and his English Method, and natural, God-gifted athletic ability in the form of the dark-haired, blue-eyed Buck Miller.

The race had been set for high noon on 21 August, and Boone had made certain that Main Street was closed to traffic for an hour beforehand. Macy had been commissioned to clear the street of horse-shit and, using a small army of Chinamen, had also raked and flattened it. Moriarty had also insisted on separate stringed lanes for each runner — Sheffield, England style — and as no one had ever seen such a construction it was left to him to instruct Macy on their setting up.

There had, however, been problems in appointing suitable officials, since it was difficult to find anyone in town who did not have a stake in the race. Finally it was agreed that Judge Perry (who freely admitted to having fifty bucks on Billy Joe) should be Chief Finish Judge and Timekeeper, and that he enlist five God-fearing non-gamblers who, though they might lack experience in judging foot-races, could be guaranteed to act fairly in such a serious situation. And Judge Perry's team of a bank clerk, a school teacher, a pastor, a 7th Cavalry Lieutenant and a muleskinner was not lacking in training for the day. Indeed, they practised assiduously for a week, holding their own races outside town between the local children for prizes of candy.

So, on the morning of 21 August 1875, two stringed lanes four feet wide stood in Main Street — two narrow corridors within which the hopes and dreams of Canyon City would rest for just a few brief seconds. That morning folks had walked past the race area in awe, whispering to each other as if they were in a cathedral. An hour before the race the street had been completely cleared and crowds had begun to gather on the boardwalks and at the windows of shops, saloons and houses above the race-area. A quarter of an hour before, Judge Perry's team had solemnly assembled at the finish, stopwatches finally checked by the local cobbler, Paul Schwarz, Judge Perry reckoning that a Swiss (even a Swiss shoemaker) would be liable to know more about timepieces than most ordinary folks.

Ten minutes before the start Judge Perry summoned the two rivals to the front of the Last Chance, where he stood on the stage of Professor Moriarty's Theatre of the West. First he called Buck to the stage from behind the swing doors of the Last Chance. Buck walked out dressed in his customary white long-johns, over which he wore dark blue shorts and his black Sears Roebuck spiked shoes. As he mounted the stage he raised both hands above his head, to loud and raucous applause.

Judge Perry then called upon Billy Joe, but when the 'Texan Challenger' appeared there were gasps and a hubbub of discussion while the ladies hid their eyes. For Billy Joe Speed was wearing white, knee-length shorts, his thick hairy calves fully exposed to public gaze.

The judge held up both hands for silence.

'All parties concerned have already discussed the question of Billy Joe's apparel and no objection has been raised by Buck

Miller or any of his backers. There ain't no sporting rules pertaining to a man's clothing, save what's within the bounds of decency, and it's my belief that these have been observed. I want to declare to both competitors that I wish them the best of good fortune and to make it clear to every man here that I wish only a fair race and no favour.'

Thus saying, he descended from the platform and strutted along the street towards the finish.

The starter, Father McCarthy, ordered the two runners to approach the starting line. The two men descended from the stage and McCarthy tossed a silver dollar to decide lanes. Billy Joe lost, the men shook hands, and Buck chose the lane nearest the Last Chance Hotel, closest to his main body of supporters.

Father McCarthy had no need to call for silence. As the two men walked to their marks a hush travelled along Main Street, covering the one hundred and thirty yards of the race quicker than any Fast Man had ever done.

'Get to your marks . . .'

Buck and Billy Joe stood on the scratch line, toes to the line, legs flexed, each man staring glassily at the ground in front of him, the point at which the first stride would land.

'Get set . . .'

Both men raised their arms straight; one arm back, the other forward, and for a moment they were like characters in an ancient frieze.

The gun unleashed them, releasing too the roar of the crowd. Billy Joe and Buck got off the mark at the first attempt, as one man, their first strides perfectly synchronised, like dancers. For the first twenty yards the two men were locked together, not an inch between them, still matching strides. Then Billy Joe started to edge ahead and at fifty yards there was daylight between the two. But Boone and Medina, watching from the balcony at Mulligan's, had seen Buck give away a yard or more before and finish like a god, and were not troubled.

For ten yards the gap remained steady, with both runners,

despite the roar of the crowd, appearing to move in some still, silent world all their own. Then Billy Joe's whippy, high-stepping stride stretched his lead to a yard and at Macy's Livery, with fifty yards to go, the gap increased further to a yard and a half.

'C'mon Buck, start your rush,' hissed Medina to himself. But at ninety yards Billy Joe had increased his lead to two yards, and was going away.

Then came Buck's rush, the grandstand finish that had put so many greenbacks in the pockets of the citizens of Canyon City. In ten yards he had picked up a foot, then in the next ten another foot, and the same again in the next.

But Buck had run out of time. Billy Joe preserved his pumping, high-knee action right through the tape, to win by a clear yard. Judge Halsey's shouts of 'Thirteen point two! Thirteen point two!' were lost in the roar that swamped the two men, as Buck, head down, hands on knees, was almost bowled over in the rush as the crowds poured off the side-walks to get at Billy Joe, Canyon City's new Fast Man.

Above them, Medina and Boone, stricken, looked at the teeming throng in disbelief. Boone checked his watch.

'Got Buck at thirteen and a quarter,' he said. 'Fastest he ever ran hereabouts.'

'But not fast enough.' It was Moriarty, on the balcony behind them, his face straining hard to conceal his delight.

Buck had left town before nightfall, though no one had seen him go. He had, however, publicly met his debt to Moriarty in the bar of the Last Chance — three and a half thousand dollars, every cent that he had earned that sweet, swift summer in Canyon City. Folks were sorry to see him leave, for everyone was agreed that he was a fine fellow. But he was a loser, and folks had no time for that, especially when their hard-earned bucks were riding on his back.

Moriarty had been magnanimous to a fault. With ten

thousand bucks from Halsey, five from Medina and five from Boone he could afford to be. It had been drinks for everyone all round at Mulligan's, and none of your panther piss or Taos Lightning either. No, it was your genuine Paris, France champagne, crate upon crate of it at fifty bucks a box.

Nor was there any ill-feeling from the principals. Moriarty, Halsey, Medina and Boone stood drinking together at the rail, while over in the corner, where they had first encountered him, Billy Joe, the travails of the English Method far behind him, was whooping and hallooing it up with half the riff-raff of the neighbourhood.

Mulligan stood behind the bar, his great fat face glowering. He had lost two hundred bucks on Buck.

'You best find yourself another line of work, Medina,' he said, pushing a fresh bottle of champagne across to the cardsharp. 'This one sure don't fit your pistol.'

Medina scowled and poured some of the bubbling liquid into his glass. 'I got no beef,' he said. 'It was all fair and square.'

'No question,' said Boone. 'We caught Buck at thirteen and a quarter seconds, a tenth faster than he ever ran here.'

'Just Billy Joe ran one yard quicker,' said Medina.

'But you *clocked* him,' hissed Halsey as Moriarty turned to collect another bottle. Medina gestured Halsey to keep his voice down, and withdrew his stopwatch from his fob pocket. He surveyed it, shook it, held it close to his ear, then shook his head.

'Must be full of prairie dust,' he said finally. 'You in need of a timepiece, Mulligan?' He flipped the watch to the barman who caught it and examined it with interest.

'Just don't time no fast men with it,' said Halsey.

'I got to hand it to you, Moriarty,' said Boone, stroking his walrus moustache. 'Your English Method had us all beat.'

Moriarty tapped the side of his nose. 'The wonders of modern science, Marshal,' he said. 'Billy Joe simply proved to be an ideal vehicle.'

48

'Never thought to see all that sweating, shitting and running bringing a man to such a pitch,' growled Boone.

Moriarty did not reply, but sipped his drink, coughing as the icy bubbles hit the back of his throat. 'No,' he said. 'The deciding factor had nothing to do with the English Method. It was something quite different. A new element in athletic training, some might say a revolutionary one.'

'And what was that?' asked Boone.

'Well, the sweats and the Black Jack, even the punch-ball training, that was all part of the Captain's regime, followed, I might say, to the very letter. But I've watched a parcel of foot-races in my day and I've seen many a fast man fall apart in the final twenty yards. "DOA", we call it in the profession.' He sipped his drink.

'DOA?' said Medina, his brows furrowed.

'Dead on Arrival,' explained Moriarty. 'They tighten up, 'cos they don't have the bottom.'

'Bottom?' prompted Medina.

'Endurance,' said Boone testily.

'So l decided, let's have Billy Joe do his fast work at Macy's, starts and so on, but out at Blanco Canyon I'll pace me out one hundred and forty yards, ten more than the racing distance . . .'

'One hundred and forty?' said Halsey, spluttering on his drink.

'Yes,' said Moriarty, blithely. 'My walking stride is exactly thirty-nine inches long and l took one hundred and thirty paces, which measures just over one hundred and forty yards. It certainly paid off, because I knew that Buck had a big rush at the finish. But I must say Billy Joe held him off good.'

The three men round the Professor could scarcely bear to look at one another. Moriarty reached back to the bar to pick up a fat leather-bound volume. He put it under his left arm and drained his glass.

'I must go. Virginia City next Saturday, so Eleanor and I

must make an early start. *Hamlet*. I must say that it's been a pleasure doing business with you gentlemen.'

He shook each man by the hand.

'What was the name of that stuff you fed Billy Joe?' said Medina.

'Black Jack,' said Moriarty. He reached into his inside pocket, withdrew a small slip of paper and passed it to Medina. 'Here's the recipe.'

'I'll start tomorrow,' mumbled Medina.

'Then take this,' said Moriarty, handing him the volume. 'The Works of William Shakespeare. It'll help you pass the time in the john.'

It was almost dark, and in the gloaming Moriarty's wagon could just be seen in the light of his flickering camp-fire, while, a few feet beyond, the waters of the stream glinted as the moon passed from behind a cloud. The evening was still and the approaching lone horseman could be heard for miles before Moriarty saw him finally break the gloom and enter the perimeter of their camp.

Moriarty was busying himself with the basting of a chicken on a spit when the rider's identity finally became clear

'Buck!' he said. 'Come join us. Just in time for supper.

Buck Miller dismounted, taking off his hat in deference to Eleanor, who had that moment come out of the caravan, carrying four tin plates.

'Thank you, Mr Moriarty. Evening, ma'am.'

He sat down on a log, warming his hands, but hardly had he settled than there was the sound of another horseman, this time galloping. It was Mandy Boone who trotted into the light of the fire, her pinto wet and foaming. Moriarty and Eleanor were pleased to see her but hardly surprised, for it had been clear to them for weeks that Mandy had no heart for school-marming in Canyon City and that her real interest lay in acting. Mandy, indifferent to Buck's presence, babbled on endlessly about her ambitions over the Arbuckle's at the camp-fire and they were glad to indulge her. Eleanor nevertheless made it clear to her that Moriarty's Theatre of the West was no Niblo's Theatre, New York. She also made it clear that Mandy's disappearance would be a severe blow to her father, a betrayal which he was unlikely to forgive. But Mandy Boone was adamant. At twenty-one she was old enough to make up her own mind, she said, and if they would only have her she would accept whatever terms they offered. Moriarty looked across the fire at Eleanor and her nod was sufficient. The company had a new member.

The last visitor arrived half an hour later, the sound of his horse clear for miles in the still night. The rider stopped and dismounted in a single movement. He walked swiftly into the light of the camp-fire, rubbing both hands together as he did so.

'Evening, folks,' he said. 'What's for supper?'

Moriarty rose and reached into his back pocket, withdrawing a fat money-clip.

'Fifteen thousand dollars, Billy Joe,' he said.

4

THE MAKING OF MORIARTY

The dark and secret paths of pedestrianism were second nature to Moriarty, who had been virtually born into the sport, by courtesy of his father, Alan Cameron, late of Sutherland, Scotland.

It was 1848, and Moriarty had been eight years old — named 'Douglas' after his grandfather — when famine had struck his home town. The population, already ravaged by the brutal clearances imposed by the Countess of Sutherland in order to free the land for sheep-farming, had been almost entirely dependent on the potato harvest. But that year the crop had been attacked by blight and the crofters left with only an evil black slime.

Douglas's mother, Morag, had died of tuberculosis that first bitter winter following the failure of the crop, and his father had hacked the frost-bound ground in the churchyard for two days and nights in order that she might be given a decent burial. That night, in March 1848, he and his father had sat huddled round the peat fire in the dim light of a candle in the freezing croft.

'We're done here, son,' said his father, as if Douglas were an adult. 'We're off. Away.' He had paused. 'When I get strong.'

The next morning he had slaughtered their only surviving animal, an ancient cow, and they had spent the next two days dismembering its teaky carcass and salting down the beef. The two Camerons had virtually lived off salt beef and porridge for the next eight weeks, until the snows had melted from the sour mosses of Glencalvie. And each day his father had left Douglas on his own for the two hours between 10.00 a.m. and noon, returning mysteriously on each occasion red and sweating, and breathing heavily.

On 28 June they had packed their belongings. It had not taken long, and neither Alan nor his son had taken a backward glance at the croft as they had trekked up the glen towards the kirk at Glencalvie. Once at the church, Alan had informed the minister that his furniture and what remained of the beef should be disposed of amongst the crofters, as the minister saw fit. After a few moments at his ife's grave, Alan Cameron and his son walked south, hand in hand.

That week of walking would always be sharply etched in Moriarty's memory. Luckily the weather had been good and man and boy made fifteen to twenty miles a day through Sutherland's mountain-ranges, their harshness now mellowed by the warm summer sun. Though the eight-year-old Douglas was well-shod in sturdy, hand-made brogues, his young legs could not take the long miles. But the boy's pride would not accept his being carried, and somehow he kept going, never knowing how long the next painful stint might be.

Every night they would find shelter beneath an overhang or a tree, and his father would devise a makeshift bed of heather. There, covered in their Cameron plaids, they would sleep till early morning, Alan Cameron hugging the eight-year-old lad closely to him.

Moriarty would later reflect that those few short days had irrevocably bound him to his father.

Each morning they had slaked their thirst from the mountain streams that slashed the bleak Highland mosses and used the water to make their porridge, his father adding the necessary salt from a leather pouch. Then it was onwards south, the lonely figures of man and boy dwarfed by mountains looming over them like sleeping monsters.

At Altnaharra, on the second day, they had stopped at a crofter's house to buy milk, and the little boy, already quivering with fatigue although they had only covered some half-dozen miles, could hardly hold the bowl of creamy milk to his lips. His father had spoken to the crofter in the Gaelic, for the man had little English, and Douglas had strained to catch a wisp of their conversation. But the words he had picked up had meant nothing to him. 'Games' were mentioned, and sums of money, but he could make little of it.

On the fourth day they had reached the village of Lairg and there, their salt beef depleted, had bought their first meat. Douglas had never before eaten a meat pie and he devoured it like a hungry dog, as if somehow its nourishment might immediately revive his jaded body.

Bonar-Bridge was reached a day later, and there father and son had sat by the river, allowing the cold water to run over their tired legs. Then it was on to Dingwall, the first town which either Douglas or his father had ever seen. They had spent the day wandering wide-eyed through its cobbled streets, gazing at its immaculate grey-stone, two-storey houses and goggling at the gentry in their carriages. Douglas felt happier when he felt his father's grip strengthen as they made their way south, out of Dingwall, and the signs began to show 'Strathpeffer'.

That last morning, long before they had reached Strathpeffer, they could hear the wail of pipes, floating down the sunlit glen towards them, guiding them to what proved to have been their immediate destination. Alan Cameron's grip on his son's hand had tightened once again, and they had quickened their pace.

Then, suddenly, below them lay Strathpeffer, nestling in the summer sunshine, two lines of cottages. But at the entry to the village, in a grassy bowl, hundreds — perhaps thousands — of people had gathered, wreathed in the sound of a score of pipes.

'The Games,' said his father, without explanation. Half

an hour later they had reached the gamesfield and Alan Cameron had made his way through the milling crowds to the Secretary's tent. There a tam-o'-shantered little man swamped by bristling muttonchop whiskers sat at a collapsible camp table, scratching busily with a quill pen.

'Well, ma man?' he said gruffly in English.

'When are the running events, sir?' asked Alan.

'You're no' a local man then?'

'No.'

'Then ye'll have to compete in the open races, at three o'clock. Which events?'

'All of them.'

The little man's eyebrows rose but he said nothing and duly entered Alan Cameron's name for every event from the 100 yards to the hill race. Then Douglas's father had gone to the competitors' tent to rest till the afternoon, leaving the boy to wander about the games field.

The Strathpeffer Games were known in the area as 'The Gathering', for that was what it was, a gathering of country folk after the rigours of a Highland winter. No one could remember when they had first been held. Certainly it had been before the horrors of Culloden Field in 1746, when the Jacobite clans had been slaughtered by the king's forces under 'Butcher' Cumberland. The Games, under pressure of restrictive laws, had then lapsed until 1786, when they were revived, and now even the once-banned kilt was permitted.

These were the hardest times, a time of the destruction of the Highland population by the lairds as the subsistence farming of crofters was brutally replaced by sheep-farming. Many Highlanders had died in the famine, while tens of thousands had emigrated to the Dominions or moved down to the industrial towns of central Scotland. A culture was dying, and the gatherings were one of its last manifestations.

Young Douglas had watched all that morning as the local heavies had launched putting-stone and sledge-hammer, struggled with the giant two-hundred-pound Strathpeffer caber, and finally battled to lift the Clach Cuid Fir, the Stone of Manhood, weighing over two hundredweight. Then had come the wrestling, Cumberland style, an exhausting physical exchange that left sturdy Highlanders limp with fatigue.

It was two o'clock when Douglas had wakened his father for the first event, the 100 yards, and half an hour later Alan Cameron, dressed in white long-johns and shirt, and barefooted, stood poised at the start of the sprint final, having finished second in his heat. A blast of a trumpet signalled the start and the ten runners bounded up the narrow bumpy track, jostling and elbowing. From the start, Alan Cameron struggled in the middle of the field, never able to catch the leaders and always under pressure from the runners behind him. Cameron had a loping, tangy stride, but there was no thrust, no power in it, and he ended in fifth position, out of the money.

Half an hour later, in the 220 yards, it was the same story, though this time Alan Cameron ended fourth; but there were only three prizes. His first success came in the quarter mile, where he was placed third, earning himself five shillings.

By the time the half mile (with a first prize of £1) had arrived, the thousand-strong crowd had begun to notice the lean, leggy Sutherland man, and there were shouts of encouragement as he came to the starting line. At the blast of the trumpet Cameron bounded off into the lead, his long legs devouring the ground. At half-way he was twenty yards ahead, and with only a furlong to go he held on to fifteen of those yards. But coming into the final straight his legs began to weaken and he was being drawn in on a long rope by a stocky young Ballater runner. When he reached the finishing line and fell to the ground on the rough grass beyond it he was only inches ahead — but he had finally come first. Douglas rushed to his father as officials levered him to his feet, and walked proudly beside him as he was half-dragged to the competitors' tent.

There, in a corner amid the steamy moistness of the tent,

Alan Cameron sat on the damp grass, sweat pouring down his lean open face, while his son crouched anxiously in front of him. Cameron sensed Douglas's unspoken question.

'We're going to America, laddie,' he said, speaking in gasps. 'Just the mile and the hill race to go. Then it's on tomorrow to Ballater Games and Aboyne. That's where the big money is.'

Suddenly Alan became aware that there was someone else in the tent. There, standing at the tent-flap, was a plump little moustachioed man in bowler hat and loud check suit, a thick cigar projecting from his lips.

'America, is it?' he said, in a thick Glasgow accent. 'You'll no' get as far as the Broomielaw Dock on the Clyde, no' the way ye're going.' He crossed the tent and bent down to extend a soft fat hand.

'Edward Bell,' he said. 'Supporter of Scottish pedestrianism.' He bent down further so his face came in line with Alan Cameron's.

'Now, you've got bottom, lad, and a wee bit of pace.' He said. 'And a heart as big as a pumpkin. But you're no' using the heid.' At this he took out a watch from an inside waistcoat pocket. 'Ah clocked you at inside sixty seconds for the first quarter mile out there. But the second lap, that was closer to eighty.' He wagged a finger. 'Ye've got to *pace* yerself, man. Pace yeself.'

Alan Cameron did not reply. The pulse in his left temple was still throbbing, the perspiration continuing to pour down his face.

'How much have ye won?'

His father said nothing. 'One pound five shillings,' volunteered Douglas.

'Ye'll no' go far on that,' said Bell, not unkindly.

Alan Cameron coughed, and involuntarily spat a gob of phlegm on to the grass in front of him.

'I'll run at Ballater and Aboyne,' he said.

'Ballater? Aboyne? It'll be a week afore you're fit to run

again, man,' said Bell. 'And the best footracers in Scotland, they'll all be there. Ye won't pick up five bob at Ballater or Aboyne, ye can take Edward Bell's word for that.'

Bell checked his watch. 'It's an hour to the mile and an hour after that there's the hill race. If ah put yer prize-money on a wee double with one of the gentry, ah can put twenty-five quid in yer pocket. But ye've got to follow my instructions. Run to orders. What d'ye say?'

'Does that mean I've got to win both races?'

The little man nodded. 'Ye can do it. As I said, ye've got bottom and ye've got a wee bit o' speed. All ye've got to do is to pace yerself. Use the heid and we can both come out with a few pounds. What d'ye say?'

This time it was Alan Cameron who nodded, and Bell began to talk to him in a low, urgent voice.

An hour later the Sutherland man, leading the field, duped the following runners into a slow first three-quarters of a mile and strode away in the final quarter-mile to win easily, to be handed a guinea in prize money.

The hill race was less easy, for the fatigue of a week's walking and the day's racing had caught up with Alan Cameron. But the hills had been his life and his legs were well used to the localised agonies of fell-running. He came home to win by a good ten yards – and to a prize of thirty shillings.

The Strathpeffer Gamesfield was deserted when Edward Bell drew open the flap of the tent and entered. He held in his hand a thick wad of notes, more money than Alan Cameron had ever seen.

'Ah got better odds than ah thought,' Bell said. 'Forty-two pun' fourteen shillings. Ye can go to America first class.'

And so on 1 August 1848 the Camerons had set sail for the United States. '

Alan Cameron would not for worlds have admitted it, but he knew as little of New York as his young son. For his only

58

experience of a large town — Dingwall had hardly been that — had been the three weeks they had spent together in Glasgow, living at a grimy tenement boarding house off Argyll Street, as he and Douglas waited for the departure of their ship.

Glasgow was like a decayed tooth, its dark, wet alleys lined with poverty like a scale-furred kettle. The two Camerons were glad to see the back of it as they sailed on the *S.S. Troy* from the black, greasy waters of the Broomielaw Quay.

Alan Cameron had heard terrible tales of the steerage trip to America, from letters that had come back to Glencalvie from the New World since the late 1780s, when the first of the terrible Clearances had begun. They were stories of vomiting agonies in the depths of sea-washed, rat-infested holds, and he had therefore resolved that even if he were to arrive in New York penniless he and his boy would travel in comfort. Thus he had secured a small, well-appointed two-berth cabin.

Next door was lodged a man who was to change both of their lives, Gregor McGregor.

McGregor was a strapping giant of a man, fully six feet four and sixteen stones. He was making his way to the New World to appear on the stage of the Park Street Theatre in a revival of *Rob Roy, the Highland Rogue*, having previously distinguished himself in that role in London and Leeds.

Each night, after (and sometimes during) dinner Gregor would regale his fellow passengers with readings from *Rob Roy*, *King Lear* and *Richelieu*, booming on endlessly in his sonorous Highland bass. Cameron and his son sat transfixed, the older man amazed that anyone could possess so many words, let alone remember them or repeat them in such tumbling profusion. Fortunately for Alan, Gregor was complemented by another Thespian, an Irish comic actor, Dennis Flaherty, also bound for New York to play a supporting role in the Irish farce *Brulgruddery*. Flaherty had an endless flow of stories and kept his audience helpless with mirth so that even

59

the normally shy Alan Cameron lost his reserve and joined in the general laughter.

But for young Douglas Cameron the rantings of McGregor and the banter of Flaherty triggered off something at his very core. He observed each night the faces of the other passengers and noted how they hung on every word of the two actors, saw how the tears streamed down their faces as McGregor became the mad King Lear and yet how only moments later more tears, this time of laughter, poured forth as Flaherty told stories of his Irish past. It was then that Douglas Cameron resolved to become an actor.

The giant McGregor and his tiny Irish friend Flaherty decided between them to take the Sutherland man and his son under their wing. Flaherty had been in New York ten years before, in the palmy days of the great tragedian, Junius Brutus Booth, and knew it to be a tough town for penniless immigrants, offering even the toughest Irish labourers only a miserable twenty dollars a month. It was therefore resolved that Alan Cameron and his son would stay with Flaherty, at least until they had found their feet.

On their arrival in New York McGregor was greeted by the management of the Park Street Theatre like royalty and was met on the quay by a carriage. So Flaherty and the Camerons arrived at Flaherty's flat above the Burton Theatre in some style.

New York was a city beyond the Camerons' wildest imaginings, a seething maelstrom of broad streets, houses five storeys and more high, of thoroughfares loud with the squeal of horses, the bellowing of street traders and the grind of carriages. Alan Cameron had cause to be glad that Flaherty was giving them shelter, for he had, in that first confused day of arrival been shocked and disturbed by the brutal world he had seen through the carriage windows. To the Presbyterian Cameron, New York was a Babylon, a melée of all the races of the world clawing, jostling and elbowing for position. Life in Sutherland had been hard, but it had related to the simple demands of the land. Here he felt lost.

Unlike McGregor, Dennis Flaherty was a practical and sensitive man, and he realised that the Camerons would have difficulty in surviving without help. Despite rehearsal demands he made sure that Alan Cameron was fully employed helping backstage, as a carpenter, paying Alan seven dollars a week wages out of his own pocket, then, under pressure from the proud Scotsman, taking back three in rent. Meanwhile, Douglas Cameron wandered freely about the wonderland of the Park Street Theatre, his head full of dreams.

But it was, surprisingly, from Gregor McGregor that the Sutherland man's big opportunity was to come. McGregor had been a hit in *Rob Roy* in more ways than one. Each night at the Park Street Theatre Rob Roy had several –stage battles, all of which McGregor pursued with manic — and often alcoholic — fury. The result was that in the first tumultuous fortnight the Scot had put four of New York's finest stage-swordsmen in hospital.

During the voyage on the *S.S. Troy*, Alan Cameron had frequently practised with McGregor on deck with wooden sword and quarter-staff and could easily cope with him with both weapons. It was therefore to Cameron that Hamblin, the manager of the theatre, came, at McGregor's prompting,to ask him to play three separate parts, for the salary of thirty dollars a week.

Alan Cameron could not believe his luck.

Thus six nights a week, and on Saturday matinées, Alan Cameron battled with Gregor McGregor with claymore and quarter-staff on the stage of the Burton Street Theatre. Soon, as their battles became stereotyped the two men began to think of ways in which they could develop their 'fights', which had become a popular feature of the play. Alan saw that one way lay in the reconstruction of the sets, using different levels, so that jumps could be employed. Then he created a springboard

61

so that McGregor could soar from one level to another, and finally added ropes so that he and 'Rob Roy' could swing across the stage.

The fights in *Rob Roy* became a feature of the New York season, one which embraced works as diverse as Edwin Forrest's *Hamlet*, Marty's *Havana Opera*, the Irish farce *His Last Legs* and P. T. Barnum's sundry offerings at his Museum.

At one end of the scale, in the 'stews' of the Bowery, rats scuttled between the legs of an audience who had paid 12½ cents to sit on hard wooden benches; at the other, a dollar changed hands in order to witness Shakespeare at Niblo's Gardens.

For Alan Cameron, Rob Roy had been a perfect opportunity to make his way in the strange fantasy-world of theatre, itself a salient part of the fastest-growing city on earth. But he had no desire to spend the rest of his life staging sword-fights. He had discovered, at the Park and then at Burton's, that he had a talent for the building of sets, and when in February J.P. Marsh looked for a set-designer for a musical play, *The Enchantress*, it was to Alan Cameron that he came.

On 26 August the play opened with its first big set-piece, 'Pirates' Ship at Anchor', which drew spontaneous applause. *The Enchantress* was a slim piece, little more than a series of linked musical sketches and tableaux, but its sets were impressive, and one of the final scenes, 'The Regent's Palace on Fire', was so realistic that it nightly drew forth screams from ladies in the audience. At curtain-call Marsh was forced to break with tradition and bring his young Scots set-designer before the audience.

Alan Cameron was made. In the autumn of 1849, he moved with Douglas to a fine three-storeyed house in Park Avenue. For Douglas, his father's turn of fortune meant that he could now live in a world in which he already felt completely at home. However, Alan Cameron's feelings for his homeland were strong, and he soon linked up with other Scots expatriates, members of the New York Caledonian Society. Douglas was sent to a Scots school on Fifth Avenue, where an inflexible Glasgow dominie called Alexander McCanna taught him the basics of Reading, Writing and Arithmetic.

There, in the tiny one-room school, the young Cameron daily scraped away upon his slate-board and recited his tables in constant fear of Mr McCanna's leather tawse upon his palms. But the world that he longed for was that in which his father now lived — that of the theatre. When Niblo's Gardens sought a Puck for their 1850 production of *A Midsummer Night's Dream*, twelve-year-old Douglas begged his father for the chance to audition for the part. Alan Cameron agreed, and Junius Brutus Booth himself was engaged to coach him for the role.

Booth, now old and almost mad, had been the great hope of the American theatre in the early part of the century. He had originally come from England and had in 1825 returned to put himself to the test against Edmund Kean, who had already established himself as the greatest Shakespearean actor of his time. But Booth soon realised that he was not in the same class. The English actor showed Booth that he had no 'bottom', that he simply did not have the psychic endurance for the great classic roles. Booth realized that he had cruised through the greater part of the plays, saving himself for the big dramatic speeches; this was not great acting, rather merely a form of dramatic oratory. He returned to the United States a wiser man.

Whatever his limitations as an actor, the eccentric Booth was an excellent teacher. Shakespeare was his home territory and Douglas Cameron was taught how the rhythm of the verse gave weight to the words. Booth also devised all manner of play-activities and word-games to enliven the monotony of learning. He taught Douglas not only the fundamentals of diction but, equally importantly, set him daily voice-projection exercises to enable him to throw his voice from the diaphragm rather than the throat.

On the afternoon of 15 January 1851 the twelve-year-old Douglas auditioned for the part of Puck in the Niblo's Gardens against twenty-five youthful aspirants of both sexes. Gregor McGregor, Flaherty (himself playing Bottom) and the boy's father, Alan Cameron, sat in the almost empty theatre, trembling on the outcome. But mad old Junius Brutus Booth had done his work well, and Douglas secured the part, showing admirable control under the pressure of the audition. It was then that his proud mentor dubbed him 'The New Moriarty' after an outstanding child actor of half a century back. Douglas thought that it was a fine name, though his father and Mr McCanna had doubts, for it was certainly not a Scottish one.

The Niblo's Theatre 'Dream' was an outstanding success, not least because of Flaherty's marvellous performance as Bottom. The production centred on Flaherty, ignoring the romantic and poetic elements of the play, pivoting rather upon the drolleries of Bottom and his mechanicals. Flaherty drilled his bumpkins till they became an uproariously funny comic team, and Niblo's 'Dream' ran well into the spring of 1851.

But the young Moriarty's performance was not lost in the lunacies of Bottom and his bumpkins. Moriarty gave a splendid account of Puck, making up for what he lacked in dramatic experience by the gymnastic vigour of his acting. Alan Cameron devised a series of invisible pulleys for Puck's flights and, using concealed trampettes, gave Douglas natural-seeming 'flights' which enraptured Niblo's audiences and drew sighs and loud applause.

Early in 1852 Moriarty acquired a mother — in the personable form of Mary Sweeney ('the Irish Nightingale'), a young singer from Kerry who had achieved considerable success on the Eastern seaboard. Mary, though sharing her husband's belief in the formality of a Scottish education, was sensitive to Moriarty's enthusiasm for the stage. Under her patient tuition he developed as a singer and in the recitation of comic monologues.

This final part in Moriarty's dramatic development began, appropriately, at the point when his earlier tutor, Junius Brutus Booth, died, in May of 1852; for Moriarty had grown to like and respect the strange old man.

It was also in 1852 that Moriarty was first to show his abilities in the athletic world, winning a handicap youths' half-mile in the New York Caledonian Games, from a generous start, at the Myrtle Gardens.

Since his eleventh birthday, Moriarty had been a member of the German Gymnastics Institute which stood only a few blocks away from his home. Excited by the physical challenges of the gymnasium, with its horizontal and parallel bars and vaulting horses, Moriarty also found above the gymnasium, on the balcony, a curved track, one hundred and forty-five yards round, and he was encouraged by Herr Steinbach, the burly, mustachioed trainer who managed the Institute, to run a couple of miles daily on its board surface. In 1852, at the age of thirteen, he had, clocked by Steinbach, run just over six minutes for a mile on the cramped curves of the Institute track.

The prizes at the New York Caledonian Games were generous; they could afford to be, for the Gathering drew crowds of over 20,000 at up to 50 cents a ticket. Thus young Moriarty saw for the first time professional foot-racers, men who made their living at the sport of pedestrianism, for runners from all over the Eastern seaboard flocked to New York for the big money prizes.

But though the Scottish expatriates dominated their traditional throwing and jumping events, few of them could cope with hardened 'peds' from St Louis and Chicago, an élite capable of running close to even time for a hundred yards and well inside five minutes for a mile.

In 1853 and 1854, Moriarty tried his hand successfully at other Caledonian Games in Boston and Chicago. After again winning the youths' mile in New York in 1854, off a modest start, Moriarty decided in 1855 that it was time to compete with the men on scratch terms. He was now close on six feet, broad-shouldered and muscular from his years at the Institute, his freckled face and twinkling blue eyes set off by a mop of curly black hair. Moriarty always looked as if he had just heard a joke, or was just about to tell one. His years of formal Scottish education under Mr McCanna, an innate Scots Calvinism, and his pleasure in physical skills had retained in him a lack of guile, an innocence rare in someone in the theatrical profession.

So, in 1855, a rapidly-maturing Moriarty entered for the men's open mile, taking on the half-breed Steeprock and the recently-arrived Scottish 'ped', Ewan McIlwain.

Before a crowd of 25,000 and urged on by his father, two of the Booth sons, Edwin and John Wilkes, and most of New York's theatrical population, Moriarty clung to Steeprock and McIlwain for the first three laps. Then, throwing caution to the wind, as the trumpet sounded for the final lap he sprinted into the lead. The two 'peds', who already had an 'agreement' that McIlwain would win, were taken by surprise. But the nut-brown Indian, Steeprock, responded, his long, thin legs eating up the four-yard gap which Moriarty had created. Behind him the veteran, McIlwain, slip-streamed, only a foot behind, all the way up the back straight.

Then it happened. On the final bend, with only two yards spanning the three men and Moriarty, gasping, struggling to retain his slim lead, Steeprock reached forward and tapped Moriarty's rising right heel. The touch was enough to send the young runner tumbling, off-balance, into the infield.

Steeprock looked to his right at McIlwain, nodded, and the two men prepared to stage a mock 'battle' up the final hundred yards of the home straight. They would give the crowd a good show.

But Moriarty was not finished. Somehow he regained his balance and, rubber-legged, returned to the curve of the track, now seven yards down on his two adversaries.

Anger momentarily engulfed his fatigue. He began to sprint, pumping his knees high in front of him, his breath raging in his throat. With eighty yards to go he was only three yards down. Fifty yards from the tape he was a mere yard away.

Then, just as he was drawing level and with thirty yards still to go, the two 'peds', acting according to plan, made their dash for the tape. For ten yards Moriarty held them, before the accumulation of fatigue caught up with him and his legs, unable to support his weight, gave way and he fell past the finishing-line on to his face, well behind Steeprock and the pre-ordained victor, Ewan McIlwain.

Those New York Caledonian Games had been a revelation to Moriarty. First he had discovered that there existed men like Steeprock and McIlwain to whom footracing was a trade; he had learnt too that the race does not always go to the swift. But most of all he learnt that he had a talent, like his father, for distance-running.

At the same time he saw no clash of interest between his developing acting career and his involvement in foot-racing. In this he was supported by Edwin Booth, the most talented actor of the family. Edwin, frail of body himself, argued that an actor's physique was part of his capital and that Moriarty's athleticism could only be of value in his professional career — it was common knowledge he said, in the acting profession, that the legs were always the first to go.

By 1857, at the age of eighteen, Moriarty was playing everything from Irish farce in such deathless dramas as *Mother Grogan's Daughter* to Laertes in *Hamlet*. His father's thriving stage-design business now spanned New York, Boston and Philadelphia, and Moriarty would not only play in theatres in these towns but also visit plays in rehearsal, watching such Shakespearean stars as Charlotte Cushman in preparation, and observing how, in the dusty anonymity of the rehearsal-room, performances were built.

At the other end of the scale, back in New York, the young

Scot was able to visit the many circuses and freak-shows which battled for survival there. He learned the rudiments of horse-manship (Colonel Farrell) and acrobatics (Young Hengler) and the elements of conjuring (Professor Anderson, the Wizard of the North) at Phineas T. Barnum's American Museum.

When Moriarty was not greedily absorbing all that the stage had to offer, he was exercising his body mightily at the German Gymnastics Institute. Steinbach would not permit his young charge simply to run round the gallery track.

'No,' he said in his fractured English. 'Runner must be all-body strong.' Moriarty therefore daily pursued a rigorous routine of exercises created by the great German physical educationist, Jahn.

Though the pedestrian activities of New York and district were not as dense as its theatrical life, there were weekly matches between local runners and, less frequently, with visitors from towns as far apart as New Orleans, St Louis, Chicago and Boston.

During 1857, Moriarty, now eighteen, took on three matches against local opposition over half a mile and a mile and was victorious in every race, earning himself and his backers a total of over five thousand dollars. In late 1857, he was matched with the Irish 'champion' Muldoon over three-quarters of a mile and took the Irishman on the tape, winning — judiciously — by a bare yard. The New York Irish demanded a re-match and on 1 January 1858, for a wager of two hundred dollars, Moriarty gave Muldoon the kiss of death in the final straight over the same distance, to win this time by a clear ten yards.

Barnum, the shrewdest of Moriarty's mentors, advised that he lie low for most of 1858, and wait for rich pickings from runners coming from outside town. Thus, during the spring of 1858 he played in the Irish farce *Tom The Tyler* and then as Demetrius in *A Midsummer Night's Dream*, while daily keeping in condition at the Institute.

Other aspects of Moriarty's education had not been lacking.

In July 1858, when he was playing Demetrius at the Park for the first time, Mrs Alice Clay, playing Queen Titania, had thrown her regal status to the winds when he had visited her dressing-room between acts, carrying a replacement prop – the substitute crown. Mrs Clay had been standing behind a screen when he had entered her dressing-room.

She had been nothing if not direct. 'Bring it over here, young Moriarty,' she had cried in her deep, languorous voice, only her head and shoulders visible above the screen. He had stood, hesitantly, in front of her.

'Put it down there,' she said, pointing over the screen to her candlelit dressing-table. Obediently he had done as he was told.

'Come round here a moment,' she ordered, beckoning with her right hand. He moved to the right of the screen.

As he reached its edge he felt his knees go soft. For Mrs Clay was completely naked. His first shocked impression was of curved whiteness and of two great pouring pink nipples, perched on massive breasts. He had never seen a naked woman before and he felt a sweaty redness engulf his face and neck.

'Not much time, young man,' she said. 'So let's see what you're made of.'

She briskly pulled down his tights and cod-piece and his genitals flopped out, his penis stiffening visibly. She leant back and surveyed him.

'Not bad. Not bad at all.'

She turned to a little table behind her, dipped her hand into a pot of cold cream and slapped the cream between her legs.

'Now this is what I'm going to do. I'm going to lie over there.' She walked over to a couch in the corner, lay down and spread her legs. 'Fine,' she said. 'Now come over here.'

Numbly, Moriarty obeyed. She pulled him down on top of her and deftly slipped him inside her.

'Okay, Demetrius,' she said. 'Let's go.'

Instinctively, he drove down and felt her hips press up into him in response. Alice Clay's breathing soon began to quicken.

'It's close,' she groaned. 'Jesus, it's close.'

Suddenly her rhythm increased and for the first time during the encounter Alice Clay was no longer in control.

'Hit me, hit me, hit me!' she exclaimed, and he thrust hard down into her.

'Man, man, man!' she shouted, shuddering and scratching his shoulders and back. Then she subsided, though Moriarty involuntarily kept driving down on her, and in a flurry of thrusts he was gone, exploding into her, shouting as he did so.

She looked him in the eyes, her deep, curved lips smiling. 'Not bad,' she said. 'For a first attempt.'

There was a knock and she looked out over the screen as a stage-hand poked his head round the door.

'Two minutes, Mrs Clay,' he said.

Alice Clay smiled serenely and nodded over the top of the screen as the stage-hand's face disappeared. At her side Moriarty was desperately trying to rearrange his clothing.

The production of *A Midsummer Night's Dream* lasted a further four weeks, and in that short month Alice Clay took Moriarty through a lifetime of sexual experience. For although Mrs Clay's first assault upon him had been perfunctory, she was, in the comfort and luxury of her Park Avenue apartment, to show him a gentler, if still erotic side to her nature. Moriarty learned about foreplay, learned to dominate, if temporarily, his more experienced partner, both by teasing her towards a climax and by suddenly rushing her towards it without warning. Thus, when Alice Clay left for Boston — to play Lady Macbeth to Edwin Forrest's Thane — their sexual relationship, if not yet one of equals, was achieving a satisfactory balance.

News of Moriarty's sexual prowess was not long in travelling through the world of New York theatre, for Alice Clay was nothing if not garrulous, and the young actor-athlete was soon followed in both his Thespian and footracing pursuits by a devoted claque of young ladies. However, his innate Scottish Calvinism, coupled with his Spartan zeal in his training at the gymnasium, made him sparing with his favours. This in turn only increased the ardour of his followers and the period from 1858 to 1860 was rich in sexual experience.

His first experience with Alice Clay had been a shock to Moriarty. For he had discovered in himself a carnality which he had not expected. He had always liked girls, but from a distance, in an abstract way, being engrossed on the one hand with the development of his acting career and on the other with his athletic prowess.

But now, even though his sexuality had been aroused, it was neither random nor promiscuous, for by some strange personal rationalisation Moriarty reckoned that there was nothing much wrong with copulation if the ladies came to him rather than him going to them and if they were unmarried.

From the beginning, Moriarty's main backer in his pedestrian pursuits had been the ebullient showman Phineas T. Barnum. To Barnum, who was no sportsman himself, all life was a gamble. What else could it be for the man who had, single-handed, created the American Museum, who had brought to the American public General Tom Thumb and Jenny Lind? From the day that they had first met, Barnum had taken to Alan Cameron and his precocious son and helped the young Moriarty to develop a plethora of skills from the artistes in his Museum. When Moriarty had shown a talent for the running-path, Barnum, with Edwin Booth, had been his most enthusiastic backer, and he had picked up good money on him in the handicaps in Boston and Pittsburgh and in his match-races. So far Barnum had resisted the temptation to put Moriarty up against the hard men of pedestrianism, the 'cracks' of the East Coast or touring English professionals. But now his sensitive antennae told him that the young Scot was ready to take on one of the top-ranked footracers — and there would be long odds, since Moriarty's form had not yet been fully exposed

So in December 1858 a match was made against the Frenchman, Yves Latour, to take place in February of 1859

Latour had whipped everything set against him in the South, even beating a horse (running four laps to its eight) in New Orleans and achieving four and a half minutes for the mile in so doing, the first man in the United States to run such a time

The Frenchman, a Basque, had started, like many from the Basque region, as a jumper, and in 1853 in his late teens had cleared five and a half feet in the high jump and twenty-one feet in the long jump, and was unbeaten on the East Coast. Then, at nineteen, a heel injury had ended his jumping career and turned him to middle-distance running. Latour had shown an immediate talent for the distances and had cracked five minutes in his first mile at New Orleans Race Course in a thunderstorm. He had not been beaten since 1856, and came to New York with over ten thousand dollars on his back. Barnum and Booth got odds of between three and five to one against Moriarty for a match on 4 February at the Manhattan Island Race Track.

The race against Latour took place on one of the coldest days of a bleak, snowbound February. Phineas T. Barnum and Latour's backers agreed upon stakes of $500, and ensured a flat course of packed snow. At two o'clock that afternoon Moriarty and Latour stood at their marks, arms raised, frozen men in a frozen landscape. Then thick, swirling snowflakes began to fall, covering the runners and the two thousand spectators who had gathered at the rail of the course and on the fleecy mound of snow above the track on the infield.

The one-mile race was to be a single lap round the Manhattan Race Course. On the gun, the swarthy Frenchman bounded into an immediate lead. His backers had done a little checking on the young New York man; he was a novice, had only run against local boys, never been really pushed to his limits. More, Moriarty was an actor, so he would have seen plenty of the good life and would not have the 'bottom' for a really hard race. Thus Latour had been told to push hard from the start. So the Frenchman, clad in black long-sleeved vest and long-johns, churned up the snow a couple of yards in front of Moriarty as they pounded into the thin winter mist, their breathing throwing plumes of vapour in front of them. The going was surprisingly good, though both men could feel the cold through the soles of their thin moccasins. As they passed the first quarter-mile post, where Barnum, his father, and Edwin Booth stood with Latour's backers, by their steaming horses, the snow thickened, matting Moriarty's eyebrows and causing moisture to engulf his eyes, like tears.

'Sixty-nine, seventy,' roared Barnum, as Latour's men shouted their advice. 'Stay close, m'boy.'

He then turned, with Booth and Cameron, and they mounted their horses and galloped off, churning through the snow and mist towards the half-mile post.

The pace was fast and the snow was swirling down thickly as they took the long left-hand curve towards the half-mile post, and the crisp, firm path was now overlaid by a skin of fluffy snow, making it slippery and uncertain. Moriarty pinned himself grimly to Latour's right shoulder, the steam rising from his all-white vest and long-johns, as they closed in on the half-mile post.

Suddenly Moriarty felt Latour slacken and before he knew what had happened he was in the lead, making his own path through the white wall of snow, increasingly aware of his breathing and the burning, sweaty sensations in his face and neck. Somewhere in the far distance he could hear the roar of the crowd, which for its part was still quite unable to see either of the runners, but, eyes on their watches, knew that both men were less than two minutes away.

They passed the three-quarter-mile point with Moriarty

in a one yard lead, but this time only Barnum and his father were at the post, Barnum's roaring 'Three minutes forty-six seconds. Whip him boy, whip him!' lost in the blizzard and his own gathering fatigue. For Moriarty's breath was now raging in his throat and his legs were beginning to tire. Ahead was only the roar of the crowd, the finish-line an infinity away. The snow and his fatigue merged into a great frozen pain, and it was at that moment that Latour passed him, his choppy, powerful strides throwing snow back into Moriarty's face. It was then, with three hundred yards to go, that Moriarty felt core-fatigue, pain far beyond his muscles, for the first time in his life. He knew that he had dug deep and that there was nothing more left. Latour was only a dim, wraith-like figure moving away from him, and Moriarty felt he was no longer racing: simply surviving.

Then with a furlong to go, as the roar of the crowd came more strongly, piercing the cocoon of snow which enfolded him, he heard a clear bell-like voice. It was that of Edwin Booth, who sat astride his mount at the furlong point.

'The moment, Moriarty! The moment!'

They had often talked of 'being in the moment' during rehearsals, of being completely absorbed and committed to a role. That was the point at which all cohered, all became true and real in any drama.

Somehow, Booth's words reached deep inside Moriarty, touching something beyond his pain. His opponent was no longer in sight, but that did not matter, for what was happening no longer had anything to do with Latour, or the wager, or anything material.

Moriarty started to sprint, his breath rasping in his throat like fingernails on emery paper. Somehow, his flagging legs were driven on, the softness of the snow ignored. With a hundred yards to go Latour was in sight, only ten yards away. The New Orleans man's hips were low, his feet hitting the ground heel-first — a sure sign of fatigue.

But Moriarty was beyond picking up clues to his opponent's condition. He ran like a machine, his arms working like pistons, driving into the snow. With fifty yards to go, he could almost touch the fading Latour. But the impulse of Booth's words had nearly melted from Moriarty's psyche and the two yards between him and Latour seemed an impassable gulf.

Then it happened. With thirty yards to go, Latour took a single, desperate look over his right shoulder. That was enough — the confirmation that the Frenchman hurt as much as he did, the confirmation of the man's frailty, his humanity, penetrated Moriarty's isolation. He launched himself forward; all technique lost in a void of suffering. With five yards to go he had caught and passed Latour and he toppled through the tape, furrowing the snow beyond it.

It was a week before Moriarty was allowed to leave hospital and even then, seven days after his triumph, he was still the hero of New York, applauded before the curtain at plays as diverse as *Hamlet*, *Mother Carey's Daughters* and *The Heroes of Fort McCoy*. He was unable to work for a month and Phineas T. Barnum provided, in addition to his share of the wager and the side bets amounting to $1500, all hospital bills and two months' salary. Then, five weeks after the race, Barnum linked with the Booths, Forrest and other New York theatrical luminaries to hold a gala benefit which raised eight thousand dollars on Moriarty's behalf and two thousand for the gallant Latour.

In early April Moriarty went to his next appointment with Doctor Sutherland, who had conducted his treatment since the race. He left Sutherland's surgery a broken young man. For the doctor's advice had been categorical: Moriarty had 'athlete's heart', and all thoughts of pedestrianism must be discarded for ever.

5

THE FURTHER MAKING OF MORIARTY

The first night of the three-week voyage Moriarty dreamt of jungle drums. The second morning he fancied he heard a rhythmic thud somewhere far above him, but it faded, to be replaced by the familiar slap of waves on the hull of the *S.S. Troy*, as it steamed on a placid Atlantic, bound for Liverpool, England.

The years since the match with Latour had been fruitful ones. Moriarty's friendship with the Booths had brought him a host of good roles in New York, while he had also toured several times with the eccentric and volatile John Wilkes Booth as Laertes to his Hamlet.

But it was his friendship with Barnum which had extended his range. Barnum had encouraged him to play in comedy and melodrama and introduced him to gymnasts and equestrians, so that before long he became, somewhat to his surprise, an accomplished rider and acrobat. Edwin Booth had supported this policy, reasoning that the wider the range of Moriarty's skills the more he would have to offer in all branches of theatre.

Moriarty's marriage of 'serious' drama with farce, circus and melodrama was in perfect accord with the melting-pot of the mid-century New York stage; it also answered something within Moriarty himself, an intense desire to acquire every possible skill. He realised well enough that he was not in the same class as Edwin Booth as a tragedian, and never would be. But he did have a range which even Booth would never possess; he was, as Barnum put it, 'an inch deep, but a mile long'.

Thus, when in late 1861 Booth decided to tackle the English stage, as had his father thirty-six years before him, and asked his young friend to accompany him, Moriarty jumped at the chance. His enthusiasm was heightened by two other factors. The first was that Alice Clay, now Mrs Millard Cohen, the wife of a ruthless New York millionaire, had made it clear — before departing in September 1861 on the Grand Tour — that she had already tired of her corpulent, middle-aged spouse and would look to re-establish their relationship on her return. But Moriarty had no desire to tangle with any of Cohen's ex-prizefighter henchmen, even for someone as beguiling as Alice Clay.

The second was that England was the home of pedestrianism, and Moriarty was eager to view the greatest footracers in the world. Only a year before, the English impresario George Martin had brought the cream of British professional running to New York and they had thrashed the best that America had to offer. There had been calls in the New York press for Moriarty to return to the running-path to face the all-conquering English. He had, quite rightly, demurred.

Not that he had followed Sutherland's advice to the letter. Moriarty found it impossible to give up athletics, and only a few weeks after he had been cleared by Dr Sutherland he returned to the Institute gymnasium and began a programme of light gymnastic exercises. By September 1859 he had started to trot round the curves of the gallery, at first only a mile a day, at a gentle seven-minute mile speed. Two years later he was cruising round the indoor Brooklyn track, three miles every day at only a few seconds outside five minutes per mile. Thus, by the combination of skeletal exercise, using Indian clubs and dumbbells, and a gentle, progressive running programme, at the age of twenty-three Moriarty had unwittingly made himself again into a powerful running machine, with reserves that he had not possessed before, even in his competitive days.

But although he trained rigorously Moriarty resisted the temptation to race again. Training was physical but racing was emotional. Thus he saw no contradiction between Dr Sutherland's diagnosis of 'athlete's heart' and his ability to turn out mile after mile of quality running round a cramped Brooklyn gymnasium. Moriarty desperately feared that extra five per cent of effort that competition demanded, and although he had longed to challenge the great English athletes he knew he no longer possessed the courage to compete at such a level. If he did push himself, he knew it might prove fatal.

There it was again, that steady, rhythmic thudding above him on the deck. It was no dream.

He swung both legs out of bed, pulled on his dressing-gown and thrust his feet into leather slippers. He opened the door of his cabin and ran along the narrow corridor towards the companionway that led to the deck, bumping his shoulders against its oak walls as the ship rolled in light waves. As he pushed open the door at its end. The morning sun and the wet salt sea-breeze rushed down into the corridor as Moriarty made his way up the steps, ignoring the door swinging behind him.

He looked up the planked deck, towards the ship's bow, as the *S.S. Troy* cruised easily through the light morning swell. Empty. Then he heard the thudding again, more dimly, on his right, growing in intensity. Suddenly he realised what it was — the footfall of a runner.

A moment later a tall, heavily-muscled man, aged about thirty-five, dressed in thick polo-neck sweater and white long-johns and moccasins, ran into view. He stopped just above Moriarty with his back to him, unaware of the other man's presence, and put both hands on the ship's rail. He proceeded to bend and straighten his knees, breathing in deeply as he did so.

Moriarty scrutinised the man. The runner had long, jet-black hair tied in a bow at the nape of his neck. Even from behind, Moriarty could see that the man's skin and hands were nut-brown. He coughed lightly.

The runner turned to face him. He had sharp, clearly-defined features and piercing brown eyes — like a hawk, thought Moriarty, walking towards him, right hand outstretched.

'My apologies if I've interrupted your training.'

The runner extended his right hand to Moriarty in a firm grip. 'No,' he said. 'I was just finishing.'

'My name's Moriarty.'

'Moriarty?' said the man, nodding.

'And yours?'

'Louis Bennett,' said the man. 'Some call me Deerfoot.'

Moriarty had heard of Bennett, a full-blooded Seneca Indian, the only American runner to have seriously challenged 'Clipper' White, 'Crowcatcher' Lang and the other great English professionals who had so thoroughly whipped the Americans during their tour of the Eastern seaboard. Now, Bennett soon explained, he was being brought to England by the bookmaker, William M. Bunn, and George Martin, the P. T. Barnum of English pedestrianism, to take on the best English runners on home territory.

During breakfast, Bennett discussed his forthcoming tour. There were to be genuine races against English runners, from three to twelve miles. Matches against time were also to be undertaken, his central aim being to run twelve miles inside the hour. Finally, George Martin was planning a travelling 'circus' of top pedestrians, looking for crowds of up to twenty thousand at each venue. Bennett looked forward to a highly lucrative four weeks.

Moriarty mentioned his own pedestrian background and Bennett was dismissive of Dr Sutherland's diagnosis. The

Indian nations were a running culture, he said, and this way of life had absorbed the introduction by the white man of the horse in the eighteenth century, and still had a rude and healthy existence. Thus racing, which was deemed to have a religious significance, enriching the earth and stimulating the crops, was still a central feature of Indian life. So, if there were any such condition as 'athlete's heart', centuries of Indian running had failed to produce evidence of it.

Next morning at six the thud of Moriarty's footfalls was added to that of Deerfoot's as the two men matched stride for stride around the cramped deck of the *S.S. Troy*. The clocking for that first day was a modest twelve minutes for two miles but within a week they had together sliced a minute from that performance, and a week later were inside ten minutes for the first time.

Deerfoot was undoubtedly an athlete of the highest calibre, fully capable of going inside half-an-hour for the six miles, something no man had ever done. Moriarty's only doubt was that Deerfoot, though intelligent and articulate, had little experience as a professional athlete and might find the cut-throat world of English pedestrianism too hard. Barnum had some experience of England, and had told Moriarty of a dark world of 'fixes' and ringers, where runners had been 'stopped' with drugs or bought off. Deerfoot, a simple, natural athlete, could flounder and perish in such a world.

The three-week voyage allowed ample time for rehearsals, though Edwin had, through his agent, already arranged to pick up most of his supporting cast in England. Booth and Moriarty rehearsed *Richelieu*, *Richard III* and *Hamlet*, with Booth's wife, Mary, already well into her first pregnancy, filling all the women's roles. When Moriarty expressed surprise at such activity Mary Booth regaled him with countless tales of actresses who had performed on stage until well into the final month of pregnancy. Fortunately, she was not about to face that situation herself, as her husband planned to prepare casts of English actors for each production.

Edwin Booth was the dramatic opposite of his father. Not for him Junius Brutus's cruise through the great roles, punctuated by sustained ranting in the big speeches. Rather, Edwin had an interior nervousness, an unfocused energy, which bubbled beneath the surface of each performance.

Alas, the manic streak of his father lay deep within Edwin too. He drank five bottles of wine a day, despite Moriarty's pleas for moderation, and his sexual life had always been wildly exuberant. Moriarty reflected that of Booth and Deerfoot it was the actor, for all his inheritance and his dramatic skills, who was the more uncertain. Had he chosen the right plays, the best theatres? Would he have adequate supporting casts, decent scenery, good costumes? What did the English public already know of him? These questions nagged at the introspective Booth throughout the long sea voyage.

Deerfoot, in his innocence, had no such doubts. He had discovered that English runners, though they honed themselves into superb condition for match-races or big handicap events, allowed themselves to go to seed between races, debauching themselves in the taverns which were the hub of English pedestrianism. Deerfoot was of a different feather. He came from a running culture, one in which men ran regularly as a part of the very fibre of their daily life.

He also had another weapon in his armoury. The British footracers who had come to the Eastern seaboard had only one tactic — to run from the front at a steady, even pace. But Deerfoot had trained assiduously using a different technique. It involved using regular devastating bursts of speed over distances between a furlong and a half-mile, in order to destroy the rhythm of tracking runners. This was a tactic which the hidebound, conservative English had never faced.

Edwin Booth was soon to find Deerfoot as engaging as Moriarty did, and the Seneca Indian was a frequent visitor to their dinner table. At breakfast on the deck of the *S.S. Troy* on the morning of their arrival in Liverpool, Moriarty and Deerfoot reached an informal agreement, for it was clear they were both in England in search of fame and success.

'I will pray for the success of your ventures,' said Deerfoot, as the Troy slowly moved into the dock, 'and will keep watch on them.'

'And I yours,' said Moriarty, shaking the Indian's hand.

The tour started disastrously. On setting foot in Liverpool Booth found that vital letters to him had passed him on his way to Great Britain. There had been problems in booking theatres; his English business manager, Alfred Thrush, had been ill; it had been a bad winter for London theatre. To top it all, British public opinion on the war between the States was for the Confederates — and Booth was a confirmed Yankee. Thus Philip Barrett, who had taken over from the ailing Thrush as Booth's English manager, had hastily penned a letter to Booth in New York advising cancellation, or at least postponement. Still, they were now here, and a tour of sorts had to be cobbled together; but it was a despondent troupe who departed by train for London and their first engagement at the Haymarket.

They sat in silence as the miles clicked by, Booth's face set as he sat hunched in a corner of the carriage opposite his wife. Intensely superstitious, he reflected to Moriarty that he had brought it all upon himself. He should never have given away his birth-caul, just before leaving New York. And he should have brought with him the skull of Lovett, a horse thief, which he always used in the gravedigger scene in Hamlet.

Moriarty felt almost as low as Booth, but decided to try to be cheerful, and by judicious prompting egged Booth on to recall various stories from his acting past. By such means the trip to London passed more pleasantly than it might otherwise have clone, and Philip Barrett and his American visitors arrived in the capital that evening in good spirits, and were installed in apartments in Sloane Square.

Booth pondered mightily over the choice of his first play at the Haymarket, now just three weeks away. Finally, he decided to play Shylock to Moriarty's Bassanio in *The Merchant*, and auditions were held four days after their arrival. Fortunately, a touring company had recently finished playing the piece in Birmingham and Booth was able to engage them virtually *en bloc*, though the company's Portia would never again glimpse forty. The supporting cast, Moriarty excepted, was not of high quality, but Booth had little choice. Shylock was a role which he had played to great effect in the United States, and it was the part with which he wished to make his first impact with the English public.

Alas, sets and costumes were of even poorer quality, the former being battered and patched from six months on tour and the latter an ill-fitting assembly of clothing spanning several centuries

Booth, undeterred, spent the next fortnight knocking his tatterdemalion company into shape, his energies undiminished either by his vast daily consumption of alcohol or by the fact that Mary was now only two months away from the birth of their first child.

He even had time — along with Moriarty — to follow Deerfoot's first British appearance. This was against Edward Mills, better known as 'Young England,' at Hackney Wick, over six miles for a purse of £500, and before a crowd of ten thousand. Sadly, though Deerfoot gave Mills a race all the way to the line, he had still to recover from his ocean voyage and lost narrowly in a modest time of 32 minutes 30 seconds. But a few days later, after crowds had broken into the Salford ground to catch a glimpse of the Indian 'wonder', Deerfoot had whipped Jack White, 'The Gateshead Clipper', one of the team of runners George Martin had brought to the US.

Moriarty remarked that at least one American now seemed to be winning; perhaps they could, too.

Booth's opening performance as Shylock showed him at his best, in a subtle and compassionate interpretation which affected even his mediocre English supporting cast, some of whom were stimulated to performances of which they had not realised they were capable. Moriarty could feel the power of Edwin's acting, feel himself being drawn into it, and even Mrs Moody, their arthritic Portia, seemed to shed her years

The audience's reaction was strong but restrained, for this was not the Shylock of their experience. Moriarty took a carriage from their lodgings to Fleet Street in the early hours of the next morning to pick up the first reviews and bring them back to Sloane Square. The English critics were, at best, reserved: 'Mr Booth, in avoiding the excesses of his late father, has taken to the other extreme and at times his performance is barely audible,' said *The Times*. 'So complete is Mr Booth's disgust for ranting and play-effect that he adopts the opposite extreme,' noted the *London Review*. Moriarty read the reports with increasing dismay as his carriage trundled back through the night. At best, the London critics damned with faint praise; at worst, they were downright offensive. Heavy-hearted, he handed the reviews to Edwin.

Booth was in despair; the critics had wounded him. He had started off with his best classical part — what could he now do to sway London audiences, before he moved north to Manchester and Leeds?

Moriarty intervened. Why not try *Richelieu*, he suggested, a role in which Edwin was well versed? There were two weeks to audition and rehearse, and before that the invitation of a long weekend to recuperate at the Earl of Grafton's estate up in Cumberland. Booth agreed, auditions began three days later, and a cast was quickly chosen.

The Graftons had long been known as benevolent eccentrics. Junius Brutus Booth had met the late Earl during his ill-fated

English tour of 1825 and found that they shared a common interest in wine and wenching. Junius Brutus had also met the then-teenage Maurice, Grafton's son, who had revelled in the American's acting and in his fund of tales. Grafton's meeting with Booth had stimulated a lifelong interest in drama and he had built himself, in his grounds, a hundred-seat theatre equipped with every modern facility. There it was his custom to hold amateur theatricals, mixing local gentry with farmers and shepherds, or, for lavish fees, to bring leading actors of the calibre of Macready to perform in professional productions.

Now Maurice was Lord Grafton, a 52-year-old veteran of the Charge of the Light Brigade, a man who would spend all day with the best pack of foxhounds in the nation and rant Othello in the evening to bewildered rustics.

As their carriage passed through an arch of silver branches up the sunny, mile-long gravel path to Grafton's home, Moriarty prayed that their stay in Cumberland would repair Edwin's confidence. In his heart Booth knew that his Shylock was the best he had done, felt certain it had a truth that answered something central in Shakespeare's Jew. On the other hand, there were the critics, so could he trust his instincts? Moriarty knew that this problem gnawed at Booth every mile of their journey.

When they viewed Grafton Hall, it was as if they had come home. For the old Earl had built his house as a copy of a Southern mansion, of the type, alas, under cannon-fire from Union troops at that very moment. Four soaring white marble pillars towered above the Booths and Moriarty. At the top of a broad stairway stood the fifty-eight members of staff, from shepherds and butlers to cooks and gardeners, in two lines. And at the doorway the Earl himself, a lean, towering man of six foot four with a ruddy face and a massive shock of grey hair. He wore the breeches, white stockings and waistcoat of a Regency buck. Beside him stood his wife, three sons and a daughter.

The actors got down from the carriage, blinking in the bright sunshine, Edwin and Moriarty supporting the pregnant Mary as she descended.

'Edwin!' roared Grafton, running down the stairs. Booth was surprised, for they had never met. He was immediately engulfed by the giant Earl and drawn, with his wife and Moriarty, up the staircase into the house. Moriarty looked around him as they moved through the doorway: this might just be what Edwin required.

Grafton's little theatre proved a delight, containing a small, well-lit proscenium stage equipped with the most modern mechanical devices for speedy and effective scene-changes. The lush velvet seating was luxurious, better even than the best of London and New York theatres, and the auditorium's sight-lines and acoustics were faultless.

But it was in Grafton's performance in excerpts from Othello that the hairs on Moriarty's neck started to prickle. Grafton was undoubtedly a physically impressive Moor, though this only highlighted his dramatic deficiencies, particularly as he had requested Booth to play Iago.

However, it was the Desdemona of Eleanor, the Earl's twenty-year-old daughter, which was to capture Moriarty. Eleanor was no professional. She showed it in the way she moved, the manner in which she allowed even an amateur Othello to upstage her. But she had a warm, lustrous voice and, most important, she had stage-presence. When she spoke, she drew the audience to her like filings to a magnet.

When, later in the evening, his own turn came and he acted the King to Booth's Richelieu and then performed Hamlet's soliloquy, he played to her and to no one else.

At the interval, Booth and Moriarty joined the audience for drinks in the crowded foyer. 'Capital!' roared the Earl, champagne in hand, still in his Othello robes, enfolding them both in his arms. 'Ever played Petruchio, m'boy?' he asked his younger guest.

Moriarty replied that he had understudied the role. The Earl turned and beckoned to his daughter. As she moved through the crowds towards them Moriarty's eyes were drawn to her — slim, bright red hair, full, soft lips and high cheekbones, all accentuated by stage make-up which seemed to heighten rather than coarsen her sensuality. He felt himself flush.

The Earl put one arm on Moriarty's shoulders and the other on Eleanor's. 'How about the last couple of pages of the "Shrew"? You know it by heart, Eleanor — done it a thousand times up in the Hall. Your best part, woman.'

Eleanor did not reply, but turned her head to look squarely at Moriarty. Meanwhile, her father blustered on.

'Trouble is, Moriarty, Eleanor always takes all our Petruchios apart. Browbeats the poor young fellers. So perhaps what's wanted is the professional touch. What d'you say?'

'Perhaps that is what is needed, Father.' The girl's voice was tremulous, and her eyes avoided those of Moriarty. 'The professional touch.'

'So where shall I begin?' said Eleanor, her hands in her lap.

Eleanor and Moriarty were facing each other in the candlelit stillness of the Green Room. The tension between them was almost palpable.

Moriarty swallowed. He looked down at the text in front of him.

'Here we are,' he said, sitting, aware of her perfume as she stood and bent over his shoulder. 'Just before your big speech.' He put his finger on the page. 'I come in with — "I say she shall: and first begin with her." And then you go into your big final speech.'

'Where it says, "Why are our bodies soft, and weak, and smooth"?'

'That's part of it,' said Moriarty, feeling his voice tremble. His finger found the line. 'It starts -- "Fie, fie! unknit that threatening unkind brow." '

87

Eleanor did not need the text. She moved to stand in front of Moriarty in her green velvet gown, and Kate's final speech simply flowed from her. Moriarty, trapped in the moment, let her give what was essentially a recital, but all the while he made his own mental notes. When she had ended, the words came from him sharp and clear. In the short term, there were three key points in the speech which, if improved, could substantially change its dramatic impact. Moriarty made his suggestions with confidence and authority, aware as he spoke that the balance between them was changing, that he was now in charge.

Eleanor was also aware of what was happening. She nevertheless responded well to his coaching. They ran through their entire parts three times in all, sitting facing each other throughout. Moriarty let each run-through take its course, uninterrupted, accepting her minor errors in order to preserve the dramatic momentum.

Then, as they reached the end of their final scene for a third time, there was silence. Eleanor sat in front of him, her eyes scanning the lines as if they had yet to give up some special secret. Moriarty looked at her intently. The girl was completely absorbed. He realised that here was a keen dramatic intelligence at work. More: sitting in the stillness of the shadowy little Green Room, among the props of productions long past, he was aware that for the first time he was with a woman with whom he was completely at one. But he was also aware that this was no Alice Clay, and that he had simply no idea of how to approach such a woman.

Eleanor looked up from her text.

'I'm ready,' she said, standing up.

'For a full rehearsal?' said Moriarty. 'Without books?'

'Yes,' she said. They pushed back the chairs to give themselves space. Soon they were in full swing, until it had reached the point where Moriarty cried,

'Why, there's a Wench! Come on, and kiss me, Kate.' As she

said the words Moriarty froze, unable to summon the courage to lay hands upon his partner.

In a moment, he was assaulted by her soft, yielding mouth as her arms pulled him to her. He tried to pull away but she held him fast. Moriarty's head swam. Then finally, gasping he was free.

'Well done, Moriarty,' she said, laughing. Later, he was to remember that this was the first time she had omitted the appellation 'Mister'.

In the performance itself, an hour later, when the time for the kiss came Moriarty decided to risk all, and to throw caution to the wind. Ignoring the audience, he kissed Eleanor tenderly and passionately; Eleanor responded at once, her own tongue darting, active in response.

He could feel her pull him in towards her, the light, butterfly touch of her hand at the back of his neck. Moriarty held the kiss as long as he dared, though not as long as he would have wished, and there was no resistance. He swept Eleanor off to resounding applause, his heart throbbing as quickly as it had in the races of his youth; albeit for different reasons.

The evening had been a resounding success. After the play Moriarty was the life and soul of the party, entertaining his hosts with stories of America, of the Wild West, and of his plans for the future. Both Mary and Edwin, as well as Lady Grafton, had been quick to note the true nature of Moriarty and Eleanor's final embrace, but Lord Grafton, oblivious, was determined that his guests' time should not be wasted: the Saturday morning would be spent in riding in the magnificent Cumbrian countryside, while the afternoon — as it happened — was allocated to attendance at Ambleforth sports.

The Ambleforth meeting had been held for centuries on the village green, which nestled between two mountains, Black Tor and the Combe. It was essentially a local meeting, though wrestlers and fell runners came from as far as Carlisle and the

Scottish borders to contend for money prizes worth as much as three months' wages for an agricultural labourer.

The various contests were no more than an English version of the Highland games, minus the throwing events. Not for these hardy men of Cumberland and Westmoreland the spiked running shoes worn by the crack pedestrians of London; indeed, many ran and jumped in bare feet. By contrast, the bulky Cumberland wrestlers wore gaudily-decorated costumes and, indeed, there was even a prize for the best-dressed competitor.

Throughout the afternoon the Earl and his family and guests sat, sheltered from the sun, in a specially-constructed stand made of canvas and wooden scaffolding. In a tent nearby their servants dispensed iced champagne and hors d'oeuvres. Moriarty looked at the dalesmen in the arena — wiry and lean, faces thin and lined — and reflected that here were the 'two nations' from which he and his father had fled back in 1848. Through chance, he now had a foot in both these worlds, but he knew that his true interests lay with athletes running their guts out for a few shillings.

Grafton's suggestion to him that he should run in one of the races had come out of the blue. Booth had let it drop that Moriarty had been a champion footracer and Grafton's response had been immediate.

'The fell race!' he had said. 'The last event of the Games!'

Moriarty had begged to be excused, observing that his medical advisors had counselled against serious racing. But Grafton, bluff and imperious, had insisted. Then, still bent on refusal, Moriarty had caught Eleanor's eye over her father's shoulder. It was clear to him what she wanted him to do. He was lost.

An hour later, as Moriarty lined up with twenty-seven other runners for the race, he looked up to the top of the Black Tor, a thousand feet above. At its peak was a stone cairn round which the runners had to turn before making their way down.

From the gamesfield, the mountain appeared a mixture of brown and green, the clouds casting shifting shadows across its blend of grass and rock, the single snaky path to the summit only partly visible. About a half mile to the top, thought Moriarty: perhaps eight minutes' hard running. He looked around. The age-range of the other competitors surprised him — everything from smooth-chinned teenagers in moccasins to grizzled, white-bearded veterans in walking-boots.

On the report of the gun, Moriarty sprinted into an immediate lead, aiming to get to the path first. He reached it with twenty yards to spare and scrambled up its pebbled surface, throwing up a spray of dust and stones behind him. But there was no rhythm to this type of running, and after only a couple of hundred yards of twisting and turning up the bumpy, tussocky path he felt the fronts of his thighs begin to ache. Twenty yards later two runners passed him on either side, elbowing him as they went past. Twenty yards later three more passed, two of them wearing walking-boots. With only three hundred yards of Black Tor covered Moriarty was in deep trouble, for the fronts of his legs were close to spasm and he was having difficulty even in trotting. When six more runners passed him in the next hundred yards he was almost beyond caring; his legs had gone, his breathing was beginning to go and he wanted to retch. This was not like any normal race – it presented him with problems that he had never faced before.

By the time he had staggered round the cairn at the top of Black Tor he was back in fourteenth position, sweat pouring into his eyes as he struggled for breath.

Moriarty's heart thudded like a hammer inside his chest. Somehow, despite his fatigue, he was pleased. So much for medical advice; he had scaled a mountain and was little the worse for it. Then it came up, his lunch, spilling out in a bitter green stream on to the grass below him. Moriarty, gasping, shook his head and looked down the mountain. Far below he could see Grafton's white marquee. Nearer him, the dalesmen, ignoring the path, were taking the fastest way down, covering it in great bounds. This is it, he thought. Do or die. Taking the mountain anywhere his feet could find it, he launched himself down Black Tor, somehow holding his balance on thighs that he hardly dared ask to support him. Despite the uncertain and unpredictable nature of the rocky terrain, he somehow found a rhythm, quite unlike that of conventional running, and half-way down had picked up seven places and was only a hundred and fifty yards away from the front group of runners. With a hundred yards to the foot of the hill he was just eighty yards from the four leaders, who were crossing the main road before entering the games-ground for a final lap. By the time they had entered the ground he was a bare fifty yards down and closing fast, his breath coming in great, greedy gulps.

As he passed the Earl's stand on his right, every occupant stood; but Moriarty was now flat-footed, legs bent, in a sweaty, desperate approximation of running. The leaders, thirty yards ahead of him, he saw as a confused blur.

Then, with a furlong to go and Moriarty only ten yards behind, it happened. His running dropped to a wobbling, stumbling trot, an athletic grotesque, as he fumbled for the cues that would re-activate a muscular memory long forgotten. Somehow he kept on his feet, staggering from side to side, only blind, animal instinct keeping him from falling.

The three leaders hit the tape. Moriarty still kept coming, oblivious to the crowd's roar as other runners entered the ground behind him. Eight yards from the line, he fell to his knees and dropped forward on to his hands, sweat pouring into his eyes. Then suddenly triumph pierced through his pain, the glorious realisation that he had done it, had pushed himself to his limits. And nothing had burst, nothing had broken. He was *alive*.

He thought of Eleanor all the long way on the train back to London: he seemed to have a lump stuck at the base of his throat which, however much he tried to clear it, would not be removed.

After the race, he had seen nothing of her. For Eleanor had been hustled off by Lady Grafton, who had seen enough to know that the relationship between the American and her daughter had gone far beyond play-acting. That evening, when Moriarty had fully recovered, it had been time to take the train south, and when Grafton had seen his guests off at Ambleforth station Eleanor was nowhere to be seen.

The Booths noted their young colleague's unnatural silence and, sensing its source, were themselves quiet and restrained, Edwin confining himself to discussion of the forth-coming production of *Richelieu* at Covent Garden. Lytton's play was a hoary old potboiler, but always went down well, had plenty of big moments and gave Booth an opportunity to express the flamboyant side of his nature. The cast was already chosen, and Barnett had been busy in London assembling costumes and creating sets. Moriarty, recalling how he had tried to tease Booth out of his melancholy on their arrival from the United States, appreciated his friend's concern, but found it difficult to raise enthusiasm for the enterprise. He knew that in Eleanor he had come up against someone outside his experience, someone who, because of her class and background, made his stage chivalries and Green Room banter seem trivial and irrelevant. Whatever the figure he cut before the flickering footlights of the New York or London theatre, and whatever his New World views on the British aristocracy, the fact was that he was at best a mere actor, at worst the son of a crofter. He travelled to London with the Booths in silence, his thoughts far from Richelieu and Covent Garden.

The omens for *Richelieu*, however, were good from the outset. Deerfoot had climaxed a series of seven successful races in three weeks, an arduous schedule, by whipping three of the best men in England, White, 'Crowcatcher' Lang and Richards,

93

over six miles, before 15,000 spectators at the Copenhagen Grounds, Manchester, forcing all but the Crowcatcher to retire from the race. Deerfoot's policy of injecting repeated bursts of speed had found no answer from the hide-bound English professionals.

And, sure enough, *Richelieu* too was a triumph, Booth's art overcoming the flimsy plot. Even the London critics came close to admitting that they might have been a mite hasty in their earlier assessments. 'Mr. Booth, in his great final scene, seemed visibly to *grow* in the part' acknowledged *The Times*. Moriarty had smiled wryly on reading that particular review, for he knew that Edwin, dressed in a flowing gown, in that particular scene had stood on tiptoe throughout.

Booth was buoyant, and the decision was made to retain *Richelieu* to within three days of their departure for Manchester with *Richard III*, *Hamlet* and *The Merchant*, leaving precious little time for rehearsal in the North.

The company left for Manchester on 16 August. Moriarty's first glimpse of the city did little to lift his lovesick spirits, for even in summer the sun was blotted out by the pall of grit that spewed remorselessly from its factories and mills. As the train trundled through the seamy rows of back-to-back houses and factories Moriarty recalled his days of touring in Iowa and Kansas, and the endless open spaces of the West. It was difficult to believe that Manchester and Kansas were even on the same planet.

The performances went well, with Booth in top form, but it was from a new young supporting actor, Henry Irving, that Moriarty was to learn most. For it was immediately clear to him that Irving was exceptional, a man who put his stamp on everything he played. When he was Iago to Booth's Moor there was no way even Booth could dominate the stage: it was a meeting of equals.

The month in Manchester passed quickly, despite Moriarty's

melancholy. Both he and Booth continued to follow Deerfoot's progress, though now through the sporting magazine *Bell's Life*. Things were not going so well for the Seneca athlete. For Martin's Grand Tour of Champions had turned into a shabby, tattered crew, lacklustre and weary, trudging from venue to venue and carrying their portable 'arena' with them. This arena consisted of several hundred yards of canvas and fencing which the athletes themselves had to set up on convenient stretches of grass to form an impromptu stadium, before charging the public sixpence a time to watch their 'contests'.

It soon became clear to the sporting public that the races, occurring almost every day of the week, were hardly more than exhibitions, bearing little resemblance to true athletic competition. Rumours had begun to circulate that Deerfoot had a liking for firewater and by the middle of the tour it was obvious that the Indian was well out of condition. By the end of August Martin was forced to cancel the remainder of the programme in a blizzard of litigation. For the first time, the parallel progress of the tours of Booth and Deerfoot had diverged sharply.

However, during his stay in Manchester Moriarty had developed other contacts with English footracing, for the town was a hive of pedestrian activity. Match-races were held daily on any stretch of open space in the area, with the big handicaps at the Copenhagen Grounds just outside the city.

It was here, in the soot and grime of Manchester, that Moriarty was to complete his athletic education, to learn of runners competing in lead-soled shoes to deceive handicappers, of 'ringers' from outside the area, introduced by bookmakers to clean up local competition before moving on to another part of the country, of the secrecy in which trainers would enshroud their charges in order to prepare them for a match-race or a big handicap. It was thus in Manchester that

Moriarty first began to plan his future — as actor, runner and manager.

Old Junius Brutus had always said he should never look at the audience; not at least until the final curtain. It was a dictum that Moriarty had no difficulty in following, for if he were truly 'in the moment' the audience was an irrelevance.

But, for some reason he would never understand, on that final night in Manchester, while playing Laertes to Booth's Hamlet, Moriarty's eyes had strayed to the front row of the stalls. And there sat Eleanor. For a moment he almost lost his concentration, and struggled to respond to the next lines — 'I embrace it freely and will this brother's wager frankly play. Give us the foils. Come on,' which introduced the duel with Hamlet.

When at last he had recovered himself, he embarked upon the fight with a ferocity which surprised his partner. Fortunately their choreography had been well-planned, and Booth was able to hiss a warning to his colleague to back off. The words brought Moriarty to his senses. For the rest of the duel he was under control and 'died' perfectly.

It was another agonising twenty minutes at least before Moriarty was able to take his curtain-call. Eagerly his eyes roamed the front row, seeking out Eleanor. Her place was empty. He felt his heart sink, and Booth had once more to hiss a warning – 'Bow, you fool!'

A few minutes later Moriarty was making his way slowly backstage, his head down. At his shoulder, an exuberant Edwin Booth was full of talk, bubbling with delight at the audience's enthusiastic response. As soon as they reached their tiny dressing-rooms, deep in the bowels of the theatre, Moriarty went into his room and closed the door behind him. For a few moments he sat staring into the cracked mirror. With a long sigh he peeled off his moustache and reached for his pot of cleansing cream. He smeared the greasy white substance on his face with both hands, still staring into the mirror. With another sigh he picked up a cloth from the table and lifted it to his face.

It was then he heard a light knock on the door behind him. Moriarty did not even bother to wipe the cream from his face. He leaped for the door, overturning his chair as he did so.

Eleanor, dressed in blue velvet, and a marvellous, massive floral hat, stood before him, her dark eyes sparkling.

She looked him squarely in the eye, her lips trembling as she stifled a laugh. Moriarty hastily wiped the cream from his face.

'That's better,' she said.

For a moment Moriarty stood immobile. Eleanor wrinkled her nose, mock-seriously.

'So when do we go, Moriarty?'

'Go?' The words tumbled from him. 'Go where?'

'West, of course,' she said. 'To America.'

Moriarty would always be grateful that the Earl of Grafton was a few bricks short of a dozen. For when back in July after the actors had left Cumberland his daughter Eleanor had told him her first lie — saying that Moriarty had proposed to her — Grafton, unlike his wife, had been enthusiastic. Like the rest of his family, he had been entranced by Moriarty's tales of the Wild West, and it seemed only reasonable to him that a fine, well set-up lass like Eleanor should wish to set off with such a strapping fellow to the New World.

All that then remained for Eleanor was to bring Moriarty into her little lie. For Grafton's daughter had no doubt what faced her if she spent the rest of her days in England. Within a year she would be wed to some vague, aristocratic nobody, within five years there would be a couple of children and she would be marooned on some vast estate, dedicated to a life of country sports and charitable works. She had known that Moriarty was her man from the first moment she had set eyes upon him. *The Taming of the Shrew* had merely set the seal upon their union, even if Moriarty, in his own words, was not yet 'in the moment'. She was realistic enough to know that their life would bear no relationship to the tales of Western derring-do with which Moriarty had regaled Grafton and his guests, but that was of no matter. Moriarty was the man, and if he were to be a pioneer then they would pioneer together.

The Booths postponed their return to America in order to attend the wedding. Which was fortunate, for Mary Booth gave birth to a son, Edwin, on 16 September. Three Booths therefore attended the wedding of Douglas Cameron and Eleanor Sinclair on 25 September in the tiny chapel on the Grafton estate, and Edwin, in celebration of the happy event, performed a series of excerpts from Shakespeare, including, for Eleanor's benefit, that fateful sword-fight from Hamlet.

Mercifully, Lord Grafton, involved as he was in the wedding-preparations, required less dissuasion than usual from performing Quasimodo in *The Hunchback of Notre Dame*.

The next day the couple made their way south with the Booths, just in time for a final view of Deerfoot, who, his reputation in tatters after the ignominy of Martin's 'circus', was tackling the world one-hour record.

On 10 October 1862 Louis Bennett stood at his mark before 10,000 spectators on the cramped little 260-yard track at Brompton, London, the cream of British foot-racing stretched around the track in front of him. The Indian had decided to finish his tour in style. He had given starts to every English runner in the race, from a quarter of a mile to the veteran Jackson down to a hundred yards to England's best, 'Crowcatcher' Lang.

Deerfoot, now with a month of solid preparation behind him, was again lean and hard, and throughout the next hour picked off his opponents with ease, subjecting any who tried to stay with him to devastating bursts of speed which left them straining in his wake. With a lap to go, having taken world records for nine, ten and eleven miles, he had only the great Lang ahead of him, just twenty yards away, all the other runners having retired.

The Indian went after his man with a will, the English crowd rising to him. With twenty yards to go the runners were almost level, but Deerfoot, spent, could make no further impression. The two men staggered across the line locked together, to be engulfed by the crowds.

To the Booths and Moriarty it seemed a dead heat. But the smart money had been on Lang and the decision was given to the Englishman, with Deerfoot having to be content with a new world one-hour record, one that was to endure far beyond his lifetime.

The tour was, for all practical purposes, over. Booth gave two dramatic readings in London and two more in the universities of Oxford and Cambridge, and the company became tourists for a week, on Edwin's insistence spending several days at 'the great man's birthplace' at Stratford-upon-Avon.

As Moriarty and his new wife boarded the *S.S. Galatea* at Southampton he reflected that both Booth and Deerfoot had, in the end, come through in England, despite adversity. But he, Moriarty, who had travelled only in hope, had come back with the best prize of all.

Eleanor had decided on the stage-name of 'Eleanor Cameron' during the honeymoon trip back to New York.

It was also on the voyage from Liverpool that Eleanor first began to keep a diary. She felt that she was travelling to a new life and this was therefore an ideal time to keep a record of events. At first she wrote in secret, in the confines of her cabin, but when Moriarty came upon her and gently teased her on her 'secret journal', she decided to keep the diary openly, knowing that her husband would respect her privacy.

It had been a working voyage, and Moriarty and the Booths had drilled her remorselessly in the basic elements of acting.

Eleanor was an apt pupil and quickly absorbed the mass of advice proffered to her. She proved an equally apt pupil when the day's dramatic lessons were concluded. Eleanor had now travelled beyond her first nights with Moriarty when she had been stunned by the outrageous messages which her nerve-ends had sent to her brain. The couple were at that most thrilling point of any relationship, when they would explore every square inch of their partner's flesh, sharing the surprise and delight of every new discovery.

She knew that Moriarty would take a long time to know, for both as athlete and actor he had lived a life of self-concern, always working within the boundaries of his own imagination and his own desires. But within him lay a great generosity, even a kind of nobility. She resolved that her task in life would be to turn Moriarty into a more complete human being.

6

THE MAN FROM ST LOUIS

In their first years in the New York theatre and in their occasional forays into the boondocks of Iowa and Kansas, Eleanor Cameron learned the actress's craft, and learned also to be a resourceful and loving partner. And in 1865, with the assassination of President Lincoln by Edwin Booth's brother, John Wilkes, it was her strength of character which helped to bring Edwin through a period of despair during which even his wife Mary could not reach him.

Then, in 1869, came Booth's disastrous venture in theatre management, with his purchase of Booth's Theatre at 6th Avenue and 23rd. Within a year the project had collapsed in a plethora of debts. Again, Eleanor was a tower of strength, in 1871 helping Moriarty to bring Booth back to the finest acting of his career. But the Moriartys' forays to the Mid-West had stimulated a taste in them for the thrill of touring. After the War, the whole nation seemed to be moving West out into the dry vastnesses of the Great Plains, and it was there, they reasoned, that a new audience waited, eager for drama. In late 1871, Moriarty and Eleanor sold everything they had and set off. Moriarty's first Theatre of the West was born.

They had met Bern Muller in the summer of 1874 at the St. Louis Fair

Bern was the only son of Karl Muller, a former member of

the Hanau Turnverein. This was a politically radical German gymnastics club which had, in the year of revolution of 1848, when Prussia and other reactionary German states had invaded the state of Baden, held out with its six hundred poorly-armed members against the finest army in Europe. But after four weeks of bitter fighting the Hanau volunteers had finally been defeated. About two hundred and forty of them, including Karl Muller, had reached the Swiss frontier and the rest had been killed in action or shot as rebels after capture. Muller had made his way by foot across Switzerland and into France and for a few months had scratched a living as an acrobat in a Paris circus. Then, in May 1850, like thousands of other political refugees he had travelled across the Atlantic to the United States.

Karl Muller settled in Boston, where in 1851 he found a position as a teacher of gymnastics in a German private school. Two years later, he married Marita Mauermeyer, a Latin teacher at the same school, and in January 1854 Bern Muller was born.

Even before he could walk, young Muller was familiar with a variety of physical skills. By the age of eight, he was accomplished on parallel and horizontal bars and at nine could perform a forward somersault from a run. Turnen competition began at eight in Boston's German community, and young Muller was not only victorious in his first competition, but went on to win every year until he was fourteen, in 1868. That was the year when he was first taken to the Boston Caledonian Games.

Bern had never before seen athletes in action. The Scots and Irish amazed him with their feats of strength in hammer, putting-stone and caber, for he had never believed it possible that any man could hurl such heavy weights such vast distances. But it was the jumping and running which fascinated him most, and in particular the sprinters, their spikes clawing the soft turf of the Boston gamesfield.

It was the totality of the effort that attracted him — the perfect, utter commitment to cover short distances in a blaze of speed, without hint of reserve. From the moment he first saw sprinters, he knew that was what he wanted to be.

In 1869 he entered the junior hundred-yard dash and, competing against boys at least two years older, finished third. In 1870 he won the junior race and finished last in the final of the men's open hundred-yard dash. A year later, at the age of seventeen, Bern entered for the men's hundred yards and the furlong and finished fourth in both.

By now Bern was acting as assistant gymnastics instructor to his father at the school, his body like a rock from years in the gymnasium. He did no specific sprint training, relying instead on the hard core of fitness he had developed under his father's tutelage.

Bern's father believed that gymnastics was central to all sporting skill, providing as it did a complete vocabulary of movement. He believed too that his son should be exposed to a wide variety of disciplines; thus by his early teens Bern had competed with distinction not only in local swimming meets but also in horseshoe-throwing and rifle-shooting.

By 1871 he had become a regular competitor at 'picnic' games in the Boston area during the summer months, making good money at every event from hundred yards to high jump, but a win at the Boston Caledonian Games eluded him. There, the running events were dominated by hard match-racers from New York to St. Louis, men like the Irish sprinter Reardon and the great distance-runner Moriarty; there was little hope for a local boy against professionals of such calibre.

Then, in July 1873, after finishing third to Manderson at Boston in the hundred yards, Bern met William Cummings.

Cummings, plump and swarthy, introduced himself as a backer and manager of fighting men and footracers. In his black suit and shiny bowler hat, his belly straining at the

103

buttons of his check waistcoat, Cummings seemed to have made a good living from his work.

The manager had come to Boston for a match between his protegé Hutchings and the young Irish star Reardon for a wager of $200. Hutchings had gone down to Reardon by a yard, losing Cummings over two grand in bets, and the gambler had stayed on for the Caledonian Games, hoping to recoup his losses.

But Hutchings had gone down again in both dashes, and it was the young Muller who had caught Cummings's eye. The Boston boy was raw, but he had run six yards outside even time on rough grass. With preparation, reasoned Cummings, he could trim four yards off that time, taking him into championship class — St. Louis class.

After the race Cummings had approached Bern. Two months' preparation deep in the Adirondacks, twenty bucks a week folding money, win or lose; then down to St. Louis in September to take on the fastest men in the States, for the St. Louis Sprint Sweepstake. This meant each one of between ten and twenty runners putting up $200, winner take all. If Muller won he picked up the total cash, and Cummings would cut him in for ten per cent of all bets, which could come to another $2,000.

Cummings, an Irishman, was persuasive. Bern could not lose, he argued: even if he lost the race he would still have a couple of hundred bucks in his pocket and a trip to St.Louis behind him. And his chances were good, for two yards over evens would be enough to win, and Cummings reckoned that a couple of months with his trainer Sergeant Routledge would guarantee that time. So what did he say?

It did not take Bern long to answer. A week later he was established in a rough log cabin deep in the Adirondacks, a few miles south of Lake Placid, with a surly little ex-Union soldier called Archibald Routledge. The one-eyed Routledge was an American disciple of the great Captain Barclay. At first Bern had thought that the Captain might have been Routledge's commanding officer in the Union Army, but Routledge soon made it clear that the famous captain was an Englishman, the father of modern athletic training.

The first week was spent in clearing Bern's bowels of all waste, using an evil black potion of Routledge's own devising, and Bern's main sprinting was done between the cabin and the log privy twenty yards away. This cleansing of the bowels was accompanied by daily 'sweats' which were accomplished by long runs in the heat of summer clad in long-johns, woollen jersey and balaclava, followed by an hour in bed swathed in blankets.

It might have been thought that, with all the sweating, Bern might have been allowed the relief of a modicum of liquid. But not so, for Sergeant Routledge had extended the Captain's already harsh regime by denying his charge all but the minimum of fluids. Bern Muller therefore spent most of the day dehydrated, dementedly seeking water. Once, when Routledge had caught Bern desperately licking moisture from the leaves of bushes after a sudden rainfall, he had punished the young sprinter by pushing him out on yet another torrid hill run.

Routledge was not a coach, but he was a conditioner of men. He viewed it as his primary task to bring Bern Muller down to one hundred and fifty-five pounds of bone and muscle, and this he would do even if he had to kill Muller in the process. Thus, within a month, by which time Bern had reached his target weight, Routledge had achieved his main aim. For the next four weeks he confined himself to gun-starts and time-trials, gradually honing and sharpening Muller by trial and error into an efficient sprinting machine. By a week before departure for St. Louis, Bern had run 10.3 seconds for a hundred yards on a flat stretch of grass on the meadow below the cabin, under the scrutiny of his backer, William Cummings.

It was then that Cummings had asked Bern to choose a

nom-de-guerre, which was the custom of all professional runners. Bern had read many a dime novel featuring a buckskin hero called 'Buck Brady — Terror of the plains', and he immediately chose Buck for his first name. Although he spoke hardly a word of German, he was proud of his German antecedents and for his surname decided on the English equivalent of Muller. Thus, on 1 August 1874, Bern Muller became Buck Miller.

Buck's trip to St. Louis was undertaken in conditions of the utmost secrecy. Before leaving the Adirondacks he had, on Routledge's orders, grown a moustache, and, wearing clothes more appropriate to a man of fifty, he was shepherded to Chicago, where he was sequestered for a day on the top floor of the Grand Union Hotel. Thence he was taken, in the company of Sergeant Routledge, on 7 September, two days before the race, to a farmhouse just outside St. Louis to stay with an elderly Irish couple called McCarthy.

The St. Louis Fair was dedicated to the holy pursuit of the fast buck. Centred on the newly-built St. Louis Racecourse, the Races were a hotbed of gambling based on horse-racing, foot-racing, prizefighting, cockfighting and dogfighting. The Races were therefore a magnet to every gambler, pickpocket and whore in the West, offering as they did a full four days of dedication to the goddess Chance.

Billy Joe Speed had arrived two days before Buck and promptly lost all but his last hundred dollars on a trotting horse called Pretty Sally. He had at once entered a one-hundred-and-fifty yards handicap dash. Billy Joe's handicap, he being a stranger, was not generous at three yards, but he was nevertheless giving away up to ten yards in starts, with such 'cracks' as the Irishman Reardon and the Indian on scratch behind them. However, Billy Joe had picked up his field by one hundred yards and was still a short yard ahead of the fast-closing Indian when he hit the tape. The prize of a hundred dollars plus five hundred in side bets gave him a renewed feeling of confidence in his left-hand hip pocket, but he decided not to risk another handicap race against Reardon and the Indian where the handicapper, having now seen him in action, would undoubtedly pare down his start to a more realistic level.

So Billy Joe had allowed himself some relaxation, and had been booze-blind for two days on a local version of Taos Lightning before returning to the Races to view the final day's sport.

In those two days of Billy Joe's debauchery, Moriarty had distinguished himself in another way, winning both half-mile and mile handicaps from scratch. But the shorter distance had been a close-run thing, both Moriarty and a young Southern boy called La Salle hitting the tape together at exactly two minutes four seconds, the fastest time ever recorded in St. Louis. Moriarty reflected that, at thirty-six years of age, some of the sap had gone out of his legs and that this was beginning to tell over the shorter distances. But in the mile he had shown a clean pair of heels to a field of thirteen runners, some almost half his age, winning easily in a fifth of a second inside four minutes forty seconds.

In the stands, Eleanor watched with a mixture of pleasure and dismay, for as long as Moriarty could still whip the best of American footracers, so long would he continue his wanderings and delay his plan to set up a permanent Theatre of the West in San Francisco. Still, she could not complain, for already thirty thousand dollars lay snug in the San Francisco vaults of A. P. Wagstaffe, banker; fifty thousand more and the Theatre of the West might become a reality. And today's haul of a thousand dollars would swell the coffers even further.

The St. Louis trip had been more athletic than aesthetic. Thus it had ever been since their first visit there in 1866. They had presented no full-length plays, or even excerpts, instead confining themselves to two drama readings at the Barn Theatre and a guest appearance at Colonel Blincoe's

Hall of Fantasies. St. Louis had, however, given Eleanor the breathing-space to repair costumes and purchase fresh horses for the final part of the season, which would start in Dodge. St. Louis was fun; it gave Moriarty the opportunity to be young again and earn money at the same time, while for Eleanor it was a brief respite before a period of intensive travel.

Moriarty had sought out Billy Joe and Buck directly after his first victory, for he had long been looking for one partner, and possibly two, for a speculative venture which contained, he told Eleanor, 'all the best elements of both sport and drama.' But Speed had vanished from sight immediately after his victory, while Buck had been closely guarded by Cummings' bruisers. Then, in a mêlée in the refreshment tent on that last day of the Races, Moriarty had suddenly come upon Billy Joe standing by his side, whey-faced from his two days of drinking, downing a beer. Moriarty introduced himself to Billy Joe, who seemed to know nothing of the older man's victories, and invited the young Texan to sit in the stands as his guest. Billy Joe agreed, and so, on the morning of 11 September 1874, he, Moriarty and Eleanor sat watching the heats of the hundred yards sweepstake, while Moriarty explained the nature of his venture. The race-course was no place for fast times in the dash, for the grass, pock-marked by the hooves of six heats of trotters earlier in the day, was bumpy and uneven and the sprinters were running into a stiff head-wind. Fifteen runners had each put up two hundred dollars and had been divided into three heats, with the first two in each heat going into the final.

Moriarty had liked the look of Buck Miller from the beginning. The Boston boy won his heat easily in six yards outside evens, two-tenths of a second faster than the next fastest, a little Mexican called Gomez. Hutchings, who had whipped Buck in Boston, only just made the final, finishing second in the last heat.

Moriarty decided to give young Miller a few moments to

cool down, then walked down through the milling racecourse crowds towards Buck's tent behind the stands. But as he approached he saw that it was guarded by two of Cummings' prizefighters who stood impressively, arms folded, their faces an argument he couldn't win. To Moriarty it made sense: with only a couple of hours to go before the final Cummings was keeping a close watch on his man. He therefore decided to put a little more on Buck's back, and made his way to his bookmaker, the little Jew, Len Levine. He was surprised to find that the odds on Buck had gone up to evens from two to one on, while Hutchings' odds had dropped to evens from three to one against. So something was up. Big, late money was therefore being laid on Hutchings, indicating that there was a coup in the air. Moriarty made his way back to Buck's quarters, this time taking a back route, so that he would reach the rear of the tent.

With two hours to go, Buck was feeling good. He lay back on his camp-bed while the impassive Routledge gently rubbed liniment into his legs. The semi-final heat had been easy and he had had two yards or more to spare, of that he was certain. With fifteen runners in the sweepstake, it would be three thousand silver dollars waiting for him in the stakeholders tent at the finish. He could already feel the money heavy in his pocket. It had all been worth it — the laxatives, the sweats, the endless miles in the Adirondacks — and now it was only a couple of hours away.

Suddenly, he realised Cummings was standing over him.

'Dandy,' he said, in his soft Irish brogue. 'A fancy piece of running, if ever I saw one.'

Buck sat up on both elbows. 'Thanks, Mr. Cummings,' he said.

Cummings leaned over the bed and Buck winced as be took in the stale smell of beer and cigars.

'And how are you feeling about the final?'

'I can take it for you, Mr. Cummings.'

'Of course you can, m'boy,' said Cummings, his patron. 'Only man here can beat Buck Miller is the Indian hisself, eh Routledge? And he ain't running.'

Routledge nodded and continued to knead Buck's calves.

Cummings withdrew from his coat pocket a transparent glass bottle which appeared to contain a dark brown cough mixture.

'Got a little pick-me-up for ye here, Buck. Give you an extra yard.'

Buck lay back. 'No need, Mr. Cummings, thank you kindly.'

Cummings gave Routledge a veteran's look and the trainer stopped massaging Buck's legs and wiped his hands on a rough towel. He made his way to the entrance of the tent and closed the flaps before making his way back to the bed.

'Money in the bank, Buck me boy,' said Cummings softly, taking a large spoon from a table beside the bed. Something in Cummings' voice caused Buck to rise again on both elbows. He saw that the two bruisers now stood, with Routledge, above him, one on each side, as Cummings slowly poured the brown fluid on to the spoon.

'Part of the training programme, Buck me boy,' said Cummings softly.

Before Buck could move the two thugs had pinned him to the bed. At the same time Routledge swiftly pulled open his jaws. Cummings ladled the spoonful down Buck's throat. He coughed reflexly, splattering the two heavies. It made little difference. Cummings poured out another large spoonful and again ladled it down Buck's throat; this time it stayed down as Buck strained, impotently, tears and sweat streaming down his cheeks. Cummings nodded to his three helpers and Buck, spluttering and coughing, was released.

'Run your heart out, me beauty,' Cummings said. 'You got no chance.' He nodded once more to the other men and slipped the bottle and spoon into a jacket pocket. Even before they had left the tent Buck had begun to retch.

Moriarty, standing at the rear of the tent, heard it all. Even before Cummings had left the tent he was running through the crowds towards Professor Tancredi's Medicinal Show. He had a good idea what Buck had been given: a violent emetic, calculated to bring him to the line a mere shadow. He cursed himself for not having seen it earlier, when the odds on Hutchings had suddenly started to drop. Hutchings had been their man from the beginning, from the summer when he had lost to Reardon and had gone down again at the Boston Caledonian Games. Buck had merely been the decoy.

As soon as he reached Tancredi's tent he blurted out to 'The Professor' what had happened. Tancredi's response was swift. Of the potions which he sold most were merely alcohol-rich placebos, but some did work and Hiawatha's Snake Juice was one of them, being an excellent antidote for stomach upsets. Armed with a bottle, and having advised the Professor to put a hundred dollars on Buck's nose, Moriarty rushed back to the tent.

It was no longer guarded; there was now no need. When Moriarty entered Buck was on his hands and knees on the floor, green bile spewing from his mouth. Moriarty pulled him to his feet and on to the edge of the camp-bed. He dragged a sheet from the bed and ripped off a corner, wetting it in a bucket of water that stood by the side of the bed. With this he wiped the sick from Buck's face. The runner's eyes were closed, his mouth open and slack.

'Now listen to me,' hissed Moriarty, taking the stopper from the bottle which he withdrew from his pocket. 'And listen good. You're going to come out of this smelling of roses.'

Buck opened his eyes and Moriarty answered his unspoken question.

'Doesn't matter who the hell I am,' he said. 'I've got money on your back, that's all that matters.'

He handed Buck the bottle. 'Get this down you,' he said. 'We'll make those sons of bitches pay.'

Buck blinked and took a tentative swig, coughing as he did

111

so. It tasted like liquid chalk. Moriarty gave a sidelong glance at the entrance to the tent and tapped the bottle.

'Take some more,' he said. Buck took another swig, the tears spurring from his eyes.

'Now lie down,' said Moriarty, withdrawing his watch from his pocket. 'We've got exactly one hour to go. So just you pin back your ears, and run to orders.'

An hour later, when Buck Miller emerged from his tent, he looked dreadful. Pale and unsteady, and enveloped in a blanket, he walked with Cummings and Routledge through the crowds to the start of the race, pausing occasionally to give a racking cough. By the time he had reached the start, odds against him had risen to three to one and Moriarty had put on another three hundred bucks.

It was a good race, for Hutchings was no slouch. At thirty yards he and Buck were locked together, with the others at least two yards back. At fifty yards Buck edged ahead and from then to the finish gradually eased away from the older runner, taking him by a clear yard at the line. But Buck did not stop running. Instead, he maintained his speed, zig-zagging through the crowd towards the prize-tent, a hundred yards beyond the finish.

Behind him, an enraged Cummings and his henchmen stumbled through the milling crowds in hopeless pursuit.

Entering the tent, sweat-streaked, Buck demanded his stake, as a few yards away, on a megaphone, the track referee announced his victory. Seizing his pouch of three thousand dollars from the official, Buck rushed out again and vaulted over the race-track rail, sprinting for the road leading from the track. There stood Moriarty and his wagon and behind him a mounted Billy Joe Speed and a spare horse. Within minutes they were galloping on their way west, far from the clutches of Cummings, Routledge and their cronies.

7

THE KANGAROO START

It was a day in mid-August, 1875, and the guns had not stopped since dawn.

Billy Joe and Buck had begun by practising their speed of draw with empty pistols, each taking turn at 'calling' his partner, standing there like statues in the morning mist, first side by side, then facing each other. Neither man took count of the number of draws, though somehow by some unspoken agreement each knew when it was time to conclude one area of practice and move on to the next. Second had come the draw and fire practices, using some old Arbuckle's cans placed twenty yards distant, perched on rocks. Here the men were matched perfectly, the cans spinning off into the dust almost simultaneously as they drew, as if jerked away by some ghostly hand. Finally, the cans were thrown into the air and hit in flight. There had been occasional misses, but precious few.

By the end of the practice session no one watching the two men could have separated them with confidence, for no matter who 'called' both often appeared to draw, cock and point simultaneously. Surprisingly, it did not appear a competitive affair; rather, each man constantly helped the other, suggesting changes in stance, hand-position and angle of gun-butt. It was as if Billy Joe and Buck sought together for some absolute moment when reaction, reflex and action would flow into a fluid and perfect whole. But behind the co-operation, the striving for perfection, there was, too, an unspoken struggle, tinged with bitterness. As ever, it all came easily to Billy Joe. Two-gun cross-draw, fanning, left-handed draw — whatever new practice they turned to, it was the Texan who was the first to master it. Behind him plodded dour, dark Buck, taking twice as many attempts to reach what the golden-haired Billy Joe achieved immediately, with ease and grace. But Buck, performing repetition after repetition, would eventually get there and in the end was often a shade faster than his friend. And Billy Joe would never know how much practice went on at night, long after he was asleep.

Well satisfied with their morning's work, Billy Joe and Buck walked up towards the wagon, where Eleanor and Mandy Boone were preparing breakfast.

Moriarty looked up as the two men approached the pit-fire, above which stood a three-legged skillet spluttering with bacon. He pulled out his watch from his waistcoat pocket and inspected it.

'You boys must have worked up a fair appetite out there,' he said in his deep, morning voice, turning the bacon with a fork in his other hand. 'Sounded like Bull Run.' He beckoned them to sit on their saddles, which lay beside the camp-fire.

Mandy came from the wagon and handed them each a tin plate, smiling. 'You know what they always say. Practice makes perfect.'

'Practice makes permanent, more like,' growled Moriarty. He sat in front of the fire as Mandy doled out the biscuits and bacon. He poured some steaming Arbuckle's and handed it to Buck just as Eleanor joined them, immaculate as always in her gingham dress with its high, white collar.

'Who's top man? Still Billy Joe?' she asked, mock-innocently.

Buck, his face masking his displeasure, nodded. 'Not much in it,' he said. 'Wouldn't like to live off the difference.'

Moriarty grunted and handed a mug of coffee to him as Buck added: 'But it don't tell us much.'

114

'How d'ye mean?' said Billy Joe. His tone too was level, betraying nothing about his feelings.

'Just like I say,' said Buck. 'It ain't real.'

'I think I know what Buck means,' said Eleanor, glancing at each of the younger men in turn. 'Firing at cans and rocks: it's a bit like us rehearsing. You may know the lines, but it's never the same as being in front of a live audience.'

Moriarty forked a piece of fried bread and placed it on his plate. 'Mandy's father said it all, back in Canyon City,' he said. 'You got to be willing. Your fancy-dan shot isn't used to having the split part of a second between his living and his dying. The gunfighter is schooled to kill. He's not a man whose nerves trouble him in a tight moment.'

Buck nodded. 'You got it, Moriarty,' he said. 'If he ain't an apt scholar at his business in the early beginning he gets killed and never is heard of no more.'

'This is no fit subject for breakfast discussion,' said Eleanor, aware of how the conversation was developing. 'I've never seen much point in all this gun-practice every morning anyway. Just tell me this — has any of you ever fired one of those wretched things at anyone?'

There was silence. Buck and Billy Joe chewed on, both men gazing sullenly forward into the fire.

'It's a dangerous world, Eleanor,' said Moriarty. 'The boys have got to learn how to take care of themselves.'

Eleanor looked at Buck and Billy Joe. There was no point in arguing. Her face relaxed into a smile. 'I suppose you're right,' she said. 'So what are our future plans, husband?'

Moriarty scratched his nose. 'No point in trying the English Method again for a while,' he said. 'Takes too long to set up, though the money's good. We'll try Diamond City first. Then maybe Fort Hall. And there's a street dash up in Virginia City in three weeks: always good pickings there. We'll play it straight as usual: let Billy Joe run on his merits.'

'And what about me?' asked Buck.

'I reckon we'll call it a day for you for this season,' said Moriarty flatly.

Buck's face fell and Eleanor nudged Moriarty in the ribs.

'Leastways, for the big-money races,' he quickly added. 'But I've got great plans for you, Buck. I see you taking on the long sprints next year, a furlong, maybe longer. You've got bottom, we all know that, but we've got to find you the *right* race. Meantimes, we've got the shows to put on, and in Virginia City it's Iago for you, Desdemona for Mandy here.'

Buck shook his head. 'I hate Iago,' he said. 'He's so 'ornery.'

'Then you got no problems,' said Billy Joe, laughing. 'Just act natural.'

Buck scowled.

'But you do it well, Buck,' insisted Eleanor, providing him with another thick rasher of bacon whilst applying her toe to Billy Joe's rump.

Buck, mollified, turned towards her. 'You think so?'

'Eleanor's right,' interjected Mandy, replenishing Buck's mug and studiously ignoring that of Billy Joe. 'You're the best Iago ever came to Canyon City.'

Billy Joe grunted and, leaning forward, poured his own coffee. 'And just how many times you seen *Othello* in Canyon City?'

'Twice,' said Mandy, fiercely. 'And excerpts at the drama club. And none of them a patch on Buck here.'

Buck's spirits visibly revived. He shook his head. 'That Iago,' he said. 'If'n only I knew *why* he was so godamned 'ornery.'

'No one knows that, Buck,' said Moriarty. 'Not even Shakespeare himself, though we can take a good guess. I've seen it played every which way. Perhaps it's because Othello's a nigra with a white woman, perhaps it's just envy, 'cos he's a leader of men. But whatever the reason, you've got to play him as a scheming son-of-a-bitch.'

116

Buck nodded. 'And are we doing *Davy Crockett*?' he said. 'Do I get to play Crockett? I'd like that.'

Moriarty speared the last piece of bacon from the skillet and smiled. 'Whatever you say, Buck,' he said. 'Iago one night, Davy Crockett the next.'

So it was decided. After Diamond City, Billy Joe, then Moriarty, Mandy and Eleanor would meet at Fort Hall, entering the camp a day apart. There might be fancy pickings from the boys in blue who always had a fast man. Buck would take a separate trail to Virginia City to arrive first and assess the situation with their local 'spy', the schoolmarm Belinda Fyfe. Two days later Moriarty and his party would arrive, start rehearsals and 'discover' a promising young travelling actor, Buck Miller, and bring him into their company. Billy Joe Speed would then arrive a day later and show more capacity for the alcoholic pleasure of Taos lightning than for the running-path.

From the diary of Eleanor Cameron, 28 August 1875
The reviews in Diamond City were excellent. I had thought Moriarty over-optimistic in casting Mandy so early in the lead role in *The Drunkard's Daughter*, for taradiddle of this type needs to be played to the hilt, and this is usually difficult for a novice. But our little ingénue came through with flying colours, even if she did dry up half-way through the second act.

Certainly, Moriarty was delighted, as he had every reason to be.

He was equally pleased with Billy Joe's performance (running under his real name, Clark) in the handicap street race. Giving starts of up to ten yards, he won by a clear yard, gaining us a thousand dollars. Then he challenged any man in the town over fifty yards on scratch terms, he to be handicapped by carrying a 28lb rail on his shoulders. Moriarty staked a thousand dollars at three to one on Billy Joe, who just took his challengers on the line.

From all this competition Buck was kept apart, as Moriarty is holding him under wraps for another attempt next year at the English Method. This makes sense, with a mustachioed Billy Joe running here in disguise; but it is clear that Buck is still unhappy at all the attention that Billy Joe is being given. Moriarty assures him that it will even up, in the long run, but I seriously doubt if Buck sees it that way.

Now on to Virginia City, where our 'spy' tells us the best footracers in the territory will soon gather. For myself, I look forward to playing Gertrude to Moriarty's Prince in the bedroom scene, and to tutoring Mandy to play Desdemona in *her* bedroom scene in *Othello*.

Buck Miller read and re-read the letter all the way to Virginia City, in particular the part relating to the Street Dash. By the time he had reached the town the letter was crumpled and stained.

'. . . the distance of the Dash is said to be one hundred and forty yards, but I have paced it several times at a hundred and forty-six, so Billy Joe's swift finish could be of considerable value. It is uphill for the first forty yards and bumpy, then a dip at Turk's Livery Stables, which is often shitty, so Billy Joe must watch his footing there. The final fifty yards take a slight curve and there is another sudden slope twenty paces before the finish.

'I know of one local boy, a barman, Wallace by name who has disposed of most of the fast men around this vicinity. He has clocked fifteen seconds for the distance, but rumour has it that he has run two yards faster in a secret trial for his backer, a tinhorn gambler called Cyrus O'Shaughnassy. Word here is that a swift Scotchman called Baird is being brought in from San Francisco and an Italian, Dalla Barba, from Los Angeles, both rumoured to be speedy, but I have no clockings for either of them. I look forward to your arrival, as the past two months here have come hard to me. I sincerely trust that this information has been worth all the trouble.

'I hope to see you all soon and advise you, as usual, to get moving and pump all the way to the finish!

Yours,
Belinda Fyfe'

This was the second time that they had used Belinda Fyfe as a 'scout', the first occasion having been at Blade City, Kansas, a year before. Belinda, who had been the resident postmistress, had been entranced by the Theatre of the West and had kept Moriarty posted on the doings of the Blade City sporting fraternity through her discreet questioning of an eight-year-old pupil, the son of one of the town's leading gamblers. Belinda's inside information had resulted in Moriarty's wallet being two thousand dollars heavier on his departure.

Belinda longed to be an actress but, though possessing an attractive face and figure, she had no talent for the stage. Virginia City would be her last work for them, for she was now betrothed to a banker, Marcus Allen, now mercifully away on business in San Francisco.

The letter had been addressed to Moriarty, and they had picked it up at Fort Hall, where Billy Joe had won two hundred bucks in bets in a fifty-yard sack race against some soldiers, and later had given the camp's best runner ten yards' start in a race for another two hundred dollars. Then, starting on his back, Billy Joe had picked up the camp's best sprinter on the tape, and gave him a further five yards' start in a decider, pocketing another two hundred dollars. 'Like taking candy from children,' Billy Joe had sighed contentedly.

Billy Joe had entered Fort Hall separately from Moriarty, a day behind him, as he intended to on his arrival in Virginia City, for they planned to keep their distance from each other before the Virginia City Street Dash, in order to give them freedom in laying their bets. Any hint of a direct link between Moriarty and Billy Joe would have twitched the sensitive

119

antennae of O'Shaughnassy and other Virginia City men of a sporting disposition.

Moriarty had decided upon his *Selections from Shakespeare* for Fort Hall, and had enrolled the wives of the officers to take part in minor supporting roles, always a popular device to attract large and attentive audiences.

Their three days at Fort Hall passed pleasantly and profitably. All was now ready for the last big hit of the summer season, the Virginia City Street Dash.

The man had entered Belinda's darkened bedroom stealthily, carrying his spurred Mexican boots in his hands. He stood in the gloom at the door, watching as the young woman took her afternoon siesta.

He undressed slowly, as if the disengagement of each button might awaken the sleeping girl, lowering his vest and shirt gently to the ground beneath him, then his trousers. Finally, he unbuttoned his white long-johns and peeled them off.

Belinda gave an involuntary sigh and turned in her sleep as the man, tiptoeing towards the bed, suddenly trod on a loose floor-board. Belinda continued to sleep, the sound of her breathing filling the darkened room. The intruder placed one knee on the bed, causing the springs to creak. Belinda awoke abruptly and, turning, propped herself up, pulling her nightgown over her bosom.

'Sir! I do declare!' she cried, fumbling with the buttons of her gown. 'You have me at a disadvantage.'

'I sure do hope so,' said Buck, crawling towards her along the bed, pulling the blankets over him and drawing her to him. For a moment they kissed each other greedily, then she pulled herself away.

'Moriarty got my letter?' she said.

'Yes.'

'Then recollect what I advised.'

'Committed it to memory,' he said, nestling into her. He

120

paused. 'You know: human beings are the only animals that make love face to face?'

Belinda shook her head, and her head continued to shake, only soon to an inner rhythm, as Buck's attentions became more insistent. Gasping, she gathered herself and put both hands on Buck's shoulders.

'You never heard tell of preliminaries?' she reproached him.

'You knew I was on my way, so I reckon you have been doing your preliminaries all afternoon,' he replied, moving back into a steady rhythm.

'You haven't answered my question,' she said, gulping.

'About your letter?'

'Yes.'

'Get moving and pump all the way to the finish? No problem, that's exactly what I plan to do.'

Moriarty and Eleanor were staying at the Eldorado, and had begun to play, as a preamble to *Othello* and *Davy Crockett*, excerpts from *Richelieu*, *Mose in New York* and *Rory O'More*. A week later Buck and Billy Joe had arrived, a day apart. Buck established himself at the Palace and Billy Joe at the Excelsior, the stomping ground of Cyrus O'Shaughnassy, the leader of Virginia City's gambling fraternity.

There was still a week to the Street Dash, and as Billy Joe casually strolled the main street on that first still Sunday morning he found that Belinda Fyfe had done her work well. The distance was indeed one hundred and forty-six yards exactly, and the terrain just as she had described it in her letter. She had also been useful in checking out such matters as the likely entrants, the honesty of judges and timekeepers and the most reliable bookmakers.

Moriarty's arrival in Virginia City could not have come at a better time, for Eustace L. Chanfrau, the son of Frank S. Chanfrau, the creator of Ned Buntline's character 'Mose', which he had played with great success in New York in the

1850s, was in town with his wife Sarah. Chanfrau, rubicund and bucolic though only in his mid-thirties, and an inveterate gambler, was no longer an actor, but was now, with Sarah, peddling Dr. Spooner's Snakewater Oil and the Incredible Magnetic Belt. He was, however, delighted to make a few extra greenbacks by playing nightly in Moriarty's Theatre of the West.

The rest of Moriarty's casts were local amateurs and it was in their training that Eleanor and Moriarty were to find their greatest pleasure. It always amazed them how even the most repressed Baptist matron nursed a secret desire to perform on stage. Equally, it surprised them how much raw talent often lay behind a facade of whale-bones and high-necked bodices. It was all there: it only required release. And that was their job — to let out what was within.

Ultimately it often came down to a few simple mechanisms. Thus Eleanor and Moriarty would have their amateurs play charades in order to relax them, and a few slugs of Spooner's Snakewater Oil (90 per cent alcohol) would complete the task.

'Unless ye become as little ones ye cannot enter the kingdom of art,' Moriarty would boom as his volunteers pretended to be flowers or trees. Then, as his pupils began visibly to glow, 'Take the stage as the bird takes the air; it's your medium, ladies and gentlemen.'

Whatever the limitations of Moriarty's charges' performances, there was never any question of modifying Shakespeare's plays or playing down to his audiences, for many knew the classics off by heart. Thus, although Moriarty produced *Othello* with a cast which doubled up on parts, the text was played to the letter. More liberties could be taken with *Davy Crockett*, and there Moriarty allowed Buck to ham it up outrageously.

In the second act the heroine, Eleanor (played by Mandy) reads to Davy (played by Buck) the ballad of Young Lochinvar, but just then the howling of wolves is heard. Soon the wolves are throwing themselves at the door of the cabin.

Eleanor: Nothing can save us.

Davy: Yes, it can.

Eleanor: What?

Davy (kissing Eleanor): The strong arm of a backwoodsman.

(Davy bars the door with his arm. The wolves attack the house. Their heads are seen through an opening in the hut and under the door).

CURTAIN

The curtain to that second act always dropped to a standing ovation and Buck milked it for all he was worth. Even Billy Joe, frowning at the back of the hall as Buck and Mandy embraced, was usually drawn to reluctant applause.

The Chanfraus' final performance in *Othello* as Cassio and Emilia ended less successfully. Eustace Chanfrau was in debt to the Mayor for two hundred dollars on a game of stud and Moriarty could hardly keep his face straight as, thrusting a dagger to his chest in the final scene, he watched in the wings the 'dead' Emilia, played by Sarah Chanfrau, hurriedly packing in preparation for a quick getaway with her husband, a 'dismayed' Cassio, still onstage.

From the diary of Eleanor Cameron, 14 September 1875
Never have we played *Othello* with such success. Even hardened Southerners, who have in the past voiced audible objections during the love-sequences, were swept away by the quality of the production. Buck was a particular success; he seems to have an intuitive feeling for the part of Iago, for the cancer of envy of Othello which consumes him. The Sawmill Theatre is one of the best in the West, its stage a perfect size for our smaller productions, thus removing the need for large numbers of amateur players.

Davy Crockett, which we played on two consecutive nights,

alternating casts, is a dreadful piece of old rubbish, but the denizens of Virginia City loved every minute of it, cheering and halooing when Buck slew four Indians in the final sequence. Alas, the truth is that many of our followers see little difference between the mawkish melodrama of Mayo's *Davy Crockett* and the true red meat of Shakespeare's classic. But we can only do our best, whether it is Shakespeare, Ned Buntline or Frank Mayo. And that we are assuredly doing.

One small cloud has, however, appeared upon the horizon. At the curtain of Davy Crockett, with Mandy playing the female lead, Buck pulled her to him and kissed her on the mouth, ending the play as we always do. As I stood in the wings I caught sight of Billy Joe's face. There can be no doubt as to where his interests lie.

The Dash was a big money race, being a $100-a-man sweepstake, offering anything up to $3,000 to the winner, plus side bets.

Billy Joe was not known in Virginia City and his entry for the Dash caused little comment, for the race had always drawn entries from optimistic cowhands whose only credentials were that they had whipped the best men on their ranch. They were invariably left for dead in the first twenty yards by the hard men from Los Angeles or San Francisco, and from their standpoint their $100 entry money might as well have been thrown down the nearest drain.

Moriarty found that he could place money on Billy Joe at as high as three to one, and he and Buck duly laid bets quietly through the week, all over town, until they had well over five thousand dollars on Billy Joe's back. In the meantime, the Texan maintained a low profile, keeping his spiked shoes well hidden in the bottom of his chest of drawers and avoiding any discussion of running or runners during his frequent forays to the bar of the Excelsior. Billy Joe in fact drank little, for he hated liquor, but Moriarty thought it essential, to keep the odds up, that Billy Joe appear a drinking man. So each night Billy Joe took a bottle of redeye up to his room and poured its contents into the roots of a potted plant, which amazingly survived for three days before expiring.

Dalla Barba arrived on Thursday, Baird on Friday, and Buck was duly despatched to check them out. The Italian was short for a sprinter, barely five foot six inches, but Buck could see that, even in his street clothes, the man was thick in the thigh and big in the haunches, and that meant he was probably swift over the first fifty yards. Baird, on the other hand, was a tall, angular Scot, a red-haired giant who sported a tiny chin-beard. He gave all the signs of being a man well-versed in the business of professional running. Moriarty sounded him out one night after a performance of *Othello*.

It turned out that Baird had run at the renowned Sheffield Sprint Handicap in 1873, coming first in a blanket finish. He had been brought to San Francisco in 1874 by a Scots gambler called Fraser to race over a furlong against a local fast man, a Frenchman by name of Charles Le Ventre. But Baird had pulled a muscle in the final week of his preparation, had gone down by five yards to Le Ventre, and been abandoned by Fraser. Since then he had picked up odd races in Los Angeles and San Francisco, though he had kept clear of Dalla Barba, who was rumoured to be mustard over short sprints. But Baird was still a Sheffield man, and that meant he had done some fancy running.

By Friday evening, therefore, Moriarty had the field sized up. Dalia Barba might provide trouble at the start, but the long-legged Baird would be more liable to stay the distance and come through fast. The others were an unknown quantity, being composed of local boys such as Wallace, who had beaten off all recent contenders, but Moriarty did not reckon Wallace to be better than four yards over even time. By Friday evening, on the eve of the Dash, Moriarty considered he had everything under control. He therefore blacked up for Othello feeling confident that come Saturday evening he would play the Moor fourteen thousand bucks the richer.

When Buck recognised, in spite of his beard, the man called the Indian checking in at the Excelsior he broke even time getting across to the Sawmill where Moriarty had just strangled Eleanor to perfection.

Moriarty was not surprised that the Indian was wearing a beard. When Buck expostulated that Indians could not grow beards, Moriarty explained that the Indian was not an Indian.

'He's Welsh,' said Moriarty, without turning his gaze from his dressing-room mirror. 'Name of Nythbran.'

'Welsh?'

'Yes,' said Moriarty, continuing to apply grease to his face. 'Claims his great-grandfather was the great Guto Nythbran. He ran twelve miles in an hour about a hundred years ago against a soldier called Prince — back in seventeen hundred and God knows when. Then he keeled over, stone dead.'

Buck whistled through his teeth. 'Twelve miles in an hour. I'm not surprised,' he said. 'But then how come he's called "the Indian"?

'His father,' said Moriarty, wiping his face clean with a rag and surveying himself. 'Spent a lot of time up in the Indian territories with the Blackfeet. They called him "the Welsh Indian". So people started calling his boy "the Young Indian". When he started running, he cut out the "young".'

'So what do we do?

Moriarty completed the cleansing of his face and stood up. 'Stay cool. We can't spill the beans on the Indian or he'd do the same to us and we'd all be in hot water,' he said. 'We've just got to make sure that Billy Joe does some fancy running.'

First came the camel-races. These animals had been brought out to the South 'West in 1855 by the Army, and by 1857

126

seventy-five of them had been quartered in Camp Verde, Texas, which became known as 'Little Egypt'. However, the experiment had never looked like succeeding. Veteran cavalrymen, whose legs were permanently callipered to the dimensions of a horse, were unable to stay on the beasts, while rookies became violently 'seasick'.

The Army programme was therefore abandoned and the camels sold to a San Francisco-based camel-importing company, and camel caravans were established in the South West until the 1860s. The Civil War then put an end to the venture. The herds were split up, many finding their way into zoos and sideshows, while others were left to wander off into the wilderness. It was the progeny of these strays which were yearly used in Virginia City for racing purposes.

After four heats of camel-racing the boardwalks of the Main Street filled again, for the first heats of the Dash were less than an hour away, and final bets were laid. Somewhere in the crowd Moriarty knew that Claud Feeney, the Indian's manager, would be laying quiet money on his boy, with half a dozen others doing the same. Moriarty had never seen the Indian this far west, certainly never under wraps, and even he had difficulty in recognising him under the heavy, black beard.

The Indian was a class runner, and from 1871, when they had first met in New Orleans, Feeney had handled him beautifully. Six foot tall, one hundred and sixty-eight pounds and split to the ears, Nythbran was a perfect running machine. Feeney had used him sparingly, making only two or three big hits a year, taking the big man to Cuba in 1873 to whip a trotting horse over fifty yards and to Paris the year after to cane the best men that Europe had to offer. The Indian had been regularly clocked at even time for a hundred yards on level ground and, in New Orleans in 1874, two yards inside evens for one hundred and thirty yards. Now twenty-six years of age, he was at his peak, a full yard or more faster than Billy

127

Joe by any reckoning, and just as much a master of his craft as Deerfoot had been over a decade before.

The heats started in the heavy heat of the midday sun in a Main Street narrowed to a stringed five-lane funnel, with spectators pressing in heavily on the outside lanes. The Indian took the first heat in 14.7 seconds, scarcely breathing hard as he hit the finish five yards up. The local boy Wallace took the second four-tenths slower, only just holding off a feisty little Mexican called Aquido. Baird and Dalla Barba took the next two heats easily in the same time, 14.9 seconds, and Billy Joe the final heat even more easily, again in 14.9.

Watching from the balcony of the Eldorado, Moriarty saw that, though Billy Joe was running well, there would still be a clear yard between him and the Indian. That yard was made at the start where Billy Joe, never quite in balance, could not match the Indian's fluid surge from the gun. Once he was off his mark, Billy Joe could equal his opponent, but that was academic — the result was a foregone conclusion.

With three hours to go before the final, Moriarty repaired to the Sawmill Theatre to confer with Billy Joe and Buck.

There he found Billy Joe on his face on the dirt and sawdust floor of the passageway of the improvised theatre. Above him stood Buck, his expression a mask of frustration.

'You speak to him, Moriarty,' he said, shaking his head.

'He's gone plumb loco.'

Billy Joe turned to sit facing his manager, and wiped himself down.

'I can win this one,' he said. 'I can taste it.'

'Of course you can,' said Moriarty, placatingly.

'No. I mean it,' insisted Billy Joe. 'Just you hear me out.'

At this he got up and sat on a bench on one side of the passageway, while Moriarty and Buck did likewise on the other. He leant forward, elbows on knees.

'Now what's the worst part of my dash?'

'The start,' said both the other men simultaneously.

Billy Joe grinned. 'Right,' he said. 'I start like this, standing up.' He got up and stood frozen in the standing-start position, facing towards the darkened stage.

Moriarty nodded. 'I've seen all this before,' he said.

'Now I can't ever get my balance right?'

'That's true,' said Moriarty.

'And I don't seem to be able to push off good?'

Moriarty nodded, then stood and raised both hands in exasperation. 'Where's all this getting us? I've seen you run hundreds of times. You're a lousy starter.'

'Only because I can't get my balance.'

'Balance?' said Moriarty. 'Who d'you think you are — Blondin?'

Billy Joe smiled a patient smile.

He got down onto his front on the soft dirt, facing away from the stage.

'Now we've taken a parcel of money from suckers by me starting face down, while they're standing up, haven't we?'

'Yes,' said Buck. 'That's because they're suckers.'

'And I can usually pick them up in the first ten yards, can't I?'

'Right so far,' said Moriarty.

'It's because I've got a better push when I turn around like this.'

Billy Joe turned round swiftly and got into an all-fours position, now facing the stage. 'Then off I goes like a bat out of hell!'

Billy Joe stood up, dusting himself down.

'Where's all this taking us?' said Moriarty. 'Are you saying that you're going to start in the final lying on your face, pointing in the wrong direction? Is that what you're trying to tell me?'

Billy Joe shook his head. 'Look at this,' he said, turning again to face the stage. He got down on to his marks, right knee opposite his left instep, facing forward. He leant forward, placing both hands on the ground. His fingers and thumbs formed a triangular shape a shoulder-width apart, a foot or so ahead of his left toe.

'Say "on your marks",' he said.

'On your marks,' said Buck, sullenly.

Billy Joe settled himself. 'Say "set".'

'Set,' growled Buck.

Billy Joe raised his hips, so that his spine was parallel with the floor.

'Go,' said Buck, automatically.

Billy Joe sprinted down the passageway, only just managing to stop before he reached the stage. He turned, smiling.

'See what I mean?' he said.

'No, I don't.' said Moriarty. 'I saw you get down. Then I saw you get up. So why the hell get down in the first place? It doesn't make sense.'

'It's not scientific,' said Buck.

'That's it,' said Moriarty. 'You got it, Buck. It's not scientific. It stands to reason. Why go down when you've got to waste all that energy just to get back up again? You try that against the Indian and he's going to take you by five yards, not one.'

'In other words, you think my idea stinks.'

Moriarty stood up and made to leave. 'Not in other words,' he said. 'Those would be exactly the words.'

He walked down the aisle. 'You try to talk some sense into him, Buck,' he said. 'See you at the race.'

No question of it, Billy Joe had drawn the best lane, plumb in the centre, with the Indian on his left and Dalla Barba on his right, with Baird to the left of the Indian and Wallace to the right of Dalla Barba. Thus he would have pressure on either side of him, all the way to the finish.

But when Mayor Beauregarde brought the runners to their marks, there was a burst of chatter when Billy Joe Speed went down on one knee and placed both hands about a foot beyond the line.

'Stand away from the line, gentlemen,' said Beauregarde from his position on a raised stage in front of the Excelsior.

All but one of the runners did as they were hidden. The exception was Billy Joe.

'Mr. Speed?'

Billy Joe looked up at the starter. 'Yes, sir?'

'You do have a passing acquaintance, sir, with the rudiments of starting?'

'Yes, sir, I think that I do.'

'Then please get to your mark, sir, and do as the others do.'

Billy Joe stood up, put his hands on his hips, and his clear blue eyes stared up at Beauregarde.

'I got a new way, sir. A new method of starting.'

Beauregarde looked around him in exasperation. 'There's only one way of starting, sir. Sheffield-style. The straight standing-up way, like a man, not on all fours like a coyote.'

Billy Joe shook his head stubbornly. 'I got both feet behind the line,' he said. 'That's what it requires in the rules, sir.'

'That's right, judge.' It was Moriarty from the balcony above; sticking up for Billy Joe no matter what. 'Nothing in the regulations says that a man has to stand up. I have it here. Sheffield Rules.'

He threw a small brown book down to Beauregarde, who caught it surprisingly deftly in his right hand. The Mayor perused it for a moment, shook his head, then looked again at Billy Joe.

'You're right, young man, I got to admit it. Nothing in the Sheffield Rules says that a man can't get down on all fours if he has a desire to. But I warn you, sir, look to yourself.'

He paused to regain his composure. 'Gentlemen, get to your marks.'

The runners returned to their positions, the Indian muttering in Welsh under his breath as he took his mark. It

131

was impossible to make out whether it was an imprecation or a prayer.

Billy Joe scratched a shallow hole in the dust with his left foot. He screwed his foot into the hole, then bent to place his right knee on the ground opposite his left foot. Finally, he placed his hands in front of him in the brown dust as precisely and delicately as if he were playing the piano. The Indian watched for a moment, transfixed, then suddenly turned to face up the track, his focus now upon the race.

'Get set.'

A child scuttled across the track at the finishing mark, probably hoping to get himself a better view. Then Main Street was cathedral-still, and only the banners flapping over the start could be heard. Billy Joe slowly raised his hips.

The gun exploded, filling the silence. It released them with a rush and Billy Joe went into an immediate lead, coming off his mark as if someone had thrust a red-hot poker to his rump.

To Moriarty, watching from the balcony above, it was a revelation. Billy Joe was three feet up on the Indian at twenty yards, with the others nowhere. He was running as if he had somehow come from a point ten yards behind the start, already in motion. He surged out now, each stride rangy and fast, making even the Indian look sluggish. At fifty it was only Billy Joe and the Indian, with the others threshing around a couple of yards back.

Billy Joe held his yard into sixty, cutting through the roar of the crowd. Had there been no others with whom to compare him, he would not have seemed to be moving at speed, for there was no sign of effort, no hint of tension. For he ran as if to a sure and certain inner rhythm, oblivious of the race and its imperatives. He is beautiful, thought Moriarty; win or lose, you got to give it to him. My boy is beautiful.

But the Indian was not finished. By seventy he had clawed back a foot, and at ninety yards another foot. At a hundred he was nearly level — Billy Joe could almost feel him. But the

132

Texan held on and as they hit the tape both were as a single man as the watches stopped at 14.4 seconds.

Buck, in line with the finish, knew it was close, with probably only six inches between them, but felt in his gut it was Billy Joe's race. As the runners were engulfed by the crowd the chairman of the judges' panel, Sheriff Kennedy, boomed from the balcony of the Excelsior that the judges were going into closed session to decide on the result.

Buck and Moriarty did not dare go near Billy Joe as they waited for the decision. Somehow the outcome was a very secondary matter: it was the fact that for the first time Billy Joe had put it together, the start, the middle, the finish, all fused into one fine coherent whole.

Twenty minutes later, the plump, white-haired Beauregarde, dressed in morning coat and top hat, stood on the balcony, with a crowd of two thousand standing expectantly below.

'There is a split decision,' he said.

There were boos and hisses from the crowd. 'The winner, by a majority verdict, is Dai Nythbran, in a time of fourteen point four seconds.'

Billy Joe Speed sat slumped on a bench in the dark, empty theatre. It was nearly eight o'clock in the evening and as far as the others were concerned he had vanished from sight with a bottle of redeye directly after the race. Moriarty had let him go, and had also counselled Buck and Mandy to leave him be. He had never seen Billy Joe drink for real, but this was as good a time as any. He had told him that it was a fix, that Beauregarde and Kennedy both had money on Nythbran, that they knew for certain that Billy Joe had beaten the Indian. But the Texan was inconsolable. He sat in the front row of the theatre, staring at the empty stage, and was unaware of someone standing behind him.

The Indian coughed. Billy Joe looked round, his eyes vacant.

The runner put out his hand and Billy Joe saw that it contained a wad of notes.

'Take it,' said the Indian. 'You won it fair.'

For a moment Billy Joe was nonplussed.

'Come on,' said the Indian. 'I ain't never been beat before, but I do know when I am. Take it.'

He sat down beside Billy Joe. 'Where the hell d'you ever learn to start so fast?' he said. 'I never saw no man start that way.'

'Science,' said Billy Joe, blearily, passing his bottle to the Indian.

'Could you show me?' said Nythbran, taking a swig.

'No problem,' said Billy Joe, standing up a little unsteadily. He got down on the sawdust floor and the Indian, checking each movement, got down parallel to him.

'What do you call it?' asked Nythbran, looking sideways at his fellow runner.

Billy Joe paused for a moment. 'The Kangaroo Start', he said. 'I call it the Kangaroo Start.'

Mandy had never seen Billy Joe Speed so down in the mouth. Since Virginia City he had ridden silently with Buck alongside the wagon while she sat beside Eleanor and Moriarty. They were making their way to Ogden and the railhead where they would embark for their winter quarters in San Francisco. Nudged by Eleanor, she attempted to engage him in conversation about his past, and gradually Billy Joe began to relax.

Billy Joe's father, Adam Clark, had been an Englishman, he told her, a miner from Kent, transported to Australia in 1843 for attempting to set up a trade union.

Adam Clark had escaped from Australia in 1850 and had made his way with other ex-convicts to San Francisco via Hawaii. There the Sydney Ducks, a lawless band of Australian expatriates, almost an alternative government, were in the city, but Adam had refused to join them, siding instead with the Vigilante Committee, headed by the equally ruthless and ebullient politician Sam Brannan. By 1852 the Ducks had been wiped out by Brannan and his vigilantes who had mobilised the law-abiding citizens of San Francisco into a fighting force, and Clark had made his way south to San Antonio to scratch out a living by ranching, and in 1854 had married a Spanish girl called Maria Ordonez.

William Joseph had been born a year later, and almost as soon as he could walk he was running. In his youth Adam Clark had been a runner too, part of a Kent culture which had for centuries raced village against village, using a running game called 'Prisoner's Bases'. When Billy Joe was five his father, then thirty, could give him fifty yards' start in a hundred. Seven years later, Billy Joe's start on his father was down to a mere ten yards, and in 1868, at the age of twelve, Billy joe did what he had aimed to do for nine years — he beat his father from scratch.

That night, they sat side by side at the camp-fire, twenty miles short of Ogden. Near them, seated on saddles, Moriarty and Buck rehearsed Macbeth while Eleanor repaired damaged costumes.

Somehow Mandy felt closer to Billy Joe in his failure than she had in his success. For the first time he seemed vulnerable. But as the gloaming began to envelop them Billy Joe grew quieter and she could feel that he was again re-living the disappointment of Virginia City. As Billy Joe stared into the fire Mandy felt that she could almost see in its flickering flames that desperate finish with the Indian.

'And how did you come to find out that you could really run fast?' she asked. 'Outside of San Antonio, 1 mean.'

Billy Joe's reply was immediate. 'Because of a doughnut,' he said. 'Want me to tell you about it?'

8

THE DAY OF THE DOUGHNUT

Billy Joe Speed would always be able to declare with absolute certainty the exact moment that the course of his life had irrevocably changed. It was 7 June 1873: the Day of the Doughnut.

It had been the eighteen-year-old Billy Joe's first trail-drive for the Circle X, and he had thus ridden drag for the first three weeks, breathing in the choking dust of seven hundred beeves being driven north from San Antonio to the Union Pacific at Ogallala, Nebraska.

They had made good time, for the trail-boss, Cal Prenn, a leathery, six-foot-four Texan of thirty-six, had an excellent remuda of horses, while his beeves, Texas Longhorns, had plenty of bottom and could make fifteen miles or more a day. Billy Joe had picked himself out from the remuda a fine sorrel fifteen hands and one inch high, with a thick belly and fleshy haunches which would help him stay over long drives.

The trail had gone well until the Red River. Only seventeen beeves lost, ten to a 'friendly' Kiowa chief who would in any case have had his braves help themselves to another ten had they not presented them to him as a 'gift'; five to an Apache chief who claimed them as tribute for passing through land which he did not own; and two on river crossings.

The rivers had been unusually high for the time of the year, but the Red River, just beyond Doan's Store, presented a special problem, for it was over a hundred yards wide, four to six feet deep and had a vicious undertow. This, together with a quicksand bottom which would bog a saddle blanket, forced Cal Frenn to reconnoitre several miles north and south to check on more suitable fording-points. There was none.

The only alternative was to wait it out for a couple of days, in the hope that the level of the river would drop. But Frenn decided to take a chance and the crossing was made. His driving philosophy was simple — 'Never let a beeve take a step in any direction that is not towards his destination' – and this he followed on the crossing, by putting forward the best swimming horses to lead the herd.

Only, from the beginning, everything went badly. Two drovers, Ben Tate and Bobby Rice, were thrown, and Billy Joe was forced to leave the herd, pull the men to safety, then drag their horses from sucking quicksands. Next, several of the wagons, which had been placed on rafts, broke clear of the ropes which held them, and in re-securing them Frenn had gashed his knee against a wagon wheel.

It took over six hours to make a crossing which should have taken two, and in so doing three horses were lost and twenty-five Longhorns. It was therefore a sodden, bruised and bedraggled bunch of cowboys who straggled in for dinner that evening on the north bank of the Red River.

Frenn was a good leader of men. He ordered Stumpy, the cook, to fix a mess of son-of-a-bitch stew, and in no time at all the Circle X men were savouring the smell of a brown, bubbling hash consisting of liver, sweetbreads and the choicest parts of a Longhorn which had drowned that morning in the river. Stumpy had always claimed that he put in 'everything but the hair and the holler', and after a couple of helpings of son-of-a-bitch the world was beginning to look an altogether better place.

Half an hour later, after two wedges of apple pie washed down by endless mugs of Arbuckle's coffee, some of the boys were ready to tackle the Mississippi, let alone the Red River.

Even so, the gamble on the crossing had not paid off, and

Frenn elected to cut his losses. He himself was injured, the cattle and the horses were bushed, and few of the boys of the Circle X had any stomach for an immediate return to fifteen miles a day of dry mouth and dust. He therefore decided on two things. The first was a two-day rest. The second was that Stumpy should produce his *piece de résistance* — hot doughnuts.

Now Stumpy Wood's doughnuts had a lustre and a fame in Texas camp-lore not far short of Jim Bowie, Davy Crockett and the other doughty defenders of the Alamo. Indeed, men had been known to forsake spring round-up, four aces and the comforts of hearth and home for Stumpy's confectioneries. But although his creations were light, they were not to be taken lightly, and Stumpy would no more attempt to produce doughnuts in the course of a daily stint of fifteen miles than Michelangelo might leave off painting the garden fence to start work on the roof of the Sistine Chapel. No, Stumpy's doughnuts were more art than craft, and the respite afforded by Boss Frenn was just the sort of period needed by Stumpy for work of such sophistication.

So, on the next morning, he set to his task with a will, while the boys of the Circle X got to work repairing the ravages of the river crossing. Lots were drawn to decide who would ride ahead to check out the next couple of day's trail, the unlucky losers, Jess Holt and Sam Peck, being assured that their ration of doughnuts would be guarded and waiting for them on their return. Thus mollified, the two men had early that morning ridden north, the smell of Stumpy's cooking already wafting temptingly in the morning air.

Then men began to appear from nowhere. By noon ten cowboys had appeared at the camp, offering their services free for the day, and by the middle of the afternoon seven more, so that the visitors now outnumbered the crew of the Circle X itself. Though nothing was said, it was clear that Holt and Peck had spread the news of the confectioneries far and wide, and that the Day of the Doughnut had indeed arrived.

By dinner-time that night chores which would have taken a further day had been mopped up by men driven south by the maddening promise of Stumpy's preparations, odours of which seemed to cover tens of acres of Texas land.

Sitting that night by the camp-fire, Billy Joe made a rough estimate of the total mileage that had been covered that day in pursuit of the Holy Doughnut. A conservative guess was five hundred miles, but there was not a man amongst them who did not think his trip was worth it.

The men gobbled down the son-of-a-bitch wolfishly, not merely because they were so hungry, but rather because it would bring them more speedily to that which they longed for, hungered for, lusted after. Stumpy teased out the moment, doling out helping after helping of the stew, until the cook-pot was empty. Finally even Frenn could stand it no longer. He gave Stumpy what the men knew as the 'Iron Eye', at which the bearded, bandy-legged little cook shuffled off, muttering, into the darkness, towards the chuck-wagon.

When he returned it was with a skillet heavy with hot, moist doughnuts, rolled in cinnamon and sugar. That first helping went down so quickly that they barely touched the back of the throat, and Stumpy replenished the men's mugs with more Arbuckle's. His recipe for Arbuckle's coffee was simple. 'Damp it down with water for two hours then throw in a horseshoe; if it sinks, then the coffee ain't ready.'

Another glare from the Iron Eye and Stumpy returned with a fresh batch: fluffy, light and warm, the aristocrats of the doughnut world. These went down with the same speed, again washed away with black draughts of Arbuckle's. From then on there was no need for the Iron Eye, as Stumpy, warming to his task, was remorseless, bringing tray after tray of steaming doughnuts as if he were monarch of a kingdom of confectionery. Billy Joe ate in a sweet dream, releasing notch after notch in his waist-belt, then finally discarding it altogether.

Finally, bloated, the men could eat no more. They sat round the circle of light spread by the camp-fire belching and sighing, as down beside the river the Longhorns lowed contentedly.

When the two groups of cowboys got to talking it was of horses and Indians, and the lead was taken by O'Grady, a grizzled veteran in greasy brown buckskins who had been one of the men lured into camp by the Siren of the chuck-wagon.

Most folks didn't realise, stated O'Grady, whose accent still bore traces of his childhood in County Kerry, that your Indian didn't have a horse till about a hundred years back. No, they were running men, with plenty of speed and bottom and, indeed, when they caught a white man they often took pity on him and allowed him the Run of the Arrow.

This meant that they shot an arrow about a hundred paces away and then, when the prisoner had reached it, he set off at a lick and the fastest braves got to hunting him. Not many white men had ever survived such an ordeal, and to O'Grady's knowledge only Daniel Boone and Davy Crockett had ever laid claim to such a feat.

It had been the Spaniards, stated O'Grady, warming to his story, that had first set the Indians up as a horse people, for it was they who had first brought horses to the West. Your Apache took as natural to horse-thieving as a duck to water, and it wasn't long before they were breeding them and on the way to being the best horse-soldiers in the world, a match even for your Tartars and Cossacks.

None of the boys had ever heard of either Tartars or Cossacks; indeed, some assumed they must be Indians from up Canada way. So it was, said O'Grady, that the Indian with his sheaf of arrows was often more than a match for the pursuing white man – at least, till the middle of the century. So perhaps the white man did have a musket, but it was too damn slow to reload, and this gave the Indian ample time to launch a volley of arrows. The equaliser was the revolver of the 1840s, and the relationship between white man and Indian had never been the same since.

Talk then drifted on to the speed of horses, and again O'Grady was a mine of information. Your Kentucky race-horse, he said, that was an endurance animal, capable of going close to forty miles an hour for a mile and a half. Your trotter pulling a sulky — that could only make thirty miles an hour over the same distance. But for real, blazing speed it was the quarter-horse that could run better than forty miles an hour over a quarter of a mile; and turn on a dime, moreover. And he, O'Grady, had one jim-dandy of a quarter-horse, the fastest animal west of the Mississippi.

At this point Frenn interjected, in his slow, measured tones. He had viewed O'Grady's steed, he said, and he would not give two nickels for its chances against any one of six of his fastest quarter-horses from the remuda. O'Grady had not responded immediately, digesting the last of his doughnut with a draught of the now lukewarm Arbuckle's.

When he laid down his cup, he looked around him at the faces of the men of the Circle X and grinned all over his grey stubbled face. 'Looks like I've got me a race,' he said.

O'Grady had gone back north to Doan's Store for a couple of days to complete some business and pick up some money. He then returned from town ready for the fray, and the terms of the wager were laid. It was to race his horse, Blackie, over a quarter of a mile, over an out and back course, against the Circle X's best man and the best horse in the remuda.

Whilst O'Grady was at Doan's Store the cowboys of the Circle X held their trials. It was clear that Lightning, a sturdy little grey owned by Cal Frenn, was the fastest horse over a quarter; it had already put money in Frenn's pocket in races in Austin and San Antonio and was particularly good on tight turns. The Circle X trials were simple. Every hand was to have a time-trial on Lightning and another on the next fastest horse, the pinto, Diablo, both runs to be clocked by Cal Frenn. The rider with the lowest total time on the two runs would represent the Circle X against O'Grady and Blackie.

141

The result was close. Billy Joe clocked 24.2 seconds on Lightning and 24.8 seconds on Diablo, while the next fastest, the little Mexican, Louis de Gama, did 24.6 seconds on Lightning and the same on Diablo, so Billy Joe scraped home by only a fifth of a second, a margin just as likely to rest on the accuracy of Frenn's timing as on any difference between himself and the Mexican.

The camp was scoured for money but Frenn was adamant that the wages for the trail-drive were not to be touched and that no saddles or horses were to be bet.

The night before the race, Stumpy, who claimed to have trained the fastest quarter-horses in Kansas (though no one had ever heard of a fast horse from Kansas), spent two hours rubbing down Lightning with a foul liniment of his own devising and then an hour pummelling Billy Joe with the same malodorous concoction. After that, both man and horse were given a dose of Thunderer, an evil black laxative, and every hand was warned to stay well clear of them until race-time.

When O'Grady returned from Doan's Billy Joe was still out, down by the swollen river, evacuating his bowels, and the Irishman was kept busy taking bets.

The Circle X cowpokes laid heavily on Lightning, and O'Grady took everything they offered — over five hundred dollars, almost all the money in the camp. That morning, 10 June 1873, the track was cleared of stones and branches and all was ready for the race, to be started by the report of Boss Frenn's shotgun.

Frenn himself had laid a hundred bucks on Lightning's back and half an hour before the race could be seen earnestly conversing with Billy Joe at the side of the chuck-wagon. The Circle X hands took this as good medicine. Frenn knew Lightning well, and but for his bum leg would undoubtedly have run the horse himself against O'Grady.

Finally, at ten o'clock all was ready. The sun was hot but not too heavy and there was not a hint of a breeze as Frenn called

142

both riders to a start-line drawn in flour by Stumpy on the rough, brown surface of the plain. Ahead of them, a furlong away, stood a cactus eight foot or more tall which would serve as their turning-point. Frenn and Billy Joe knew that it was essential to get there first, then turn tight and neat before hitting back for home. Half a length there could be worth more than a length at the finish.

As they came to the start, Billy Joe ventured a glance at O'Grady. The Irishman had shaved and had removed his battered Stetson, revealing a brown, bald head. His greasy buckskins had been replaced by a suit of clean, light brown-skins: somehow the effect was to make O'Grady look leaner and lighter. Certainly this was no longer the cracker-barrel raconteur of the camp-fire three days before. Alexander P. O'Grady had come back to the Circle X loaded for bear. Billy Joe, for the first time in his life, could hear the beat of his heart as he sat, coiled, at the start by O'Grady's side, tasting his sweat as it trickled warm and salt down into his mouth.

When the gun went, the two horses surged off to the whooping and hollering of the Circle X boys. Over the first hundred yards the horses were locked together, O'Grady riding high, eyeing Billy Joe on his right as he put leather to his mount, a sturdy thick-haunched black. As they approached the cactus they were still level but on the turn Billy Joe, spattering stones and grit behind him, turned best and came out a vital half-length ahead.

At once he dug in his heels and laid his quirt to both sides of Lightning's neck as, leaning forward, he made for the cheering knot of Circle X men roaring Lightning home. And his steed responded. Billy Joe could feel the sudden quickening of the pulse of the little horse beneath him. But suddenly O'Grady and Blackie were there at his side, a menacing blur on his right. With fifty yards to go, Blackie was a neck ahead and going away for ever. There was no catching him. O'Grady left Billy Joe for dead over those last fifty yards and finished up close on a length ahead, to a stunned silence from the men of the Circle X.

Billy Joe did not dare to look at his supporters as he dismounted, shaking his head. His opponent got down and patted his own horse on its sweating rump. 'Just like l told you boys. I got me a regular jim-dandy here.'

O'Grady, grinning, held out both hands, palms up, and in a few moments he was five hundred dollars the richer. Billy Joe paid over his own wager of twenty dollars, fighting back the tears.

'Another race, O'Grady,' he said. 'Double or quits?'

O'Grady looked up from counting his money. 'You got another horse? Just give me an hour to rest up and Blackie and me will race against the best you have.'

The Irishman walked away, continuing to thumb through his money, towards the chuck-wagon. Billy Joe followed him.

'No, O'Grady, not a horse-race.'

O'Grady turned. 'Not a horse-race, Billy Joe? Then in Jesus name what?'

'Me. just me against Blackie.'

Behind them Cal Frenn and the cowboys of the Circle X had heard the exchange. They stopped talking and slowly began to gather behind Billy Joe.

O'Grady stuffed his winnings into an inside waistcoat pocket, the thick wad of notes standing out like a woman's breast. From his back pocket he withdrew a crumpled red handkerchief and wiped his sweating face.

He shook his head. 'Now let me get this straight, Billy Joe. You saying that you want to *run* against Blackie? A footrace?'

Billy Joe nodded.

'You're not joshing, Billy Joe? A man should always take a bet serious.'

Billy Joe shook his head. 'Blackie against me. A footrace. I lay my wages for the drive.'

'No, you don't, Billy Joe.' It was Frenn's voice from the back

144

of the crowd. 'No ways you bets your wages. I told you that.'

O'Grady rolled his tongue beneath his lower lip as he looked at the cowboys clustered around him.

Then — 'My horse and saddle,' replied Billy Joe.

O'Grady shook his head. 'No ways I take a cowboy's horse and saddle, boy.'

There was silence.

'I'll back him. Two hundred bucks — one hundred for me, forty for Billy Joe and sixty for the rest of the boys'. It was Frenn, who had pushed his way to the front of the group. He pulled out a wad of notes and peeled off two hundred.

O'Grady smiled, the sweat still pouring down his smooth face. 'That's good enough for me,' he said. 'Okay, cowboy — what are your terms?'

The distance agreed was fifty yards, but the unusual feature of the race, on which Billy Joe had insisted, was that both he and Blackie were to face away from the direction of the finishing line, with Billy Joe actually lying on his stomach. O'Grady had agreed readily, but the money from the rest of the Circle X was slow in coming, and only started to be laid when the Irishman, who had taken an evens bet from Frenn gave odds of two to one against the young Texan.

But two to one were tastier odds, for they could recover all they had lost on the horse-race and more. Thus every scrap of spare cash remaining in the camp was rustled up, with Frenn allowing each man to bet twenty-five bucks from his wages for the drive. By two o'clock that afternoon over four hundred dollars had been laid on Billy Joe's back, though no one could explain why they should lay money on an eighteen-year-old, starting from a prone position, racing against a quarter-horse.

The fifty yards was measured out at noon on the prairie surface in stride-lengths by Cal Frenn, closely observed by Alexander P. O'Grady, who then checked it with his own crabby little strides and pronounced it to be fifty yards or as near as could be reasonably estimated. Then Frenn and his men went over each yard of the track which Billy Joe would run, clearing it of large stones and twigs, after which Stumpy brushed it meticulously with a broom. Finally, Frenn laid his last hundred bucks on Billy Joe at two to one just five minutes before the start of the race.

When Billy Joe came to the mark the boys saw that he had discarded his boots. Now he wore a pair of brown, Indian-style moccasins. Further, he had stripped to the waist and was clad in pristine white long-johns. O'Grady scrutinised him as he mounted his horse, his gaze lingering for a moment on the moccasins. Meanwhile Cal Frenn ordered Stumpy to lay out a fresh starting-line in white flour on the brown dust of the prairie. This the cook did with all the ritual of a Catholic priest at Mass.

Frenn, six-gun aloft, called the two men to their marks. There would be two starting-commands, as required by the laws of pedestrianism, laid down in Sheffield, England, then the gun. As he walked to his mark, Billy Joe looked down the track to the finish where Stumpy and de Gama held a strip of white cotton which would serve as the finishing-tape.

On the command 'get to your marks' Billy Joe lay face down on the dust, while O'Grady steadied Blackie, both men as agreed facing away from the direction of the race. On 'get set', Billy Joe placed his hands directly beneath his shoulders and dug both toes into the soft ground. When Frenn's six-gun exploded Billy Joe quickly pushed himself up into the horizontal press-up position, turned on all fours and bounded off.

Billy Joe was eight yards up before O'Grady had even turned Blackie round, ten before the Irishman had propelled his horse forward. Meanwhile, Billy Joe was on his way to the finish as if the hounds of hell were behind him. Blackie came after him fast, his hooves throwing up stones and dust behind him as he gained speed. O'Grady, leaning forward high in the saddle, applied his quirt to his mount's neck and Blackie somehow responded again, but this time it was all too late, for Billy Joe was two yards up and there was now no catching him. He finished hands held high, a long yard ahead.

It was a chastened Alexander P. O'Grady who sat that night at the Circle X camp-fire, munching the last batch of Stumpy's doughnuts. He did not consume them with the vigour of the first, marvellous tasting. When he had finished O'Grady sipped the remains of his coffee and beckoned Billy Joe away from the Circle X men, towards the shadows of the chuck-wagon, about twenty yards away.

The two men sat on the ground against the wagon wheel and O'Grady withdrew from a pouch on his waist-belt a stick of chewing tobacco. He pulled out his knife from its sheath, cut himself off a chew, then held the stick out to Billy Joe, who shook his head.

'S'pose not,' said O'Grady ruminatively. 'An athlete's got to keep away from baccy and such things. Keep himself in shape. Live clean.'

He chewed steadily for a moment, as if considering his next words with care. 'You cleaned me out good, out there today,' he said at last. 'I swear to God I never saw any man run so fast. Quicker than a shithouse rat.'

He spat a long ribbon of brown tobacco juice at a spider scuttling a few feet away.

'You had it coming to you, O'Grady,' said Billy Joe.

'I don't quite take your meaning,' replied the Irishman, looking straight ahead.

'You had two horses,' said Billy Joe. 'The first one, the dog you had here on Doughnut Day, that one couldn't run fast enough to scatter its own dung. The second one, Blackie, must've been its 'zact twin, but it could run like a stag.'

'You got any evidence to support this? Them are mighty serious charges, young feller.'

Billy Joe nodded. 'The night you left, I marked your horse with a piece of black tar underneath the saddle. When you came back today there was no tar.'

'So, how come you didn't tell all the other boys?'

'Boss Frenn knew, but we kept it close.'

O'Grady shook his head and chuckled. 'I should have knowed it,' he said. 'When I seen them moccasins. I seen Injuns' running shoes before.' He spat another brown line of juice on to the ground. 'I thought I was some bunco man, but I can see I been buncoed real good.' He shook his head. 'But I'm a gambling man. I been in over my head more'n once.'

He cut himself off another piece of tobacco, still chuckling, and put it in his mouth.

'You thinking of staying a cowboy for the rest of your natural span, Billy Joe?'

Billy Joe considered the question. 'I never thought of much different. Maybe, perhaps, save what I can and buy myself a spread.'

O'Grady scowled. 'Cowboys.' He gestured towards the Circle X men sitting at the camp-fire. 'That's what they all say. Used to say it myself when I was your age.'

He shook his head. 'But there ain't no profit being a cowboy, Billy Joe. Just end up at forty with a sore ass and busted legs.'

He pointed again to the camp-fire where the Circle X men were now singing. 'Those boys over there, they ain't got much else, never will have. But you, Billy Joe, you've got fast legs. That's what I would call a negotiable commodity.'

Billy Joe sensed something in the air. 'How d'you mean?'

O'Grady chewed for a moment. 'I mean that not many men can move their ass like you. One in a million, maybe, throughout the whole of the Union. And there's plenty of sawbucks for those that can.'

'Where?'

The older man cut himself another plug of tobacco and replaced his knife in its sheath.

'The real big money's in New York and St. Louis, in the towns, so I've been told. But all over, there's street dashes in

Kansas, Missouri, Arizona. Every town's got its Fast Man, Billy Joe. We could live off the fatheads of the land.'

The implication was not lost on the younger man. 'So what would *you* do?'

O'Grady smiled and spread both arms, palms open. 'I'd be your manager. Fix up your races, put down the money at fancy odds, do all the planning and arrangements. All you'd have to do is move your legs like a fiddler's elbow a coupla times a week.'

Billy Joe thought for a moment. 'And what's the split?'

'Fifty-fifty.'

Billy Joe shook his head. 'No. If I got to do all the running, then I get the thick end. Seventy-thirty.'

O'Grady pondered for a moment. 'Seventy-thirty but only if you meet your own training expenses.'

Billy Joe looked back at the Circle X men at the camp-fire. Then he nodded and put out his hand. 'Partners,' he said.

'Partners,' replied O'Grady.

Alexander O'Grady had always been firm in his belief that the great issue of the nineteenth century had not been Secession, but rather the more esoteric question of whether or not in a sack race a man should try to run inside his sack Missouri-style or bounce two-footed, as in Ireland. Billy Joe resolved the question one baking Saturday afternoon in Virginia City on 21 July 1873 over sixty yards, winning three hundred bucks in the process. The fact that he did so in a massively broad sack of his own construction was neither here nor there. He had clocked eleven seconds, had won by a clear ten yards and there the controversy rested — at least, as far as O'Grady was concerned.

O'Grady was cunning, but not always wise. Money that he had earned during the day by the sweat of Billy Joe's brow was often lost on the turn of a card that night, or on crazy bets on jumping frogs or the speed of a bed-bug. The Irishman loved to live on the edge of disaster, for that for him was where life was lived at its fullest. Billy Joe, despite his youth, was more prudent. For him there was no such thing as gambling, only betting on the certainty of his own speed and agility. So perhaps occasionally O'Grady would give some greenhorn half a yard too much of a start and they would end up on the wrong side of the money; but that was simply bad judgement. With frogs and bed-bugs and the like it was all in the lap of the gods rather than the lip of O'Grady.

During the summer and autumn of 1873 a strong bond of friendship was forged between the Irishman and the young Texan. O'Grady was a bunco artist extraordinary, no question of it, but with Billy Joe he was completely straight. He did, however, insist that if Billy Joe was going to take up pedestrianism as a career then he would have to acquire a pseudonym. It was the standard practice in pedestrian circles in England; some runners had more than one, as a means of confusing the handicappers. And he wanted a real jim-dandy pseudonym, none of your ordinary Smith, Jones or Brown. So, in September 1873, William Joseph Clark became Billy Joe Speed.

Most of Billy Joe's races were of a more conventional variety, from fifty to a hundred and thirty yards, up in the little mining towns of Montana, where every town had its strong man, its best 'rassler', its fast man. The miners, whose very lives were a gamble, loved a bet, and there O'Grady saw to it that Billy Joe learned that it was not always wise to run his fastest. Rather, he would instruct Billy Joe to try, on the first race, to take the local champion on the line, winning by feet rather than yards. This meant that if, in a re-match, Billy Joe had to give the local boy a start, the distance given would be modest, perhaps only a couple of yards, when the real gap between the men was closer to double that distance.

Also, the mining boys always liked novelty events, and Billy Joe earned good money in hopping-races, backwards running and his favourite, stone-picking, which involved four hundred yards of running out and back to pick up ten stones placed twenty yards from the starting-line. But by the coming of autumn of 1873 both O'Grady and Billy Joe had exhausted the possibilities of the Montana mining towns and O'Grady, flush with dollars, had decided to winter in the fleshpots of San Francisco, leaving Billy Joe to return to his parents in San Antonio. The two men agreed to meet in Wichita the following spring for an assault upon the pockets of the citizens of Kansas.

Back in San Antonio, on his parents' ranch, Billy Joe found that his father, Adam, approved of his son's new profession. Years before, his father had told Billy Joe of the Men of Kent who had regularly raced village against village for centuries. The nineteen-year-old Billy Joe, who had never really understood the significance of his father's tales of running in far-off England, now listened with attention. The older man was able to pass on to his son running lore from long past, of the purgatives essential to cleanse the system of its wastes, of the need for strength-building meat, of the value of regular massage. But it was an old English newspaper which his father had picked up in Austin that was to fan the younger man's enthusiasm for running.

The newspaper was yellow and tattered, but still readable, and was *Bell's Life of London*, dated 2 March 1871. The front page was unremarkable, consisting of sundry advertisements for stallions, lost property and horse-race meetings. The opening inside pages contained reviews of plays, Naval Intelligence, Court News and reports of race-meetings. All of this was interesting, giving as it did a glimpse of a world of culture and taste remote from the life of a Texan ranch, but the page which caught Billy Joe's attention was that on pedestrianism, four whole columns of news of English footracing. First there were the challenges — 'Higgins of Barnsley, having defeated Figg of Bolton, Smith of Norwich and Batten of London, all of whom were acknowledged Champions of the World, now lays claim to this title and offers to run any distance from one furlong to a quarter of a mile, against any man breathing'; 'Carr of Preston, having received no satisfactory reply from Clowrey of Glasgow or Sherdon of Newmarket, will give ten yards' start over a mile to any man in the kingdom'; and many more.

The page was full of such stuff, together with reports of foot-racing matches and 'pedestrian carnivals'. It was clear to Billy Joe that the world of foot-racing was a serious business, and that if he were to flourish as a runner then he would have to be professional both in thought and deed. He was fast, no question of that; but it would not always be a matter of beating hicks for a few hundred bucks. One day, perhaps soon, he would have to line up with other Fast Men, some of the swiftest in the Union. Mere talent would not be enough to deal with them.

Thus, each day, after doing his daily chores on the ranch, he turned his mind to his preparation for his spring pedestrian offensive. But he had little idea of how he should set about his task, short of repeatedly sprinting on a hundred-yard stretch alongside the corral.

So, one night in November of 1873, Billy Joe and his father sat in the ranch-house in the dim candlelight as the sharp wind whistled outside, while Maria Clark sat by the fire darning socks. Adam Clark had a good analytical mind. The first thing in any dash, he suggested, was to get fast off the mark. They would therefore have pistol-practice at least twice a week to sharpen Billy Joe up, running over twenty yards. Then it was important to stay the distance, what the Kentish men called 'bottom'. It was obviously essential to run beyond the furthest sprint distances, possibly up to a furlong: that seemed to make good sense. And Adam Clark remembered that, in his youth, when he had seen runners stripped, they had revealed well-defined stomachs, like washboards. It would be necessary to strengthen the stomach with exercises. Finally, it stood to reason that a man could run best if he were scoured of all fat, like a racehorse. 'Muscle carries you, you carry fat,' was Adam's view. Between them they decided that they would check regularly on Billy Joe's 'fighting weight', which they reckoned to be one hundred and fifty pounds. It would matter little if it rose in winter — that was only natural —as long as he could pull himself down to the necessary one hundred and fifty by the time it came to rejoin O'Grady in the spring.

At the end of each day's training, both men would spend half an hour on the most enjoyable practice of all, with their six-guns. Adam Clark had learned during his Vigilante days with Sam Brannan in San Francisco the importance of skill with a gun. He himself was not fast, but deadly accurate with a six-gun at up to twenty yards. Billy Joe, on the other hand, was obsessed with quickness of draw, and his father had difficulty in convincing him that speed was useless without accuracy. Billy Joe was a quick learner, for he relished the challenge of new physical skills. By the spring of 1874 he would have become in every way a Fast Man.

Then came a letter from O'Grady himself, which Adam Clark had picked up in San Antonio. While waiting for service in a San Francisco sporting house, O'Grady wrote, he had come upon a Sears Roebuck catalogue. There, nestling on page 125, was an advertisement for patent leather, spiked, running shoes – 'as used by the Champion Pedestrians of England and the Antipodes'.

O'Grady had torn out the advertisement and posted it with his letter, and the two male members of the Clark family had devoured its text. The shoes looked like black moccasins, with six sharp spikes on each sole, and were claimed to have been used by such great English athletes as Hutchens of Putney and Gent of Darlington. They were priced at $10 the pair, postage included, and remembering the pulpy, slimy streets of the mining towns on which he had run Billy Joe reckoned that they would be good value for money. He promptly despatched $20 for two pairs.

The shoes had arrived in San Antonio in mid-February. Billy Joe could not wait to run in them, but his father counselled caution. It stood to reason, he said, that these new-fangled

153

spiked shoes might well change a runner's action, might even cause a muscle-pull. Billy Joe had dutifully taken a few easy strides in his new shoes, gradually increasing the speed as he felt more confident. But after six runs along the track beside the corral he decided to give it all he had. It was a revelation. For the first time, he felt that he gripped the ground beneath him, particularly in the first strides of acceleration. Somehow he could feel, as never before, force being transmitted from the thick muscles of his thighs and calves down into the ground. Somehow, too, he felt that even when he was running at top speed he had another, deeper reserve of speed on which he could now call.

O'Grady asked him, in a further letter, to meet him in Wichita on 21 May and told him to bring all the money he could raise. What O'Grady did not say was that he had squandered his own nest-egg of the previous autumn in the sporting houses and gambling dens of San Francisco. Billy Joe had saddled his sorrel and packed his Sears Roebuck spiked shoes and set off north to meet O'Grady in the Palace Hotel, Wichita.

Billy Joe had taken his time getting to O'Grady, making plenty of stops, as too much time in the saddle was bad for the legs. He reflected that he had never in his life seen a good bow-legged sprinter. Every two or three days he would find a suitable spot, usually in a valley or box-canyon, and stretch his legs with an easy run. He was a pro, he told himself, and from now on mind and body would be focused on that narrow corridor between start and finish.

But when he arrived at the Palace, on the evening of 20 May, O'Grady was not there. There was nothing to do but wait. For two days Billy Joe, eager to start his first real season with his mentor, performed hundreds of push-ups in his room, interspersed with a re-reading of the now papyrus-like copy of *Bell's Life*, which he felt he now knew by heart.

Then the letter arrived. It was nestling in a pigeon-hole

behind the hotel clerk when he came down for breakfast on the morning of 23 May. It read:

Ellsworth,
Kansas
3 May 1874

Dear Mr Speed,

I have not had the pleasure of making your acquaintance and sincerely regret that I must be the bearer of bad tidings. They are that your friend, Mr. Alexander P. O'Grady, is no longer with us. Three days ago, Mr O'Grady entered into dispute with a gentleman by the name of Curly Bob over a horse-race. It appears that Mr. O'Grady may have been guilty of the crime of substitution, and when brought to task by his accuser attempted to draw on him. This was a serious error on the part of Mr. O'Grady, resulting in his taking two slugs in the chest from which he died two days later. Before expiring, he asked that I contact you to the effect that you would have to continue your pedestrian career without him, and wishing you all possible good fortune in the future.

Yours sincerely,
Elias Crane (Undertaker)

P.S. There is a small matter of four dollars fifty cents for the burial (which I have met from my own resources) which I would be pleased if you will meet, if you ever have a mind to pass this way

Billy Joe had stood frozen in the foyer of the Palace staring at the letter. He felt a great lump at the back of his throat. For the first time in his adult life, tears streamed down his young cheeks.

A day later Billy Joe was wending his way through the crowded, dung-strewn streets of Wichita, north towards Ellsworth

The town had, until the end of 1873, been the biggest of all the trail-towns, but it was beginning to decay, its traders having begun to price it out of business as early as 1871. Now Dodge City, fed by the Aitchison Topeka and Santa Fe railroad, was beginning to boom in its place, and the red lamps of the railroad crews would dangle outside Dodge's sporting houses, creating the first 'red light' districts

On 1 June 1874, Billy Joe was standing, bareheaded in the morning sun, above O'Grady's grave on Boot Hill outside Ellsworth. The Irishman had not even merited a proper cross, the undertaker having found only two dollars fifty cents on him after Curly Bob had divested him of his winnings and both his horses. Crane had lashed together a couple of spars of wood from a crate and burnt on them 'A. P. O'Grady, 1821-74', for a seven-dollar funeral. Billy Joe was surprised: he had always thought his friend and manager much older.

Billy Joe went down to Elias Crane, paid off O'Grady's debt and for twenty-one dollars bought a cross. On it he had inscribed 'Alexander P. O'Grady, Bunco Artist Extraordinary, 1821—1874. R.I.P.' He thought O'Grady would like that.

While the inscription was being made, Billy Joe enquired of Crane after the whereabouts of Curly Bob. It appeared that O'Grady's killer was still in town, resident at the Bella Union Saloon, one of the town's three best boarding houses; and that he had claimed O'Grady's horses and had already success-fully raced Blackie twice since his master's death.

Somehow, intuitively, Billy Joe knew what he had to do. He checked his Colt 45, greasing, cocking and re-cocking it, before pulling in his gunbelt a notch and tightening his leg-thong. He then mounted his sorrel and, perspiring heavily in the midday heat, trotted down into Ellsworth.

It was only when he pushed his way through the swing doors of the Bella Union that he felt the sound of his own heart, which seemed to throb through him like some deep, insistent drum. As he made his way up to the curved wooden bar of the saloon he was aware of the dryness in his mouth. The saloon was a good deal less than full — maybe twenty men strong. He ordered a beer and moments later relished the cold feel of the liquid at the back of his throat. For a few brief seconds the thudding within him seemed to recede.

Billy Joe laid his left elbow on the bar and half-turned to look round the almost deserted saloon. The chuk-a-luk and the keno tables were empty. In a corner, three drunks were snoring off their exertions of the previous evening beneath a painting of 'The Stag at Bay'. In the centre of the room four men were playing poker, the only sounds their calls and the movement of chips across the table.

He looked round at the bartender, a weasel-faced little man with a droopy moustache, who was breathing on some glasses as he polished them. The thudding of Billy Joe's heart began again.

'You seen anything of Curly Bob?' His voice, though strong, wavered.

The barman continued to polish the glasses. Over at the table a bald, bullet-headed man in a red check shirt laid down his chips and looked round.

'I'm Curly Bob,' he said.

The thudding was becoming unbearable, and for a moment Billy Joe wondered if they could all hear it. But somehow the words he needed came out clear and strong from a throat as dry as a powder horn.

'Then you're the man who killed my friend O'Grady.'

Curly Bob slowly picked up his chips again, took the two cards that he had been given and added them to his three.

'Yup, I'm the man who killed that Irish son-of-a-bitch bunco artist. You any kin of his?'

'No,' said Billy Joe.

'Then I have no quarrel with you, young feller.' His gaze fell to his cards. 'I'll up you twenty,' he said, looking across at the white-bearded man across the table.

'I don't see it that way.' It was Billy Joe who spoke, but the words seemed to come from somewhere else. This time Curly Bob slowly laid down his cards and stood up. He was a big man, but with a fair gut on him, his belly swelling over his black gunbelt. He pulled back his chair, its legs squeaking against the board surface of the floor as he did so. Curly Bob's eyes now focused on those of Billy Joe and his heavy features were a solemn mask. He stepped forward to face Billy Joe and the men at his table hurriedly cleared away to the side.

A great stillness came over the saloon. For a moment it was like a tableau, only the buzzing of a fly above the bar disturbing the silence.

Everything happened slowly. Billy Joe saw the gambler's hand quiver at his side then move to his gun. Then his own gun was in his hand, cocked and ready. Curly Bob's weapon had not even cleared its leather casing.

The gambler's jaw went slack and his fingers released the gun, which dropped back into his holster. Sweat beaded on his bald head, and started to run down the side of his face. Curly Bob gulped, and when he spoke it was a croak.

'Jesus Christ,' he said. 'Don't kill me.'

As Billy Joe made his way East by rail to St. Louis he sat watching the endless miles flicker by, and his mind returned constantly to that moment in Ellsworth. It had been a reflex action, the result of hours of practice and nights of dreams, dreams of that magic moment when he would draw on a man and be slick as greased ice. And it had been just as he had dreamt. He was quick, just as fast as in practice, and more important he had been fast under pressure.

But he had not fired. And he knew that under other circumstances this might have cost him his life, and the unformed question that his hesitation suggested haunted him all the long miles across the Great Plains. His speed had rendered irrelevant the central question of whether or not he could fire

158

upon a man, let alone shoot to kill. But there would be other times when that would not be enough, when he would not be so far ahead that he would have no need to fire. What would he do then?

He had taken O'Grady's horses from Curly Bob and sold them that afternoon for three hundred bucks. The man to whom he had sold them, a skinny white-bearded Scot called Angus Gordon, had haggled dourly for two hours over the sale, and seemed well pleased with his eventual purchase.

The sale over, the old Scot had become loquacious.

He would race Blackie in July in St Louis, Gordon said, at the big horse-racing and foot-racing meet; he would make himself a parcel of money on the little black.

At this, Billy Joe's ears had pricked up. The St Louis Fair was the mecca of gambling men, it appeared, and regularly attracted the best horseflesh and footracers in the country. Had done since before the War, whatever they might say about that new-fangled horse-racing track over Saratoga way. But Billy Joe was not too concerned about the horseflesh, and pressed Angus Gordon for more information about the foot-racing.

Gordon, however, had only a passing interest in the pedestrian aspect of the Fair. 'Never bet on anything on two legs, laddie, that's mah advice,' he counselled. He remembered that there were distance-races a mile and over — he had seen a fellow Scot, an actor fellow, win there once — and play Othello the same night, to boot, in a real-life theatre outside one of the main saloons. For the dashes, Gordon was of the opinion that there was one long race, about three hundred yards, and something shorter, probably closer to a hundred, both held on the same racecourse as that on which the horses ran. And big money, of that he was quite certain. Big money.

9

THE GREAT SAN FRANCISCO
HIGH JUMP

7 March 1876, Palace Hotel, San Francisco
Eleanor scrutinised herself in the mirror, pushing back her hair at the temples with both hands as she did so. She had noticed the first flecks of grey only a few months before, in Virginia City.

Still looking forward into the mirror, she puffed out her cheeks, and allowed the air to expire slowly, in a regretful sigh. If she were ever to become a mother, then surely the time was now. That she was not one already was certainly not for want of trying.

She crossed her arms and slipped her hands inside her dressing-gown, cupping them so that she could feel the full, pendulous weight of her breasts. Yes, they were still firm and full, a perpetual delight to Moriarty. The paradox was that for Eleanor her breasts had never been a source of sensual pleasure, whatever Moriarty's passionate ministrations. But she had pandered to him, performing the one-act sexual curtain-raiser till he had transferred his attentions to her intensely sensitive thighs and hips, and the real drama could begin.

For a moment, still looking into the mirror, she shifted her attention from her own body to Moriarty, lying behind her on the bed. He lay sprawled, flat on his face, his right arm dangling over the edge of the bed, like some wilful child.

At thirty-four, she was five years his junior, but Eleanor had for some years realised that it was she rather than her husband who would have to plan their future. For Moriarty was in many ways still the young athlete of the New York Caledonian Games of 1856.

Since taking up with Billy Joe and Buck at St. Louis in 1874 they had tried the English Method twice, on both occasions successfully, and with other profitable minor 'stings' in the years between had earned over $30,000 towards the permanent Theatre of the West which was his avowed goal and her fervent desire. For she was tired of the endless miles across desert plains, weary of bug-ridden hotels and rat-infested theatre barns. She was even wearier of the endless deceptions involved in the betting coups. It was surely time to settle down.

For Eleanor, her early years in the West had been a great adventure. But soon it had become clear to her that her dreams, fuelled in New York by dime novels and romantic plays about frontier life, bore little relation to reality. For the West had little in the way of drama except that brought to it by actors like herself and Moriarty. What it did provide was vast empty spaces, appalling sanitary facilities, extremes of heat and cold, occasional sudden death and in its population a consuming desire for the golden dollar

For Moriarty, however, the English Method and its athletic mutations had given him the perfect mix of sport and theatre; marvellous, flexible little dramas in which he could star and direct and come out at the curtain far richer than at the conclusion of any play. Eleanor could see no end to it, could imagine herself, grey and lined, in middle-age still trekking remorselessly back and forth across Montana, Kansas and Arizona, duping the gambling fraternities of the West, playing Shakespeare and Ned Buntline back to back in draughty barns and sawmills.

Strangely, despite his obsession with foot-racing, Moriarty's

161

dramatic performances had yearly gained in strength. Though no Edwin Booth, he had considerable dramatic range and even in the heavy Shakespearean parts such as Richard III and Macbeth was beginning to show himself an actor of ability. Similarly, Eleanor, though lacking her husband's depth of dramatic background, was now, in her mature years, proving herself an actress of great talent.

As for the others, Billy Joe Speed never ceased to surprise her. Acting, like running, came easily to him. Shakespeare, Dickens, Buntline, Marlowe — it was all the same to Billy. She was sure that he did not understand half the language in Shakespeare, yet the verse flowed from his lips in perfect balance, as if new-minted. Buck, too, was good, often even better than Billy Joe, but for him, as with the running, it came hard, and he sweated nightly over his lines while Billy Joe played keno and blackjack.

Mandy had been a revelation to everyone. She had from the beginning shown an immense appetite for the theatre, devouring manuscripts voraciously, and was now word-perfect in all their major classical productions as well as at least a dozen of the potboilers. Her main worries — as they had been with Eleanor fourteen years before —lay in voice projection and in the mechanics of stage-movement. Her occasional tendency to forget the right positions had, on more than one occasion, almost resulted in catastrophe.

Overall, Eleanor reasoned, this was surely the time for them to leave the unreliable world of gypsy theatre and the English Method and to settle down, form a small repertory company at an established theatre like the Jenny Lind in San Francisco, and start acting in earnest. Their yearly winters in that city only confirmed her in this belief, for in the security of its theatres they produced some of their best work.

But whatever it meant to Eleanor and Mandy, to Moriarty, Buck and Billy Joe the winter in San Francisco was only a respite, a time to plan fresh coups for the spring and summer of 1876.

Eleanor got up and sat on the edge of the bed. Perhaps she was wrong to be so hard on Moriarty, because from the outset his life with Barnum, Edwin Booth, Alice Clay and Junius Brutus Booth had itself been like a dream. Indeed, part of that early life had surfaced the previous spring in San Francisco in the shape of Gregor McGregor.

Gregor, in his early fifties, now playing character parts at San Francisco's Palace Theatre, had come to Moriarty with a hare-brained scheme to prospect for gold in the Black Hills, where traces of the yellow metal had recently been reported. 'Chunks of yellow stuff, big as turkeys' eggs,' McGregor had roared. So perhaps there *was* a treaty with the Indians, so perhaps General Crooke *had* strict orders to keep out all prospectors; but for a grub-stake of five thousand dollars wasn't it at least worth a try? Moriarty had been intrigued, and staked McGregor and five tough young Scots miners. In March 1875 the actor and his companions had duly set off East, vowing to make themselves — and Moriarty — rich men on their return.

Eleanor had not grudged McGregor the money, even though part of it was hers. She knew that without the generosity of the actor the Camerons would never have survived that first bleak New York winter of 1848, and Moriarty was never a man to forget his friends. She did, however, feel that Moriarty had overreached himself now. For it was only a few weeks before that the Great San Francisco High jump had been brought into being.

It was all Phineas T. Barnum's fault. The showman had made and lost several fortunes since his last involvement with his Scottish friend. His Museum had been destroyed in 1865 during the Confederate plot to burn down New York, and Barnum had been forced to supplement his income by embarking upon the lecture circuit. But the man who had brought to the world the Mermaid from Fejee, General Tom Thumb, the Cardiff Giant, Chang and Eng the Siamese Twins

163

and the White Whale, was not to be deterred by fire, plague or flood, and had soon taken to a yet more spectacular branch of the entertainment business. 'Barnum's Circus' had arrived in San Francisco in early January, had established its massive three-ring marquee in the Exhibition Grounds at the corner of California and Pine, and had done thriving business. Only a few blocks away was the Jenny Lind Theatre where Moriarty, Eleanor and Mandy (with occasional support from Buck and Billy Joe) were disporting themselves in a winter season of drama which extended from selections from Shakespeare to Ned Buntline farce.

Barnum had summoned 'at massive expense' from Newmarket, England, 'the Equestrian Wonder of the Age, Captain Whitby and his noble steed Salamander'. The huge mare's great achievement was to clear ten hurdles, each five feet high, spaced ten yards apart, 'a feat never before achieved in equestrian history'. No one had challenged Barnum's claim.

'Captain Whitby' was, surprisingly for Barnum, a real captain. At the age of twenty-three, during the Crimean Campaign of 1856, Lieutenant Mark Whitby had acted as aide-de-camp to Lord Raglan. Dim and imperious, Whitby was a classic example of the least endearing of the English upper class. In Darjeeling, in 1869, having risen to captain and after six years of whoring, debauchery and polo, he had been found *in flagrante delicto* in his quarters with his colonel's wife and strongly advised to resign his commission. He had drifted to the United States in 1870 and in 1871 had set up a riding school for the offspring of the gentry near Hartford, Connecticut.

Salamander, a magnificent white mare standing a full sixteen hands high, had been brought to Whitby by a local farmer, Herbert Kranzlein, who had been delighted to accept a hundred dollars for his beast. Salamander had already been jumped by Kranzlein, but under Whitby's expert tutelage became a magnificent leaper. The mare possessed that rare quality of always taking off in perfect balance and of responding sensitively to Whitby's subtle promptings in the space between barriers. She also appeared to have no fear of even the heaviest of hurdles, whatever their height, and Whitby had taken her regularly close to five feet even in her first few months of training.

Whitby's problem was that there was, in Connecticut, no real means of capitalising on the mate's abilities, for appearances at local fairs barely covered the mare's feed-bills.

It was in late 1874 that Phineas T. Barnum had entered the Captain's life. Barnum had come to Hartford in quest of an eight-foot German 'giant' and had, as was usual in these pilgrimages, discovered that the 'giant' was substantially overstated — on this occasion only six foot ten inches tall. However, whilst in Hartford he had heard of Captain Whitby's mare and had travelled out to the Englishman's stables to investigate.

A quick look round Whitby's crumbling establishment had shown the perceptive Barnum that the Captain's enterprise was in a bad way. But the milk-white Salamander was magnificent; might the Captain be tempted to leave his Hartford haven?

Whitby was at first cool. Working in a circus was hardly, after all, an appropriate life for an officer and a gentleman, even at a salary of two hundred dollars a week. That evening, however, he did decide that at a weekly three hundred and fifty dollars, with bonuses for 'world records', it might be acceptable after all.

Although Barnum found the Captain, with his uneasy mix of social pretensions and sexual promiscuity, something of a trial, there was no doubting his star quality. Billed as a 'survivor of the Great Charge of the Light Brigade' (though the gallant Captain had merely surveyed the carnage through field glasses from a hill a mile away), Whitby, with his haughty bearing and stiff-upper-lip insouciance, went down well with American audiences. And Salamander was truly splendid, appearing to conquer gravity in her long, soaring

165

leaps. So, when Barnum had brought Whitby and his steed to San Francisco, Leland Stanford's mansion was naturally his first port of call.

Salamander's performances had already caught the attention of the wealthy Leland Stanford even before Barnum's arrival. Stanford was one of the 'big four' of Stanford, Huntington, Hopkins and Crocker, who had created the Central Pacific Railway. Leland Stanford took a high view of himself. He saw himself as a horse-breeder rather than as a man who had cheated the United States Government of millions of dollars by false route-specifications. This, and the black- mailing of towns all the way from San Francisco to Promontory Point into paying 'compensation' in order that the Central Pacific would pass through their townships, had made Stanford and his colleagues multi-millionaires. Now, as a result of a bribe of half a million dollars, he was Governor Stanford, a pillar of Californian society.

The Central Pacific had been a money machine, and Stanford, Huntington, Hopkins and Crocker wallowed in riches. Of the four, only Huntington, a grim New Englander, ruthless as a crocodile, had maintained his business muscle into later life, scornfully observing his partners building mansions on Nob Hill, or gathering worthless French paintings.

Stanford's consuming passion was horses. True, he had spent a fortune building the California Street Cable Railway up to his hilltop home so that guests could get off at the front door from the cable car, but his pride and passion was his Palo Alto Farm, 9,000 acres containing two racetracks. The farm, with sixty acres of trotting park, one hundred and fifty hired hands, sixty stud stallions, two hundred and fifty brood mares and the same number of colts and fillies, grew sixty acres of carrots for the horses alone.

Thus, when on 11 February 1876 Whitby and Salamander had arrived in San Francisco it was only natural that America's greatest showman should soon bring them to the Palo Alto

Farm for Leland Stanford's scrutiny. There Barnum and Moriarty were reunited, for Leland Stanford had engaged the actor to give his *Selections from Shakespeare* at a party at his home in early March, and with Buck, Billy Joe, Mandy and Eleanor, Moriarty had travelled out to Palo Alto for preliminary discussions.

Stanford was not known for his prolixity. Bulky and slow-voiced, speaking for him was like having his teeth drawn. But as he stood in his paddock in the thin winter sunshine, watching Whitby put Salamander through her paces, the portly Stanford waxed eloquent. Never, he said, had he seen such a piece of horse-flesh, such a masterpiece of equine athleticism. Would Whitby take $20,000? But the Captain was in no position to dispose of Salamander, tempting as Stanford's offer undoubtedly was, for he was under contract to Barnum till the end of 1877, and in debt to him for ten thousand dollars, the result of raising against an inside straight, held by a midget in St. Louis.

Billy Joe, Moriarty and Buck had watched Salamander's performance with interest, all being expert horsemen, though only Moriarty had had direct experience of jumping, from his days with Barnum twenty years before.

Stanford had called for refreshment, and within minutes a stream of black servants in colourful livery had come down by carriage from the main house, bringing tables, ice buckets and crates of wine. By the time Whitby had finished his exhibition Stanford's servants had created a dining area in a small marquee previously erected beside the paddock. Stanford guided Eleanor and Mandy gently towards it. There the millionaire's staff had laid out a magnificent luncheon of cold game and meats, to be washed down with draughts of Stanford's ice-cold home-produced wine, the work of a team of vintners imported from France.

Eleanor masked a wince as she took her first tentative sip.

'Delicious,' she said, smiling serenely at Stanford. The wine had a harsh, metallic after-taste.

'The best vines, ma'am, in the civilised world, all the way from Europe,' he responded in his slow, heavy voice.

Mandy noted Eleanor's reaction and stifled a cough as she followed Eleanor's lead, her face frozen in a glassy smile as her drink was recharged. Buck and Billy Joe, both with big thirsts, knowing no better, had gulped down Stanford's wine as if it were beer. It was not long before they were joined by Barnum and Moriarty, and by Whitby, still dressed in his riding-gear.

'Ladies and gentlemen, a toast to the world's record equine high-jumper,' Barnum said, as he raised his glass to Whitby, his lumpy, florid face red with pride. Whitby smiled and raised his glass in response.

'Just what *is* the official high jump record, Phineas?' asked Moriarty, his antennae up.

Whitby answered. 'There is, sir, no official record,' he said in his clipped tones, accepting a glass of wine.

'So what you are saying, Captain Whitby, is that no one really knows for sure how high a horse can jump?' pursued Moriarty.

'No, sir, not precisely. Though we have heard of English hunters clearing close on six feet during a chase.'

'On level ground?'

Whitby shook his head. 'No, sir, it has never been accurately checked.'

'And your Salamander, Captain Whitby — it can clear six feet?' It was Stanford, his voice slightly slurred. Whitby looked at Stanford directly, but kept his normal hauteur from his eyes. 'Without question, sir.'

'And how high d'you reckon those hurdles were, out there in the paddock?'

This from Billy Joe, who was now decidedly the worse for wear. He had already consumed four large glasses of wine and was beginning to feel it.

'I can tell you for certain, Mr. Speed,' said Leland Stanford,

168

as he reached for a chicken leg from a servant hovering at his side. 'Five foot three inches.'

'Well, Cap'n Whitby,' said Billy Joe, bleary-eyed. 'I don't reckon that your Salamander was clear by much more than three inches.'

Moriarty could see Whitby's hackles rise, but the Englishman controlled his temper well. 'Are you doubting my word, sir?'

'No,' replied Billy Joe. 'I'm only saying that by my reckoning your mare can clear about five foot six inches. And that's it.'

'Do you wish to place a wager on it, sir?'

Barnum looked at both men. Nothing could be better for his circus than a bet on Salamander, made at Leland Stanford's ranch, particularly if the millionaire himself could be persuaded to throw in a few bucks. Moriarty caught Barnum's eye and grinned. His instincts were to let Billy Joe venture his own money this time, for he made it his custom never to bet in the dark. In Moriarty's view, Salamander was probably only clearing about five foot six inches; but how much had the mare in reserve?

'Yes,' said Billy Joe, as his glass was refilled. 'But I'll do more than that, Captain. I'll jump against her myself.'

Whitby let out a short bark, then, unable to prevent himself, started to laugh uncontrollably. In a matter of moments everyone in the tent, the lugubrious Stanford included, had joined in the laughter. Only Billy Joe did not share in the general mirth. Indeed, his face grew more stern as the merriment around him grew. Gradually, however, it subsided. Whitby withdrew a white silk handkerchief from the pocket of his jodhpurs and dabbed at his eyes. He looked at Stanford.

'You must forgive me, sir,' he said. He then looked across the tent at Billy Joe. 'Now let me get this absolutely clear, Mr . . .'

'Speed,' said Billy Joe.

'Mr Speed. You are telling me that you wish to compete in a jumping match with Salamander?'

'That's right,' said Billy Joe, ignoring Buck pulling desperately on his left sleeve. 'I've jumped plenty, back in Texas. Never once been beat. Never in my life.'

'You've *never* been beaten in high jump?' pressed Barnum, already visualising the headlines.

Billy Joe shook his head. 'Never a once,' he said ponderously, swaying slightly against Buck.

Moriarty saw his chance. 'What odds would you give Billy Joe in a contest, Phineas?'

The showman looked around him, oblivious of Eleanor's, grim, warning glances at her husband, but nevertheless aware that Billy Joe had only the dimmest idea of the situation.

'What's your opinion, Mr. Stanford?' he said.

Stanford's face was impassive. He scrutinised Billy Joe. 'How old are you, young man?'

'Twenty-four, sir,' replied Billy Joe, unsteadily.

Stanford took Billy Joe by both shoulders and looked him straight in the eye. He then looked at Moriarty. 'With horse-flesh, Mr. Moriarty, it always does to look at a beast's teeth.'

Billy Joe flashed a toothy, drunken grin. 'I got nothing to hide, Mr. Stanford,' he said, revealing a perfect set of teeth.

Stanford looked at Moriarty, then back at Whitby. 'You are sure your horse can clear six feet?'

For a moment doubt flickered in Whitby's eyes. 'Certain, sir.'

'Are you a Christian man, Mr. Speed?' asked Stanford.

'Calvinist,' said Billy Joe.

'I am now going to ask you a question, sir, which I require you to answer honestly as a Christian gentleman. Do you swear to do so?'

'Yes, sir,' said Billy Joe. 'Fire away.'

'What is the greatest height you have ever cleared in high jump?'

The tent was utterly still as Billy Joe gathered his thoughts. Even the waiters, who had caught the gist of what was

170

happening, stood frozen in their work. Billy Joe's voice was strong as he answered.

'Four foot ten inches sir,'

For the first time in his life Moriarty broke one of his most sacred rules; he bet on instinct. There were also, he rationalised later, good reasons for putting money on Billy Joe. At six to one, the odds against his man were juicy. There was also the fact that he had never seen the Texan beaten in any physical test, from a handicap dash to a sack race. But for Moriarty the best reason of all was to wipe that condescending smile off Captain Whitby's aristocratic face. That night in San Francisco he laid six thousand dollars on Billy Joe: only Eleanor's intervention prevented him laying four thousand more.

It had taken just a day for Billy Joe to dry out, but by that time San Francisco was buzzing with the story of the Great High jump, which event Barnum had agreed to hold a month later in a gala night at his circus.

Every level of San Francisco society became immediately involved, from the toffs on Nob Hill to the pretty waitresses who made themselves available twenty times a day down on the Barbary Coast. First, the odds rose to eight to one against, and that opening week the athlete's hotel was besieged by Chinamen, leaders of Tongs who had laid money on Billy Joe, eager to check on their investment. Then someone had the bright idea of checking on the height of the hurdles at Barnum's circus, and found that they were only just four foot nine tall: the odds immediately dropped to three to one against Billy Joe. The match prompted the *Examiner* to run a series on 'The Athletic Powers of Man', with contributions from learned professors of anatomy who argued that it was surely against the laws of nature for a man to clear above his own height: the odds rose again. A Scot called Anderson then wrote in to say that many a Scot in his time had cleared five foot nine inches, but he had heard of none who could clear six feet: though Billy Joe claimed no Scots ancestry, the odds dropped.

An Irishman, Keane, then wrote a long letter to the *Examiner* claiming that the Irish had been jumping and throwing long before the Scots had even started to walk erect. This had been in the Tailtean Games, about two thousand years before the birth of Christ. Their great champion Cuchulain had developed the technique of the 'salmon leap', whereby, by flicking his lower legs, he could stay in flight pretty much as long as he liked. In fact, claimed Keane, Cuchulain only came down from his jumps to help out the officials.

Professor Schmidt, a professor of mathematics, then wrote a complex article, containing a dozen equations, saying that if a man's centre of gravity was raised to the height of six feet six inches, then it was just possible for him to clear six feet. Though no one understood Schmidt's thesis, inexplicably, the odds dropped still further. Finally, a Methodist minister called Frewer opined, quoting scripture, that it was against God's will that any man should clear his own height, and since Billy Joe was only five foot ten tall even to attempt six feet was verging on sacrilege. The odds rose again and settled at five to one.

When Schmidt and Keane finally met on a public platform and the Irishman restated the feats of the great Cuchulain and of his 'salmon leap', Schmidt's response had been brisk. 'What,' he asked, 'about the law of gravity?' 'Oh,' replied Keane, 'he paid no attention to that.'

From all of this Captain Whitby remained aloof, concentrating instead on stabilising Salamander's approach runs. It was true that her nightly jumps at the circus were less than five feet, but in training Whitby now pushed Salamander to regular clearances of five foot six inches, with an occasional slither over five foot eight — which, had the Captain been truthful, was the best that Salamander had ever achieved.

On the other hand, Leland Stanford was in his element. He had placed a bet with Barnum and Whitby that if Salamander lost he would be able to buy Whitby's contract and the horse at a price of thirty thousand dollars. But, equally important, Leland Stanford was right in the public eye, a man of the people, possibly even, he reflected, a future President of the United States.

For Barnum it was like a dream come true. Crowds packed his circus nightly, simply to see the 'Greatest Jumping Horse in the World', soon to 'Compete against a Man to decide the Greatest Jumper in Creation' — Barnum's own phrase. Demand was so great that within a week of the wager he had added a Wednesday matinee and two weekly lectures conducted by 'Captain Mark Whitby, The World's Greatest Equestrian' on 'The Art and Science of Equitation'. The take on the matinées and lectures was never less than $500, and this Barnum split down the middle with Whitby, whose status as a gentleman had never dulled his instincts for a sharp buck.

Moriarty soon found himself sucked into a gambling fever, a fever which gripped the town. By the end of the second week he had laid a total of ten thousand dollars at odds between four and six to one, ignoring the advice of both Eleanor and his banker, A. P. Wagstaffe. But a tiny voice inside him told him that he was in way over his head — and when the first flush of the moment had faded, Moriarty's innate Scots canniness reasserted itself. The day after the wager had been made be measured four foot ten on the side of his bedroom door with a tape, marking it in chalk. Then he measured six feet, only an inch above his own height. He then stood back, hands on hips, and surveyed the two marks. Moriarty frowned. Four foot ten looked like nothing, but six feet — that looked dam' near impossible.

It was at that moment that he resolved that Billy Joe and Buck would have to be despatched out of town for special preparation. Clearly, there was no possibility of Billy Joe's training in San Francisco, for there were too many distractions in the city, too many prying eyes, too many possibilities for skulduggery. In other circumstances he would have supervised Billy Joe's training himself, but there were plays to rehearse and perform; and in any case he had not the slightest idea of how to prepare a high jumper.

Early in the morning of 21 February, Buck and Billy Joe, along with a Mexican cook called Manuel, were sent on their way to The Hacienda, a remote ranch twenty miles to the south, to prepare for the Great Match. Billy Joe, now aware of the gravity of the situation, had asked Moriarty for advice.

His response had been brusque. 'Practice, practice, practice.'

A week after they had left Moriarty, buoyed by a rapturous reception of his *Macbeth*, decided to ride down to check on his investment. He arrived there at noon on a bright spring day, and from a distance be could see Buck and Billy Joe squatting in the corral, a few feet away from two vertical wooden stands supporting a wooden crossbar. The stands had holes drilled in their surfaces at one-inch intervals from a height of four feet to their tops, which looked close to eight feet. The wooden crossbar, sagging only slightly in the middle, looked appallingly high. Buck and Billy Joe sat in front of it, eyes fixed on the bar, saying nothing, Billy Joe chewing impassively on a straw.

Moriarty alighted quietly from his horse and went over to stand behind them, sharing their silence. This was a pleasure to witness, two men clearly deeply involved in Billy Joe's athletic preparations.

At last, seemingly unaware of Moriarty's presence, Buck spoke.

'The way l see it, Billy Joe, you don't use enough psychology.'

Billy Joe looked sideways at Buck, scowling. 'The hell l do!' he said. 'I wash, I slick up, I use the best perfume . . .'

Buck shook his head, chewing on a straw.

Moriarty's expression hardened. It was now clear to him that they were not discussing high jumping.

'You don't take my meaning,' said Buck. He paused. 'You mind if l give you some advice – about Mandy?'

'Advise away!' said Billy Joe.

'You're shy, and that's the plain truth of it. You of all people.'

Billy Joe flushed. 'Keep talking.'

Buck slowly got to his feet and walked towards the crossbar. He stood under it and turned to face Billy Joe, at last noting Moriarty behind them. He nodded to Moriarty, but did not change tack.

'It's 'cos you're shy that you don't mosey up to her, ask her how she feels, tell her how good she looks, you know what I mean. Women *like* that. You've seen Moriarty do Romeo?'

'That's play-acting,' said Billy Joe sourly, looking behind him to acknowledge his manager.

Buck returned to sit beside Billy Joe.

'With women it's *all* play-acting,' he said. 'The whole dam' thing. You take my word for it. I been there times enough.'

Moriarty had had his fill. He had not ridden all morning to listen to the details of Billy Joe's social life just days before an important contest. Shaking his head, he walked forward and stood under the bar, facing the two men. The bar was a good couple of inches above his head.

'This must be well over six feet,' he said.

The two younger men did not reply, but continued to gaze morosely in front of them.

'I said, well over six feet,' repeated Moriarty, raising his voice. '

'We can hear you,' said Billy Joe, getting slowly to his feet. He was stripped to the waist and dressed in his long-johns. On his feet were his black patent leather running shoes.

'Well,' said Moriarty, withdrawing a vast white handkerchief from an inside pocket. 'Does this mean you've cleared it?'

'Are you loco?' said Billy Joe, standing underneath the bar. 'It's way over my head.'

'Jesus Christ,' said Moriarty, taking off his stove-pipe hat and mopping his brow. 'Do you two know how much we've got riding on this?'

175

'No,' said Billy Joe, measuring the space between his head and the bottom of the bar. He looked down at Buck. 'Y'know, Buck, this is one helluva height.'

Buck nodded in agreement.

'You should have thought of that before you got us all into this,' exploded Moriarty.

'He thinks by the inch and talks by the yard,' said Buck, standing up and moving to the bar. He stood under it, shaking his head as he gazed at it. 'That is one helluva height.'

'Stop *saying* that!' shouted Moriarty.

He took off his jacket, placed it on the ground and sat on it. 'Now I've ridden twenty long miles just to check on you guys. So in heaven's name let me see some fancy jumping —and Billy Joe, if you tell me you can still only clear four feet ten then I'll swing for you, so help me.'

Billy Joe turned to look at Moriarty. 'No,' he said, his face serious. 'I can do better'n that.'

'Then will you tell me why in God's name you've got it up at way over six feet?'

Buck tapped his temple with his right index finger. 'Mental,' he said. 'It's six foot two inches. So when I put it down, say at five nine, it looks low. You take my meaning?'

'Yes,' said Moriarty, nodding. 'That makes a lot of sense. But *can* you clear five nine?'

Billy Joe walked away from the bar, over to a mark which he had scratched in the dust behind him, and stood at it.

'Course not,' he said, still surveying the bar. 'That's 'bout as tall as I am.' He beckoned to Buck.

'Put it down,' he said. 'To five feet.'

'*Five feet!*' Moriarty exploded again.

'Hold on to your britches,' said Billy Joe, making placatory movements with both hands as Buck adjusted the crossbar. 'Just watch this.'

Billy Joe took three easy, springy strides then four faster ones as he closed in. He jumped in a light, lissom way, like an antelope, and cleared the bar in a seated position, with plenty to spare.

Moriarty smiled and stood up. 'Now that's a horse of a different colour,' he said.

'Put it up to five foot three.' Billy Joe beckoned to Buck, who adjusted the pegs and steadied the crossbar at its new height. Billy Joe looked at the bar for a moment, then, using the same light, springy run, cleared it easily.

'That's my boy,' said Moriarty, clapping both hands.

Billy Joe's expression was unchanging. 'Give me five foot six,' he said. Buck complied.

This time, Billy Joe took a little longer before he began his run, blinking as he focused on the bar, and rocking from one foot to another. Then he began his approach and flowed up out of his take-off into a high, hanging leap. He touched the bar on the way up but it stayed on. Then, at his high point, in the seated position, he swung his rear leg up. It touched the bar, and after he landed Billy Joe looked up to see it still trembling above him. But it stayed on. Billy Joe got up and walked back to his mark.

'Put it up to five nine,' shouted Moriarty. 'Give us five nine.'

Buck looked at Billy Joe, who nodded, so he raised the bar a further three inches.

But this time, as Billy Joe turned to face the bar, Moriarty could see that his eyes had gone. No longer was there that glazed fixity of purpose that had marked his previous jumps. Billy Joe's gaze was fixed upon the bar, trying to see himself clear of it, but his imagination would no longer take him there. He started his approach-run, ran three strides, then turned and walked back, shaking his head. Buck looked at Moriarty, warning him with his eyes to be silent.

Billy Joe looked at the bar again, a thin trickle of sweat running down his left temple, his weight moving from one foot to the other. Then once more his nose twitched like a rabbit's, and he started his run. But this time there was no guts in the approach, no certainty, and long before Billy Joe had taken off Moriarty knew that the jump was doomed. Indeed, his leap would not have got him clear of three foot nine, let alone five nine; for he virtually ran through the bar, falling over it as it hit the ground and tumbling forward on to his face into the dust of the corral.

'Shit,' said Moriarty. 'Have another jump.'

Billy Joe stood up, shaking his head. 'No, Moriarty,' he said. 'That's it for today.' He dusted himself down.

'Is that it?' said Moriarty. 'That's all? Five foot six? That's what I've got ten thousand bucks riding on? And Eleanor — she thinks it's only six thousand!'

Buck stole a worried glance at Billy Joe. 'Don't forget we've got two thousand each on it, too,' he said, handing Billy Joe his shirt.

'But five foot six!' groaned Moriarty.

He reached into an inside pocket and withdrew a faded clipping which he handed to Buck.

'You're the trainer, Buck,' he said. 'So read this. It's about jumping, by some professor guy called Schmidt. I can't make head nor tail of it. Something about the centre of gravity.'

Buck took the clipping and scrutinised it, Billy Joe peering over his shoulder.

Moriarty picked up his jacket, dusted it down and put it on. Billy Joe handed him his hat. Then Buck and Billy Joe watched as Moriarty trudged slowly back towards his horse, head down.

'Leave it to us, Moriarty,' shouted Buck after him, holding the clipping aloft.

'Yes,' shouted Billy Joe. 'Centre of Gravity, Moriarty, Centre of Gravity.

When Moriarty had returned from the ranch it had not surprised Eleanor that he had said little about what he had seen. Both boys were in good health, and preparations were going well, and of course Billy Joe, a born jumper, was going to cream that jackass Captain Whitby. That was all that her husband would say.

But Moriarty's terseness did not trouble Eleanor. She was used to the traditions of secrecy in athletic preparation, well aware that the less she knew the better, in case by any chance she gave away vital information which might influence the odds.

She was more concerned about a conversation which she had had that morning with Mandy, during rehearsals for The *Merchant of Venice*. The problem was Billy Joe Speed. Mandy had taken to him from the beginning, but despite her feelings the Texan seemed oblivious to her, if not actually hostile. Billy Joe, to whom the skills of sprinting and acting seemed to come so easily, appeared to glide in some still, silent world of his own, beyond her reach.

Buck, on the other hand, she could relate to easily. Ever gracious and attentive, plodding dourly towards levels of performance on running-path and stage which Billy Joe achieved with ease and effortlessness, he was already a firm friend. And she valued that friendship just as much as she longed for something more than that from Billy Joe.

Eleanor had been supportive. She recalled for Mandy her first Green Room experiences with an uncertain Moriarty. She had been forced to take the initiative then, and it had been worth it. Perhaps, she counselled Mandy, it was something to do with the inward, self-concerned life of the athlete. Such men had difficulty stepping out of themselves, moving towards other people. Certainly, she said, Mandy should not look upon it as any reflection upon herself, for the nightly admirers at the stage-door of the Jenny Lind Theatre were sure testimony to her charms. Mandy would simply have to be patient, and wait for her moment. It would come.

Moriarty did not know why he had even bothered to send spies to check up on Captain Whitby. It was, after all, a horse

179

they were competing against, not one of Barnum's freaks, and a horse was a four-legged animal specially designed by the Almighty for running and jumping. Okay, so Billy Joe had once beaten one over fifty yards; but that was a short distance, and Billy Joe had fixed the terms so that he was halfway to the finish before the horse had even got moving. But this time they were on an equal footing, and the reports from Moriarty's spies at Barnum's Circus only deepened his gloom. For although Whitby had always insisted on complete security during his work-outs one of Moriarty's informants, a little Australian clown called Boyle, had hidden himself in a vaulting box and had witnessed a session in which Salamander had leapt to massive heights, perhaps six foot or more. Certainly Whitby seemed pleased with his steed, rewarding her with chocolates at the end of the work-out.

Moriarty had not dared to go back down to the Hacienda to check out on Billy Joe's progress. His money was lost, and he resolved to put as good a face upon it as possible. Yet Billy Joe's disappearance only served to increase the hysteria which had gripped San Francisco, with gamblers pouring in from New York, Chicago and St. Louis. Everyone had a theory, everyone an angle on the competition, and the town was rife with rumour. There were stories that Moriarty was bringing in some new type of jumping shoes with springs in the soles, that it was all a fix, that a spring-board or a trampoline was going to be set under the surface in the circus, and a consortium of the city's sporting men had demanded an inspection of the surface by an independent jury directly before the competition — to which Barnum had readily agreed.

Moriarty responded to these stories with increasing incredulity. True, if he had been able to secure Billy Joe spring-loaded shoes he would happily have done so. But he had visited the ranch, he had seen Billy Joe barely scrape his butt over five feet six inches, and damn lucky to do so. No, Billy Joe could only clear six feet if he had somehow devised some new method of defying the law of gravity, something akin to the discovery of the Holy Grail, or perpetual motion.

The Great High Jump Match had done wonders for their presentations at the Jenny Lind Theatre, however. The newspapers, abetted by Barnum, had portrayed Moriarty as the trainer of the age, capable of turning base athletic metal into gold. The Scot had been pressed into a series of joint lectures on 'Modern Man and the Athletic Ideal', which he and Barnum gave at the Jenny Lind on evenings when no drama was playing. And Barnum had been generous to a fault, reasoning that, as the lectures were good publicity for the Circus, Moriarty could have seventy-five per cent of the take.

Eleanor had early decided that there was no useful point in discussing the wager with her husband. In the first week after the bet had been made she had contented herself with looking up at doorways (which were just over six feet) and shaking her head as she passed through them: but that seemed to have little effect. After Moriarty's first and last visit to the Hacienda it was clear to her that his first mood of blithe optimism had changed. For he would not talk to her about the visit, or the wager, and she could only assume that something awful had happened and that he realised that all was lost. Since she had assumed that from the beginning, it made little difference to her, and she therefore concentrated instead on the creation of new costumes for their April production of *Julius Caesar*.

In down-town San Francisco on the morning of 17 March counterfeit tickets were going at ten times their face value of three dollars. Inside Barnum's massive marquee, six thousand three hundred and twenty-three buzzing spectators looked down upon the raked and rolled earth surface of the central circle of Barnum's three-ring circus. Outside stood ten thousand others who had paid a buck simply to gain entrance. This was to a newly-fenced area which Barnum had constructed to surround his vast black-and-white-striped marquee. Clowns and conjurors entertained the crowd before being replaced by barkers with megaphones who provided a running commentary on the progress of the events within.

No question of it, Moriarty reflected, as he entered the vast marquee: Barnum had milked the competition for every dime and sawbuck. Posters showing Billy Joe flying through the air as if from the barrel of a cannon and of Salamander floating like some latter-day Pegasus were selling like hot cakes. Barnum had sold the food and drink concessions for monstrous sums, while there were at least twenty medicine shows and astrologers willing, for suitable remuneration, to vouchsafe the result of the competition.

At noon Moriarty was standing alongside Barnum in the central ring as the high jump stands were brought in with the sort of ceremony that might have accompanied the entry of the Tzar of Russia. The crowd oohed and aahed as if they were viewing the arrival of the Crown Jewels rather than merely a set of plain brown wooden stands and half-a-dozen ordinary hickory laths.

The stands were ceremonially placed in the middle of the central ring by tiny circus hands dressed in the costume of some obscure Ruritanian militia, and the six laths placed at the side, at right angles to them. Two of the 'militia' stayed behind each one, each standing stiffly beside one vertical upright. Barnum, who was carrying a megaphone in one hand and a handbell in the other, raised the handbell and rang it, its peals bringing almost immediate silence.

'In a scientific experiment of this awesome dimension,' he began, through the megaphone, turning slowly through a full three hundred and sixty degrees as he did so, 'it is essential that every aspect of the competition be absolutely fair and thoroughly scrutinised. It has therefore been agreed by the sporting fraternity of San Francisco that Dr. Augustus Friedrich, well-known in this area as a distinguished medical practitioner of unimpeachable ethical standards, together

182

with Cardinal Thomas Feeney and Pastor Ian McGuffie, representing the Catholic and Protestant Churches, be asked to check and validate the take-off area to ensure that there are no mechanical aids by way of trampolines, springboards, rockets' — at this there were good-natured boos and laughter — 'or the like, on the surface from which either competitor might gain advantage.'

He paused. 'I therefore call upon these three illustrious citizens who will, with Governor Leland Stanford as final arbiter, act as a jury of appeal' – Stanford stood in the VIP area, hands above his head, to accept his measure of applause — to perform this necessary official function.'

The three men stepped forward, smiling and raising their hands in response to the ovation from the crowd. Friedrich was dressed formally in a black, long-tailed jacket and pin-striped trousers and top hat, while both churchmen were in their clerical garb, Feeney in his red cardinal's costume and McGuffie in the more sober black vestments of the Presbyterian Church.

Barnum, loving every moment of it, solemnly conducted his jury to the area directly in front of the high-jump stands. The three judges, none of them quite sure what they might be expected to find beneath the earth in front of the jumping-stands, stood before him uncertainly. Cardinal Feeney finally took the lead by stamping his red-sandalled foot on the surface of the ring, then bending to scoop up a handful of its surface. Taking their cue, the other two men did the same, Friedrich stretching the moment by taking out a small magnifying glass from an inside pocket to scrutinise his own handful of grit. Moriarty could hardly keep his face straight and wondered if Friedrich had brought his stethoscope, or if Feeney might venture to bless the surface with holy water.

Next, all three knelt to pat and scrape the area before getting back to their feet.

Barnum saw that he could squeeze no more from the

ceremony. 'Gentlemen,' he roared. 'Are you satisfied that this is a true and genuine jumping surface?'

The three men nodded and Barnum handed the megaphone to Cardinal Feeney.

The Cardinal's brogue was thick but his voice was clear and strong. 'I hereby confirm,' he said, 'on behalf of me fellow judges, that the surface which we have inspected is as genuine a lepping ground as I have ever set eyes upon. Me best wishes to both of the competitors on behalf of all members of the jury.'

Led by Barnum, the three men then walked from the arena, to a sustained ovation, to join Leland Stanford.

Barnum made his way to the middle of the central ring and stood beside the stands. He again swung his handbell and the applause subsided.

'Finally,' he roared, 'in the interests of modern science, Governor Leland Stanford has asked the great English photographer and student of human and animal movement, Eadweard Muybridge, to engage in the taking of a series of photographic plates of the competition. I give you — Mr. Eadweard Muybridge!'

Muybridge, a slight, bearded man standing at the edge of the central arena with a massive square camera resting on a tripod, smiled weakly and waved at the crowd, then vanished inside the black linen folds behind the camera. Muybridge looked through the lens, focusing on Barnum. There was not enough light, but he would open the lens wide and hope for the best.

Barnum looked around the vast concourse, arms raised to his sides as if in supplication.

He then lifted his megaphone again. 'And now — let the competition begin.'

There was a full-bellied roar from the crowd, filling the marquee, as the circus band entered, playing 'See the Conquering Hero Comes'.

But still no Billy Joe, still no Captain Whitby and Salamander.

The band performed four circuits of the circumference of the central ring, then marched to its centre, behind the high-jump stands, where they halted. At a signal from their leader, they abruptly ceased playing, then marched off, leaving the centre of the ring to Barnum. Again he swung his handbell, again silence.

'And now,' he bellowed, 'the marvel of the world of equitation, the greatest jumper in the recorded history of the animal kingdom, with its rider Captain Whitby, hero of the immortal Charge of the Light Brigade . .. I give you...Salamander!'

All eyes focused on the entrance to the ring. There, pristine white, surmounted by Whitby in his Royal Fusiliers' uniform, was Salamander. Whitby pulled on the reins, causing the horse to rear almost vertically, pawing the air. Moriarty observed the scene gloomily. Her hooves, he estimated, were at least eight feet above ground level: all the beast had to do was to follow them up and she had cleared the bar. Whitby trotted Salamander round the central ring, smiling and doffing his pillbox hat in response to the crowd. Where was modesty, where was the celebrated English stiff upper lip, brooded Moriarty.

A nod from Barnum directed Whitby to the centre of the ring, where he circled Salamander, rearing on her back legs, in response to the continuing roars and applause of the crowd. Then it was Barnum again with his bell, but this time it took him several minutes to restore order.

'And now,' he roared into the megaphone, 'the greatest jumper of the western world.' Moriarty winced. Billy Joe had not, as far as he knew, ever competed in adult competition. 'A leaper extraordinary, a man who defies the very laws of gravity! I give you, ladies and gentlemen . . . from Texas Mr. Billy Joe Speed!'

Barnum turned to the entrance to the arena, right arm raised. It was empty. Then suddenly there was Billy Joe in gleaming white tights and vest and shining, black patent leather shoes, a scarlet cape flowing behind him. Moriarty groaned audibly. It was getting worse by the minute. He looked for Buck, and saw that he had quietly followed Billy Joe into the arena and stood a few yards from the entrance, head down, hands lightly clasped in front of him.

Well, this was Billy Joe's moment and he was milking it for all it was worth. He strode round the ring, arms horizontal, so that for a moment he looked like some great red and white bird. Would that he were, Moriarty reflected: then they would see off Whitby and a whole regiment of British cavalry.

If anything, Billy Joe got an even more rapturous response than Salamander. Indeed, the citizens of San Francisco got to their feet, waving programmes, Union flags, newspapers, handkerchiefs and anything else they could lay their hands upon. Moriarty felt himself curdle inside and dared not look up at Eleanor and Mandy, sitting serenely in the VIP box alongside Friedrich, the two churchmen and Stanford.

After two circuits Billy Joe joined Whitby and Salamander in the centre of the ring. With a flourish he doffed his cape and threw it back to Buck, who caught it, smiling sourly. Barnum again clanged on his bell, this time taking a full three minutes before he had established order. Moriarty went to the back of the ring to join Buck on a bench.

'It has been agreed,' shouted Barnum, again rotating slowly as he spoke, 'that the opening height should be five feet and that the crossbar should rise by three inches at a time. Each competitor will be allowed only one attempt at each height, a failure resulting in immediate withdrawal from the competition.' He paused. 'The first round of the jumping match will now begin.'

There was a roar, from crowds both inside and outside the marquee, but amid the din Whitby could be seen gesticulating furiously at Barnum, pointing at the jump-stands. Then Billy Joe joined in the discussion, and soon Whitby had stopped waving his arms and even began to smile. Barnum beckoned to the two attendants standing behind the stands, and the uprights were moved back about two yards.

Barnum again pealed on his handbell until there was silence.

'Captain Whitby,' he said, 'has complained that the placement of the uprights in the centre of the arena does not allow a sufficient approach-run to Salamander. Billy Joe Speed has shown himself a true sportsman by agreeing to allow the stands to be displaced by six feet.'

There was another round of applause, this time mixed with a volley of impatient shouts, and Moriarty wondered if Barnum was not stretching it too far. But no: the old master, unbowed, held the centre of the arena and the crossbar was placed at five feet.

'A coin will be tossed to determine starting position,' he roared. Not that it matters a hoot, thought Moriarty.

The crowd was again hushed. Barnum spun a silver dollar into the air and Buck called 'heads' and gestured to Whitby that he would like him to jump first.

The dollar hit the dirt surface of the ring. Barnum inspected it.

'Heads it is,' he boomed. 'Captain Whitby jumps first, at a height of five feet.'

Whitby raised his pillbox to the crowd, trotted to the edge of the ring, turned Salamander round and paused. There was silence. Then a slight dig of the heels and Salamander surged forward, the noise of her hooves pushing through the marquee. Her jump was merely a continuation of her run, and there appeared to be a clear foot between Salamander's white belly and the crossbar. It was a couple of minutes before the cheers started to die as Billy Joe slowly paced out nine paces to the right of the high-jump stands. As he turned there was again complete silence.

Moriarty looked at Billy Joe. There was an inner silence in the man, an indefinable quality that had not been in evidence at the ranch. Billy Joe looked at the bar for a moment, then

187

began his springy, prancing run. He jumped. It was a good leap, but he only cleared the bar by a couple of inches, landing lightly on the ground on the far side. In the crowd, amid the roars, the bookmakers put Billy Joe down to five to one against. Meanwhile Barnum's man put the bar up to five foot three inches.

Salamander's next jump was a formality, and she cleared the bar by a good six inches, with Whitby raising his hat to the crowd as he rode back to get into position for his next jump.'

Then it was Billy Joe's attempt. He rocked back and forward, wrinkling his nose like a chipmunk. Then he began his run. His take-off was strong and balanced and he cleared the bar without touching it, but Moriarty could now see only about an inch of daylight between Billy Joe's hips and the lath.

The crossbar was raised to five foot six inches, and there was no need for Barnum's bell as Whitby steadied Salamander for the jump. Whitby's face set in a mask of determination as he impelled Salamander forward in her attempt. The mare seemed for a moment to hang in flight. There was still a good three inches, perhaps four, between Salamander and the crossbar; in the bleachers the bookies stopped taking money on Whitby at any odds, and Billy Joe went up again to six to one.

Billy Joe's jump was a good one. But he reached the peak of his flight just before the bar, and there was an 'aah' from the crowd as he touched it with his hips. The bar wobbled but stayed on, and the sighs were replaced by cheers as Billy Joe returned to his mark, smiling, hands raised. The condemned man ate a hearty breakfast, thought Moriarty.

For the first time, when the bar was raised to five foot nine, it began to look high. This was possibly because Barnum had deliberately employed attendants of around five foot four in height to put the crossbar in place, and Moriarty wondered gloomily why Barnum hadn't gone the whole hog and used midgets.

Whitby faced the new challenge with his face set in the same resolute aspect as he had assumed at the previous height. If anything, Salamander seemed to be moving even faster into the jump, crouching like a great white cat at take-off. Whitby had her balanced perfectly, his weight well forward as Salamander extended her thick, powerful rear legs. It was a perfect clearance, albeit a narrow one. A smiling Whitby again raised his cap to the crowd, allowing his *sang-froid* to melt in the joy of the moment.

Moriarty looked at Billy Joe, who was now in conference with Barnum. The showman listened for a moment, then walked out of the ring towards the VIP box where sat Dr. Friedrich, the two clergymen and Leland Stanford. There they conferred for fully five minutes, before Barnum made his way down through the buzzing crowd, back into the arena. He clanged his handbell, then bellowed into the megaphone.

'We have a point of order, 'ladies and gentlemen. Billy Joe Speed wishes . . . and I use his exact words . . . to modify his jumping technique, and requests the use of a mattress for that purpose. I have consulted our jury of appeal, who see no objection.' He looked towards Whitby. 'Captain Whitby?'

Whitby raised his hat in acceptance and the crowd bellowed its approval. An English sportsman, no question of it. In a flash, Buck had vanished from Moriarty's side and returned to the arena dragging two grey straw mattresses, which he placed on the far side of the uprights, about a foot from them, one on top of the other, at right angles to the bar, at its middle.

Billy Joe moved from his previous starting-point and walked to the centre of the crossbar. He stretched his right arm, touching the centre of the bar, and stood, both feet together. Then he stepped out nine stiff-legged walking paces away from the bar and turned to face the uprights. Moriarty gazed at Buck, who had returned to his side, in mute appeal. The younger man looked him straight in the eye.

'Centre of gravity, Moriarty,' he said. 'Don't trouble yourself.'

Billy Joe now faced the crossbar head-on. Moriarty had never seen him like this before, not even in the fiercest of the street-dashes. His eyes were glazed, his Adam's apple bobbed up and down, and he moved back and forward from foot to foot as if transfixed.

This time Billy Joe sprinted forward, rushing in upon the bar as if it were a finishing-tape. When he took off, about two yards from the uprights, he leapt as if he had been shot from a cannon, his body at right angles to the bar. At the peak of his flight, his belly a couple of inches above the bar, he dipped his head so that his body assumed a jack-knife position. Then he was clear, rolling forward on to the mattresses as pandemonium broke out in the crowd.

The roars could be heard three blocks away as the information was relayed to the ten thousand spectators massed outside the marquee.

Billy Joe sprang to his feet and ran around the arena, hands raised as before. Even Salamander became fractious, snorting and champing as the roars continued, and Whitby was forced to lean forward to quieten her. This time all Barnum's frantic bell-ringing failed to calm the crowd.

Barnum put down his bell and beckoned his attendants to raise the bar to six feet. Billy Joe jogged over to Moriarty.

'Put it all on,' he hissed. 'Put all you got on my ass. The family jewels.'

Moriarty was infected by the moment. Within minutes, he and Buck had laid another two grand with bookies in the crowd at odds which had now dropped to evens.

On his return, he noted that Barnum had given up any attempt to control the crowd and was sitting on a wall at the edge of the ring apparently waiting for the pandemonium to die down.

Then, as if by common consent, the noise of the crowd began

to diminish. There were occasional isolated shouts of encouragement, mainly directed at Billy Joe, but there were hisses for silence in response. Finally there was silence and Barnum strutted to the centre of the ring, hands raised. He accepted his megaphone from a steward.

'Six feet,' he said, pointing to the crossbar. 'Six feet — a height never before cleared, or indeed attempted, by man or beast. In the event that neither competitor clears at this height, then there will be a two-attempt jump-off. If neither competitor clears successfully in the jump-off then the bar will be lowered to five feet ten inches and each competitor allowed one attempt at that height.'

There was a buzz of discussion and Barnum waited for silence, lowering his megaphone. When it had come he again raised it to his lips. 'And here, may I crave your indulgence. We must ask for complete silence during each attempt. Complete silence. Thank you, ladies and gentlemen.'

Moriarty looked at Whitby. The Englishman, poised on Salamander, now had the same glazed, distant look as Billy Joe had possessed only a few moments before. The man, for all his airs and graces, was a competitor. Somehow, too, Salamander seemed to have become part of her master's psyche, her eyes fixed on the crossbar. She snorted lightly, her muscular rump twitching and flickering.

Finally, Whitby was ready. He pressed Salamander forward and his steed flowed smoothly into her run at the jump. Her gather for the leap was perfect and she hit exactly the correct take-off spot.

Salamander's white belly had a clear three inches of daylight at the peak of her flight. There was no question of it, the jump was the most wonderful, most marvellous, ever made by any animal. But the timing of her rear legs was out, albeit only fraction-ally, as she dropped towards the landing. They touched the crossbar, which quivered and continued to wobble as Salamander landed and galloped on. Whitby pulled up his mount and turned to look at the bar for what seemed an eternity. Slowly, it dropped, the sound of its fall echoing in the hushed tent. Whitby blinked and Moriarty could see a tear in the Englishman's eye, and thought the better of him for it.

The bar was replaced at six feet, and while Billy Joe was checking it Buck carefully replaced the mattresses, one on top of the other.

Billy Joe walked slowly back to his mark and turned to face the bar.

He took a long breath which could be heard by Eleanor and Mandy in the VIP box ten rows back. Next he blinked hard and took another deep gulp, before focusing upon the crossbar. Then he started his rocking back-and-forward movement, wiping his lips with the back of his left hand as he did so.

Billy Joe sighed again, deeply. At last he started his run, rushing in as if pursued by devils. His run and take-off flowed together, a unity of speed and spring, and for a moment after take-off Billy Joe's head was well above the crossbar. Then, at the peak of his jump, came the jack-knife, and Moriarty could see clear daylight between Billy Joe's belly and the lath. Then his legs swung up and over and he landed on the middle of the mattresses, well clear.

The crowd went crazy in a blizzard of hats, programmes and handkerchiefs, and within moments the mob outside were grappling with guards at the entrance in their attempt to get into the arena. Moriarty got to Billy Joe first, as the crowds broke into the ring to get to the competitors, hugging his protégé to him.

A couple of months later news came from England that some college boy, name of Marshal Brooks, had gone over six feet, the first athlete ever to clear the height, so they said. San Francisco folks knew better. Four hours earlier on the same day Billy Joe Speed had done it, clean and easy, and those Limeys — well, they could believe whatever they liked.

From the diary of Eleanor Cameron, 18 March 1876
The Great High Jump is over, and even those who have lost heavily on the outcome somehow do not feel themselves to be losers. It is strange, this release, this joy, that men (and, dare I say it, women) gain from the witnessing of sport at its best. Perhaps it was because nothing that they saw yesterday in Barnum's arena was sham, that in the losing of their money they felt no real loss. Certainly no one who witnessed the occasion will ever fail to have it etched indelibly upon his memory, Billy Joe soaring like some great white bird over the lath. Even Captain Whitby himself accepted it all with good grace, and is with Salamander now in the employ of Leland Stanford as a riding instructor, Barnum having released him from his contract. But the ladies of San Francisco will have to be on their mettle, for Captain Whitby is rumoured to be even more dangerous as an instructor of riding than ever he was with Cardigan at the Charge of the Light Brigade.

10

RUN OF THE ARROW

From the diary of Eleanor Cameron, 24 March 1876
At the end of the first act of 'The Scots Play' (I really cannot take seriously Moriarty's superstitious insistence that the name 'Macbeth' never be mentioned) word was brought to us of the return of Gregor McGregor and a member of his party, Alistair Blain, from their prospecting expedition. I had always considered the monies given by us to McGregor over a year ago (it is called a 'grub stake' in these parts) to be of the nature of a donation rather than an investment, but this has not proved to be so. Certainly, McGregor is altogether lighter and will no longer have to go on a diet in order to play Falstaff, but he has returned to San Francisco considerably the richer, albeit with a tragic and terrible tale to tell.

By the time McGregor and his five Scottish compatriots had arrived in Dakota, in late April, 1876, the army had discovered and evicted the first group of prospectors under James Gordon, who had taken the 'Thieves' Road' (as the Sioux called it) into the territory. McGregor was only a bare few weeks ahead of others who were now forming parties and setting out from all over the United States, pouring round the patrols set up by the Army. More by luck than good judgement McGregor, unlike other 'sooners', had steered clear of both army patrols and wandering bands of Sioux, and by June had established himself and his men by a river in a heavily-wooded valley fifty miles west of North Platte, having picked up 'colour' there on their first attempt.

McGregor's party had consisted entirely of Scots. Two, the nineteen-year-old Alistair Blain and his twenty-one-year-old brother Fergus, had both mined for coal in Fife since their early teens. The other three, Jim Keir, Calum Law and Douglas Bell, had also been miners, all in their mid-twenties. They had worked on the other side of Scotland, at Leadhills in Lanarkshire, toiling six days a week in narrow, two-foot seams, for wages of fifteen shillings. Leadhills had the added advantage that its hills contained a thin streak of gold which was not worth mining, but which afforded Keir and his friends excellent experience in identifying and panning the precious metal.

McGregor's group, unlike many of the others which followed it, was well-equipped, having used oxen rather than mules to carry the provisions, heavy Dutch oven, galvanised water pails, frying pans and grub boxes essential for camp-feeding, and the spades, axes, sieves and pans required for the operation itself. They themselves travelled light, carrying sleeping-tarpaulins rather than heavy tents, and each man toted a Colt, a needle-gun and a Spencer carbine.

It took a fortnight to build the eight-foot-long wooden cradle called the 'Long Tom'. This was on rockers, open at the foot, at its head a coarse grating; the bottom was rounded, with small cleats nailed across.

Five men were required to operate the Long Tom. One dug earth and grit from the bank close by the stream, one carried it to the Long Tom and emptied it on to the grate. The third and fourth men

The sieve kept coarse stones from entering the Long Tom, the water washed off earth, and mud and gravel was gradually carried out at the base of the cradle, leaving any gold mixed with the heavy, black sand above the first cleats. Sand and gold were then drawn off through auger holes into a pan below and dried in the sun, later separated by blowing off the sand.

McGregor's first attempt was only a modest success. True, there was 'colour', but each day's ten hours of backbreaking labour was bringing in only ten dollars-worth of dust. After two months' prospecting, he decided to break camp and go deeper into the Black Hills.

Two weeks later, twenty miles further west, they set up Camp Scotia in a wooded valley at the junction of the same river with a narrow tributary pouring down from a brown, rocky hill above. It was now late June and each day the sun hit the six men like a hammer as they poured their sweat into the diggings. Again, the river showed colour, but thin pickings, still only just over twelve dollars a day.

Then, at the end of August, there was a vicious rainstorm which left the camp a sodden morass and which turned the tributary from the mountain above into a torrent. On impulse, McGregor set up the Long Tom parallel to the tributary and began to take samples from its depths.

The results were immediate, with great golden specks and flakes totalling $320 in the first day. In the first week, McGregor and his men picked up over $2,000, and by the onset of winter in mid-October the party had taken out over $60,000.

From that first day on 29 August, they worked like madmen, rotating their roles so that there was always a fresh man for the heavy work of digging. It really needed only four men to operate the Long Tom, so the free men either rested or hunted for game in the hills. The Scots filled every moment of each day with work, and the mountain above never failed to respond, even when at the end of the first fortnight after the rainstorm the flow of water began to ebb.

From early August they had known that there were Indians in the area, for there was no lack of smoke. So, although no one even caught sight of an Indian, each night a guard was set up on the horses.

The attack came only a day before, supplies exhausted, they planned to return to San Francisco. There was a swish and a thud. Fergus Blain fell, face down, in the stream, a strange surprised look on his face, hit between the shoulder-blades by an arrow. Then as Douglas Bell, also at the river, dropped his pan and ran for his rifle, he was hit in the left shoulder by an arrow and dropped back into the stream, shouting in pain, his blood mixing in the icy water with that of Blain.

McGregor reached for his Spencer first and poured shot after shot wildly up into the hill above, while Alistair Blain dragged his dying brother from the stream towards the horses. Law and Keir had almost reached their guns when they were brought down by rifle shots, Law in the hip and Keir, mortally, in the chest.

Blain left his brother's corpse and joined McGregor as they rushed for the horses, which were already saddled, while the wounded Law and Bell staggered towards them. But the two wounded men were taken out by withering rifle-fire only a few yards from their mounts. McGregor poured more shots into the hill above him, then he and Alistair Blain took to the horses and galloped madly down the valley, parallel to the river, as gunfire continued to pour down upon them.

Their first mistake was to skirt Deadwood, which was less than a hundred miles away. The town, which had grown in less than a year from a single digging to a brown, pock-marked morass of workings, was flush with miners. But McGregor and Blain, with twenty thousand dollars in their belts, forty thousand lying back in the camp and God only knew how much more still in the mountain, had no wish to give anything away to the gold-crazy men in Deadwood or to the thousands of others now pouring into the Black Hills from all over the nation.

But their main error was to ignore their own bodies. Both men had existed for almost a year on a scurvy-inducing diet of sowbelly and sourdough and a daily output of work that would have taxed the powers of even well-fed agricultural labourers. The adrenalin of gold-fever had driven them through the summer and autumn of 1875, but now, the deaths of their friends lying heavy upon them, the two Scots made slow progress throughout December, south-west across the windy, freezing plains of Wyoming.

A chance encounter with a friendly party of Sioux making their way north enabled the enfeebled Scots to replenish their depleted stores of food, albeit in return for their six-guns (though they retained their Sharps). More important, the Indians directed them towards a trading post a hundred miles south-east, itself only two hundred miles from the Union Pacific railroad.

Though Blain was now barely able to sit astride a horse, the two Scots rode on towards Evans Station, three log cabins owned by Dai Evans, a rapacious little Welshman whose family had made several fortunes serving the needs of miners since the first great gold rush of 1848. Evans Station was ideally situated for prospectors coming into Dakota from the west via the Union Pacific, and had already done well from those who had passed through between the spring and autumn of 1875.

Evans, swarthy and cunning as a ferret, sized up McGregor from the start, noting that neither he nor his young companion ever left their goods unattended, and that both were undoubtedly wearing thick money-belts. He insisted on cash, charging them a hundred dollars a week for the use of a rat-infested barn. Food was extra. Only minutes after meeting Evans, McGregor knew that he had hated him for years.

All into February McGregor, himself weak, nursed Blain with the limited medication available from Evans, which had consisted of Hostetter's Bitters, laudanum and cold compresses. By mid-February his reserves of cash had run out and he was forced to pay the Welshman in dust — though he never allowed him to see his money-belt.

McGregor's constitution was a living paradox, for at six foot four and two hundred and twenty pounds he possessed an inner animal strength that seemed to exist independent of and untouched by the excesses of smoking, alcohol or gluttony. But even he had reached its outer limits.

In late February McGregor himself went down with a raging fever, and it was the barely-recovered Blain who was now forced to cope with his older colleague in the frozen barn at Evans Station, while outside sixty-mile-an-hour winds raced across the Wyoming Plains. The actor, in his delirium, raved his way through the works of Shakespeare, Dickens and Marlowe; long stretches of them coming forth without pause or error. Had Blain had the disposition, his nursing of McGregor might well have afforded him a rare education.

Finally, in the second week of March, McGregor recovered sufficiently to travel. Thus, two thousand two hundred dollars poorer, the two Scots made their way slowly south towards the Union Pacific, which they reached on 17 March 1876, the day of the Great San Francisco High jump, catching the train at Callender, seventy-five miles east, a week later.

The discretion of A. P. Wagstaffe was legendary. By evening on the day of McGregor and Blain's arrival the Scots' gold, estimated at eighteen thousand two hundred and seventy-seven dollars, had been deposited in the vaults of the Wagstaffe bank, with no one in San Francisco any the wiser. By the end of the week Moriarty had his five-thousand-dollar grub-stake back, and the remaining money was split evenly between himself, Blain and McGregor, with four thousand dollars set aside to be divided between the four dead men's next-of-kin.

Neither Blain nor McGregor had any desire to go back to the Black Hills. It was the young Fife man's intention to return to Dakota, but to set himself up as a supplier of goods to miners in Deadwood, not to prospect. That was where the certain money was, he reasoned: in the provision of services, not in scouring Godforsaken Indian-ridden territory for gold.

McGregor's reluctance derived from a different source. It was shame. The actor had always taken a romantic view of combat, more directly related to the theatricals of Rob Roy, The Highland Rogue, than to the realities of battle. He had thought that on attack by hostiles he would fight and stand his ground, bellowing defiance to his enemies. But when Blain's blood had stained the river and bullets had begun to fly it had not been as he had expected. It had all been squalid and desperate, a rush to escape with scarcely a backward glance. Indeed, he could hardly even be certain that one or more of the four men left behind had not still been alive.

Eleanor and Moriarty's insistence that he had shown himself a true Highlander in steering the sick Blain back to civilisation did not mollify him much. By his own standards he had been tried and found wanting, and henceforth he would confine his acts of heroism to the stage. The diggings and all that remained there at Camp Scotia were Moriarty's to do with as he pleased, and a detailed map was given to the actor.

Buck and Billy Joe, still flush with the glory of the Great High Jump, devoured McGregor's story, pressing him to repeat it over and over again. Billy Joe checked the map: it would be a piece of pie to get there, he announced, for Camp Scotia was less than one hundred miles north-west of Deadwood. The camp would be virtually untouched, for the Sioux had probably only wanted the horses and guns. The dust, all $40,000 or more of it, would still be there, stashed in the men's sleeping tarpaulins. Why then, they pressed Moriarty, could they not mosey on up to Camp Scotia, travelling light, and pick up the gold? Moriarty could send up another band of fully-equipped miners to continue to work, and, if he and Buck could pick up a few choice nuggets while they awaited the second party, then all to the good.

At first, everyone else was against it, Mandy in particular. Four men had already lost their lives, the Black Hills were crawling with Indians, and General Crooke had been appointed

200

to stem the rush of prospectors there. In the end, however, one argument was crucial and it came, surprisingly, from Eleanor. As she pointed out, $40,000 was the sum that would finally enable Moriarty to take a long lease on the Jenny Lind Theatre. If any other party came upon the Scotia, however, then the mine, its $40,000 and all future earnings from it would vanish. They'd never get another chance like this.

It was rare for Eleanor to come down strongly on the side of a speculative venture, and it was this more than anything else that prompted Moriarty to agree to Billy Joe and Buck's project. But their terms of reference were inflexible. They were to find the Scotia, secure what gold they could and await the arrival of a group of miners from San Francisco which Moriarty would assemble in the next fortnight. They were on no account to mine for gold, as they had a running assignment in Cheyenne, where there was a street dash on 14 June, and on the first sight of Indians were to hightail it out of the area. When the mining party arrived they were to make their way back towards Cheyenne.

The two men were so keen on their adventure they would have signed an affidavit, had Moriarty demanded it. On I April they were aboard the Union Pacific, on their way east, armed to the specifications of a British regiment of the line.

Giving a wide berth to Deadwood, Buck and Billy Joe entered the Black Hills a fortnight later. They came upon General Crooke's men only a day after, camped on the banks of the Black River. Lacking, as they did, all the accoutrements of a mining party and, with their Sharps and needle-gun, possessing sufficient armaments to clear the Black Hills of all game, Buck and Billy Joe were easily able to pass themselves off as hunters. On the morning of their departure they were also able to relieve Crooke's soldiers of two hundred dollars as the result of a three-legged race.

Buck and Billy Joe had brought four mounts and were thus able to make their way speedily into the depths of the hills, which were now basking in the warmth of spring sunshine, a far cry from the icy bleakness through which Blain and McGregor had fled. But they were reminded of McGregor's warning on the weather in the Dakotas — 'If you don't like the weather, then just wait a minute': on the third day, when they were only fifty miles short of Camp Scotia, spring rain lashed down upon them.

They picked up McGregor's first camp a day later, its Long Tom still intact, and two days after that came upon the remnants of Camp Scotia.

The four men were still just as they had fallen, their bones long since picked clean and white by buzzards and coyotes. Two of them, the elder Blain and Law, still wore their body-belts, the gold spilling out of them from the punctures made by the birds. It was a more difficult task than either man had expected to disengage the belts before giving the Scots a Christian burial.

Altogether it was not a bit as they had imagined. A year ago, four fit young men like themselves had left San Francisco in hope and optimism. Now they were only dry skeletons in a nameless valley, their lives having been taken merely for a few horses and guns.

Nevertheless, Buck and Billy Joe set about finding the rest of the gold. It said much for the trust in which the Scots had held each other that the caches had not been buried, but were found beneath their sleeping tarpaulins. So they had it all, every cent. They transferred the gold to their body-belts and anxiously watered and fed the horses as a weak spring sun settled in the dark trees above them on their right. As darkness fell that first night at Camp Scotia both men hoped that Moriarty would not take long in organising a mining party to follow them

White Wolf had recognised the man immediately; he was one of the madmen in the valley. There he was, down by the river,

202

stripped to the waist, his body as lean and white as it had been that strange day almost a year before.

As he looked down towards them White Wolf could not believe his luck. The men were well armed: at least four rifles and two hand guns, all close by, with the Sharps and the needle-gun capable of causing considerable damage. But the men appeared to be preoccupied, shouting to each other as they dug at the river's edge and shook a long wooden trough the heat of the sun causing their torsos to gleam with sweat. White Wolf watched them for over an hour; they appeared to be oblivious to all else but their work. There was no question of it, even so. One of the men, the golden-haired one, he had never seen before. But the other was assuredly the runner. He scampered back to the camp.

Swift Dog, sitting by his tent, saw his son running towards him down the slope through the village and smiled. The little boy lived in the afterglow of his discovery of the White Eyes the year before. Try as he might, Swift Dog could still make nothing of it. For the Sioux, running was indeed a way of pleasing the gods and thus enriching the earth — had been since time began — but he had never heard of any similar customs among the White Eyes.

He reflected briefly how, since the madmen in the valley, it had been a bad winter for his people, the warriors returning time after time from the hunt with almost nothing to show for their day's work. The tribe had had to exist on thin rations of maize, eked out by an occasional rabbit or mountain deer, and even on his daughter Morning Star's betrothal to Black Fox the feast had been meagre. But the snows had melted, winter was over, and now they faced new challenges, perhaps the greatest challenge of all. For every treaty had been broken and now the White Eyes, lured by the gold of the Dakotas, were pouring into the territory. And it was clear that the Army was dedicated to the destruction of the Indians of the North Plains. So Sitting Bull had called the Sioux to him in Montana, and soon they would link up with other parts of the tribe and their Cheyenne, Arapaho and Gros Ventre brothers to face the White Eyes.

White Wolf had stopped a few feet away from him, gasping for breath, having zig-zagged through the camp at breakneck speed. Lungs heaving, sweat streaming down his face, he seemed scarcely able to speak.

'The runner,' he gasped at last. 'The runner.'

'What runner?'

'The White Eye in the valley.'

Swift Dog motioned his son to sit down and called across to the medicine man, Dark Cloud, to join them.

'Tell what you have seen,' he said.

The words poured from the little boy, and as they did so the lined, solemn face of Dark Cloud slowly creased into a smile. 'The bad medicine of the winter', he said, 'it can now be changed. Not only for the tribe, but for all Sioux.' He, Dark Cloud, would tell Swift Dog how it would be done.

When Swift Dog and the warriors arrived above the valley the two men below were dancing in the shallows of the stream, the golden-haired one holding above his head a metal dish. The Sioux had heard their whooping and shouting long before they reached the valley. The White Eyes were either mad or drunk and quite oblivious to the Sioux poised above them on both sides. When they did notice the presence of Swift Dog and his warriors it was too late. In any case, it would have made no difference if they had managed to draw their guns, for the warriors were many.

As the two white men were put under guard, White Wolf had an opportunity for the first time to see the runner close at hand. The young black-haired man was still stripped to the waist, the muscles of his abdomen and shoulders clearly defined as if carved from wood. The other man, though golden-haired, was almost identical, like a Sioux warrior in

204

the finest condition. Were all White Eyes men like this?

The little boy was, as a mark of favour, allowed to ride one of their four horses back to camp.

The White Eyes were led through the encampment, to the whooping of the warriors and the screaming of the women, who struck at them with branches as they passed, while the camp dogs snapped at their feet. Finally they were placed outside the tent of White W0lf's uncle, Black Moon.

The two men sat, hands bound behind them, in the heat of the midday sun, the sweat streaming down their bodies as some of the more adventurous of the young women of the tribe pressed forward to inspect them. Some poked them with sticks, others threw dust on to their white skins, while others simply gazed at them, giggling.

Swift Dog, Dark Cloud and the elders of the tribe sat round the camp-fire in conference. White Wolf now sought the opportunity to satisfy a burning curiosity. He scampered off, ignoring the pleadings of his friends, and made his way round the group of squaws inspecting the White Eyes, through the flap into the gloom of the tepee behind them, where lay the White Eyes' goods.

The Great Manitou, Dark Cloud explained to the tribe, had surely brought the White Eyes to them as a sign. For the two men were undoubtedly runners and therefore big medicine. Had not young White Wolf last summer seen the dark-haired one run like an antelope through the valley, towards the sun, always towards the sun? Had he not seen him naked, cleansed in the water of the mountain streams, the stuff of life itself? And what of the marks, like those of animals, along the valley floor?

It was then that White Wolf brought the barbed moccasins to his father. He had found them in the saddle-pouches of the White Eyes, two pairs of them. White Wolf sat with his father and Dark Cloud as Swift Dog scraped the dry earth with the sole of a shoe, shaking his head. What was the song they had sung the last time Black Moon and the other members of the tribe had run?

> The hawk laid out the racetrack
> The hawk laid out the racetrack
> On it the man won. Ah!
> Wild the man came here;
> A hawk's heart he won. Ah!
> Evening is falling
> Like an eagle I move
> Back and forth
> Morning is standing!
> Like a hawk I run back and forth.

Dark Cloud listened as his chief began to chant the running song, then joined him in the singing.

Since they had been captured, Buck and Billy Joe had spoken hardly a word. All the reflexes they had expected in response to their first sight of the Indians had failed them, and their capture stayed fixed in their minds, a crime against their honour, all the way to the camp.

The two men lay on their backs, bound, on the dry, brown earth of Black Moon's tent. Buck was the first to speak.

'Who are they?'

'Sioux,' replied Billy Joe.

'What will they do with us?'

Billy Joe shook his head. The possibilities running through his mind were too terrible to voice. He swore, adding, 'These savages'll slit your throat just to keep in practice.' The words felt bitter in his throat.

'What do they want?'

'Horses, guns.'

'Then they might let us go?'

'I wouldn't lay bets on it. This is their land. We shouldn't be here. No white man should.'

The tent-flap opened and a tall, lean warrior in his mid-thirties entered. He was big for an Indian, and in the light gloom they could see only the gleam of his eyes, hear the rattle of beads round his neck, smell his strange, musky sweat. He levered Billy Joe to his feet, then Buck, and pulled them out into the warm spring night. Surprisingly, the camp looked less menacing in the darkness than it had in the light of day. Gone were the yapping dogs and the squaws with their lashing birch-boughs. The tepees were shrouded in gloom, only the light of the central camp-fire visible, round which twenty Sioux sat, dressed in brightly decorated buck-skins. Their Indian guard pushed Buck and Billy Joe towards the heat of the fire and forced them down to their backsides, facing a middle-aged Indian in full head-dress across the bright, crackling fire.

'You understand any Sioux?' hissed Buck, as behind him his arms were unbound.

'Yes,' whispered Billy Joe out of the side of his mouth, rubbing his wrists as they were released. 'But don't let on.'

There was silence as the Indian held up a pair of black running shoes, the spikes catching the light of the fire as he did so.

'Shoes,' he said in English in a thick, guttural accent.

Billy Joe nodded, gulping.

'For battle?'

Billy Joe shook his head and stood up. 'For running,' he said in English. The Indian did not respond, so Billy Joe made running movements on the spot, paddling with his hands at the same time.

'Running,' he repeated.

This time the Indian nodded and looked sideways at a scrawny old brave wearing a necklace of bones, then around him. There were grunts of agreement from other braves.

'Runn—er,' said the Indian, who was clearly the chief.

'Yes. We are runners,' said Billy Joe, nodding, as he sat down again.

A young brave, resplendent in feathered head-dress, stood up, slowly walked round the circle and inspected Buck from above. Then he bent down, put a hand on each side of Buck's chest" and squeezed. It was not painful, but Buck gasped. Then the brave scrutinised Billy Joe, finally fingering his blonde hair. He pulled hard, extracting several strands, which he inspected closely before walking back to his place.

The scrawny old man sitting on the chief's left now spoke in Sioux. 'They are big medicine, Swift Dog', he said. 'They run for the White God. Their speed gives the White Eyes the earth and all it bears.'

Swift Dog's eyes turned again to Buck and Billy Joe. 'Why you run?'

Billy Joe's reply was immediate.

'For our Gods,' he replied. 'It pleases them.'

Swift Dog looked at the old man at his side. 'Dark Cloud?' he said.

'If we kill them now we kill nothing,' responded Dark Cloud. 'But if we defeat them in speed then we will assuredly weaken the White Eyes and their God, for future battles.'

Swift Dog was silent for a moment, stroking his chin. He stood up and walked round the fire to his two prisoners. He pulled Buck to his feet and felt his shoulders and abdominal muscles with both hands. Then he raised up Billy Joe till he was standing and suddenly, alarmingly, grabbed the middle of his left thigh. Billy Joe almost let out a cry of pain, while the Indian merely nodded, and returned round the fire to his place, to the grunts of the warriors and elders.

'These are runners,' he said. 'There is speed in their loins. Great speed.'

'Then our fastest warriors must contest with them in the Run of the Arrow,' pursued Dark Cloud.

Swift Dog nodded. 'You run,' he said, pointing to Buck and Billy Joe.

He held up their spikes in both hands. 'Run of Arrow. Dawn.'

The food had been delicious, particularly so because they had eaten nothing since their capture: broiled legs of rabbit and strange, sweet honey cakes, all washed down with goats' milk. Next they had been taken to the river at the edge of the village to defecate and wash, then taken back to the tepee, where they were again bound at the wrists, laid on the ground and covered in woollen blankets.

About an hour or so later, as dusk gathered, two shadows flickered for a moment on the thin skin of the tent. Buck, still awake, felt a chill sweat form on his brow and a cold spot in the pit of his stomach. He dug the sleeping Billy Joe in the ribs. The tent-flap opened and the two figures were framed in the flickering camp-fire behind them.

Neither of the two girls was more than sixteen years of age. They stood whispering for a moment, then the taller of the two put her finger to her lips, closed the tent-flap behind her and stood above Billy Joe, who was now awake. She pulled the blanket from him, scrutinising him as she did so in the shadowy gloom of the tent. Then she bent down and Billy Joe could smell the smoke of the camp-fire on her body as she timidly drew her hands through his silky blonde hair.

She whispered something in Sioux.

'What's she saying?' asked Buck.

Billy Joe did not answer.

The girl continued to speak in whispers, drawing her companion towards Billy Joe.

What's she saying?' pursued Buck.

'She says I'm beautiful,' whispered Billy Joe.

The girl spoke again to her companion, who even in the gloom of the tepee could be clearly seen to be short and plump.

'They want to take my clothes off,' said Billy Joe.

'And are you just going to sit there and let them? We got a

race for our lives at dawn tomorrow, don't you forget that,' said Buck, testily.

'Don't see that l got much choice,' answered Billy Joe.

The tall girl undid his belt and pulled down on his buckskins, motioning the other girl to help her. Her companion needed no urging to join her and together they pulled down Billy Joe's clothing, giggling as they did so. Irrationally, Billy Joe realised he was glad that his white long-johns were relatively clean. Then both girls sat above Billy Joe, each pointing at the other and shaking their heads. Buck levered himself up on to his elbows, while Billy Joe looked from one girl to the other. Then the first girl spoke and for the first time Billy Joe knew what it was all about.

'If I do it, he is mine.'

The other girl did not reply, and the first girl's response was immediate. She pulled on Billy Joe's long-johns, drawing them down to his knees, exposing him.

'There it is,' she said. 'As I have said. It is not the length of a long branch. It is just as I have told you.'

Indeed it was not, being at that moment of twig rather than branch length. The plumper girl, reassured, crawled over to Buck and quickly confirmed the finding of her friend.

From that moment on it was the plump girl who was to make the running, for neither Buck nor Billy Joe had ever seen anyone divest herself of her clothes at such speed. The girl pulled off her buckskin dress in one movement, revealing in the shadows a stocky, nut-brown body and firm, pointed breasts.

Her friend was not far behind and Billy Joe looked up, helpless, at the flat belly and fluffy, black pubic V of the taller girl. The girl pointed to herself.

'Swift Deer,' she said, in Sioux. Then she pointed at her friend. 'Bright One,' she said. Then she knelt down and took him in her mouth, as Bright One did the same with Buck. Each girl appeared to treat Buck and Billy Joe as an experiment, for there was no orifice, no area of their bodies which they did not probe, scratch, caress or explore.

At first neither man was able to respond, but in the end persistence triumphed. For the two girls were nothing if not industrious, nibbling, scratching and biting, all the while crooning and mumbling to themselves. Before long Buck and Billy Joe's sexual reflexes asserted themselves, and they began to enjoy it.

When they had finished, the girls dressed with much the same celerity as they had previously undressed, still giggling, as if sharing a private joke. Billy Joe smiled in the darkness. They were comparing notes.

Buck was the first to have something moist and sticky pressed into his mouth, by his plump partner, and Billy Joe's Indian girl soon did the same for him. Then the girls left the tent.

Buck cautiously bit on the object.

'Honey cake,' said Billy Joe, through mouthfuls. 'Suppose they reckon that they've taken something out of us, so they're duty bound to put something back.'

'Figures,' said Buck, chewing.

Then the tent-flap opened again and two further shadowy figures appeared, whispering, framed against the camp-fires outside.

'Jesus. More,' said Buck, licking his lips clear of the last remnants of the honey cake.

The figures vanished almost immediately and there was the sound of an angry man's voice outside. Then silence.

'What the hell's happening out there?' asked Buck.

'Coupla more ladies wanted to test us out,' said Billy Joe.

'The old medicine man's just chased them off. Says a runner has to have all his holy juices intact.'

'Then he's too late,' said Buck.

It was only four hours after the girls had left them that Buck and Billy Joe were led out, blinking, into the weak morning sunshine. The camp-fire was now only smoulder and smoke, and Buck and Billy Joe walked through the village past tribespeople who no longer slashed at them with birch-boughs. Instead, the women looked at them silently, nudging each other, smiling and whispering.

Swift Dog stood at the fire beside Dark Cloud, clasping a pair of running shoes in each hand, this time holding them out in front of him like offerings. Buck and Billy Joe's bonds were cut and they spent several minutes massaging their wrists. They took their spiked shoes from Swift Dog and slipped them on, lacing them tightly.

Swift Dog pointed across the camp-fire to three warriors painted in vertical stripes of blue and white and wearing only breech-cloths and moccasins. Beside them stood Black Moon, taller and broader than the others, though similarly painted and dressed.

'These our best, our swiftest warriors.' He pointed first to Black Moon. 'Black Moon,' he said. 'Hollow Stone, Grey Deer, Black Dog,' he added.

He sat down, as did Black Cloud, and Buck and Billy Joe inspected the men against whom they would race.

Each bore a quiver of six arrows, slung on a leather strap diagonally across his trunk, and a bow. Dark Moon looked a natural runner, with long legs and short trunk, though he was now clearly in early middle-age. Hollow Stone was a younger, squint-eyed little Sioux, no more than five foot four, with powerful thighs and thin, scrawny calves. Good for a fast fifty yards, thought Buck; after that he would fade. He looked at Grey Deer, a bandy-legged, rangy young man with a doleful expression, probably about the same age as himself. No power there, but he might be a stayer. Finally, Black Dog: of all of the Sioux he looked the most likely to give them trouble. At roughly five-nine in height, he was tall for an Indian and long-legged, with big buttocks and thighs; all the power in the right places. But it all depended how far they would have to run

– and how far the Sioux could accurately fire their arrows.

'What's the distance?' asked Billy Joe, echoing Buck's thoughts.

Swift Dog looked sideways at Dark Cloud. The medicine man pointed south-east, towards the distant hills beyond the plain on which the Sioux camp rested, and spoke in Sioux to his chief.

Swift Dog turned to look at Buck and Billy Joe.

'You must run to the end of our land,' he said. 'Your horses wait at Deer Leap.'

'How many paces?' asked Billy Joe.

Swift Dog shook his head. He could not compute in English.

Billy Joe looked sideways at Buck. It was too important. He threw caution to the winds. 'How many paces?' he blurted, in Sioux.

Swift Dog's eyes narrowed and he pulled on his lower lip. 'Three thousand,' he said, also in Sioux.

'A mile and a half to two miles,' said Billy Joe to Buck. He was surprised that Swift Dog had not reacted more strongly when he had spoken in Sioux. Somehow, he did not know why, it troubled him.

The two men looked out across the plain. They could see no end to it. Perhaps the chief was trying to trick them, pressing them into exhausting themselves early in the chase. Perhaps it was six miles to the horses. What if it went on for ever?

'Three thousand paces?' confirmed Billy Joe, in Sioux, his voice a question.

Swift Dog nodded. 'Your horses are at Deer Leap with your food and guns,' he added, still in Sioux. He pointed out across the plain, and, irrelevantly, Billy Joe noted the crepey, brown skin of his upper arm.

'My son, White Wolf, will fire an arrow as far as he can,' he said. 'When you reach it, my warriors will come after you.'

Billy Joe translated for Buck.

'First time we ever been given a start,' said Buck, trying to prevent his voice trembling.

Billy Joe gulped. 'We run it in bursts,' he said. 'Sprints and jogs.'

Buck nodded. 'Keep together,' he said.

'All the way,' said Billy Joe, his voice thin and hard.

Buck and Billy Joe looked around them at the Sioux. None of them was smiling. It was as if they had all wagered heavily on the race, thought Buck, but more than money. Swift Dog took his runners to the side, away from the tribe, with Dark Cloud. Billy Joe could not hear distinctly what he said to them, though the Chief's staccato barks were sharp and vigorous. The words 'gods' and 'big medicine' did, however, recur.

Swift Dog pointed to White Wolf. The little boy strutted forward, self-important, carrying his bow. The chief beckoned to Buck, Billy Joe and his runners, and together they walked through the village, with warriors, women and children following silently behind them.

They reached the perimeter of the camp, at which point Swift Dog raised his right arm and the procession stopped. Little White Wolf pressed his way to the front, paused, inserted an arrow in his bow, paused again, then unleashed it. It swished through the morning air and landed about eighty yards away, hitting the base of a yucca tree.

The chief smiled and patted White Wolf on the head.

Buck and Billy Joe stood for a moment as the arrow quivered at the base of the yucca.

'Let's go,' said Buck, walking forward.

The two men walked slowly away from the silent congregation behind them, as the four warriors stood, hands on knees, coiled, ready to give chase.

Billy Joe looked ahead but could see only the shimmer of heat-haze on the apparently endless plain, the mountains like a distant dream beyond. They were now only thirty yards from the arrow, and again Buck felt the thud throbbing in his temple and neck, the dryness in his mouth. Billy Joe broke the silence.

'Take it slow,' he said. 'No point in wasting energy.'

Buck nodded. He was beginning to feel the ground hard beneath his feet, the soft feeling leaving his legs. He concentrated on deepening his breathing. He spoke, continuing to face forward, as if the Sioux behind them could hear, 'We got to bust their balls early.'

Billy Joe nodded, also looking forward. 'When we get to that arrow, really get moving,' he said, harshly. 'Let's run the guts outa these boys early on. Burn 'em out.'

They reached the arrow. 'Now!' bellowed Billy Joe. Both men accelerated as one, their spikes gaining good grip on the dry surface of the plain, the earth spurting in their wake. Behind them came the collective whoop of the tribe as their chosen warriors raced off in pursuit.

Black Moon took the lead, running at full speed, with little Hollow Stone pattering at his shoulder and Grey Deer and Black Dog loping along two yards or so back. The Sioux zigzagged through the brush, oblivious to branches and thorns which ripped at their legs. After only a furlong it was obvious to the Indians that they were making no impression. Indeed, the white men appeared to be further away than ever, and little Hollow Stone was already beginning to labour, his breath coming in deep sucking gasps, though Black Moon, Grey Deer and Black Dog were still running strongly.

By a quarter of a mile, Hollow Stone had dropped twenty yards back, and Black Moon and the two other runners could already feel the breath begin to rasp in their throats and their legs grow heavy. Ahead of them, the white men seemed like elusive spirits of the plain, hardly making contact with the ground. They were now more than two hundred paces away. Black Moon dropped his arms and slowed to a trot, and Black Dog and Grey Deer did the same. Soon even Hollow Stone had caught up.

Buck and Billy Joe were well ahead, and they knew it. They had covered a quarter-mile at close to sprint speed, fear masking their fatigue.

They dropped to a slow trot for a hundred yards, sucking hard. 'Okay,' said Billy Joe. 'Hit it.'

The two men surged off again, this time at no more than a fast stride.

Behind them, Black Moon thought for a brief moment that he and his men were catching up. They started to increase their speed. Then the white men seemed to be stretching away again, white wraiths in the desert heat. After only half a mile Hollow Stone was reduced to a shambling trot, his breathing a bronchial wheeze, as he wobbled a hundred yards behind his companions, tripping on stones and roots. Black Moon looked behind him. Hollow Stone was all but finished, but beside him Grey Deer and Black Dog strode remorselessly on, their bodies gleaming with sweat.

Then, at a mile, for the first time Buck saw the horses. They appeared quite close, but it was difficult to judge, for the image was distorted by the heat. Strangely, they could only see the top halves of the animals.

For the next half-mile Buck and Billy Joe kept up the same tactics, but the distance was beginning to take its toll on their sprinters' muscles, and each time they began their quarter-mile dash their strides became heavier, more flat-footed. With half a mile to go, Billy Joe's breathing was harsh and his stride low, and for the first time Buck looked back.

The Indians were gaining. Perhaps they lacked speed, but they had stamina, and were beginning to pull their prey in on a long rope. They were less than a hundred and fifty yards away.

With a shout, Black Moon stopped his men and they charged their bows. The Sioux fired singly. The arrow from Hollow Stone, now barely able to support himself, was a good forty yards short of the white men, Grey Deer's and Black Dog's about twenty yards closer. But Black Moon took his time. His purpose was not to hit his quarry — he was too far off for that — it was to sap their spirits. His arrow landed five yards

216

in front of Buck and Billy Joe, thudding into the soft earth and triggering off in them a sudden, frightened spurt. For the first time they were within firing range.

But, with a quarter of a mile to go, their legs bowing with fatigue, Buck and Billy Joe could see the horses quite clearly — could see that they were saddled, and still. The sight gave fresh impetus to their flagging legs.

But Black Moon was only sixty yards behind, and sensed that he had his men. There was no escape. He beckoned his braves to stop and recharge their bows. Hollow Stone and Grey Deer fired together, their arrows splitting the still morning air. The shafts landed almost in line, thudding into the dry earth only a yard ahead of a wobbling Billy Joe. His knees buckled and he fell forward on to his face, the grit mixing with his sweat to cake his chest and arms.

Buck, gasping, stood above Billy Joe, straddling him, then bent down to pull him to his feet. As he did so an arrow landed between Buck's legs, only a few inches from Billy Joe's blonde head. This produced another convulsive spurt from Buck, but Billy Joe, staggering behind him to his feet, was gone. Buck stopped, for Billy Joe was now ten yards back. His action saved him, for Black Moon's arrow, perfectly flighted, would have landed between his shoulder blades. It whistled harmlessly beyond him.

Then, two hundred yards on, Buck saw the horses through the heat-haze again, but this time clearly. He realised why Swift Dog had smiled when he had spoken of Deer Leap. The animals appeared to be on their knees. As they ran closer, they saw that it was because the horses were on the other side of a chasm, and at least two feet below them. But it was a leap of a good five yards.

Buck looked back. Fifty yards behind them, Black Moon and the other two Sioux had dropped to their knees, gasping, with Hollow Stone staggering a hundred yards behind. Black Moon was motioning to the two men to recharge their bows once more,

217

and within moments the three men loosed another flight. But their muscles were heavy with fatigue, and the arrows landed ten yards short of the white men, who squatted, exhausted, just seventy yards away, a bare ten yards from the chasm.

Buck jogged forward to the edge of the cliff face and peered over. On the other side the horses whinnied tantalisingly. There was no way down, for it was almost vertical, and the chasm seemed to stretch endlessly on either side of them. For the first time he realised they had been on a plateau. He ran back to Billy Joe, who stood sobbing with fatigue, hands on knees. Behind them Black Moon pointed to Buck and Billy Joe.

'Look,' he said. 'They are finished.'

The four Sioux started to walk unsteadily forward towards the white men, and were soon within thirty yards of them, and in sight of Deer Leap. Then something happened that Black Moon would recount to his children all his life, even in the same breath as the victory over Yellow Hair, the white soldier. For the two White Eyes suddenly stood and rushed at the chasm like devils, launching themselves into space. The dark-haired one cleared with much to spare, but the golden- haired one was short, landing just on the edge, which crumbled, and he slid down, hanging on to the cliff-edge by his fingers.

Then the other White Eye pulled on the armpits of his friend and slowly levered him up. The two men lay, exhausted, on the other side of Deer Leap. By this time Black Moon and his men had advanced to within ten yards of the chasm, and Black Dog made to place an arrow in his bow.

But Black Moon put his hand on his arm, restraining him. He walked to the edge of the plateau, followed by Black Dog and Grey Deer, as the white men, too tired to move quickly, struggled to mount their horses.

Black Moon raised his bow high above his head in salutation, the sweat streaming down his dark body.

'Runners,' he shouted, his voice resounding in the morning air. 'Runners.'

11

SHOWDOWN IN CHEYENNE

4 June 1876
Swift Dog had never really expected the White Eyes to reach their horses. He had reasoned that Black Moon and his braves would run them down long before Deer Leap, and that if by some chance the two men did reach the chasm first they would not attempt to clear it. But the will of the Great Manitou had to be observed and respected, and it was thus that Buck and Billy Joe found two well-groomed horses, the same beasts as they had lost at Camp Scotia, on the far side of Deer Leap, with their rifles and clothing, and food capable of taking them as far as the first trading station.

The two men had said little in the first hours after their escape, concentrating instead on putting distance between them and Black Moon, for there was no understanding the Indian mind. That first day they rode thirty-five miles, making camp in a glade by a stream, an area which afforded them good vision on all sides. Billy Joe rustled up some hot sourdough biscuits on the skillet, while Buck concentrated on the Arbuckle's, and they sat by the fire in the gloaming while the horses whinnied lightly behind them.

'Thought you were done for back there,' said Buck.

'Me?' said Billy Joe. 'No trouble. I had plenty of starch left in these legs.'

'Didn't look like that to me,' said Buck, sipping his coffee. 'You looked clean tuckered out.'

'Well, it's not my distance, is it?' growled Billy Joe, sliding some steaming sourdough off the skillet on to a plate and handing it to his companion.

'A mile and a half wasn't mine neither,' said Buck, struggling to cut off a piece of the hot bread.

'Well, good for you,' said Billy Joe. 'You get the long distance medal. You can tell Moriarty all about it when we catch up with him in Cheyenne.'

There was silence as both men let the moment simmer. They chewed at their sourdough.

'Anyhow,' said Billy Joe, gulping down the remains of his coffee, 'I had me an ace in the hole all the time.'

Buck laid down his plate. 'How d'you mean?'

'I mean if'n those savages *had* turned real bad, I could've got both of us out of there as easy as pie.'

Buck stood and poured Billy Joe out another mug of coffee. 'And how exactly would you have worked that?'

Billy Joe paused. 'Shut your eyes,' he said, wiping his mouth with the back of his hand.

'What the hell—' protested Buck.

'I said, shut your eyes,' insisted Billy Joe. Buck dutifully did as he was told.

'Just you keep 'em closed,' said Billy Joe, laying down his mug and plate, standing up and drawing down his buckskins, then pulling down his long-johns and fumbling behind him. Then he pulled up both long-johns and buckskins and buckled his belt.

'You can open 'em up now,' he said, sitting down again.

When Buck opened his eyes he saw that Billy Joe was holding in his right hand in the flickering light of the camp-fire what looked like a thin sliver of steel. He took it from him and examined it, turning it over and over. The sliver was about two inches long and half an inch wide; it was sharp on one side, like a razor.

He laughed. 'So you've got a dwarf's razor — what about it?'

Billy Joe did not laugh, his face solemn as he retrieved the razor from Buck.

'This ain't no ordinary razor. This, my good friend, is a cutting edge — it can go through ropes, open locks . . .'

'I didn't see much in the way of locks back there with them Sioux — '

'You're full of piss and vinegar!' exploded Billy Joe. 'I had this hid, and hid good.'

'Where?'

'You promise not to tell?'

Buck put on a mock-solemn face and spat into the fire. 'Cross my heart and hope to die.'

'Up my ass,' said Billy Joe, winking conspiratorially.

Buck wrinkled his nose in incredulity. 'What do you mean?'

'Can't put it no plainer, Buck. Up my ass, anal cavity, dung trap. Shakespeare himself can't put it no plainer than that.'

'You really mean to tell me you've been toting a razor up your asshole?'

'That's exactly the situation.'

Buck shook his head and poured himself out another mug of coffee. 'For how long?'

'Close on three years. My pap once told me ol' Daniel Boone carried one on him since he was twelve. 'Scaped from Indians many a time because of it. But it was the Great Marko first put me on to it proper.'

'The Great Marko?'

'An escap . . . an escapamol— a magician feller I met once down in San Antonio back in '72. He used to tie himself up in ropes and chains and straitjackets, get buried in a coffin, that sort of thing. And ten minutes after he was out, cool as eggs.'

'So how did this . . . this Marko feller come to let you in on it?'

Billy Joe lifted a lump of sourdough, smelt his hand, thought

221

better of it and threw the bread on the fire. He then wiped his mouth with the back of his other hand.

'Marko was in deep to me, for two hundred wheels in a game of stud. He told me all about the razor, so I let him go clear.'

'And you're telling me that I've been a-riding these past three years with a man with a razor sticking up his backside?'

Billy Joe nodded. 'You sure as hell have, and dam' lucky for you.'

Buck stretched his bottom lip and bit on it with his top teeth. 'Isn't it a mite . . . uncomfortable?'

Billy Joe shook his head. 'Hell, it ain't like your Sears Roebuck cut-throat — exactly what kind of orifice d'you think I've got?'

'I never gave it much thought, leastways not till now,' said Buck.

'Look at this,' said Billy Joe, holding up the razor. 'It's only got one sharp edge – the whole dam' thing's only two inches long and half an inch wide. And I got it wrapped up in rawhide' — he held up a thin strip of leather — 'skinned down real thin. Anyhow, I can tell you Buck, it's my experience that the human arsehole's a mighty accommodating place.'

'Sure sounds like it to me,' said Buck, eyeing the rawhide with distaste. 'But if it ain't a question that troubles you, how about your natural processes?'

'Shitting? Stands to reason I takes it out for my natural functions, elseways it's way down the privy every goddam time.'

Buck nodded, then threw the remains of his coffee on to the fire. 'Billy Joe, just tell me one thing. How did you plan to get your hands on it back there, them being tied an all?'

'It sure as hell ain't easy. You got to be dam' supple, for starters. I spent hunnerds of hours practising — Kansas City, Ellsworth, Wichita, all over.'

'Just for this?'

'It could've paid off! We could've been in a jailhouse,

could've been anywhere. It's an ace in the hole, Buck, I'm telling you.'

Buck thought for a moment. 'Billy Joe, just you promise me one thing.'

'Anything you say, Buck.'

'You get any other ideas, like storing vittles up there, jerky and such things, just count me out.'

'I got you,' replied Billy Joe, throwing his coffee grains on the fire.

Buck stood up and looked down at Billy Joe.

'And if you've got any more surprises, such as a Derringer in your ear or a Bowie knife in a hollow tooth, just let me know, next time. Good and early.'

10 June 1876, Cheyenne

Moriarty eased himself slowly out of bed and made his way gingerly across the floor of the bedroom towards the washbowl. He carefully avoided putting his heels on the ground, for his Achilles tendons still ached as a result of a half-mile handicap run only the day before. He had been vain and foolish, having given starts of up to a hundred and fifty yards and had been beaten on the post by a beardless young Wyoming cowboy of sixteen to whom he had given a start of eighty yards.

Moriarty groaned as his right heel dropped on a loose floorboard, sending pains shooting up his leg.

'You hurt?' asked Eleanor drowsily from the bed.

'No,' answered Moriarty, turning his head towards her. 'Just some parts wake up faster than others. The running parts take a mite longer, that's all.'

He surveyed his face in the mirror. It was remarkably unlined, indeed childlike, but his mop of curly black hair now showed flecks of grey. The hair on his head did not trouble Moriarty. No, it had been finding a single grey pubic hair only a few months before in San Francisco: that had brought to him intimations of mortality. It had been a bad moment, if only because it had been so unexpected. And now he had been taken by a stripling over half a mile. He continued to stare at his face and stroked his grey-black, unshaven chin.

'Pretty soon I'll look like an old prune,' he said.

'I like prunes,' said Eleanor from the bed.

'I'm getting old, Eleanor. I'm not the man I was ten years ago.'

Eleanor levered herself from the bed, got out and donned her dressing gown.

'You're not the man you were ten minutes ago.' She joined him at the mirror and peered into it. 'You're thirty-nine years of age,' she said.

'The hell I am! I'm thirty-eight.'

She turned and walked to her dresser on the right of the bed as Moriarty splashed cold water on his face.

'You know, ten years ago I could've run with the best — Deerfoot, the Suffolk Stag, the Norfolk Chicken . . .'

'Yes, I know,' said Eleanor, pouring water into the white porcelain bowl on her dresser.

'The whole menagerie. They feel like kin to me.'

Moriarty dipped his shaving brush into the water, then circled it in his shaving bowl until he had achieved a rich, white foam.

'Eleanor,' he said, looking down at the brush, 'if it hadn't been for the war, I could've had the world ten-mile record. Fifty minutes! I could've run five-minute miles all the way.'

Eleanor lapped water on her clear white skin and surveyed herself.

'Nobody gets to be an athlete for ever,' she said. 'Let Buck and Billy Joe do the running.'

Moriarty applied the foam generously to his face, sneezing as it made its way into his nostrils.

'The hell I will. I've got one big run in me, Eleanor . . . I know it.' He scraped his right cheek, pulling down on his chin.

Eleanor dried her face. 'You're looking in a narrow mirror,' she said, turning to him.

Moriarty whetted his razor on his stropping belt. 'How d'you mean?'

She walked across the room and stood behind him as he continued his shaving. 'Since San Francisco I've begun to feel something.'

He put down his razor, turned to her and grabbed her by the shoulders, looking down at her stomach.

'You're not pregnant, are you?'

'No such luck,' she said. 'No, I mean our work. Our *real* work, in the theatre. I feel it's coming good.'

He released her, turned away, lifted his razor and started once more to scrape his right cheek. 'It's always been good.'

'That's where you're wrong.' She caught his eyes in the mirror. 'Sometimes it's been good. A lot of the time it's been awful. You remember that time in Canyon City when you played Julius Caesar?'

'When that Navajo came in when Buck and Billy Joe were killing me, started whooping with fear and rushed out before anyone could stop him?'

'Yes.'

Moriarty smiled into the mirror. 'Well, you can't blame me if a dam' fool Indian can't distinguish drama from the real thing.'

'Can you?'

'Can I what?'

'Distinguish it from the real thing?'

Moriarty completed his shaving, inspected himself and lapped his face with cold water. He turned to her, towelling his face.

'Eleanor, you're talking in riddles. It's too early in the morning.' He pulled her to him. 'What's bothering you?'

'You,' she said. 'You remember when we first came out here and you had such great plans?'

He looked at her solemnly. 'I've still got them.'

'Mr and Mrs Moriarty in Moriarty's Theatre of the West — that's what you said then.'

'And I seem to remember you said then that was one helluva lot of Moriarty.'

She grinned and fondled the hairs on his chest. Then her face became serious. 'Well, I don't feel that you want to do it anymore. Now it's all running and the English Method and high jumps against horses and God knows what else.'

'But that's what's made the money. Sixty thousand dollars back in A.P. Wagstaffe's Bank in San Francisco. We only just about break even on the shows, you know that.'

'But you still want to set up a theatre in San Francisco?'

'Moriarty's Theatre of the West'? Of course I do.'

She looked up into his face. 'I feel as if we're in a race,' she said. 'A race to get to the money we need for the theatre before . . .'

'Before, what?'

'Before something bad happens.'

'Nothing's going to happen,' he said. 'I promise.'

'Promise?'

'Yes,' he said. 'Cross my heart.'

It was on 10 June that Buck and Billy Joe arrived back in town, bearded and lean on horses that could now barely trot. Moriarty had arranged a secret meeting at Chang's Bath House for a wash and rub-down and a conference to decide the week's programme. As the two runners lay groaning in the hot soapy suds of Chang's deep wooden tubs, Moriarty extracted from them the story of their travails at Camp Scotia.

He seemed unconcerned about the money, interested only in their welfare and their experiences with the Sioux.

'These Indian girls, what were they like?' he asked.

Buck replied first. 'Kinda smoky,' he said.

'Like sourbelly,' said Billy Joe.

Moriarty laughed. He explained that the Cheyenne Dash was a short one, a hundred and five yards uphill on a lumpy, rutted 16th Street for a hundred bucks. Buck would enter the race first, immediately, then Billy Joe would enter late, having

226

established himself in Cheyenne as a drinker and trencherman over the next few days. Buck and Billy Joe got out of the tubs and made their way to Chang's steam hut, where they were soon joined by Moriarty, who placed himself between them, and the three men sat naked in the thick steam, the sweat pouring in rivulets down their bodies.

'Who's running?' asked Billy Joe.

'A local boy, name of Perkins, clocked five-tenths outside even time,' said Moriarty. 'Then there's a Sioux half-breed, name of Black Rock, never wears spikes, runs about the same. Also an Englishman, an amateur, calls himself Lord Haldane; says he can go to a yard off evens.'

'No amateur ever run near even time,' snorted Billy Joe.

'No English amateur anyway,' Buck added.

Moriarty stood and peered through the mist before locating the water bucket. He walked to it and splashed some on his head before returning to the bench.

'Don't be too sure,' he said, leaning forward, elbows on knees, the sweat from his head and neck dripping on to the wooden floor. 'Those University boys at Oxford and Cambridge, they can run some.'

'But they're amateurs,' said Billy Joe.

'That's just it,' said Moriarty: 'They've got more time than most of the peds up in the north of England, men who've got to work for a living between matches. Nothing to do but run, those college boys.'

'Your Lord Haldane, he'll have to shift some to take me,' said Billy Joe dourly.

'You think you'll be all right, after that run with the Indians?' asked Moriarty.

'I never ran faster,' said Buck. 'It was better than training.'

'It should work out well then,' said Moriarty, turning to Billy Joe. 'Money on you to win, Buck to place.'

'Why not me to win and Billy Joe to place?' said Buck sullenly.

Moriarty turned, sensing — and not for the first time — hostility in Buck's words.

'Because Billy Joe's a yard faster, that's why,' he replied.

'Was a yard faster,' said Buck. 'You should've seen it up there in the Dakotas with those Sioux. Billy Joe here was on the floor, me still running like a train.'

'It was two miles, Moriarty,' interjected Billy Joe.

'Horses for courses,' said Moriarty, placatingly.

'I'm no horse,' said Buck. 'But what law is it says Billy Joe here's always got to be a yard faster? Just you tell me that.'

'You're the slower man, Buck,' said Moriarty. 'Simple as that.'

'Says who?'

'Says twenty years in the profession of pedestrianism,' said Moriarty tersely. 'That's what says.'

Buck got up and dashed some cold water on to his naked body before returning to the bench.

'What if you trained me up, English Method, like Billy Joe?'

Moriarty shook his head, shaking a spray of sweat on to his knees. 'Buck, take my word for it, you could shit and sweat all day and never have Billy Joe's start.'

He slapped the fronts of his thighs with the palms of his hands. 'Because it's all here, Buck. In the loins. The power.'

He stood up and looked down on both of them. 'Now don't get me wrong, Buck. You've got speed, real speed. If you went to scratch with Billy Joe over a long dash, say a furlong or a quarter mile, then you might just take him. You showed that up in the Dakotas with those Sioux. You've got bottom, I acknowledge that. If we ran furlongs . . .

'If my aunt had balls, she'd be my uncle,' said Billy Joe

Buck made his reflex scowl.

So on Saturday we run on our merits,' said Moriarty. 'No faking — we never fake. Wouldn't be sportsmanlike. A little poetic licence over the betting, maybe. But once the race is on it's always for real.

He put his hands on their shoulders. 'We're a team, boys. Come hell or high water. But we run on our merits. Always.'

It all went perfectly to plan. Billy Joe established himself as a drinker of Bacchanalian proportions during the week that followed, though his actual consumption was as usual much less than the residents of Cheyenne were led to believe. While Fast Men (and imagined Fast Men) arrived in town in profusion Billy Joe made no mention of his sprinting prowess, reserving his entry to the tournament until the Friday evening. Then, after half a dozen glasses of Taos Lightning in Hannigan's Bar, Billy Joe Speed unleashed himself.

For well over an hour he kept the citizens of Cheyenne enraptured with his tale of the Run of the Arrow, a story from which Buck had been excised with the skill of a surgeon. But this was not a Billy Joe who had staggered drunkenly towards Deer Leap; no, this was a mixture of Hercules and Daniel Boone, a man who had tortured the Sioux with his devastating bursts of speed before effortlessly launching himself across a thirty-foot chasm, leaping on to his trusty steed and waving goodbye to as demoralised a bunch of Indians as ever a man did see.

The denizens of Hannigan's Bar were impressed by Billy Joe's loquacity, though they expressed — not to put too fine a word upon it — considerable reservations about his pedestrian abilities. Billy Joe, however, was in no mood to tolerate cynics. He would enter the Street Dash and show the runners of Cheyenne as clean a pair of heels as he had those Sioux, so what odds would they say? The money was not long in coming in, at as much as three and four to one against, and even Moriarty, arriving late, at the conclusion of Billy Joe's performance, was able to lay two grand at three to one before Billy Joe flaked out on the bar-room billiard table

All that morning before the race Moriarty, Mandy and Eleanor laid money quietly on Billy Joe, and by noon had put on another thousand dollars, though the odds were now dropping fast, with so much money being laid. Meanwhile, Billy Joe, his gut raging with Blackjack, had been making well inside even time in his runs to the privy since the early hours of Saturday morning. Then, his colon void of waste, he sat for two hours in Chang's Bath House, drying himself out.

The afternoon's sport began with a two-mile walk, during which Cheyenne was treated to as memorable a display of trotting, lurching and hip-wobbling as had ever appeared west of St. Louis. Moriarty observed that walking was like trying to see who could whisper the loudest, and would not lay a single dollar on the outcome. There followed sack races, children's races and a three-legged race for members of the fire department, before the first heats of the sprint were announced.

There were six heats, the winner of each to go into the final an hour later. The first was won by 'Lord Haldane', whom Moriarty now recognised as a Bronx boy by the name of Mulligan who had run at St. Louis back in 1873. 'Haldane', short and stocky, could certainly shift, but was a good five yards over evens in his heat and looked to have little more than two more yards remaining in his locker. The Indian, Black Rock, incongruously dressed in vest, long-johns and tribal feather, was a fast strider rather than a sprinter though he won his heat in six yards outside even time, as did the lanky, knobbly-kneed local boy, Perkins. The fifth heat was won easily by Buck who, using the kangaroo start, cut the field to ribbons in the first twenty yards, winning, hands up, in four yards outside.

Then, in the final heat, came Billy Joe, his face as white as his long-johns as he came to the line. As he got down to his mark, a wag in the crowd shouted, 'Don't you a-get down there, Billy Joe. You'll never get up!' There was much raucous laughter. Judge Watt, the Mayor and official starter, froze the offender with a stare and got the six runners away from the line their feet before again setting them to their marks.

The one hundred and five yards of sprint-path were no Sheffield or Hackney Wick; indeed, they were not even a St. Louis or a Canyon City. Unlaned, they provided a grooved, bumpy stretch of baked earth, scored at intervals by deep, diagonal gashes, the result of winter rains. Billy Joe reflected that it was as rough a stretch of running-path as he had ever faced. But he made it look good. He came slowly out of a standing start and was a good yard down at twenty, and two yards down at fifty, to the leader, a thick-thighed young mulatto called Snoade, and marooned in the middle of a struggling field of five runners.

At sixty Snoade still held his two-yard lead, but slowly Billy Joe pulled him in, and at eighty was only a yard back. At ninety yards it was still Snoade's race, but over the last few yards Billy Joe accelerated and took it by a clear foot, throwing his face at the tape and staggering into the crowd beyond the finish. But his time was the slowest of all the heats, seven yards outside even time, and Billy Joe's odds stayed at three to one, with Buck and Lord Haldane, who had both conclusively won their heats, the favourites at evens. Moriarty discreetly laid another grand on Billy Joe, spreading his bets around town. The mayor took two hundred, the card-sharp, Mat Gumbrell, three hundred and Joe Delaney, the owner of the Golden Nugget, five hundred, all at odds which had now dropped to two to one.

When Marshal Obadiah Boone arrived in Cheyenne that night, with a deputy and the outlaw, Josie Clamp, in custody, the talk was all of the Great Dash, of how a drunken bum called Billy Joe Speed had run a yard outside even time in the fastest, humdingingest race ever seen in Cheyenne. Boone and his deputy, Will Christie, had deposited Clamp at the jailhouse and been promised by Sheriff Clay that the $1000 reward money would be theirs when the banks opened on Monday

231

morning. He and Christie then made straight for Hannigan's Bar. Boone, his rear end sore and his throat dry as dust from his long ride, stood at the bar pouring glass after glass of cold beer down his throat, as the story of the Dash was told and retold around him, gaining with every telling.

It had all been fought out between Billy Joe and the Eastern boy, Buck Miller. Both had got down on their knees at the start, all scrunched up — the 'kangaroo start', they called it. Speed had gone off like a crazy-cat, Miller close behind. No one in Cheyenne had seen the like, two men ripping down 16th Street, legs pumping like pistons, less than a yard between them, the rest treading water five yards back. At the tape it had been Billy Joe, only a couple of feet ahead, the watches showing a tenth of a second between the men, and everyone reckoned they had seen as fair and fine a foot-race as had ever been run.

It was only when Boone had heard of the presence of the Theatre of the West, the fact that Billy Joe had been booze-blind all week, that it had all begun to come together. . . Billy Joe the runner, Buck the Fast Man, Moriarty . . . it was exactly the same cast, though in a different play, but one which always took in big profits. Boone needed no reminding that he had lost five grand and a daughter back in Canyon City a year ago, and till that moment had only regretted the latter. His next glass of beer completely quenched his thirst.

The girl placed her tongue between Buck's toes and gently licked the space between them, hearing his groan above her in the darkness. It had been strange to her that a man could be so sensitive, or that these parts of his body could taste so sweet. Then his probing fingers hit the spot, that minute area of tissue that always changed in a split second the sexual balance between them. Hannah tried to sustain her licking but it was no good: her fleeting dominance had been plucked from her. She reached up and felt for him, but he gently pushed

232

her away. It was his turn. She lay, her head against his legs, longing for that deep warm wave immediately to engulf her, but hoping that he would delay it for ever.

The light hit her like a hammer. Lamps, the hard voices of men, a room suddenly full of people, the noise of furniture being knocked over.

The girl reflexly attempted to pull the top sheet across herself, but found only the bottom corner. Then Buck tumbled off the bed towards the window, allowing her to draw the whole sheet over her. She sat, knees to chest, on the pillow, while all around her kerosene lamps dangled like pumpkin-lanterns at Halloween.

There were at least six men but it was Judge Watt's Scots voice she heard first, as Buck was dragged to his feet, struggling, by Marshal Boone.

Buck, naked, suddenly felt very weak. Boone and Christie pinned him against the wall as Sheriff Clay held a pungent lamp only inches from his face

'Is this the gentleman, Marshal?'

'I do declare it is, Mr Mayor.'

'The exponent of the so-called English Method back in Canyon City?'

'The very same.'

Boone looked sourly at Buck and replaced his gun in its holster. 'Who's the girl?' he asked.

Hannah, in shadow, attempted to pull the sheet higher, to mask her face. Watt held the lamp in front of her. He recognised her immediately.

'She's nothing,' said Watt, the darkness hiding his flushed face. 'Works in the saloon. Hannah Bliss.'

Hannah's face hardened. Watt had been pawing her only a week before.

Mayor Watt looked around at the other four men standing behind him. 'Then get you along to the Chuk-a-Luk and find that other young fellow, Billy Joe Speed. We have been cheated

233

and deceived, gentlemen. Buncoed. And for that crime there is only one answer.'

The rapidity with which Billy Joe was captured was matched only by that with which Hannah Bliss dressed and made her way from the rear of the hotel to the livery stable to saddle Buck's horse. By the time the two men had been dragged to the jailhouse she had already ridden two miles out into the darkness, away from a town now being roused into violent life.

It had taken little more than an hour for the citizens of Cheyenne to be awoken and apprised of the true facts of that Dash: that it had borne no more relationship to a true race than had the death of Caesar to a fight in Main Street.

Marshal Boone's testimony made all clear. Speed was a pro, probably one of the fastest men in the Union. His co-conspirator, Miller was even faster, but had faked the final because all the money had been laid on his confederate. Discussions among the town's sporting fraternity revealed that Moriarty and his troupe had spread over two thousand dollars on Speed from the moment that he had first committed himself to the race on Friday night. It had all been a big fix, just as it had been in Canyon City. The one man still to be called to account was clearly the so-called 'Professor' Moriarty, and a posse would have to be despatched in the morning to bring him to proper justice. But at least for the moment they had the two leading miscreants, Speed and Miller, safely in the jailhouse.

The word about the bunco and the imprisonment of Speed and Miller went round the town like wildfire. Cheyenne was in ferment, and by midnight that night the outraged sportsmen of Cheyenne were awake and dressed, and a crowd of two hundred was assembled outside Sheriff Clay's jailhouse, whipping themselves into a noisy, dangerous mob.

The outrage of the citizens of Cheyenne derived from two

sources. The first was financial, for many had placed big sums against Billy Joe; but for the majority, who had viewed the race simply as a piece of sporting drama, there was an even deeper rage.

For in the race they felt that they had seen something real, something true. They had come from the East in hope, but for most of them the West had been an intense disappointment. It had been a place where they had expected to find riches beyond dreams. Instead, they had found loneliness; endless mountains and plains; cholera and typhoid; and money-grubbing shysters that had milked them of every hard-earned dollar they had wrung out of the soil.

Now it was clear that even these two fine young athletes were both part of the same Big Bunco, and the anger felt by the good citizens was more, far more, than they would have felt had Billy Joe and Buck been mere card-sharps.

By half past twelve the Cheyenne mob was getting restless and there were shouts for Clay to bring out these fellows Speed and Miller and let them take their licks. At first there was no response. Then some of the wilder elements started to let off their six-guns while others, drawn from saloons by the noise, were sucked into the back of the mob, which started to press in on the door of the jailhouse. Those at the front of the crowd started to thump and kick on the jailhouse door, as others at the back continued to shoot off their pistols into the night air.

Inside the jailhouse, Boone and Clay advised Judge Watt that it might be wise to placate the mob by bringing out Buck and Billy Joe, letting them have a sight of them, so to speak. The runners, now in their underwear, were taken out on to the sidewalk, Boone and Clay and their deputies clearing a space for them in front of the jailhouse.

Boone had said little, but they could both feel the rage simmering within the man. For the marshal's pride had been hurt — not by the loss of Mandy, but by the completeness

235

with which he had been deceived in Canyon City, the utter perfection of Moriarty's con.

Buck and Billy Joe, held by the arms by Clay's deputies, peered out into the street. There was now a mass of nearly three hundred raging men out there, many of them carrying torches and lamps. This was a lynch mob.

Obadiah Boone looked sideways at Clay, who nodded. The Marshal pointed his Remington in the air and fired three times. There was silence, broken only by Watt's Scots burr.

'Gentlemen,' he said, holding both hands, palms out, in front of him. 'It appears we have been grievously misled.'

There was raucous laughter. Watt had defused the situation.

'You good people, and I include myself, we thought we saw a fair and honest footrace this afternoon.'

He paused.

'Fancy running. I never saw none fancier. That's what we thought we saw. A fair race.'

He paused again.

'But,' he looked sideways at Boone. 'Marshal Boone here tells us another story. And it's quite a tale, about how last year the good folks of Canyon City were flim-flammed out of their hard-earned sawbucks by these same fellows.'

Boone nodded.

'And Marshal Boone here lost much more. He lost a loving daughter to that evil man at the centre of this whole farrago, Professor Moriarty, who made off about five hours back.'

There were scattered shouts from the crowd. He paused for effect.

'What must concern us now, gentlemen, is justice. For this is a civilised country. So what I propose is that we let these young men state their case, clear and simple, here and now.'

Buck spoke for them both. He freely admitted that they had run together at Canyon City, but claimed that they had both run on their merits, that there had been no faking of the race itself. The same, he claimed, had occurred at Cheyenne.

So perhaps Billy Joe had hammed it up at the bar the week before, but the race had been fair and square — they would both swear to that fact upon a stack of bibles.

The two runners stood in the torch-light in front of Sheriff Clay's jailhouse, flanked by Boone, Clay and his deputies and the City Council, Buck shouting their defence into a crowd of three hundred outraged men and women. Buck and Billy Joe felt his words weaken and fade into the darkness beyond the crowd, for at the heart of their defence they felt a central weakness — the knowledge that, however fair and valid the race, it was all part of a drama as artificial as any of those which appeared nightly on Moriarty's stage.

As he spoke, the smell of hot, burning tar began to drift over the crowd, bringing a cold sweat to the pits of Buck and Billy Joe's stomachs.

Judge Watt raised his hand to still the shouts as Buck's final words were lost in the din.

'Ladies and gentlemen,' he said. 'This is a civilised society. Now, we've listened to Marshal Boone and we've heard these young gentlemen defend themselves. The spider at the centre of this web of intrigue appears to be Professor Moriarty, who is at present out of our reach, though rest assured Sheriff and his deputies will track him down and bring him to a true and proper justice.'

There were cheers at this, and Watt smiled. 'Now, back in Bonnie Scotland, where I come from, we have three verdicts. The first is "not guilty", the second is "guilty", and the third, unique in jurisprudence, is "not proven".'

'What does "not proven" mean, Judge?' came a voice from the crowd.

'It means that we dam' well know you're guilty but we can't prove it,' replied Watt, to roars of laughter. 'So what is it to be?'

'Guilty!' roared the crowd, as a tub of black tar was dragged in front of the jailhouse with a sack of feathers.

Watt looked behind him at Buck and Billy Joe. 'You've heard what's the people's decision, gentlemen,' he said. 'As I see it, you boys have two choices. A week from now the circuit judge will be here and you can take your licks fair and square in the court-room in front of a jury. I reckon you'll get a couple of years breaking stones in the penitentiary, at best.'

There were shouts from the crowd as Watt held up his hands for silence.

'Or,' he said. 'You have a second choice.' He paused. 'Summary justice. The law of the people.'

He looked sideways at Boone and Clay but they did not respond. Then Weir looked at the tub of bubbling black tar before him and bent down to pick up a wooden ladle. He stirred the tar, withdrew the ladle and watched the boiling liquid drip from it into the tub.

'Wrong, Mr Mayor,' boomed a voice from the back of the crowd, above the hubbub. 'You have a third choice.'

It was Moriarty, though he could not yet be seen beyond the pool of light created by the torches and kerosene lamps which lit up the street in front of the jailhouse. Moriarty, riding a black mare, trotted slowly into the edge of the light, flanked on either side by Mandy and Eleanor. All carried shot-guns raised to waist-level and pointing towards Boone and Clay. Moriarty's countenance was solemn.

Boone peered out into the street, as the crowd turned to face Moriarty. 'Moriarty,' he shouted through the hubbub. 'You're in more mess than you've a long boot to get out of.'

'Perhaps,' said Moriarty, his resonant actor's voice cutting through the night air. 'But you have no right to do what you're doing. It was a fair race: the boys ran on their merits. I swear that to you. So let them go.'

Watt regained his composure. 'Professor Moriarty,' he said, the sweat beading his brow. 'There are three of you and three hundred of us. Put down your rifle, sir.'

'Mr Mayor,' replied Moriarty. 'Myself and the two girls all

have scatter-guns pointing straight at you good people. Now neither of the ladies has ever fired a gun before and surely it will break their shoulders when they do. But in the meantime I wouldn't put a figure on the number of you people of Cheyenne who will never be quite the same again.'

He cocked his rifle, a signal for Mandy and Eleanor to do the same. The crowd backed away from them, falling over each other to put distance between themselves and the guns.

'Mandy?' Boone bellowed out to his daughter. 'You come right in, honey. We'll put all this behind us, I promise you.'

Mandy Boone's voice trembled as she replied. 'No,' she said. 'I stay here.'

Moriarty's voice boomed out again. 'Now you've heard my offer. It's up to you. We don't have much time.'

'Don't pay them any heed,' roared Boone. 'They don't have the guts.'

'Then you're going to have to pay to find out,' said Moriarty.

Watt looked nervously around him, then out at Moriarty. Moriarty reached into an inside pocket with his left hand, still keeping his rifle pointing at the crowd.

'Now, I'm a reasonable man,' he said. 'So let's sweeten the pot. You people here think that you have a reasonable grievance.'

He paused.

'I don't want to leave Cheyenne with any ill-feeling,' he said. He raised a thick money-clip above his head. 'Or any feeling that you good people have been cheated in any way. So here's seven thousand two hundred and twenty-one dollars, all the money we won here. Judge Watt, you just give me your solemn word that your posse won't follow us and the money's yours to give back to those who lost it on the race.'

Watt looked around him at the near-silent crowd. He paused. 'You can have your boys,' he shouted, his voice cracking.

Buck and Billy Joe were released, and scampered through

the crowd to leap on to the spare horses which Moriarty had brought. Moriarty handed his rifle to Buck.

'Do I have your solemn word, judge?' he shouted.

Watt gulped, the sweat pouring in streams down his face.

'You have my word.'

Moriarty tossed the clip towards the jailhouse. It landed just short of the cauldron of tar. He retrieved his rifle from Buck.

'Gentlemen,' he said. 'I swear by Almighty God you witnessed as true and fair a race today as ever you will see.' Moriarty looked directly at Boone. 'I swear too that I will kill any man who follows us. You have my word on that, Marshal.'

From the diary of Eleanor Cameron, 18 June 1876

Cheyenne must surely be the end, or at least the beginning of the end, of our pedestrian activities. This is the first occasion when things have gone seriously wrong, but it will surely not be the last. The country is simply becoming too small for such deceptions, and there is a limit to the disguises which Buck and Billy Joe can effectively employ. Certainly, there is no way by which we would again wish to face a hostile crowd such as that which we encountered in Cheyenne. Had Marshal Boone called our bluff, there is no knowing the outcome. True, we did survive, but our company is simply unfitted by our natures for such adventures. Surely, then, it is time for us to set our compass for more tranquil waters, using the money we have to set up a permanent theatre in San Francisco. I sincerely hope so. If only I could be confident that my beloved husband felt the same.

12

ENGLAND

'Would you really have fired right into that crowd?'

It was Buck. Moriarty, Eleanor, Mandy and the boys sat in a pool of light in the darkness the next evening round the campfire, having placed sixty-two miles between themselves and the angry citizens of Cheyenne.

'No means of telling,' replied Moriarty. 'I've never fired a gun at anyone in my life.'

'*I* would,' said Mandy darkly, as she sipped her coffee.

'Me too,' said Eleanor.

'Women,' growled Moriarty, shaking his head as he poked the guttering flames with a stick.

There was a brief silence, as if everyone was preoccupied with their own thoughts.

'We've used up too many places,' said Billy Joe at last.

Buck nodded. 'Too many runners,' he said. 'Too many gambling men moving from town to town, telegraphs and railroads. It only takes a Boone, a Judge Weir or a Medina to be around at the wrong time and we're dead as mutton.'

'Have you ever thought of running for real?'

It was Eleanor. There was silence while the others weighed the import of her question.

'We always run for real,' growled Billy Joe. 'You must know that, Eleanor.'

'Come on, Billy Joe.' It was Mandy. 'It's a fix, always has

been. We're the only ones who really know your merits as runners. If everyone else did then we'd be out of the money.'

'And what about the English Method?' pursued Eleanor. 'That's as phoney as a four-dollar bill.'

Buck and Billy Joe looked to Moriarty for a response.

Moriarty poked the fire with a stick, staring into the flames. 'Those boys,' he pointed the burning stick at Buck and Billy Joe, 'always run on their merits. Never fixed a race in their lives. Never will, not as long as I have anything to do with them.'

He paused and breathed deeply.

'But no question of it, we do, as the phrase says, practise to deceive. And maybe Cheyenne's just the Good Lord's way of telling us that it's high time for us to change our ways.'

'So what do we do now?' asked Billy Joe.

'Something I've planned for years,' said Moriarty. 'Go where we can find the best footracers in the world, big money, stadiums full to the brim. To the home of pedestrianism.'

'Where?' asked Mandy. 'Let's make it a long way from my paw.'

Moriarty withdrew his stick from the fire and lit a cigar with its tip, pausing to stretch the moment as he puffed. 'England,' he said. 'That far enough for you, Mandy?'

'England?' said Eleanor, smiling. 'You mean home — for a holiday?'

'Not exactly,' said Moriarty. 'First we go East to New York, put Billy Joe in some match-races there — honest ones — and pick up a few bucks' folding money. Edwin will get us some work there in the theatre.'

'And what about me?' asked Buck.

'I've got big plans for you, Buck,' said Moriarty, puffing on his cigar. 'No point in putting you out round New York. That's home territory; they know you too well there.'

'So what, then?'

'London,' replied Moriarty. 'You and Billy Joe go to the

Amateur Athletic Championships in London, April next year?

'*Amateur* Championships?' said Buck. 'We're no amateurs. We're pros, through and through.'

'Yes,' replied Moriarty. 'But they don't know that over there. And there's always big money in bets on their championships, even though the runners are all Lord this and Viscount that. They may be amateurs but that's never stopped them having a bet. So we dress you and Billy Joe real fancy like gentlemen, and we can pick up plenty and have ourselves a holiday to boot. We send you, Buck, a few weeks ahead of Billy Joe for preparation with my very good friend and the world's finest trainer of pedestrians, George Grimthorp of Norfolk, England, and the rest of us follow you up a few weeks later to England for the championships.'

Buck smiled and looked into the fire. This time he would show them. Special preparation with the best trainer in the world!

'And one other thing,' said Moriarty. 'Letters of accreditation as amateurs. To these Athletic Association people in England.'

'Now who on earth would give Buck and Billy Joe a letter of accreditation?' asked Eleanor.

Moriarty paused and looked at each one of the group in turn, puffing slowly on his cigar. 'Only the next President of the United States,' he replied, 'Buck's friend and mine, General George A. Custer.'

It had not worked out as Moriarty had hoped. Billy Joe had run two matches in July and August in Chicago and Boston, winning them both easily, but in September he had agreed to a race with an Irishman called Maloney, just landed from County Kerry and backed by a bookmaker called Seamus Flynn. Maloney, who claimed prodigious distances as a 'lepper' in long jump and hop, step and jump, was a fast, springy strider rather than a true sprinter. Indeed, it was only

243

the ferocious sentimentality of the New York Irish that had brought the match into being.

On 28 September, at Hoboken Race Course, ten thousand New Yorkers had gathered to see the contest between Maloney and Billy Joe Speed, the Texan with the Kangaroo Start. Billy Joe had given the Kerry man the kiss of death in the first twenty yards and with only ten yards to go was in a clear two-yard lead. The Texan performed as if in a sweet dream, for his running flowed effortlessly from him and all thoughts of a close, engineered finish and a re-run were lost as the speed rushed from his limbs into the grass track.

Then, as he threw himself in on the tape, it happened — the knife in the leg. For that was how it felt to Billy Joe, as if someone had inserted a blade deep into the belly of the muscles in the back of his right thigh. He pulled up abruptly, hopping, clutching the back of his leg as Moriarty, Buck and Mandy clustered anxiously around him.

It was what every sprinter dreaded — a hamstring pull, and it was a bad one. Certainly there was no question of Billy Joe following Buck to England immediately; instead, he would have to get the best possible treatment in New York and come over later to help with Buck's final preparations. And it would have to be Buck alone who would carry the flag at the Amateur Athletic Club Championships in April.

For the first time in years Billy Joe Speed was no longer an athlete. For days he walked with a limp, feeling the injury buried deep, like a cancer, in the thick wedge of muscle at the back of his thigh. From being a Fast Man, a blaze of speed on the cinder path, he felt himself a nothing, incapable of beating a matron of seventy, let alone an athlete

Dr. Gottinger, the 'anatomical expert' to whom Moriarty referred him, was useless. True, he was an able doctor of medicine, but he knew about as much about the repair of muscle-injuries as he did about the workings of the human brain. Gottinger advised rest, the water-treatment and a course of purgings to cleanse the muscular system of all waste.

The water-treatment at Gottinger's Heinrich Institute, an establishment devoted to the treatment of corpulence and debauchery, was a wilderness of cold plunges, laxatives and showers which left Billy Joe blue with cold and rippling with goose-pimples. The purges were simply a Teutonic version of the English Method — and he was in danger of pulling his left hamstring just in getting to the john.

Mercifully, Moriarty also decided on massage as a means of treatment, and daily, in the darkness of his room, Billy Joe lay on his front as Moriarty kneaded evil-smelling horse-liniment into the back of his right thigh.

But Moriarty knew that more was needed than purges and massage. Billy Joe had never been hurt before, could not leap in his imagination from this present crippled moment to that day in the summer when he would be restored to full health and vigour and capable once more of taking on the best foot-racers in the Union. So daily Moriarty retailed to Billy Joe stories of great runners of the past who had come back from injury to run better than ever. Men like Jackson of Barnsley, Wight of Jedburgh, Cole of Pontypridd. To hear Moriarty, Billy Joe's injury was a blessing.

By the time Buck eventually left a wintry New York on the *S.S. Harold*, Swift Dog and his Sioux braves had expunged forever the humiliation of Deer Leap. General George A. Custer lay dead with all his men on the Little Big Horn.

Buck was crossing first class, just as Moriarty had done all those years before, and daily in the first week he pounded the rolling, slippery deck just as Deerfoot and Moriarty had done. For this was going to be Buck's moment, when he would for ever throw off Billy Joe's shadow. Thus every dayhe trotted round the spray-swept boards, keeping the tone in his legs, and on still, dry days during that first week he even managed to put in a few faster dashes on the ship's eighty-yard straight, just to keep his sprinting muscles in shape.

He missed Billy Joe, he acknowledged; for the relaxed, easygoing Texan had many of the qualities he himself lacked. Life, like running, came easy to his friend; it was a play in which he extemporised most of his lines, but always came good by the final curtain.

The only department in which Buck had any clear lead over Billy Joe lay in relationships with women. There, Buck's relaxed charm flowed from him as easily as Billy Joe's pace on the running path. But Buck had given no more thought to this disparity than had Billy Joe to the differences between them as runners. Billy Joe, with his wit and easy ways, possessed the capacity to clear the shadows from Buck Miller's soul. The paradox was that he himself was one of those shadows.

For deep in his heart Buck believed he had the beating of Billy Joe. Each time they had set up a scam he had trained his legs off, hoping somehow to span that short yard that invariably separated him from the Texan — even though, had he done so, the whole point' of the scam would have been lost. Strangely, he knew that such a result might not have displeased Moriarty, apart from the money lost, for the Scot possessed a strange streak of Puritanism.

In England, Buck felt that he would prove himself honestly once and for all by whipping all those lords and marquises, running faster than any man had ever run, even the Indian himself. Thus, even when the *S.S. Harold* bucked and rolled in the green mountains of the Atlantic, Buck was pumping out hundreds of sit-ups and press-ups on the floor of his creaking cabin.

The *S.S. Harold* carried one hundred and forty-one paying passengers and from the first day offered a rich social life, from deck-games to bridge and piano-recitals.

To all this Buck was oblivious, as he daily vigorously exercised his body. He was now slightly heavy at one hundred and sixty pounds and hoped at least to hold that body-weight throughout the ocean voyage. He would take off the final five pounds with Grimthorp in Norfolk in the three-month period before the English Championships. Nightly, during that first week on ship, he took his meals by himself before the other guests had assembled, in the corner of the dining-room, confining himself to the bread, meat and porter which Moriarty had specified, then returning to his cabin.

By 10 January 1877, four days out, as Buck scrutinised a poster announcing a musical evening, several sporting papers in England had already given notice of his impending arrival. The first mention, in the *Sporting Life*, had appeared in December in a weekly column 'Doings on the Cinder Path', written by 'An Old Pedestrian', a pseudonym for Arthur Figg, who had run against Deerfoot on his English tour.

DOINGS ON THE CINDER PATH

News comes to us from across the Pond that two cowboys from the Wild West, by name of Buck Miller and Billy Joe Speed, will contest in the short sprints for the Amateur Championships to be held at the inaugural footracing competition at Stamford Bridge in April. No specifics are yet to hand, but the word is that Speed and Miller have run close to even time. Some of the cognoscenti are saying that when the Americans perfect their 'kangaroo start' (which appears to involve some form of crouch position) on the speedy surfaces of England they can go close to or inside even time for one hundred yards. This is a feat never before accomplished by an amateur and calls into question the status of the two Americans, a perennial problem for our amateur authorities when our Yankee cousins venture to cross the water to enter into contest upon the cinder path.

The response from the guardians of English pedestrianism had been immediate, and for weeks the columns of the sporting press had bristled with protests on the continuing vigour of

247

the British Bulldog. A letter to Bell's Life was typical of those received.

Sir,

I read with interest your intimations of 2 January of the arrival of two American cowboys to compete in our Amateur Championships. Since then other materials on Messrs Speed and Miller have appeared in the sporting press, attesting not only to their fleetness of foot but also to such matters as adventures among the Sioux and their skill with firearms.

Let me first make it clear that I bear no ill will towards our American cousins. I must, however, say that as a trainer of pedestrians over a period of thirty years (Howard of Chester, 'Crowcatcher' Lang, Jackson of Burnley, all world champions) it is my opinion that these Yanks have no possibility of running even time for one hundred yards, or even going close. The only footracers who can lay claim to feats of such calibre are your red-blooded English and Scotch pedestrians, men like Jackson of Sheffield or Clowney of Wigan, trained in the old English fashion in the Mother Country. Your native-born American is of a stock thinned by cross-breeding and your American trainer has never prepared men for big money match-races at such famous venues as Hackney Wick or Sheffield. No, sir, it is in the science of training and in the breeding that your crack sprint racer is made. That breed and that science live here in Old England rather than the Wild West, and your Yanks, Kangaroo Start or no, will prove to be no match even for our amateur pedestrians.

Yours in Sport,

Albert Clamp
(Trainer of Pedestrians)

But Buck, viewing the poster proclaiming the musical evening, was unaware of the furore seething ahead of him. He had found difficulty in sleeping on board ship, and decided that it might be best if for once he retire a little later. The musical evening, lasting as it did from 8.0 p.m. to 10.0 p.m., might ensure that he got to bed more fatigued. Anyhow, he decided, there was nothing in Moriarty's training programme saying that he could not enjoy a little culture.

Certainly the first items of the programme were nothing if not sleep-inducing. The first performer, a Cornish miner returning home from Connecticut, delivered a toneless rendering of 'Drake is Going West, M'lads', and was only dissuaded from embarking upon a series of bird-impressions by the intervention of Captain Clare himself. Then a group of Lancashire bell-ringers, fresh from a disastrous season at Barnum's in New York, filled the dining-room with their dismal clangings for what seemed like an eternity.

Next, an enormous American matron, who had nightly at the dinner table exhibited a gluttony to rival Falstaff, launched into an obscure German folk-song, her thin voice in sharp contrast to the massive frame from which it emanated

Buck looked around him in the candle-lit dining-room as the ship swayed in the light evening swell. The guests and the ship's officers sat at heavy oak tables which were secured by chains to the floor, the sixty first-class passengers filling the tiny room. On a small improvised stage Captain Clare had set a grand piano, similarly held fast by chains, on which the purser, Mr. Fenwick, had volunteered to accompany any passengers who wished to offer the assembled company a song.

Buck yawned. He could not bear much more of this. It was time to make tracks.

Then, suddenly, came Hettie Carr. Buck would never remember what it was that she sang — something about a woman called Mold and a garden — but that was of no account. Hettie Carr, pert, blonde and five foot four, dominated the room. She had a voice of power and range and was clearly a professional. Buck could not take his eyes off her clear milky skin, which was marred only by a mole on her upper lip, just above her lips. No, thought Buck, not marred, rather enhanced, focusing attention on those full lips. It was three songs more before a rapturous audience would allow her to leave the improvised stage. Buck was entranced.

For Hettie, her clear, blue eyes shining as her top notes filled the room, was lush, beautiful, almost edible.

As she returned from the stage and wound her way through the tables to return to her seat she passed Buck's table. The mole was even more wonderful than he had thought, a magnificent, a superlative mole. Hettie glanced down at him as she passed, and smiled. A moment later, when Captain Clare asked for further offers of performance, Buck's hand was reflexly raised, even though he had no clear idea what he was going to do.

As in a dream, he made his way through the tables towards the stage. He was hardly conscious of the Captain announcing him as 'the young American pedestrian who is travelling to England to take on the best English amateurs', no longer felt the sway of the ship or heard the creak of its timbers.

Buck stared dumbly at the audience in front of him as Captain Clare asked him for the second time what he wished to offer to the assembled guests. Before he could think, he had blurted out 'Richard III', and the Captain had motioned with his hands for silence. Buck had never played the part, but he had seen Moriarty do so many times, and he and Billy Joe had often mimicked Moriarty's rendering of the opening speech behind his back.

'Now is the winter of our discontent made glorious summer by this sun of York,' he began. The words poured from him but this time it was no act of mimicry. For Shakespeare's words had gone deep into Buck, found something in him and now issued from his lips renewed and refreshed.

Suddenly he was lost in the part and he reached forward to the piano, took from it the guttering, brass candlestick, and limped back to the centre of the stage as he had so often seen Moriarty do, the candle's swaying flame creating twisted patterns of light on his face. It was all terrible ham but Buck plunged ever deeper as he limped back and forward across the creaking stage. The audience, however, was transfixed. When he had finished there was spontaneous applause. Buck, blushing, nodded his thanks and stepped down from the platform.

He made his way beyond his table, towards Hettie. Fortunately, she had an empty chair at her table and he sat down beside her as the purser began a medley of popular ballads at the piano.

'You are a strange manner of athlete, Mr. Miller,' she said, her Scots voice soft and low.

Buck, heady with the success of his performance, felt as if he were drunk.

'I'm a pro,' he said.

'In the theatre?'

'The Theatre of the West,' said Buck, still flushed and pulsing from the applause

'Indeed,' said Hettie.

The words tumbled from Buck's lips, all about Moriarty and Eleanor and of their wanderings in the West, about his footracing achievements, albeit with little mention of Billy Joe: and he carefully omitted Mandy altogether.

'My father had no time for pedestrians,' rejoined his companion. 'He lost many a bawbee on those crooks, or so he used to tell me. Never bet on anything on two legs, that's what he used to tell me.'

Buck insisted that he was not one of that class of foot-racer, one who would bilk honest men out of their hard-won earnings. No, he was one of the upright breed, a man who always raced on his merits. Indeed, he was now travelling to England to take on the cream of the country's amateur runners on scratch terms. Hettie Carr seemed reassured and impressed.

Captain Clare was now introducing the ship's doctor, who was going to play Wagner upon a Jew's Harp.

Buck threw caution to the winds. Lightly squeezing Hettie's arm, he drew her to her feet and they left the dining-room.

When they had reached the deck they stood for several minutes at the ship's rail, looking out into the sea-dark, feeling the light sea-spray on their faces.

Later, Buck could put an exact time on when his shipboard preparations for the English Amateur Athletic Championships ended. It was at precisely 9 p.m. on 10 January 1877, on the ship's deck, when Hettie Carr, knocked off balance by the roll of the ship, reeled into him and he held her by the waist. Then she reached up on her tiptoes, pulled him down to her and kissed him. Her mouth tasted of raspberries. Buck had barely been able to keep his feet. He was gone, and that evening as he lay in his bunk, eyes staring at the ceiling, his mind was full of Hettie Carr.

All that next week Buck and Hettie had spent every waking hour in each other's company, talking of everything and nothing as they promenaded the decks of the *S.S. Harold*, ignoring the drenching salt spray and the howl of Atlantic winds. Hettie was a Glasgow Scot who had been brought to America in 1873 by her father, a popular comedian, and since then she had toured the West as 'The Scottish Jenny Lind'. She had been immensely successful, but it was in September 1876, whilst they had been on their way to Virginia City, that her father had contracted cholera and had died only a week later. She was presently making her way back to London to play middle of the bill at the Empire, Golders Green.

Buck listened entranced to Hettie's stories of her childhood in the bleak, rat-infested slums of Glasgow's Gorbals and of her experiences with her father in the roistering cow-towns of the West. But it would not have mattered to him if she had recited the alphabet. For Buck Miller had lost his head, and all thoughts of Billy Joe and of running those English lords into the dust, all that had gone in the daze that now hung upon him like a magic mist.

Nightly they sat together amid the dim swaying lights of the dining-room, as stewards hovered above them awaiting an order. Nightly Hettie and Buck went through the menu, and all memories of Moriarty's training diet were gone, washed away in waves of chilled Moselle.

And daily, surreptitiously, Buck Miller's body lost its athletic tone.

To Buck, Hettie was untouchable, a goddess, and his carnal instincts were consequently frozen, anaesthetised. Even holding hands, as sometimes they would do at dinner's end, was a privilege, and he would no more have thought of going further than of allowing his companion to pay for dinner.

It was strange. Buck had known many women, but they had fallen into two classes. The first had been the work-hardened females of the West, eager but invariably plain and usually sexually inexperienced. At the other end of the scale had been the 'frails' bought in desperation in trail-towns for a few bucks. Such ladies had been both vigorous and imaginative, but at ten tricks a day hardly had the motivation to be either passionate or loving. What was to happen with Hettie Carr was therefore outside Buck's experience. What occurred on the evening of 20 January 1877 came as a shock to Buck, for till that evening their days had ended in short kisses outside Hettie's cabin. Indeed, each night Buck had lain in bed staring at the ceiling, thinking of collective words for 'kisses'. For he had never before enjoyed the kiss as something in itself, rather always as a preamble to the inevitable intercourse.

A 'smother' sounded too cloying, a 'blizzard' too cold, as was a 'shower' too wet, a 'Welter' too vigorous. Buck settled on a 'melt' of kisses, the only word which in any way approximated to what he felt when he was joined so delightfully to Hettie's creamy, open mouth.

After the night of 20 January all thoughts of 'smothers',

'blizzards' or even 'melts' were made irrelevant. For it was then that at exactly 10.30 p.m. Hettie Carr had drawn him gently into her cabin.

Buck would, in future years, recall every moment of that night. And at first, in the darkness of Hettie's cabin, its gloom broken only by an occasional shaft of moonlight as the ship rolled, he felt only the touch of restless, delicate hands, and heard only the sound of Hettie's lilting Scots brogue.

Hettie's hands seemed everywhere. As she unbuttoned his waistcoat, all the while crooning his name, her other hand was on his neck, then her fingers probing and caressing his ear. And then she was behind him, pulling off his jacket at his right shoulder, her left hand between his legs, teasing him before being quickly withdrawn.

Buck was in a sweet haze, his legs barely able to support him. Hettie took his arm and gently guided him to the edge of the bed, where he sat down. Then she bent to her knees, unlaced his shoes and took off his socks, fondling his bare feet as she did so.

Next she stood up and unbuckled Buck's belt, then pulled down his trousers, all the while crooning his name. 'Buck, Buck, Buck', she intoned, almost singing the words. She pushed him on to his back and gently pulled down his long-johns. Buck, swamped by the moment, lay on the bed, his breath coming from him in deep gasps.

But Hettie did not take off Buck's shirt. Instead, she lay parallel to him, her hands moving like trapped butterflies beneath it.

Then, suddenly, Buck awoke, aware that this tiny creature, protected behind her cage of stays and swathed in endless petticoats, had so far taken every initiative.

He sat up, taking Hettie by the shoulders. He pushed her on to her face and quickly unbuttoned the back of her dress, ripping away the buttons if they did not immediately disengage themselves.

He took Hettie from the bed and, standing her up, pulled down her dress to her ankles. There was no point messing around with stays. Standing behind her, he put his hands on both sides of them and ripped them off in a single movement.

Hettie's 'Buck, Buck, Buck,' had now lost its slow crooning quality. Now a new rasp had entered her voice and his name tumbled from her lips without control.

Buck struggled with the froth of petticoats but it was no use: it was a battle in unknown territory, and short of tearing the material to shreds there was no way forward for him. But Hettie was equal to the moment. She slipped a button at her waist, reached back to undo her bodice and release her breasts, and in a moment all her softness had flooded out to him.

Buck scooped Hettie into his arms and lifted her on to the bed. For a moment he paused and they looked at each other. There was plenty of time.

'What if my Richard III had been awful?' he said.

'You mean, would I have noticed you?'

He nodded, his face deep in the pillow.

'I picked you out the day you came on the ship,' said Hettie.

'So it was just a matter of time?'

'Before I got you to notice *me*.'

For the next week, Buck and Hettie left her cabin only for meals — and rarely for them, preferring instead to have their food brought to them. Sometimes they lay in bed all day simply kissing; but Buck's 'melt' of kisses were not the simple and direct embraces of their chaste first meetings. Now they took the form of an infinity of nibblings and lickings and suckings in which the direct contact of lips was merely the starting-point for the day's pleasures. For Hettie, ever loving and attentive, there seemed to be no imagining of Buck's that was not within her compass and upon which she could not improve. A few days short of Liverpool, Buck lived in a sweet and endless dream — albeit nine pounds heavier than when he had embarked.

It came therefore as a surprise that when they were a day from Liverpool Hettie had suggested that Buck resume his morning training and, after their final coupling on the evening before, that he also resume occupancy of his room. They would meet after breakfast, she added, then disembark together and make plans for a meeting in London later that month.

That morning of 7 February, with Liverpool in sight, less than a mile away, was agony to Buck, for even a half-mile warm-up trot around the deck in the light sea mist made him gasp. He could, for the first time in his life, feel fat move on him as he ran. He had been five pounds or so above running-weight when the voyage began, but now the lack of outdoor exercise, combined with the extra intake of food and wine, meant he was a full stone overweight. There was no question of a few wind-sprints along the deck. Sweating profusely, he staggered, rubber-legged, down to his cabin to sponge down and prepare for breakfast. As he leant over the basin he saw his belly flop, white and pudgy, and he belched loudly. Thank God Moriarty could not see him now.

When he went to breakfast Hettie was not at her table, and Buck sat alone for half-an-hour before asking a steward to rouse her. Only a few minutes later the man returned.

'Miss Carr has gone, sir.'

'Gone?'

'Yes, sir. Taken off by boat by some gentlemen this morning. About seven o'clock, sir, or so I understand.'

George Grimthorp could not believe that the Buck Miller he saw before him on the rain-swept quay at Liverpool was the man whom Moriarty had described in his letter. Surely this puffy, whey-faced young man was not the fellow who had gone close to even time over a hundred yards?

Grimthorp stood, a small, gnome-like man, dressed in seal-skin jacket and trousers, his peaked cap dwarfing his lined, brown face. He walked forward along the quay, through the

256

crowds, to welcome the American. The Yank had a firm grip — that was something to be thankful for — but his eyes were dull and he seemed abstracted. Grimthorp noted that his waist was thick, his complexion pale, and there was even a hint of a double chin. The good life, thought Grimthorp acidly. It was ever thus. It would surely take more than a few weeks of physic to scour the Yank's system of its excesses.

For Buck, the trip to Norfolk was a nightmare. He felt sick in the pit of his stomach, a sickness which would not leave him, as he sat on the train opposite Grimthorp and the endless miles clicked past on the way to Norwich. From the shared rapture of the *S.S. Harold* he had come to sit with a dour stranger, with a face like a dried-up orange, looking out upon a flat, sleet-swept February landscape. Where was she? Why had Hettie gone? The questions rang like bells in Buck's head all through the train trip and the weary miles by horse and trap to the Fen Inn.

The inn stood out like a single wind-scoured gravestone on the desolate Norfolk plain. It was a grey, two-storeyed building, just off a muddy, rutted lane. Its sign creaked in the wind that swept the fen. So this was the Godforsaken spot where he was to train, thought Buck as he descended from the trap; cold as Alaska and lonely as a lighthouse.

They were greeted at the door by another man, a big, thickset young fellow with a smiling open face and potato nose. He was introduced as Sean Casey, a fist-fighter in training under Grimthorp. Something about Sean made Buck feel better despite the heart-sick feeling inside him.

As they entered the inn Buck wondered who on earth could possibly seek social communion in such a bleak, sepulchral den. For the low-beamed saloon held little more than a bar plus a few bare benches; not a splash of colour, a spittoon or a dancing lady in sight. Upstairs, his room was little better: a flat-board bed with hay mattress, a dresser and wash-bowl — that was all. Home sweet home, thought Buck — till April.

Grimthorp was well-named. He was a Lancashire man, a miner brought up in a hard school, in a world where men would bet on anything that moved. He had been a half-miler and miler in the 1840s and had run five yards behind the great George Reed, when the latter had been the first man in the world to break two minutes for half a mile. Then, in 1858, he had himself been the first runner to go inside four and a half minutes for the mile, running 4 minutes 29.5 seconds on the turnpike road at Newmarket. He had been trained by the most vigorous disciple of the Barclay School, the renowned George Hall of Formby; training, he had been taught, toughened a man, inured him to hardship, purified him. The race, when it came, after the period of preparation, should be a relief.

Buck reflected ruefully that Moriarty, using a Scots phrase of his father, would probably have said that Grimthorp 'smiled with deeficulty', and this Buck was to find in his first painful fortnight at Fen Inn. Twice daily he took his 'sweats', walking seven miles in a heavy greatcoat, then returned to lie for hours perspiring under a feather quilt. Once a day he took Grimthorp's version of Black Jack, which seemed to reach his guts before he could even make the door of his room. Even Buck's rest was supervised, for Grimthorp, ever mindful of Mary Five Fingers, had sewn a bobbin on to the back of Buck's nightshirt to keep him from lying on his back.

The only redeeming feature of that privy-bound first fortnight was Sean Casey. Each day Sean accompanied Buck out along the windswept fenland roads on his two 'sweats', enlivening the four hours of walking with an endless stream of anecdote and reminiscence. Sean was in preparation to fight Jem Smith, the Knareborough Bottlesmasher, in mid-March, bare-knuckles, an illegal event, for two hundred guineas. He had already fought twice, once in Ireland in a bout which had begun as a bat-room brawl with a lout who turned out to be the Champion of Kerry. Sean despatched the Kerry Man with a right to the jaw after only ten rounds. He had then been taken in hand by Grimthorp and a Barnsley bookmaker called John J. John and set against the Kent Man, Butcher, whose jaw he had broken in the second round. To Sean, who had earned five shillings a week and his potatoes slaving twelve hours a day on a Donegal farm, even Grimthorp's training came as a pleasure. Already he had fifty guineas safely back with his mother in Kilkerry, and after the fight with Smith, he declared, he would finish with scrapping and return to Ireland to buy his own farm.

By contrast, for Buck, for the first time training was drudgery, something which was being done to him rather than something he was doing for himself. He felt hollow inside, and although he lost five pounds in bodyweight in his first week at the Fen Inn and four pounds in the second he felt no strength flood back into his limbs. He was weak and flaccid, and Grimthorp could see it in his eyes. On 22 February the trainer despatched a missive to New York:

My dear Moriarty,
Your man Miller has now been a fortnight with me. On arrival he was in as sorry a state as I have ever seen a professional man: a stone or more overweight, pasty complexion, eyes dull — all the signs of over-indulgence of every manner.

Since his arrival he has lost close on a stone, but there is still no heart in him, no mettle in his work. Since he has begun to shed his fat I can see beneath a fine, strapping physique, much evidence of good exercise in early youth, so there is all to play for. The special exercises and the development of his running will now commence and I would suggest that we progress to Plan II, as described in your letter of 4 September, and would advise that you lay your money accordingly on your arrival. I look forward to renewing your acquaintance on 4 April.

Yours in sport,
George Grimthorp.

To Buck, Grimthorp had at first appeared another Sergeant Routledge, a martinet with a fixed and immutable programme for the training of athletes, within which there was no flexibility and from which there was to be no escape. But later, even in his lovesick state, he could see that there was something more to his tormentor. For the Lancashire man had a feel for athletes, a sensitivity which enabled him to know when to push his man and when to leave him be. That touch, that art, had made George Grimthorp one of the world's best trainers, and although it was as yet having little effect upon Buck it was showing great returns with the more responsive Sean Casey. The Irishman was now rock-hard, one hundred and seventy—six pounds of bone and muscle, capable of going fifty rounds with any man in England. Buck could almost see Sean change as he peaked towards 18 March. Daily he stood behind the heavy bag as the Irishman, wearing light leather gloves, thudded hundreds of punches into it; or watched in the gloom of the austere gymnasium in the upper rooms of the Fen Inn while sweat sprayed from Sean as he performed his dumbbell exercises. The Donegal man was showing the same level of commitment as he himself had possessed on his departure from New York in December — and which now seemed as far from him as that city itself.

Buck would have gained no confidence had he read an article signed 'Old Pedestrian' which appeared on 7 March in the sporting magazine *Bell's Life*.-

Our information is that George Grimthorp has the American 'cowboy sprinter', Miller, in hard preparation for the Amateur Athletic Club Championships at his secret training quarters somewhere in Norfolk, in harness with the Irish pugilist Sean Casey. Miller has been reported to be close to evens for one hundred yards but my spies tell me that the Yankee left his ship at least a stone heavier and ten yards slower than when he embarked, and is as yet showing no vigour in his preparations. Other intelligences are that the Barnsley sportsman, William Bunn, has laid heavy on the fast young Scotchman McDougall for the 100 yards in the Amateur Athletic Club Championships at Stamford Bridge come 28 April, so all eyes will be on the Scot and the Yankee.

The letter for Buck arrived on the morning of 17 March, just as their party was leaving for Casey's match against Jem Smith. In the excitement of the moment Buck stuffed it into a top pocket as he ascended the trap. Having followed every aspect of Sean's preparation since his arrival he was now immersed in the fight, and Grimthorp had agreed that he could work the sponge in Sean's corner.

The party aboard the trap comprised Casey, Grimthorp and the bookmaker John J. John, together with a couple of gnarled, flat-nosed bruisers whose task it was to protect the Irishman on his way to the ring. All was secrecy, for the police had known for months the date of the 'mill', but not the venue, and it would go hard with them if the law were to discover it.

They travelled a mazy, circuitous forty miles that first day, stopping at the King's Head, Downham Market, for the night. They were just a few miles short of the border of Lincolnshire. For all Buck knew, they could have been in Lancashire or Timbuctoo.

When at last they stopped, he was deputed to share Sean's room, to ensure that the Irishman got a good night's sleep: any sign of unrest and he was to report immediately to Grimthorp, three rooms away down the narrow corridor. Too much was at stake for the smallest detail to be ignored.

The group, unnaturally quiet, enjoyed the same frugal meal as Sean: underdone lamb chops, bread and porter. It was only when they were all about to retire for the night that Buck remembered the letter. As Sean undressed behind him, Buck read by the light of a flickering lamp. The letter, two tiny scented pages, was throughout scarred by crossings-out of half-written words or even whole phrases:

261

Palace Theatre,
Leeds,
Yorkshire
10 March 1877

My dearest Buck,

How can I describe to you the despair that I have felt since we parted, my guilt, my shame? But first let me be honest with you, and leave it to you to take what action you may see fit.

My father was in debt to an English bookmaker named William Bunn before he died last year, having borrowed the money to finance our American tour. The debt had, alas, not been fully paid on my father's death and I expressed to Mr Bunn my feeling that I had a moral obligation to pay the remaining sum.

A few days before I left New York for England, I was approached by an American friend of Mr Bunn's, a certain Mr Flynn. He told me of you and of your mission to the English Athletic Championships in London. He and Mr Bunn had already placed considerable sums at long odds on another runner, a Mr McDougall. Mr Flynn put it to me that if I were to effectively deflect you from your daily training on the *S.S. Harold* then he would absolve me of my remaining debts, and meet the costs of my passage as well. This I foolishly agreed to do.

Here I must ask you, dearest, to accept the absolute truth of what I am about to say. All the intimate occurrences of our crossing (and I dare not, from modesty, commit them to paper) came truly from my heart and not as a result of my agreement with Mr Bunn.

Buck, dear heart, you are the last thing on my eyelids at night and the first thing in the morning. Thus, even if you never wish to see me again I feel that I must place on paper, shunning all modesty, that which I truly feel for you.

Your dear
Hettie

Buck sat in the candlelight, face flushed, his heart thudding as his eyes raced across the pages of the letter. Their contents rushed into him, filling,him, and the tears flowed from his eyes, staining the pink surface of the paper. He felt that he must read the letter again, to convince himself that it was real. He laid the pages on the bed, wiping his eyes with the tail of his nightshirt. This time he read the letter slowly, savouring each word. Then he leapt to his feet, holding the letter aloft, and danced a jig on the creaking floorboards of the room. Sean, at the wash-bowl, stopped lapping water against his face and stood stupefied.

'Sean,' Buck shouted. 'She loves me!'

But the young boxer's thoughts were elsewhere. He forced a distant smile.

'Aye, Buck,' he said quietly. 'She loves you.'

By the time George Grimthorp's party had completed their circuitous route and arrived at their destination, at 7 a.m. on the morning of 18 March, there were at least two thousand members of the Fancy milling about in semi-darkness on the broad, grassy Lincolnshire field. They had come from as far away as Glasgow, Paris and Dublin, a motley band of gambling men, whores, pickpockets and prize-ring cognoscenti. Since before six that morning they had come by carriage, on horse or on foot, and had laid their bets with bookmakers who had set themselves up with their blackboards on a ridge above the roped-off square of cropped grass in the centre of the field.

The bookmakers drank from hip-flasks, while the Fancy had to settle for hot tea and chocolate from vendors who had disposed themselves in makeshift canvas stalls on the fringes of the field.

The smart money was on Smith, who had taken only nineteen rounds to reduce the Yorkshireman Ned Bolt to a helpless pulp in September 1876, and only two rounds to lay senseless in deep snow a Frenchman by the name of Lacoste who had foolishly ventured across the Channel in January. Betting ceased at 8 a.m. as the preliminaries for the contest began in a ring wreathed by morning mist, with Smith now at six to four on and the odds against Sean Casey varying from two to one to nine to four against. Buck laid fifty pounds on his training partner at two to one.

The mob, held back from the ropes by a team of bruisers employed by John J. John and Smith's backer, Albert Gunn, pressed in on the ring as the referee, a flat-nosed Welsh pug called Dai Gabriel, called both men to the scratch.

To Buck, Smith at fourteen stone three pounds looked over-weight and out of condition. True, he had a sturdy, powerful trunk and massive arms, but his waist was thick and puffy with no sign of abdominal definition. By contrast, Sean Casey, though a good two inches smaller and two stone lighter than his opponent and clearly outreached, had not an ounce of spare flesh on his body. The Donegal man glowed with fitness. As they came to their marks, Buck laid another twenty pounds on Sean.

The three men stood, a tableau, swathed waist-high in mist as a raw red winter sun rose on the grassy ridge behind them. Sporadic shouts from the crowd broke the silence. Buck was glad that he was well clad in a sealskin coat as he sat with Grimthorp in Sean's corner with the mob straining around them. He would always remember the two smells that pervaded the fresh morning air: the stale smell of whisky and the freshness of wet cut grass. That and the goosepimples on Sean Casey's white back as he stood at the scratch facing Jem Smith.

Neither man had been recognisable since the twentieth round. Then, half-way into the twenty-fifth, Jem Smith, his face already a bloody gargoyle, had split Sean Casey's nose, causing the blood to spout and mat on Sean's hairy, sweating chest. Now, after one and a quarter hours and in the forty- eighth round, it was hardly a question of who would win: rather of which of the men would survive.

But it had been the sound of the first big hit that had shocked Buck. It was in the fourth round and Casey had gone down at once, blood from his split cheek staining the damp grass below him. The noise was the same one that Sean's own fists had made when he practised on the heavy bag; it was the knowledge that this time contact was being made with his friend's flesh that gave the sound an extra significance to Buck.

From the beginning the roped-off square of grass had been defined as much by the noise around it as by the ropes themselves. It was a haying sound, of men watching something harsh, something at the same time both fine and awful. By contrast, the happenings within the ring were relatively silent; the gasping of men whose lungs felt hedged by thorns, the thud of hits and the groans as they were received, the thump as the contestants were smashed or thrown to the wet ground.

To Buck there was nothing noble or manly about this, whatever the courage of the contestants; the bout, for all its London Rules, was simply ritualised butchery, as inhuman as any bullfight. Sean, the gentle, joking Sean, had become a beast, using hardened, whisky-soaked fists as bludgeons to batter the blubbery Smith into submission.

Up till the fortieth round it had been going Sean's way. Smith's mouth was open, blood and sweat pouring down his face, and his breathing had gone. His corner were having trouble getting their man back to the scratch at the prescribed time of thirty seconds. Sean, though badly cut about the face, kept away from Smith, peppering him with cutting blows, while the giant Smith had tried desperately to get in close, to use his superior wrestling skills.

Then, a round later, had come the rains, lashing down, cold and relentless, from the grey March sky, and soon reducing the ring to a quagmire. It was clear that Sean could no longer be sure of his footing on the slimy surface, and in the forty-second round Smith caught up with him, cross-buttocking him into the mud.

After that, the Irishman had gone down time after time and started to slow up. Now the lumbering Smith began to make contact with his own blows, reducing Sean's lips to a red blubber.

By the forty-eighth, both men were red, muddy nightmares, impervious to the hissed advice of their trainers between rounds and the raving of the crowd, remote to everything except the desire to survive and conquer. Each time Buck sponged Sean down he kept his eyes from the pouting, jagged cuts spurting blood which Grimthorp now made no attempt to staunch.

In the forty-ninth neither fighter made any real contact, swinging wildly, then falling upon each other in the centre of the ring, exchanging pathetic half-blows to the body before falling forward in a single heap in the mud, their blood mingling with the black slime. Both men were done, only animal instinct keeping them erect.

Then came the shriek of whistles. It emanated from the grassy ridge directly above the ring, as a row of black- uniformed policemen appeared as silhouettes on the skyline. The policemen, about fifty in number, and all wearing distinctive top-hats, descended in a line with their batons upon the mob, which dispersed, skidding and falling over in the mud as they went.

'Get out!' roared Grimthorp, throwing down his bucket and sponge.

Buck reflexly threw off his coat and sprinted blindly through crowds that squelched and slipped and slithered in the wetness of the vast field. Behind him, Sean and Smith disengaged from their grappling and moved with a speed that belied the forty-nine rounds they had just endured. In a flash, they were under the ropes and bullocking their way like enraged animals through the panic-stricken mob now rushing from the whistles and batons of the Lincolnshire Constabulary. Back in the ring two policemen were wrestling with a fat bookmaker. Grimthorp, who had been at Buck's

266

side only a moment before, had vanished. All was shouting, whistling and cursing as two thousand men scattered across plough and grass, through hedge and over fence.

Buck, fifty yards from the ring and in the middle of the field, looked about him, the rain running in streams down his face. Surprisingly, he felt no fear. The main body of the police had come from one direction, the ridge above the ring, and were dispensing rough justice with their batons as they dragged struggling miscreants back towards a row of carriages that stood at the top of the ridge ready for their new occupants. Most of the mob had scattered sideways to left and right through gaps in the surrounding hedgerows, but were being driven back by' policemen who had lain there in wait for them. Thirty yards ahead lay a water-filled fifteen-foot wide ditch and beyond that a four-foot-high barred wooden fence. Buck sprinted towards it, weaving his way through the escaping crowd. He cleared the ditch without mishap, only just missing the head of a spectator below him who was desperately wallowing his way through its muddy waters. Buck took the fence in a vault, slithering on to his face in the slimy mud on the other side, then getting to his feet to splatter through a doughy, ploughed field. He had not moved so fast since the Run of the Arrow: even the clogging clay of the field could not interrupt his rhythm. Buck flowed over it, and in a few hundred yards was well clear of the whistling and hallooing behind him.

It was only when he was aware that he could no longer hear the noise of police-whistles that he realised that he had been running for at least two miles. He looked around him, but could hear nothing but the wind and the screech of birds.

He was surprised to find that, despite the speed of his flight, he was hardly out of breath. He had run two miles across this cold Godforsaken country and yet he was feeling good. It was surely the same as it had been in the Run of the Arrow . . . Not only did he have pace, he had endurance, that rare ability to sustain speed. Buck smiled to himself as he squelched along

267

the muddy lane, steam beginning to rise from him as the rain stopped and he started to dry off.

For over an hour he wandered about in the mean winter sun, finding no sign of man or dwelling, only endless fields divided by muddy ditches. Then the rain started again, pouring down in steady streams. It ran down Buck's face, mixing with the mud and grit; he could even feel it pouring in streams inside his shirt. He looked around him, across the sodden fields, more keenly aware of the cold and the fact that he had not the slightest idea where he was. There was no one to be seen, and he had no idea how he would find his way back to Grimthorp and the Fen Inn. Where was Norfolk anyway — north or south? Buck took stock. Then, plodding along the side of a hedge, he caught sight of a farm-road on the other side defined by deep, grey wheel-tracks. He made his way towards it, his feet slopping about inside his shoes, and scrambled through the hedge, ripping his legs.

After he had gone about half a mile along the cart-track the rain stopped, again the clouds cleared and the weak March sun re-appeared. In the distance Buck could see a thin spiral of smoke. He squelched along the grassy centre of the farm-road towards it, his clothes chill upon his body, feeling the goosepimples rise on his back. About a hundred yards short of a grey-brick farmhouse was a large wooden barn and Buck jogged towards it, his legs uncomfortably stiff and tight.

The door of the barn had been pulled to, but it was not locked. Buck cautiously pushed on it, closing it behind him as he made his way into the smelly gloom. He felt cold, sick and tired. Then, as he peered into the shadows of the barn, a shaft of sunlight pierced through a crack in the wall, revealing a shadowy bundle in the hay in a corner. The bundle moved. Buck went closer. The bundle snored. Buck was now above it. He smiled and shook his head. There, lying in the hay, arms around each other and sound asleep, lay Sean Casey and Jem Smith.

13

CHAMPION OF THE WORLD

Billy Joe had been surprised at Moriarty's placid reception of the damning cable from Grimthorp. There had been no rage, no tantrums, even though it was very clear that Buck had let everyone down. Billy Joe knew the cause could only have been a woman, for nothing else could possibly have deflected his friend. He hoped that she had been worth it — that the lady had done Buck over good and proper: it would serve him right for all the advice about Mandy he had ladled out. No, Moriarty had taken it all in his stride, though Billy Joe also knew that it would now need more than the rigours of the English Method to hone Buck into any sort of sprinting shape by April; especially if a lady were involved, for it would not merely be a problem of fitness, but one of conviction.

Moriarty, however, although quite unconcerned about Buck's poor condition, clearly attached a great deal of importance to a meeting on their arrival in England with the officials of the Amateur Athletic Club, one at which he would have to present Buck's amateur *bona fides*. To Billy Joe this seemed irrelevant. They were going to England to pick up a packet on Buck creaming all those lords and marquises; if Buck were not in good shape it was surely better to forget about the championships altogether and simply enjoy a vacation. For once, Billy Joe could not understand Moriarty; and nor it seemed could anyone else.

With only a few weeks to go till their departure for England the Texan, his injured hamstring still giving him trouble, was feeling generally depressed. Moriarty was absorbed in rehearsals, Buck was in dire straits in distant England, and his own relationship with Mandy had just reached a new low.

This last set-back followed immediately on her performance as Cordelia to Booth's Lear at Niblo's Theatre, which had been occasioned by the late withdrawal through illness of the famous actress Charlotte Hall. Mandy, though delivering a brave performance, did not yet possess the technical equipment to cope with the vastness of Niblo's or the charisma of Edwin Booth. Her voice had indeed been 'gentle and low', but what had commended itself to Lear had made less impression on the audience.

The play itself had been a success, the cast taking five curtain calls, and Booth, though cognisant of Mandy's limitations, had been generous in his praise. Later, there had been a party at Booth's little Park Avenue apartment. The cast had poured into its brown, lamp-lit interior, admiring its walls decorated with pictures of past successes of Edwin and his father, Junius.

Mandy, still high from the magic of the performance, had been, like so many actresses, hungry for the slightest morsel of praise. Radiant in a yellow silk dress, she stood sipping champagne and surrounded by the bubble of the cast's excited chatter.

At her side, Moriarty and Eleanor were fulsome in their praise. Then Booth, looking at Billy Joe, who had sat down to rest his leg, asked the Fast Man's opinion of Mandy's performance.

'Good — leastways, as far as it went,' responded Billy Joe thoughtlessly, rising stiffly from his chair to make his way through the crowd of actors and stage staff towards a waiter offering champagne, seemingly unaware that Mandy was listening.

'Jesus,' he said as he limped awkwardly back across the room. 'This hamstring, it's still not healed up, Moriarty — doctor or no doctor.'

Moriarty did not reply, instead looking sideways at Mandy. He knew that she was struggling to control her distress.

Billy Joe sat down gingerly and, still oblivious of the coolness of the atmosphere, sipped his drink.

'Have you any other advice?' Mandy asked him at last.

'Just that it wasn't big enough,' he said tersely. This time Mandy did not respond, but the tears began to well in her eyes. Billy Joe went blithely on.

'You got to fill the stage, Mandy, like Edwin here. Grab the moment – that's what you always say, isn't it, Moriarty?'

Moriarty stood silent. No question of it, Billy Joe had put his finger on what had been missing. But why had he chosen a time like this to be so goddam honest?

It was Eleanor who tried to salvage the evening. 'When will the reviews be in, Edwin?' she asked.

But Mandy would not be deflected.

'I *know* I wasn't Charlotte Hall,' she said, her voice kept deliberately even. 'But it was the best I could do. I'm not like you, Billy Joe. I'm more like Buck — I've got to work at it. And that's something that someone like you isn't even interested in trying to understand, so you never will. Never!' Bitterly she repeated the final word.

Now Billy Joe's face flushed deep red. He looked up to Eleanor and Moriarty for support; but help there was unforthcoming. Muttering his apologies, he rose and limped off across the room. He opened the door and made his way downstairs, out into the street.

As he trudged aimlessly through the dark midnight streets, he acknowledged to himself how far away he must now be from becoming the person that Mandy wanted. If ever he had had a chance of getting through to her, his thoughtlessness this evening had ruined it. He found himself wishing he were with Buck in England, enjoying the simple pleasures of the Norfolk countryside.

Buck fell headlong over the top of the sandy ridge onto his face. He tried to vomit, but he did not have the strength. Instead he turned over onto his back, allowing the cool east wind to fan his sweat-soaked body, and wiped the grit from his lips.

He was dimly aware of Grimthorp above him, in black pin-stripe suit, waistcoat and bowler, a massive egg-shaped 1/100-second stop-watch in his hand. 'Fifty-one and three-tenths, give or take a hundredth,' said the trainer. 'Three seconds to go.'

They had visited the Sands twice a week since early March, Buck braving their cutting winds to run endlessly up their steep sandhills. But it was the Windmill Run that from the beginning had forced Buck to dig deep. The run, most of it made on soft sand, involved a distance of three hundred and thirty yards, first around a dilapidated old windmill rotting on the seashore, then back along hard beach sand and up fifty yards of soft, near-vertical sandhill to the finish. The first time Buck attempted it he was forced to crawl the final fifty yards, and spewed all over Grimthorp's polished shoes at the top. That had taken a lung-bursting sixty point four seconds.

From the outset, for no reason that Buck could understand, Grimthorp had insisted on forty-eight seconds as the target time for the 330 yards. Buck, carefully pacing himself, had cut it to fifty-six seconds on his second attempt, and now, on his sixth, had brought it down almost to fifty-one.

He sat up as Grimthorp draped a dressing-gown over his shoulders to protect him from the cold March breeze.

'That's it, Mr. Grimthorp,' he said. 'I don't have a yard left in me. Not a goddam yard.'

Grimthorp knelt down and sat on the sand beside Buck. 'We've got a saying up Lancashire way,' he said. 'Them that never gives up is them that's never beat.'

Buck wiped sweat from his face. 'And we've got a saying

back in Connecticut too,' he said. 'You can't get blood from stones.'

Every time they returned from Cromer Buck was left with an unspoken question. 'What in God's name had all this pounding up and down sandhills got to do with speed, with sprinting? True, he had come down in weight and was only five pounds off competition-weight. True, his muscles were now hard and strong. But Buck knew his body well enough to realise that there was no snap left in his legs, no punch, nothing to give power to the Kangaroo Start which he had at last mastered. So perhaps he had a heart as big as all outdoors; but that was going to do him little good over a short dash in April.

He had resisted putting the question, partly out of respect for Grimthorp and partly because of the guilt he still felt over the poor condition in which he had arrived in England. Maybe this was simply Grimthorp's way of carving out the broad outlines of fitness, and perhaps the honing and sharpening would take place later, in the next three weeks before the Stamford Bridge race. If so, Grimthorp was cutting it fine.

But Buck was in good heart. The letters from Hettie came in almost daily, letters which put in words things it made him blush to read. Grimthorp had a good idea of the source of the perfumed envelopes, but he let it pass. As long as his man was pursuing his preparation diligently he could ask no more. Grimthorp knew that Plan II was working to perfection. All that was needed now was Moriarty.

2 April 1877, Randolph Hotel, Oxford
Moriarty could feel the coolness in the atmosphere the moment he entered the hotel's committee room. There they were, seated formally round the long shining table, the worthies of English amateur athletics, the same class of stiff-necked, arrogant bastards as those who had forced his father to leave Glencalvie almost thirty years before. Moriarty was beckoned

273

to sit down at the end of the table by the chairman, Sir Murray Clark, a bald man in late middle-age with thick mutton-chop whiskers.

Clark, flanked by six committee members on each side, rustled through some papers in front of him before withdrawing one and peering at it through a monocle.

Here we are, Mr Moriarty,' he said. 'An entry form for the Championship Sprints, from a Mr Buck Miller, for whom I believe you act as a referee.'

Moriarty nodded.

'Miller?' said Clark. 'English?'

'No,' said Moriarty. 'German.'

There were grunts from both sides of the table.

'Just so,' said Clark. 'Now, Mr Moriarty, let me make my position — and indeed the committee's position — quite clear. We are able to establish the amateur credentials of our English athletes with no great difficulty. This is because most of them come from a class of professional men rather than from the ranks of the artisans.'

'Of course.'

'Where there *is* doubt then the committee has a responsibility to the sport to ensure that no one without *bona fide* amateur credentials is allowed to compete.'

'Indeed.'

'Now, your entry for Mr Miller presents us with certain problems. This is because, as yet, there is no amateur body in the United States able to validate the status of American athletes.'

Moriarty pondered for a moment.

'Might I ask the committee a question?' he said.

Clark nodded.

'As I understand it, your English amateurs regularly lay wagers on the outcome of their races.'

'Indeed they do, Mr Moriarty,' replied Clark.

'But this doesn't make them professionals?'

'No,' said Clark, smiling. 'These are private wagers between gentlemen, Mr Moriarty. There is therefore no question of racing for a money prize. That is quite a different matter.'

'I see,' said Moriarty, his face impassive. So it was really nothing to do with money, but everything to do with the kind of person who was wagering it. Run up a mountain for a pound in the Lake District and you were a 'pro', but wager a hundred guineas with Sir Murray Clark and you were still a true-blue amateur.

Clark sighed and laid down the entry form. 'Now, as you can see, Mr Moriarty, Mr Miller's proposed participation places us in somewhat of a quandary . . .'

'You mean you won't take my word?' said Moriarty.

'I wouldn't exactly put it that way,' said Clark.

'Then what way would you put it?'

'I mean that we require some further, and indeed some *substantial* proof that Mr Miller has never on any occasion competed for a money prize.'

Moriarty looked round the room, at the assembly of frock-coats and starched collars. These men would on 28 April open the world's finest stadium at Stamford Bridge and hope to draw to it a large crowd of fee-paying customers. The cowboy with the kangaroo start might put at least fifteen thousand on the gate, close on three hundred pounds of gate money into the struggling Amateur Athletic Club. And here was this august committee solemnly debating the status of possibly the one person who could make their meet a success.

'So what do you want from me?' he asked, his face expressionless.

Clark steepled his hands beneath his chin, his elbows on the table. 'Some further assurances of Mr Miller's status . . . With no disrespect to you, Mr Moriarty, from someone of standing, someone of whom we have heard.'

'I see,' said Moriarty. He reached into his inside pocket

and withdrew a white envelope, which he laid on the table. 'Perhaps this would do.'

The envelope was passed up the table to Clark, who inspected it and broke the seal.

'Could you read it out?' asked Moriarty.

Clark cleared his throat. 'I hereby declare that Buck Miller is an athlete of amateur status, having never competed for a money wager or prize.'

There was silence. 'It is signed and sealed,' Clark added, laying down his monocle, 'by the late General George A. Custer.'

3 April 1877, Norfolk

It was perfect, just as Moriarty had imagined, though Eleanor and Mandy thought it spooky. The Fen Inn, stark and austere, jutting from bright, windswept Norfolk fens now freckled with early spring flowers, was the ideal spot for the training of a pedestrian. Moriarty breathed in deeply. The air was like wine. A month here, four weeks of cleansing and purification, and even he himself might be able to take on the miler Tulloch and all those other 'peds' he had read about in the English sporting press.

But he would resist that temptation, for all his thoughts were on the English Plan. Grimthorp had done exactly what he had asked of him, for Buck appeared in excellent condition, with that drawn, sucked-in look and brightness of eye that betokened true fitness.

Buck, for his part, had been delighted to see Moriarty and his party, Billy Joe in particular. Now they were all together again, and they would see what he, Buck Miller, could really do.

A day after their arrival, they went to Cromer for a final trial. Grimthorp had brought with him a canvas windbreak and some chairs, and Mandy and Eleanor took what refuge they could, cowering within the windbreak as the cold east wind whipped around them in the bright spring sun.

Soon Grimthorp, along with Moriarty, Buck and Billy Joe, was standing at the top of the sandhills. Grimthorp explained to them the windmill course. He asked Billy Joe if he would like to try it, but the Fast Man declined, pleading injury: he could see that it was not a sprinter's course.

Soon Buck was set upon his way and he bounded off, the second-hand on Grimthorp's watch flicking round its big dial. At the windmill, roughly half-way, Grimthorp noted that Buck was a good second inside his best time, at twenty-four seconds; but the return trip along the beach was into a strong wind.

Buck, evenly pounding along into the wind on the hard beach sand, felt as if he could run for ever. Then came the final hill, the fifty yards of sand-dune up to Grimthorp and the others, and it was at that point that the pace of his previous running caught up with him. Suddenly his legs went soft and heavy and Buck had to drive hard with his arms as he struggled up the silky yellow sand towards Billy Joe and Moriarty, trying to give impulse to his flagging calf muscles. He did not hear Grimthorp's cry of 'Fifty seconds dead!' as he fell on his face in front of him.

28 April 1877, Stamford Bridge, London
The gates had had to be closed at one o'clock, two hours before the first event, and the band of the Scots Guards was prevailed upon, on the promise of four pints of beer per man, to start its performance an hour early.

The main draw was undoubtedly the Yankee, Buck Miller, the cowboy with the kangaroo start, the fellow who had run the Sioux off their feet and who, so the papers said, had been the only man to survive the massacre of Little Big Horn. Forty-two thousand five hundred and seventy-one spectators poured into London's newly-built stadium, all eager to set eyes upon the man reputed to be the fastest fellow ever to don a spiked shoe.

Certainly the Yank seemed to be a fine, well-set young man, and the ground was hushed as he got down to his mark in his heat, kangaroo-style, just as the sporting papers had predicted. The Yank left his men early and cruised in, to the cheers of the crowd, in 10.8 seconds, clearly reserving himself for the later rounds.

The semi-final was closer, with the Yank finding another two yards to win, by a yard, in 10.6, over the Oxford fellow Le Mesurier, with the Scotsman, McDougall, running two yards faster to win the other semi-final.

The rest of the day's sport was merely a prelude to the final of the Dash. True, some fellow from Oxford had gone close to six feet in the high jump and Shepherd from Ulverston had managed ten feet in the pole-vault, but that was your German gymnastics rather than your true English athletics. Athletics was running, and running was what forty-two thousand English men (and a fair sprinkling of ladies) had come to Stamford Bridge to see.

It was five o'clock when the starter got the finalists to their marks, and the bookmakers had stopped taking bets on the Yank, who was now three to one on, with McDougall at evens and the rest of the field at three and four to one against. It was clear that the American had not shown the full power of his kangaroo start in the heats because he had come out of his holes in line with the other runners, only going on to win in the final forty yards; but the betting fraternity were not to be fooled. When the kangaroo start was given its full expression it was reputedly worth another two yards, possibly more.

The Yank had held up the start for several minutes while he used a trowel to scoop out his starting-holes. Then the starter got all the runners to their marks, the Yank low down, right knee on the ground, the others standing above him in stiff, frozen poses. On 'get set' the Yank raised his hips, while the others assumed their statuesque standing-start positions, arms high.

Then the gun, and the runners were released. But it was the

Scotsman, McDougall, who showed first at twenty yards, with Miller struggling two yards back, in fourth position. So much for the kangaroo start. At fifty the Yank had closed to third, only a yard and a half back, but it was still McDougall. Thirty yards on and the Yank had pulled in another foot, still in third position, but as they hit the tape it was McDougall by a long yard, in 10.2 seconds, with Miller second. The bookmakers cheered loud and long.

To the cognoscenti of pedestrianism, who had laid no money on Miller, it was just as they had expected. The Yankee, kangaroo start or no, was simply not up to snuff, and all the tales about running away from Redskins showed only that your Indian was even less of a match for an Englishman than a Yankee. No question, though, that it was a fair race, for Miller had given all he had; as he walked, head down, towards the tunnel leading under the stand it could be seen, clear as crystal, that the Yank was a much saddened man.

Buck could taste the tears as they ran down his cheeks, and he paused to wipe his eyes before continuing his slow walk towards the tunnel, where waited Grimthorp, Moriarty and Billy Joe. It had all been wrong from the start, and not merely because of his debaucheries on the *S.S. Harold*. Simply, Grimthorp's training had taken the snap out of his legs. He could have run forever at his finishing speed but was incapable of generating any *thrust* in the first twenty yards: he had been left with too much to do. He had been strong, but he had not been fast.

As he walked through a blizzard of boos and programmes which fluttered down from the terracing the result was posted on blackboards and carried to the corners of the ground by white-coated stewards. Three thousand miles, to be whipped good by a college boy, an amateur. Yet, for all his sense of shame, as he approached the others he saw that Moriarty was smiling.

'Good run,' he said. 'Under the circumstances.'

'Good!' exploded Billy Joe. 'He ran like a toad.'

'Of course he did,' said Moriarty, enigmatically. 'What else could he do?'

'I should've won,' growled Buck.

'No,' said Moriarty. 'That wasn't the plan. It never was.'

'The plan? What plan?' said Billy Joe.

'For Buck to run against the fastest man in the world,' replied Moriarty. 'A pro.'

'But he's just been beaten by an amateur,' said Billy Joe.

'Yes. But that was over a hundred yards. And I told you — that was never my plan, or Grimthorp's. Not from the beginning.'

'What are you up to, Moriarty?' said Buck, suddenly aware that there was something in the wind.

'To race you over a quarter of a mile,' came the reply.

5 May 1877, Barnsley, Yorkshire

'Ah'm champion of t'world, tha knows.' Josiah Headley's features were barely visible through the coal-dust which covered them, but his eyes were bright blue in the white skin of their sockets. On his head he wore a brown sack and his body was entirely covered in what appeared to be a black leather smock, tied at the waist with thick rope. He looked down upon Moriarty, Buck and Billy Joe from a coal-cart, holding reins which kept in check two emaciated black ponies.

It had begun to rain, and the water caused white stripes to form on Headley's face. As they stood on the slimy cobbled streets of Barnsley looking up at him, Buck could not believe that this was truly Josiah Headley, the man who had broken forty-nine seconds for a quarter of a mile.

'Never been beat,' said Headley, wiping his face with the back of his hand and smearing the coal-dust in a grey paste across his mouth and cheeks.

'So how do you wish it to be arranged?' said Moriarty.

Headley put two fingers to his nose and cleared it. 'You'd best see my manager,' he said. 'Mr Bunn.'

A week later the following statement appeared in the *Sporting Life*:

> Mr. William Bunn wishes it to be known that on 1 September 1877, at the Victoria Running Grounds, Barnsley, Josiah Headley will contest with the American Buck Miller, over the full quarter-mile distance, for a purse of £200 per man, winner take all; and a World Championship belt; and that Sir Edward Astley will put up a further £ 1,000 for any man who goes inside Dick Buttery's world record of 48¼ seconds. Articles have already been signed at the King's Head, Barnsley, the gate to be split evenly between the runners.

For it had been the biggest con of all, one spanning three thousand miles, and one in which Buck himself had been well and truly taken in. It had never been Moriarty's aim for Buck to win at Stamford Bridge. Indeed, it had been quite the opposite. Bunn's use of Hettie Carr to lead Buck astray had been a bonus, for she had unwittingly guaranteed the success of Moriarty's plan, which was for Buck to lose over the short distance, thus building up big odds for the later challenge against Headley over the long sprint. Grimthorp's training in Norfolk on the windswept Cromer Sands had been geared not only to blunt his speed but to give Buck a base of endurance. This training might have taken the edge from his sprint-speed, but it was to be the platform for later preparation to take on Josiah Headley, the fastest 'ped' in the world, a man who had never been beaten in match competition at any distance from a furlong to six hundred yards.

Buck's child-like belief in Grimthorp, unquestionably one of the greatest trainers of footracers in the world, and his guilt over his shipboard excesses, had blinded him to the nature of the training to which he had been subjected. Grimthorp's insistence on flat-out effort over forty-eight seconds at Cromer had been part of the build-up to the race with Headley. All of this was now clear to Buck, and his disappointment over Stamford Bridge was quickly put behind him.

Josiah Headley had won more money by his fleetness of foot than any man since the famous Captain Barclay himself. Bred in a mining community where men would bet on anything from the speed of cockroaches to fighting dogs, Headley had been carefully nurtured by William Bunn since, as an eighteen-year-old novice, he had won the great Sheffield Sprint Handicap at long odds. Bunn had made ten thousand pounds that day. Headley's share had been two hundred pounds — all of which had been lost on a greyhound called Lucky Lou only a week later.

For Headley was a compulsive gambler, and the twenty thousand pounds which he had won since the Sheffield of 1866 had all long since passed into the hands of bookmakers. Since 1866 he had taken on everything England and the Empire had to offer, and no man would now face him on scratch terms. Burke, the deaf Australian, had come to England in 1870 and been whipped over three hundred yards, as had the Frenchman, Prost, over a furlong in the same year. From Canada had come the half-breed, White Rock, in 1873, to be run into the ground over six hundred yards. Then a year later Headley had buried the best Scottish 'ped', Manchline, over a quarter mile, breaking fifty seconds on packed snow in midwinter.

This time Headley intended to keep his money, for he had no intention of spending the rest of his days bent over like a half-shut knife as a coal-beaver. At the age of twenty-eight he had only a couple of years' good running left in him, perhaps four big-money matches, and he had to make them count. With a new wife and four children — and another on the way — Josiah Headley was fighting for his life, and no Yankee Cowboy was going to take his title from him.

For the bookmaker William Bunn it was not a matter of

survival, for with a £40,000 Gothic mansion in the best end of Barnsley and twice that much snug in the bank, he had no worries on that score. But, like most self-made men, he had as much respect for a shilling now as when it had represented a week's wages to him. He had already dished the Yank at Stamford Bridge and, although Miss Hettie Carr could no longer be used to take a few yards from Miller's legs, there was no way Moriarty was going to return to the States with much more than a shirt-stud. For Moriarty had laid ten thousand pounds on Buck Miller at four to one against and, with the odds on Headley at three to one on, the man in the street was not being tempted to lay his hard-earned shilling to earn a miserable four pence. So much, indeed, of the working man's money was now coming in on the Yank that Bunn was forced to drop his odds to two to one, and finally to evens.

Bunn had no doubts about the race itself. The Barnsley man had never let him down yet. Headley would, as usual, be taken to Cumbria, to a cottage just outside Whitehaven. There, with his trainer, the redoubtable Arthur Formby, he would in a mere twelve weeks be made into a running machine. Formby was a sprint specialist, a man who had himself run the American sprint-wonder, George Seward, to a short yard back in 1848, and who had since 1860 carved a dozen Sheffield sprint winners out of unknowns. The Lancashire trainer would reduce Josiah Headley from one hundred and sixty pounds to one hundred and forty-eight pounds of sprinting power, capable of running inside forty-nine seconds from the front or of cruising behind a front runner for three hundred yards before leaving him for dead with a devastating turn of speed over the final stretch.

But William Bunn had not made his fortune by leaving anything to chance. He had checked with his American sources on Miller's background, and, apart from a race in St Louis back in 1873 and some minor races in the Boston area in the 1870-3 period, Miller, though clearly no dilettante, appeared to have no record of performance at top level. Certainly, he had never gone as far as a furlong, let alone the sapping quarter-mile. And Miller had already shown himself to be weak of will with Hettie Carr who, his music-hall informants told him, was now again communicating with the American. Perhaps she, albeit no longer with the spur of her father's debts as motivation, would deplete the bodily fluids of the Yankee even further. But on this point Bunn could not be sure, and spies were despatched to Norfolk to keep an eye on Miller's romantic aspirations.

But the American and his entourage had gone, the landlord of the Fen Inn knew not where. Bunn discovered about the ladies easily enough; they had been despatched to Cumbria, to the estate of Lord Grafton, Eleanor's father. The men, however, had vanished into thin air. Spies were sent to

Cumbria, to keep watch on incoming and outgoing mail, and also to Hackney Wick, Sheffield, Pontypridd, Newcastle, Birmingham and Edinburgh, all the main training grounds; but of Miller and his supporters there was no sign. They had gone to ground.

9 July 1877, Glasgow

It was like a prison cell. Buck and Billy Joe peered into the gloom and smelled the odour of sweat, a salt, sickly perfume which drenched the tiny tenement room. Everywhere there were black, bulbous barbells and dumbbells — on the floor, on racks, on the walls. And, standing in the centre of the room, dressed in dungarees, heavy boots and black, turtle-necked sweater, was a tiny white-haired man.

At first Buck thought the figure was a dwarf; but the little man, his arms folded across his chest, his shock of white hair standing out from his head, was perfectly proportioned. Indeed, though he was clearly in his sixties, he was superbly built, with narrow waist and powerful barrel chest, sharp, clearly defined shoulder muscles and thick thighs and calves.

'Jock Weir,' said Moriarty, pressing them forward into the cramped Gallowgate room. It was what Glaswegians called a 'single end': a room within which anything up to four people could live. To one side there was a bed let into the wall; to the other, an enamel basin and a dripping tap. In the middle of the wall facing them a coal fire smouldered.

'The strongest man in the world,' said Moriarty, as Buck and Billy Joe stumbled in the gloom over the training apparatus towards the little old man.

'At ma weight, Mr. Moriarty,' said the old man gruffly, taking Buck's hand. 'At ma weight.'

Buck felt as if his fingers had been gripped by a vice. He winced and withdrew his hand, shaking it, as Billy Joe got the same treatment.

'I'll leave Buck in your good charge then,' said Moriarty. Buck noted that Moriarty had a Scots thread in his accent which he had not previously noticed — except in *Macbeth* and *Rob Roy*.

'Aye,' said Weir. 'Just you come back in two hours, Mr. Moriarty.'

He looked up at Buck and Billy Joe. 'Noo, which wan of yiz goan tae run against this English rascal, Headley?'

Billy Joe pointed to Buck. 'He is,' he said.

Weir reached forward and grabbed Buck by the arm with his powerful little hands, then tapped him on the stomach. Finally, testingly, he placed both hands on Buck's right thigh.

'Let's see it, man,' he said. 'The engine room.'

Buck tensed his muscles and Weir considered. 'No' bad,' he said. 'Strip off.'

Buck peeled off his jacket, shirt and trousers and stood in long-johns and shoes as the little man surveyed him. Weir beckoned Buck to lie on a low wooden bench, at right-angles to which there was a black, bulbous barbell resting on a pair of iron stands, then moved round to the back of the stands.

Standing directly above Buck's head, he lifted the weight with both hands in an overarm grip.

'Ready?' he rasped. 'Lift yer hands.'

Buck lifted his arms straight above him to receive the barbell. It was all that he could do to support it, and he felt his arms quiver.

'Bend yer airms,' ordered Weir. 'Slowly, now.'

Buck bent his arms, feeling the weight accelerate down on to his body, as his muscles failed to respond to his desperate urgings. The barbell now lay heavy, black and dead across his chest.

'Push!' roared Weir, his voice filling the little room. Buck pushed but the barbell did not even twitch. Weir snorted, lifted the weight from Buck's chest as if it were a child's toy and replaced it on the stands.

'A lassie,' he said with no attempt to hide his scorn. 'A big lassie.'

He lifted the weight from the stands and replaced it with another, smaller barbell. Again he held the weight above Buck and again Buck received it. But the result was the same: the weight would not budge, no matter how much Buck heaved and strained.

'Jesus Christ,' said Weir, shaking his head. 'Ye could nae lift a wet poke oot o' a puddle.'

The next hour was a purgatory for Buck. Weir took him round the little room from one exercise to the next, from dumbbell curls to power cleans, then on to the military press and finally to squatting with a weight that would have crushed Atlas himself.

The sweat spurted from Buck as Billy Joe sat watching, expressionless, his back to the fire, while Weir, the very Torquemada of exercise, drove Buck from agony to still deeper agony. Pity did not seem part of the little man's mental equipment.

'God,' groaned Buck as he wilted under yet another ponderous barbell.

'Dinna ask Goad for help, laddie,' growled Weir. 'Goad's nae guid. Goad's a rascal.'

This final touch of atheism was too much for Buck. He sank helplessly to the floor, the weight behind his neck, and Weir stepped in to take it from him, shaking his head.

'Ah've seen you runners afore,' he said. 'just a pair o' legs wi' a heid oan top.'

He beckoned Buck to the fire, where he sat, sweat streaming down his body, beside Billy Joe. Weir reached up to a clay pot on a shelf above the fire and took from it a clay pipe and a plug of tobacco. He shredded the tobacco and pressed it into his pipe, then reached again to the shelf for a wooden taper and lit it from the fire. Weir put flame to his pipe and drew on it.

'Ye'll come here three times a week,' he said. 'Ah'll make ye the strongest runner ever wore a spiked shoe.'

He puffed on his pipe.

'And if ye don't whip this fella Headley, d'ye know whit ah'll dae?' He took the pipe from his mouth and spat a stream of brown spittle into the fire. 'Ah'll gie ye tae the Catholics.'

10 July 1877, Leadhills, Lanarkshire

The next day, Buck required Billy Joe's assistance simply to get dressed, for his arms (and indeed his whole body) felt as if they had been pumped full of lead, then hammered for days on end. The four of them — Buck, Billy Joe, Moriarty and Grimthorp — had moved to a cottage outside Leadhills, a mining village in Lanarkshire a few miles south of Glasgow. There, at a disused pit, was a black, U-shaped strip 460 yards long which had previously held a railroad track serving the mine. The surface was flat and hard; perfect for running. But for the week following his visit to Weir's Gallowgate gymnasium Buck did not even put on a spike. Indeed, he spent two days recovering from Weir's first ministrations, then he had three more sessions in Glasgow with the weights, with a day's rest between.

Despite the pain of that first session, Buck did not complain. This was his chance — to make it big in England, the home of pedestrianism — and every day he could feel Grimthorp's eyes assessing him as he worked away in Weir's gloomy little gymnasium. The combined stimulus of Grimthorp's scrutiny and Weir's remorseless driving provided a challenge to which Buck responded with enthusiasm. By the end of a week, barbells which had previously seemed to be nailed to the floor were being cleared to shoulder level, and great, thick-handled dumbbells were being punched overhead at speed.

Within ten days Buck could feel the change in himself, feel the thickening of his arms and thighs, almost see the muscles of his shoulders grow.

And he loved it, relished the muck-sweat, the throb of muscles gorged with blood, and his joy as previously immovable weights began to move fast and easily at his will. Then, when the outdoor training began at Leadhills, he could feel the power he had gained with the weights transfer itself through his limbs to the firm hard cinders of the running-path.

In the first painful days when he had started training under Weir, Buck had questioned the need to work under two trainers, particularly when the ministrations of Weir appeared to be destroying the earlier work of Grimthorp. But Moriarty had been firm. Headley was the fastest man on earth over the distance; it would take more than mere running-training to deal with him. And that was where the strength gained in Weir's gloomy little dungeon would pay off. 'You can't fire a cannon from a canoe' had been Moriarry's final statement on the matter.

28 July 1877, Lord Grafton's Estate, Cumbria
For Eleanor, the days passed sweetly in the summer sun. Little had changed at Grafton since that far-off day back in 1862 when Moriarty had first come into her life. Her father was still there, simply older and shaggier, his eccentricities

growing with the years, and above them loomed Black Tor, the mountain on which Moriarty had run for her, his lady, all those years ago.

Lord Grafton's enthusiasm for the drama had not dimmed, and the little theatre in the grounds still echoed to his Shakespearean ravings as bewildered rustics were dragged into productions as diverse as *The Red Barn* and *King Lear*.

It had been Buck who had suggested that Hettie should join them while he prepared for the match with Headley. There had been a fleeting and passionate meeting in London after the disaster of the Amateur Athletic Club Championships. 'One night off,' Moriarty had told him. 'You've earned that.'

The couple were desperately in love, so desperately that there was no need for Buck to make any formal proposal of marriage. For Hettie had made it clear that she would wait for him wherever he went, and Buck was therefore able to travel to Leadhills for his final preparations stronger of heart than Moriarty had ever known him. Moriarty also knew that Buck would dig deep against Headley just as he himself had done on Black Tor for Eleanor all those years before.

Moriarty, Eleanor and Billy Joe had immediately taken to Hettie Carr. Although she was primarily a music-hall singer, she had a wealth of experience of sketches and knock-about banter with her father, and possessed a strong stage personality. She had no experience of the classics, but everyone felt she would be able to make an immediate impact in farce and melodrama. Moriarty's description of her as 'a feisty little all-rounder' fitted Hettie perfectly, and she was delighted to accept Eleanor's invitation to travel north with her to Grafton Hall.

Mandy for her part had continued to worry away over her performance in New York. She knew in her heart that Billy Joe had been right, that in Moriarty's athletic parlance she had not 'stripped big'. Her technique was still too thinly-based

289

to handle a classic role in a major theatre, particularly when opposite someone of the calibre of Booth. In *Lear*, she had been merely competent, and that for her was not enough. On the voyage from New York she had discussed the matter with Eleanor, and they had both come to the conclusion that she now needed formal training. Eleanor had agreed to arrange a drama coach for Mandy while they were at Grafton Hall.

Mandy had been told that her coach would arrive on the Monday morning, the day after they arrived at Grafton. She had not known what to expect, but when the slim, reserved man who was introduced to her as her 'coach' was announced as Henry Irving Mandy could not believe her ears. Moriarty and Edwin Booth had played with Irving fifteen years before in Manchester when Booth had been the star and Irving merely a supporting player. Now Irving was England's greatest actor, and for the next month he was, courtesy of Lord Grafton, to be at her disposal.

Irving was the perfect teacher for Mandy. Gentlemanly and diplomatic, he teased performances from her, showing her the hidden balance in the great lines of Shakespeare, a balance that gave them strength and meaning.

Like all good teachers, he used all available materials as examples. The most substantial of these was Hettie Carr, whose ability to project her voice exceeded even that of Irving himself. True, Hettie, with her powerful diaphragm, was a natural rather than a trained performer, but Irving was able to analyse the basis of her powerful projection and to press Mandy towards the same levels through mimicry. And although the main focus of attention was on Mandy, all the women daily pursued the drills and exercises that Irving was prescribing for his young charge, for they were of value to each of them.

Mandy seemed to grow in confidence almost visibly. She practised Irving's drills eagerly, working long into the night at Grafton's tiny theatre, until the actor had to beg her to rest. He swore to her that he had never met a lady with such a capacity for work.

Thus, while in Scotland, in the bleakness of Leadhills, the men prepared Buck for the greatest challenge of his life, their women worked equally rigorously for their future challenge, the Theatre of the West.

14

REAL THING

They said little, these miners of Leadhills, but they knew why
Moriarty and his men had come to the village, for they knew
running, and runners. As Moriarty and his party sat at a table
in the stark saloon of the Leadhills Arms he felt a kinship with
these grimy, coal-racked men, men with backs pitted and
veined like Stilton cheese. For they were what he might have
been, had he and his father not set sail for New York those
thirty years ago. In six days of burrowing like a rat in a three-
foot seam these men could earn less than a pound — less than
a thousandth of what he could pick up on one single con.

Moriarty had early made contact with the men's leader, a
man called Alec Docherty, at thirty-eight about the same age
as himself, but looking ten years older. A gaunt cadaver of a
man, Alec Docherty had led his miners through three unsuc-
cessful strikes, while mining families had eaten grass. If Buck
Miller won at Barnsley a thousand pounds would go into
Docherty's strike fund, Moriarty would make sure of that.
And in the meantime the miners of Leadhills would make
sure that no word of Buck Miller's presence would reach the
outside world. The deal was struck.

25 August 1877, Leadhills
All around him, sitting on the black slagheaps, were miners,
at least three thousand of them, drinking cold tea and eating

sandwiches, as below Buck prepared for his final trial, over the full quarter-mile distance. At his first attempt, a month before, he had taken fifty-one seconds flat. He had paced it badly, having run the first furlong in an over-fast twenty-three seconds. The last hundred yards had felt like the sandy, 350-yard Windmill Run back in Cromer. Then, in his second attempt over the distance, a week later, he had been overcautious, running the first furlong in twenty-five seconds, but he had come back strongly in just over twenty-five, clocking 50.2. Now, sharp and supple at one hundred and fifty-five pounds with the volume of his training sharply reduced, he sought that fine, fragile pace which would enable him to cruise at just the right effort-level to take him close to forty-nine seconds.

Moriarty and Grimthorp had arranged that the track was sifted and rolled for his final trial; Docherty's men had seen to it, spending a whole working day bringing its surface to that perfect light hardness essential for sprinting. And now it was ready.

Moriarty, Billy Joe, Grimthorp and Weir stood at the start, fidgeting from foot to foot. They felt just as nervous as Buck, and even the laconic Billy Joe was infected by the moment. Moriarty pulled a pristine white handkerchief from his top pocket and held it aloft in the sun; it did not move. It was an ideal day for quarter-miling.

Next Moriarty took from an inside pocket a thick stopwatch, and looked at Grimthorp at his side.

'Only one curve,' he said. 'How much faster does that make it than the Barnsley track?'

Grimthorp clicked shut the cylinder of his starting-pistol and sniffed. 'Two-fifths of a second,' he said. 'No more.'

The gun was fired. Buck ate the ground, covering it with a fluency of stride which he had previously experienced only in dreams. Everything was over in a rush. As he hit the tape fatigue hit him suddenly and his legs wobbled, but up till that point there had been no feelings of tiredness, only the rhythmic flow of power from his legs to the sharp cinder surface.

Billy Joe ran to him with his dressing-gown. Above him on the slag heaps, the miners shouted and whistled.

Grimthorp looked over, Moriarty's shoulder as he consulted his watch. 'What did you get?

Moriarty wrinkled his nose. 'Forty-nine and a fifth,' he said.

'Good,' said Grimthorp.

'Not good enough,' said Moriarty, scowling.

As he looked around him in the bright sun Billy Joe thought he caught a flash of light from the top of a slag heap about a quarter of a mile away. He looked again, but it was gone. Billy Joe did not know it, but more than one watch had been placed on Buck's run. It had recorded forty-nine seconds flat, and in six hours its owner and his news were to be with William M. Bunn in Barnsley.

30 August 1877, Grafton Hall, Cumberland

Moriarty was nothing if not a good psychologist. The hard training at Leadhills was now over, so there was nothing more in the physical sense that could be done for Buck. What was needed was a little relaxation, a *reculer pour mieux sauter* before the mental 'peaking' for the big race on 1 September. He had therefore decided to call in at Grafton Hall on the way south. Grimthorp and Weir would travel ahead to Barnsley to their base at the Albert Hotel to check on all the last-minute details.

When, on their arrival, Irving and the ladies had proposed a little dramatic evening at Grafton's theatre, Moriarty had expected a night of light entertainment. Thus, after he, Buck and Billy Joe and an audience of local worthies had watched the lights dim about them he was surprised to find that Irving had chosen excerpts from Lear, playing the main part himself with Mandy as Cordelia, Eleanor as Goneril and Hettie as Regan. Irving lifted each one of his players beyond themselves. Moriarty was impressed by the improvement in Eleanor, but

294

it was Mandy who was a revelation. For the girl now had both vocal and dramatic range. True, Grafton's tiny theatre did not require great strength of voice; but Moriarty could at last see in Mandy, as with a great athlete, a high cruising speed. She would be able to hit the back of any theatre in the world but, more than that, she had dramatic depth, the capacity to relate to other actors in a scene, and to capture attention by the tiniest inflection of voice or movement of her body.

Irving did not lack ambition for his protégée. In an excerpt from *A Midsummer Night's Dream* he had Mandy play Titania to his Oberon, then, to end the evening, he put her alone on stage as Portia for the 'quality of mercy' speech.

Billy Joe, in the darkness of the audience, could feel the hair rise on the back of his neck. For this was it, the real thing. No longer was this Marshal Boone's stage-struck schoolteacher daughter reciting chunks of Shakespeare to farmers in the boondocks. Mandy was right up there with Moriarty and Eleanor and Booth, able to hold her own.

Billy Joe had no intellectual understanding of acting. He had, however, excellent instincts, and he knew that Mandy had made — as with an athlete learning a new physical skill — a sudden and important jump from mere competence to something not far from excellence. For now he felt himself forced to look at her, drawn to her, and that was what acting was about, not mere 'beautiful' recitation of lines

When the performance was over, the whole audience applauded till their hands were sore.

Billy Joe could feel tears well in his eyes. As the gas lamps began to bathe the little theatre in light, he reached into his jacket pocket for a handkerchief and blew his nose. Muttering his apologies to Moriarty and Lord Grafton, who were making their way out into the foyer, he strode off to his left, through the crowds now leaving the rapidly emptying theatre, to a side door, leading beneath the stage to the Green Room. Billy Joe ducked under the low doorway and descended rickety wooden steps, then made his way along a dark narrow passage choked with painted flats, curtains and other remnants of long-past performances. The passage smelt of perfume, talcum and dust, a strange mix as redolent of a theatre as horse-liniment of a stadium dressing-room.

Tentatively, he knocked on the door of the first dressing room on his left. There was no reply. He opened the door. There a white, half-naked Henry Irving stood surveying himself in the mirror. Billy Joe was surprised at the man's slight stature, for a few moments earlier he had appeared to fill the stage. Irving turned and immediately recognised his visitor. He smiled and jerked his thumb to the left.

'Next room,' he said. 'Good luck.'

Billy Joe nodded and closed the door behind him. He knocked lightly on the next door.

'Come in!' came Mandy's voice.

He cautiously stepped into the room.

He found himself in semi-darkness, with the gas-lamp low. He could barely see Mandy in the gloom, but even in the bad light he could see that she was only partly clothed, and stood before him in stays and white tights. She seemed small, and for the first time vulnerable.

'Mandy', he said awkwardly, feeling himself flush. 'I take back all I said. I never in my life thought you could be so good?

Her face showed a grinning line of white teeth. 'You got to take some of the credit, Billy Joe,' she said. 'Back in New York, you didn't pull any punches. So Eleanor got me some coaching with Mr. Irving. It's just like being an athlete: you're right, you've got to grab the moment.'

He nodded. 'I never in my life did anything like I saw you do tonight,' he said, moving towards her. His eyes were growing accustomed to the light, and he could now see her clearly.

'Maybe one day you'll get *your* chance,' she said, without any trace of bitterness. He had never heard her voice so soft before.

'My chance?'

There was a long, almost palpable silence. Above them they could hear the buzz of conversation and thump of footsteps as the last members of the audience made their way through the foyer back to the main house.

For a moment they stood as if suspended in time, the short distance between them alive with feeling. Billy Joe could sense the depth of her passion. For the first time in his life he felt clumsy — indeed, he stepped forward exactly the same moment as Mandy did, so that they collided in the centre of the room. Neither of them moved away. They stood, hands by their sides, each unable to take the initiative.

Then Billy Joe felt Mandy's hand, warm and tender, on his arm. His right hand slipped slowly up her arm to her shoulder, then to the shell of her ear and finally to the nape of her neck. His left hand was more direct, making its way immediately to the same spot, and for a moment Billy Joe looked down at Mandy, her head cupped in his hands.

'I'm sorry I wasn't what you wanted,' he said.

'You are now,' she said, reaching up to kiss him.

1 September 1877, the Victoria Running Grounds, Barnsley
The grounds had been full at noon, two hours before the appointed time of the match. Fifty-one thousand, two hundred and ninety-six people had either paid sixpence to crowd shoulder to shoulder on the terracings or a shilling to enjoy the relative comfort of a seat in the main stand. Upwards of five thousand had paid nothing, but had escaped the attentions of the constabulary by squeezing through spaces in the railings or by risking more serious injury in scrambling over walls crowned by broken glass. Outside the grounds, some further ten thousand devotees, unable to achieve entry, milled around, betting freely with bookmakers based in the crowd.

The Barnsley police had provided an escort for the carriages containing the two runners, both of whom had arrived just after noon, making their bumpy way over the cobbled streets through the seething crowds.

Buck had ventured a glance through the carriage windows. Barnsley, even on this sunny day, was his idea of hell: greasy black cobblestones, dingy, soot—crusted buildings, a sky always sullen with the spewings of a forest of factory chimneys. Yet . . . this was the only place on earth where fifty thousand men would fill a stadium and pay a day's wages just to see two 'peds' run in a match-race for less than a minute.

Buck had already travelled to the track with Moriarty from their base at the Albert Hotel the previous evening, to get the feel of the stadium. There was always something strange and frightening, he felt, about an empty stadium, and Buck had known a sickness in his stomach as he looked at the bare terracings, at the steel and wood advertisements ringing the track: 'Cadbury's Cocoa'; 'The Two Infallible Powers — The Pope and Bovril'; 'Scotts Electric Comb'; 'Harlene' for the Hair'. It was odd how such ephemera gave him a sense of the place better than more substantial structures.

He had lifted a few grains of the fine cinder track in his hand and clenched them in it; when he loosened his fingers most of the cinders had remained stuck to them. That was good: it meant there was clay in the surface, that the track would be both hard and springy.

But Headley had never been beaten at the Victoria Running Grounds in a match-race, never in his life seen a man's heels at the tape. . . Again Buck could feel the cold spot at the base of his stomach. As twilight gathered he looked at the track, and for a moment could hear the even, rhythmic scrape of spikes on cinders.

His reverie had been broken by Moriarty, who knew that at such times thought could be an enemy. The rest of the evening at the Albert Hotel was spent in silence; even the adroit Moriarty had not been able to raise Buck's spirits.

Now, with half-an-hour to go, Buck lay half-naked in the

dark underworld of the stadium on the massage table in the austere bareness of his dressing-room, as Grimthorp began what he called his special 'match-massage'. It was a ritual handed down from somewhere in the dim recesses of pedestrian history.

First, Grimthorp took a mouthful of cold Water. Then, cheeks bulging, he stood over Buck and lightly sprayed the water onto one of Buck's thighs and gently teased the thick, loose muscle. It took him over twenty minutes to complete the process over both limbs, but by the finish Buck's legs felt warm and loose.

Moriarty's preparations had been less to his liking. Just before noon, William Bunn had asked to see him privately at the Bell Tavern just outside the ground. There he had made it clear to Moriarty that he had gone beyond simply taking bets on Buck's defeat. He had now taken on a massive personal wager of £10,000 at three to one that Buck would lose by a full second. Bunn was prepared to be generous. A discreet muscle-pull for Buck or, even better, a gradual fade over the final hundred yards would be enough to put £30,000 in Bunn's pocket, and ten of those would go back in the *S.S.Harold* with Moriarty and his party.

The alternative wasn't pleasant. Certain of Bunn's pugilist friends would ensure that Moriarty and his entourage left Barnsley very much the worse for wear.

Moriarty had not refused outright. It was clear that Buck had somehow been 'clocked' by one of Bunn's men at his final trial and that Headley's own trial had been faster, albeit not ten yards faster. Bunn wasn't scared about Headley not winning, but he wasn't at all sure that he could win by a full second — not fairly, at any rate. Moriarty saw that there was no point in antagonising Bunn, thus risking interference with Buck before the race.

It was common practice. Someone in the crowd would 'accidentally' trip your runner, water would be tampered with, or even food: Moriarty had seen it all before. And Barnsley was Bunn's patch, so it was wise to keep a low profile. So he had smiled, poured Bunn a double whisky and said that as long as they could all come out of it a few bucks in profit then where was the problem in helping each other out? Buck, Moriarty assured Bunn, shaking him warmly by the hand, would play his part to the full. The good people of Barnsley would see the kangaroo start and a cracking race. Buck would make it look good. No one would be able to complain that he had rigged it.

The quarter-mile tactics of Josiah Headley were as fixed as the war dance of a Zulu. They were to slow down the first part of the race by getting to the front early, then to ease off, lulling his opponent into a false sense of security. When the opposing runner decided that the pace was too slow and moved ahead, Headley would tuck in behind, then strike over the last fifty yards with a devastating burst of speed. The strike was so late and so powerful that no opponent had ever been able to respond sufficiently, and Headley had won several matches by this means, often in relatively slow times.

Occasionally an opponent had made an early break before the end of the first furlong, but Headley had always had the pace to cover the break and still hit hard in the final straight. Front runners suffered the same fate. Headley would shadow them into the final straight, then leave them wallowing with a vicious sprint only fifty yards from the tape. Nevertheless, Moriarty's advice was that Buck should run even and fast all the way, from the front, to take the sap out of Headley's legs. Buck should run at the pace he knew he could handle, rather than let Headley dictate the tactics. That was surely the way to victory.

He said nothing about Bunn's offer, for this was Buck's moment, and no taint should be attached to it. If Buck were whipped it would be because he, Moriarty, had made a mistake when the coup had first been planned back in the autumn of

300

1876 – and because Buck was simply not of a championship feather.

The stadium was silent, like a cathedral. Buck ventured a glance at Headley. The man bore no resemblance to the grimy collier of four months before. White, lean and sinewy, with thick bulging thighs and light calves — that was Buck's immediate impression. 'A pair of legs with a heid on top' would have been Weir's description.

He became aware that Headley was also scrutinising him. And what would he see? Undoubtedly the same strength, the same symmetry of limb. But Headley would also see a big cavernous chest and thick, powerful shoulders and arms. And that would surprise him, perhaps even shock him, for that was not how runners were normally built.

'Gentlemen?' It was the starter, an angular, moustachioed man in a grey single-breasted suit. He stood at a wooden table on the infield, where sat four similarly dressed middle-aged men,

'My name is Mr Garforth. These are the officials, gentlemen, who are all Sheffield-trained: Mr McAllister, Mr Gore, Mr Penrose and Mr Winterbottom.'

Each of the officials nodded and Garforth turned to face the runners. 'In case of any dispute l shall be the final arbiter.'

He reached into his right fob pocket, fumbled for a moment and withdrew a gold sovereign. He nodded to Buck.

'As the challenger and our guest, will you shout, sir?'

'Heads,' said Buck. His voice sounded to him as if it had come from someone else.

Garforth flipped the coin and it dropped on the back of a thin left hand. He covered it with his right then withdrew it.

'Tails,' he said. 'Your choice, Mr Headley.'

'Ah'll tak' inside,' growled Headley, scowling towards the track.

Garforth nodded. 'Then please prepare yourselves, gentlemen.'

He moved to the table, picked up his starting pistol and opened it. He spun the barrel, lifted the gun and let off a trial shot.

The report of the gun released a pent-up roar from the crowd. It came deep, from the gut, from men who had put a week's wages on a man's back or from others who had simply come to see the Yank with the Kangaroo Start take on the great Josiah Headley. They had paid their sixpence for this moment and by God they were going to get their money's-worth.

Buck peeled off his dressing-gown and went to the side of the track where stood Moriarty, Billy Joe, Grimthorp and Weir. Up in the stands, holding each other's hands grimly, eyes fixed on the track, sat Hettie, Mandy and Eleanor. Buck handed his dressing-gown to Weir. The little man looked him straight in the eye.

'He's only a man,' he growled. 'Just use yer airms. Ah'll let ye know when.'

Buck smiled, and trotted to the inside of the track as Garforth mounted a set of steps on the infield at the starting-line. When the starter reached the top of the steps and stood, gun aloft, the roaring of the crowd stopped as if on command.

Headley now no longer looked at Buck nor he at Headley. The Yorkshireman took his position on the inside lane, his front foot almost on the line, ready for a standing start. Buck, crouching beside him only inches away, ventured a glance up the track. The crowd at the end of the straight was a grey blur: he could see only the hard, virgin blackness of the cinder, the straight which would suck them into the left-hand curve.

'Get to your marks . . .'

He could hear the flapping of the flags above the grandstand as he took his place, his knee just behind the line, his fingers behind his knee.

'Get set . . .'

He could no longer hear the flags. Buck lifted his hips, his weight now balanced on front foot and hands. The momentary

302

pause was an agony to him. It hung, denying him the release he required, demanded.

The blank charge exploded like a cannon, releasing both the runners and the roar of the crowd. Headley leapt into an immediate lead, his stride long and rangy. Buck started fast, but the champion was a yard up in twenty, Buck pinned on his right shoulder.

They were at the first curve in a rush of legs. Buck felt easy, cruising behind his man, pulled along by the power and pace of the Yorkshire runner. In the stands, Moriarty checked his watch and swallowed hard. It was not going as expected. The first hundred yards had been run in better than eleven seconds. Headley was dragging Buck to disaster. He shook his head, looking sideways, but Billy Joe and Grimthorp had their gaze riveted to the track. Weir's eyes were tight shut.

On the curve Buck stayed close, accepting the spurt of the cinders from Headley's spikes on his chest, running not an inch further than necessary. He was running easily, the speed flowing from him without effort. The crunch of his spikes seemed in time with an inner rhythm of what he instinctively knew was ideal quarter-miling, sprinting on that fine edge between power and fatigue. And he was running on that edge with perfect balance.

But so was Headley. Moriarty, seeing him in action for the first time, realised the enormity of the gamble he had taken back in December when he had despatched Buck on the *S.S. Harold*. For the man was beautiful, his great white legs devouring the untouched cinders of the back straight, dragging Buck with him on an invisible thread. For fifty yards the men ran in unison, strides perfectly synchronised, a sweet and simple ballet of effort.

Moriarty checked his flickering stop-watch as the two men closed in on the furlong mark.

'Twenty-two seconds,' intoned Grimthorp beside him.

'Jesus Christ,' groaned Moriarty. Buck was a dead man; he

had run a second slower over the first furlong at Leadhills and had still ended up a wobbling wreck.

But Buck did not seem to think so. As Headley crossed the furlong mark Buck surged into the lead, his spikes throwing black cinders into Headley's face. From the crowd came an 'ooooh' sound as the two runners pounded into the third quarter of the race, into the final curve, Headley a full yard behind.

Buck was running tall. He could taste the tape. Behind him, Headley had pulled in a couple of feet and he could hear him on his shoulder, but he did not care, for his breathing still came easily and his legs felt fresh and fluid.

But in the stands Moriarty and Grimthorp could see that Buck's leg-cadence was dropping.

Then Headley struck. Twenty yards before the end of the curve leading into the final straight he moved out and cut past Buck, on the outside, setting up a one-yard lead of his own, and adding a further half-yard as Buck was forced to check as Headley cut in to the pole position.

For the first time, Buck felt his breathing, felt the hard suck as he dragged in more breath.

The two runners hit the straight with Buck almost two yards down.

Moriarty shook his head. Headley was running high, holding form like the champion he was. Josiah Headley knew that he had his man. All that he had to do was to hold form and the money was his.

A hundred yards to go, and both men ran through an endless roar. But in spite of the roar Buck, his eyes glued to the back of Headley's vest, remembered one thing. It was the Windmill Run. He had been here before, in this land of pain, of muscles clogged with waste. And he had passed through and survived. He took a deep breath.

He pulled back a foot in the first twenty yards, then another foot in the next twenty. But with fifty yards to go the gap was frozen at a short yard, and Buck, his legs bowing, sensed that he was lost.

'Use yer airms, lad. Use yer airms.'

Moriarty looked down at his side. Weir had his eyes open now and his harsh voice cut through the roar of the crowd.

Buck heard Weir's shout and somehow through the haze of his fatigue the Scotsman's words triggered off something deep in him. He drove hard with his arms, arms still fresh, untouched by the tiredness which had engulfed the rest of his body.

The action brought new life to his legs, adding vital inches to each stride. In a matter of yards he was level with Headley, their breathing rasping together in a terrible parody of the unison their legs had enjoyed in the back straight.

Somehow, through his own pain, Buck could feel Headley's agony and in that sharing there was respect. But still he kept digging with his arms, driving himself towards a tape that seemed to recede with every stride. And suddenly Headley was gone. For a moment Buck enjoyed the snap of the tape on his chest and then, as he staggered on to the grass infield, Headley fell on top of him.

The men lay together on the grass, unable to rise, as their helpers rushed towards them.

It was Headley who was the first to climb unsteadily to his feet, dragging Buck with him. The two men wobbled across the track in front of the grandstand. The Yorkshire-man pulled Buck's arms aloft as Garforth shouted out the time of forty-seven point eight seconds, the fastest a man had ever run, through a megaphone into the raging crowd.

'You're champion of t'world, Yank,' said Headley.

15

CRISIS

It was a trouble-free departure from the Victoria Grounds through the grimy streets of Barnsley towards the railway station. A few quiet words by Moriarty with the miner's leader, Alec Docherty before the race had ensured that the four bruisers who had been sent by an irate William M. Bunn to their dressing-room to dispense summary justice had ended up — minus several teeth and plus an assortment of cuts and bruises — in the slimy murk of the Barnsley canal.

For the miners of Leadhills dealing with Bunn's men had been a pleasure, a welcome release from the pent-up emotions of the match. Buck's victory would ensure a strong trade union for years to come and guaranteed a warm, well-fed winter for their wives and children. Docherty had also senta small detachment of his men with Moriarty to Liverpool to ensure that Bunn would not follow them to their ship, and in due course Moriarty and his party walked gratefully through an applauding line of miners up the gangway on to the *S.S. Harold*. As they cast off, Moriarty reflected that, after fifteen years, Deerfoot had at last been avenged. The Yanks had come back across the Pond and given it to the English good and proper, and in the heart of professional foot-racing itself.

As for Buck Miller, Moriarty knew, whatever he did for the rest of his life, he would remember that moment when he had

306

been the fastest man in the world, when he had been beat all ends up but had come back in front of fifty thousand people and showed what sort of stuff he was made of.

For Eleanor, the race had also been a moment of understanding, for she realised for the first time just what Moriarty had striven for in his own running, what the second-rate match-races in cow-towns could never give him, however much he won in bets. She had seen two men at their limits, athletes at their finest, competing at the very peak of their powers. And there was no denying it, it was something fine, something marvellous. Which only made what she intended to say to Moriarty all the more difficult.

For Eleanor knew that their future must lie away from the cinder path, in the theatre. Moriarty and his men must think beyond their fleetness of foot. The basis of the Theatre of the West was there now in Eleanor, Mandy and Hettie, and in a less willing Moriarty, Buck and Billy Joe. Moriarty had already shown flair as both director and manager. Given a permanent base, he could develop an acting talent as yet still only partly realised. They all could.

The matter had come to a head on the first evening out from Liverpool, at the circular dinner-table in a corner of a slightly swaying, half-empty dining-room, as Moriarty dispensed champagne all round. They sat together in the flickering lamplight, the glow of Buck's Barnsley victory still warm within them.

'All out in the open from now on,' he said, looking across the table at Buck. Moriarty was already slightly tipsy. 'No more English Method. We don't need it. Let 'em come, the best footracers in the world. You'll take 'em on, Buck, on level terms.'

Buck grinned, unaware of Billy Joe's lack of response or of Eleanor's serious countenance. He in particular was still high from Barnsley. As Moriarty came to fill Eleanor's glass she put her hand over it.

'No,' she said, 'not for me.'

Instead she poured herself some water and glanced at Mandy and Hettie, both of whom returned her look, nodding. Eleanor sipped her water, then replaced her glass, holding its stem with both hands in front of her on the table.

'We've all got something to say to you,' she said.

Moriarty poured out Billy Joe's champagne, then stopped.

'Who's "we"?' he asked, aware that something was in the wind.

Eleanor again glanced at Mandy and Hettie. Both women were looking at her expectantly.

'Mandy, Hettie and I,' she said. 'You see, while you were getting Buck prepared for the race at Barnsley we were doing our own preparations at Grafton Hall.'

Moriarty continued to pour out the champagne, taking Hettie's glass. 'I know,' he said. 'And I saw the results. We all did. It was marvellous, the best you've ever done. We all thought so, didn't we boys?'

Buck and Billy Joe raised their glasses in acknowledgement.

'But it wasn't just what we did at Grafton, the entertainment,' said Eleanor. She drew in a deep breath. 'We all decided.' She paused. 'We're ready.'

'Ready for what?' said Moriarty.

'For settling down. For San Francisco, Denver, a permanent base. For the Theatre of the West.'

'But Eleanor,' said Moriarty. 'Buck's a world champion, Billy Joe's leg's healed up good, and me, I've still got some good runs in these legs. We've got all our lives to act. But running, that's for now.'

'So's the theatre.'

It was Mandy's turn.

'Look, Moriarty,' she said. 'I owe you a lot. But working with Mr Irving at Grafton Hall I saw what I really could be, the same way Buck and Billy Joe have done on the track.'

'Mandy's right.' Hettie's soft Scots voice had hardened. She faced Moriarty directly across the table. 'You lads have got to grow up. Booth and Irving, they're professionals, just like Headley's a professional. But your Theatre of the West, that's not professional, at least not yet. Being a pro's not just a matter of earning money, it's a way of looking at things. Your work's good but it's not good enough. And it won't be until we all start working at it.'

Moriarty looked at Buck and Billy Joe but both, for once, appeared speechless.

'We've got enough money.' It was Eleanor again, her voice gaining in strength. 'All we have to do now is to lease the theatre and set up our own company. And if we don't make out in, say, three years, then we can all go back on the road, with nothing lost. Just give us the chance, Moriarty. You owe us that.'

Moriarty gulped his champagne and tried to assemble his thoughts.

'What do you say, boys?' he said, across the table to Buck and Billy Joe. There was no response.

Billy Joe looked at Mandy and she nodded.

'I got no beef,' he said. 'I'll settle for San Francisco.'

Moriarty looked at each one of his group in turn.

'Then it looks like it's all settled,' said Moriarty, pouring himself out another glass of champagne. 'Anyone got any other surprises for me?'

Billy Joe again looked at Mandy for a moment and reddened.

'Mandy and me . . .' he began.

'We're getting married,' interrupted Mandy.

Hettie nudged Buck. He coughed.

'Same with us,' he said. 'Spring next year.'

Eleanor beamed. 'Congratulations,' she said, kissing each of the girls. 'It can be a double wedding.'

For a moment, Moriarty was nonplussed. He had felt certain that both Buck and Billy Joe would stand four-square behind him. Then his good nature prevailed and he ordered a magnum of champagne to celebrate the two announcements.

Their glasses charged, Moriarty raised his in toast.

'To Buck and Hettie, Billy Joe and Mandy,' he said.

They sipped their champagne.

'And a second toast,' said Eleanor, raising her glass. 'To the Theatre of the West.'

No resistance was to be offered either by Buck or Billy Joe, who had spent the first three days out of Liverpool in their cabins with their respective loved ones.

But there were soon ominous signs that the beast of pedestrianism was not yet dead. Three days after departure, Moriarty was again padding the decks as the *S. S. Harold* glided west on blithe, blue seas. Three days later, he was joined by Billy Joe, a day after that by Buck. True, rehearsals of *Richelieu*, *Macbeth* and *Lear* were pursued with diligence every hour that was available; but each morning the sound of feet endlessly pounding above reminded the women that there were contests yet to be won.

It was a good winter for all of them. In November, at the Astor Palace Theatre, Mandy and Hettie received rapturous notices for their performances as Cordelia and Goneril to Edwin Booth's Lear, with Moriarty playing the Fool. Buck and Billy Joe now took daily lessons in voice-production, though Eleanor noted that, egged on by Moriarty, they regularly seemed to manage to sneak in a couple of hours' training at the German Gymnastics Institute.

In January, Hettie and Mandy played at Niblo's in the Irish farce *Rory O'More* to packed houses, while Buck and Billy Joe made their debuts in the New York theatre at the Park as Rosencrantz and Guildenstern to Booth's Hamlet, with Moriarty playing an over-young Polonius.

A month later, Moriarty took out a month's lease at the Palace in a new farce by Ned Buntline, *Paddy in the Bronx*, one in which they all had meaty parts. Buntline's play was no masterpiece, but Moriarty's troupe, aided by sets newly made by his father, squeezed it for every laugh, and *Paddy in the Bronx* played for five weeks.

Wagstaffe had been contacted in early October.

There had been an immediate acknowledgement from their banker, then a letter in mid-November saying that negotiations for the Coliseum, Denver were proving unfruitful, and that Wagstaffe was actively pursuing the owners of the Jenny Lind. Then, in January, Wagstaffe informed them that an entirely new theatre, the Grand, had been built in Albuquerque, and might be secured on a long lease at exceptionally favourable rates. The banker soon sent detailed drawings of the theatre, and Moriarty and his company spent many hours discussing the merits of gambling on the new theatre in Albuquerque rather than taking the established Jenny Lind, where they had already experienced some success. In February, they finally settled on the Jenny Lind, and a letter was despatched to Wagstaffe enjoining him to end all discussions on the Grand and to secure a deal with the management of the Jenny Lind by the spring, the company to take up occupation in the first week of September.

It was on 11 March that news came of the A.P. Wagstaffe Bank, San Francisco. The bank's doors had been closed and there had been riots and violence as angry depositors had stormed them. Other, more adventurous souls had made the climb to Nob Hill to A.P. Wagstaffe's Palladian mansion, but the banker was nowhere to be found. Neither was his priceless collection of French paintings and Ming vases: the house had been stripped, gutted of everything of value. All that remained were some furnishings and a dozen bewildered Negro servants who knew only that 'the massa' had left as usual on the morning of 8 March and had not yet returned. This was not unusual, because Wagstaffe had a strong predilection for dusky Mexican 'waitresses', and had been known to stay away for days in their pursuit. The red light district was scoured, but to no avail. Yes, A.P. Wagstaffe was well-known in the area and had spent many a night there with Mexican girls in the opium dens and cribs; but he was not there now.

Back in New York, the news of Wagstaffe's defection hit Moriarty and his group like a body-blow. One hundred and twenty-five thousand dollars had been in Wagstaffe's vaults, all that they had earned in four years of running their guts out. True, they had retained ten thousand dollars of the stakes won at Barnsley, but that was just living expenses. The Theatre of the West was gone for ever, lost somewhere in A.P. Wagstaffe's saddlebags. They were back where they started.

When the initial shock had, dispersed, Moriarty's nimble mind swung back into action. On 14 March, in the Green Room at Niblo's Theatre, a council of war was held with Buck and Billy Joe. At first Moriarty said nothing, staring ahead, chin cupped in his hands.

'Mexico,' he said at last, abruptly.

'Why Mexico?' asked Billy Joe.

'No mention in those reports of Wagstaffe going West by boat, China-way — anyhow, he hates the Chinese, and who wants to live in China?' replied Moriarty. 'If he comes East the Pinkerton boys will pick him up, sure as eggs. No, A.P. Wagstaffe's always had one weakness. Mexican girls, they're an obsession with him.'

'How do we know he's still got the money?' asked Buck.

'We don't,' replied Moriarty. 'The reports in the papers say he's reckoned to have lost over a million on horses and cards. The bank's assets were over a million and a half. Sure as hell he's kept some. And Wagstaffe's high-tailing it south for Mexico right now. I'll stake my life on it.'

Thus it was that later that day Buck and Billy Joe made their way west by train. In Albuquerque they would each pick up two horses and ride south into Mexico. Moriarty followed behind, a few days later, having settled their affairs in New York.

312

Only two days after Moriarty's departure, during the bedroom scene with Hamlet, Eleanor, playing Gertrude, swooned, falling on to the bed as she normally did. But on this occasion, she did not rise. The curtain was hurriedly dropped and a doctor summoned. A day later the company was informed that Hamlet's mother was two months' pregnant.

25 April 1878, Chihuahua, Mexico
Carlo Montes bit off the head of the cock and spat it on to the bloodstained sawdust of the pit. He hated a runner. It was said that Spanish cocks never ran, but this one had, and he had lost two thousand pesetas on it.

Montes threw the twitching body of the bird into the ring and wiped his mouth delicately with a white handkerchief, the blood staining its smooth silk surface. He ascended the creaky steps leading up into the four rows of crowded wooden bleachers that encircled the pit and squeezed his way into the front row, still dabbing his lips.

The Mexican, plump and avuncular, sat distracted as around him finger-bets were being made on the next fight. He watched as the two cocks, a Grey and a Black, were 'billed', cradled by their handlers about two feet apart, so that they could peck at each other. The cocks had never met before but they were already mortal enemies.

Montes looked around him. Mostly sweating peons, scum of Chihuahua, they stank like a farmyard, but among them were also gentry from as far away as Mexico City itself.

Such was the lure of cockfighting — probably the only true contest left in modern sport, Montes reflected.

On the top tier were the two young US deputy sheriffs, who had just arrived. The gringos, Speed and Miller, had lost steadily since morning, at least two hundred dollars apiece. But their losses were a trifle compared with the fat one who had arrived at the Olympia Hotel just a fortnight before and who had divided his time between cockfighting and whoring for twenty hours a day. The Americanos would never learn. Cockfighting was more art than science, and the gringos had no art, no culture. Montes reached down between his legs for the leather-covered flask of tequila beneath his bench. He unscrewed the top, uncorked the flask and poured a measure of the drink into the flask-top. The fluid roared against the back of his throat, then burned slowly in his stomach. He poured himself another measure and put it down quickly. Things were looking better.

In the ring, the first pitting had begun. The Black had broken off the Grey's bill and the Grey's handler was sucking blood from its broken beak and spitting saliva down into its open mouth. Montes smiled, nudging spectators on both sides of him. He was a sportsman, and this was what he liked best. Good, clean sport.

Carlo Montes was quite clear when the two deputies enquired of him about gringos who had recently come to Chihuahua. Yes, a portly, middle-aged hombre had been in town for a fortnight, a prodigious man, an athlete. At this point they thought they might have the wrong man. But Montes explained that he meant sexual athlete, a libertine of prodigious lusts. He had taken six ladies a day since his arrival, and the hotel had been loud with the shrieks of even the most hardened of the damsels of Chihuahua. For the gringo's equipment was prodigious. Indeed, many said that, had it been available to the Texans for the defence of the Alamo, it would all have been up with Santa Anna and his men.

The stout American seemed to have a particular penchant for young girls, possessing the naive belief that Mexicans in their early teens were virgins. The young ladies of the town had indulged him in his fantasy, and indeed that very morning Montes had seen a peasant girl barely in her teens slip into the hallway of the Olympia. So he now directed the two young gringo lawmen to the said hotel. The blonde-haired deputy

314

observed that it might be as well to wait until their quarry had finished his business with the girl, but his colleague was inflexible. The two men therefore left the cockpit immediately, apparently on their way to the Olympia and their fat rich compatriot.

Buck and Billy Joe tiptoed along the creaking surface of the landing on the first floor of the Olympia Hotel, guns in hand. They stopped at room number seven.

'You think we should knock first?' asked Buck uncertainly.

'The hell we should,' said Billy Joe. He put his finger to his lips, then his ear to the door.

'Can you hear anything?' whispered Buck.

Billy Joe shook his head. He found the silence ominous.

'Perhaps he's all done?' Buck continued.

Buck made an impatient move to edge past his colleague, but Billy Joe put his left hand on the door knob and barred his way, still shaking his head. Then he slowly opened the door and went in, closing it behind him, leaving Buck in the hall. Buck pressed his ear to the door but there was no sound from the room.

Then the knob turned and Billy Joe slid out, once more closing the door behind him. He frowned.

'What the hell,' hissed Buck. He put his hand on the door-knob. 'Come on. We got money in there.'

Billy Joe shook his head yet again. 'Wagstaffe,' he said. 'He's cashed in his chips.'

'The hell he has,' growled Buck, this time forcing his way past Billy Joe into the room.

The tiny bedroom was gloomy, its curtains half-closed, but even in the dim light Buck could see that it was a mess, with papers strewn all over the floor, around an empty saddlebag. He moved to the window and wrenched the curtains open: the bright midday sun flooded in.

As he turned, his gaze immediately fell upon the bed. Wagstaffe lay crouched in a foetal position, unmoving. The

315

pillows and the white sheets around him were spattered with blood.

Buck took a deep breath. He forced himself to take his eyes from the ugly red slit running diagonally the length of Wagstaffe's throat and looked once more around the little room. It was a shambles, with Wagstaffe's blood-spattered clothes mixed with documents, letters and other papers on the brown wooden floor.

Buck moved quickly to the door. He had seen enough.

An hour later, Buck and Billy Joe sat at the deserted bar of the Olympia on their fifth drink. Billy Joe reached into his inside pocket and pulled out a clip of notes.

'How much did he have left?' asked Buck, refilling their glasses.

Billy Joe thumbed through the notes. 'Exactly twenty-three dollars.' He paused, reached into a fob pocket for some coins and withdrew them. 'And twenty-five cents.'

'Whoever rubbed him cleaned him out good.

'No knowing,' said Billy Joe. 'I hear he'd been throwing money around like a crazy man.'

Buck sipped his drink meditatively. At that moment Carlo Montes, swatting flies with his sombrero, pushed his way through the swing doors into the bar.

'Gentlemen.' Montes sat himself down without ceremony in the spare chair at their table. 'You have found your Mr Wagstaffe?'

'Yup,' said Billy Joe. 'Dead as mutton.'

Montes mopped his brow with his white handkerchief. 'That is very sad,' he said. 'But your friend, he led a full life, no?' '

'Very full,' said Billy Joe.

'But no friend,' said Buck.

Montes continued to mop. 'You know of two gentlemen by name of Mr Hogg and Mr Taggart?'

Billy Joe shook his head, looking behind him to the barman for a glass for Montes. A moment later he had filled the Mexican's glass with tequila and pushed the salt across the table to him. Montes poured a trickle of grains on the back of his hand, then licked them off and put his tequila down in a single gulp.

'This Mr Hogg and Mr Taggart, I have been told they arrived in town this morning, while you were still at the cockfights. They are at the cockpit now,' said Montes, his voice low. 'They, too, were looking for Mr Wagstaffe.' He paused, his fat face registering his unhappiness. 'I think, senors, that they found him before you.'

'Then they've got our money!' exploded Buck.

Montes shook his head. 'Your Mr Wagstaffe had already lost much, at the tables, at the pit,' he explained. 'I do not think there was much left.' He paused again. 'This Mr Hogg and Mr Taggart, they think that you, as deputies, may be pursuing them.'

'We ain't no real deputies,' muttered Buck, looking down at his badge.

'Shut up,' said Billy Joe sharply. 'Mr Montes, could I ask if you would go to the cockpit to these . . . gentlemen, and tell them that we are not deputies, and have therefore no interest in them. You understand?'

Montes nodded, as Billy Joe reached into his pocket, withdrew some coins, and pressed them into the Mexican's hand. Montes nodded once more, rose and waddled towards the swing doors out into the afternoon sun.

He returned a quarter of an hour later, to stand at the door, as if it were unwise to venture further in.

'They do not want to talk,' he said.

Billy Joe rose and walked to the window, slowly drawing apart the dingy lace curtains. 'One of them in black and got a beard?' he said, looking through the parting in the curtains.

'Yes,' said Montes. 'That will be Mr Taggart.'

317

'And the other, kinda brown, looks as if he's got some Injun blood in him?'

'That is the man,' nodded Montes. 'Mr Hogg.'

'Perhaps they just need a bit of reassurance,' said Buck.

Billy Joe withdrew his Colt and opened it. 'I think not,' he said. He loaded the gun from his belt, whirling the cylinder.

'Fill your hand,' he said. 'These boys mean business.'

Billy Joe sounded cold, somehow different. Buck got to his feet and drew his Colt as Billy Joe tightened the gunbelt on his thigh.

'Move that cylinder.' Billy Joe pointed to Buck's gun. 'Is it greased good?'

'Perhaps we should try to talk to them first,' Buck said, abstractedly.

Billy Joe grabbed his friend by both shoulders, his face set and grim. 'Wipe them drippings from your mind,' he said, spitting out the words. He struggled to catch Buck's eyes. 'Buck,' he said. 'Those boys Hogg and Taggart are real. And willing. Never mind whether they've got cause or not. They *think* they have — and that's enough, however crazy it seems.'

Billy Joe looked down and spun the cylinder of his Colt again. 'Make sure your strapping is tight,' he said.

He drew and re-drew his gun, pointing, legs flexed, as Buck at last strapped his holster tight to his thigh. Billy Joe pulled Buck with him to the window-curtain.

'The guy on the left — Hogg — he's yours. Taggart leave to me. They twitch, we draw.'

He looked out through the curtains on to the deserted main street, silent in the heat of midday. There at the hitching-rail in front of the Hotel Hacienda opposite stood the two men, looking intently towards the doors of the Olympia.

'You ready?' said Billy Joe.

'Ready,' Buck whispered.

'The best of good luck, gentlemen.' It was Montes, behind them.

318

The two men hardly acknowledged Montes but slowly walked to the swing doors and out of the hotel. But the street was empty now, the sun hitting its baked surface like a stone.

Billy Joe looked to his left, then to his right: no sign of either Hogg or Taggart, despite their presence seconds before.

'Perhaps they don't want trouble,' said Buck, likewise surveying the deserted street.

'Perhaps,' echoed Billy Joe.

Buck thought he sounded disappointed. Billy Joe again looked to left and right. 'Maybe they're just biding their time.' He detached the deputy's badge from his shirt and placed it in his inside waistcoat pocket. Buck did the same, shaking his head.

'This idea of Moriarty's, being deputies . . .' he said.

'Not a good idea,' said Billy Joe. 'Come on, let's get out of here.'

They walked cautiously across the street towards the livery stable, a hundred yards to their left, just beyond a cantina.

They entered the shadowy building, finding its cool, dung-sweet atmosphere a relief after the sun outside. Billy Joe placed two dollars on a wooden ledge just inside the door, to pay for the stabling of their horses, and they walked to the far end of the stable towards their mounts.

Though neither man spoke to the other, there was a silent sense of urgency as they quickly saddled their animals. Then there was a whinny of horses behind them at the stable door. They turned to see two men framed in the bright light at the entrance. They could not see their faces.

'I think we're wanted,' growled Billy Joe.

Together they walked slowly towards the open door.

'That's far enough,' shouted the man on the left.

Billy Joe raised both hands well clear of his gun.

'You gentlemen names of Taggart and Hogg?' he said. There was about fifteen feet separating them.

'You got it,' said the smaller man, on the right. 'I'm Taggart.'

319

'Then we have no quarrel with you,' said Billy Joe. 'This man Wagstaffe, he was nothing to us.'

'That's not the way we see it,' said Hogg, on the left.

There was a pause, a stillness that seemed to be without end.

Neither Buck nor Billy Joe looked directly at Hogg or Taggart, but they had now fixed them standing in the light, exactly in the compass of their awareness, to the inch. The men's right hands were suspended by their guns, their knees bent.

Taggart was the first to make a move, but he was down, hit in the chest, before he had even cleared his holster, thrown yards back into the street behind him as Billy Joe's Colt erupted like a cannon. Hogg too had only just cleared his holster when he faced Buck's drawn gun. But, pistol cocked and pointing, Buck froze and Hogg lifted his gun and fired wildly. The bullet took the tip off Buck's left ear-lobe, spattering his cheek with warm blood. Reflexly he fired, taking a chunk off the top of Hogg's head. The man fell forward on to his face, his blood spurring on to the soft surface of the livery stable.

It had all happened in a moment, but now it was over. The two men lay, grotesquely contorted, Hogg flat on his face, his feet splayed, Taggart on his back, his right leg twisted crookedly underneath him, his white shirt and black waistcoat drenched in blood as buzz-flies quickly settled on his beard and moustache. Only moments before these men had been alive, menacing, capable of ending both the friends' lives; now they were carrion.

Buck and Billy Joe stood together, sweat streaming down their faces, their guns dangling limp and hot from their fingers, not daring to look down at the two dead men. Around them the horses in the stable neighed in alarm. Buck felt a bitter taste come up in his throat.

'I got to go,' he said, putting his hand on his mouth.

'Me too,' said Billy Joe.

Together they stumbled to the back of the Hacienda Hotel, to the water pump. Billy Joe pushed desperately on the handle, but the vomit came up before the water did, splattering out on to the scrub grass. Billy Joe's sickness acted as a trigger on Buck, who spewed a moment later. The two men vomited until they had nothing left to bring up but a thin, green bile, and even intermittently after that.

They sat side by side at the pump, heads between their knees, saying nothing for what seemed to be hours. If only Hogg and Taggart had been willing to talk, thought Buck. They could have kept the money, for all he cared. Perhaps the couple had been legitimate creditors, just like them, though God knows they should never have killed Wagstaffe.

'It should have been easy,' said Billy Joe, sniffing noisily and spitting on to the surface of the street. He loosened his gunbelt, withdrew his gun from its holster and emptied its contents into his hand. 'They were both slow as molasses.'

Buck felt the rage rise in him. A hundred yards away lay Taggart and Hogg, cold beneath a swarm of buzz-flies, dead for no reason.

So they now knew that they had fast draws, they had proved that: but being a Fast Man with a gun was nothing like sprinting up Main Street to con some greenhorns. It was about taking half a man's head off, or blasting away great red lumps of muscle and bone. It was fast, it was certainly skilful, but there was nothing romantic or noble about it.

Billy Joe spun the empty cylinder of his revolver, examined it, then replaced it in his belt. He stood up, stretched, refastened the belt round his waist and rejoined his friend. Finally he looked sideways at Buck.

'You froze,' he said.

'The hell I did,' said Buck, wiping his mouth with the back of his hand, and fingering his left ear-lobe. It was only a flesh wound, and had already stopped bleeding.

Billy Joe looked at him. 'No question of it,' he said.

Buck sat, head down, trying to control himself.

Of course he had frozen. He had initially failed to fire because the act of firing a gun at another human being had been beyond him. He had not, in Marshal Boone's terms, been 'willing'. Buck felt a mixture of shame at both what he had done and what he had failed to do — and rising anger that Billy Joe could treat the matter so casually.

'You froze,' said Billy Joe again. 'Like a goddam rabbit.'

There was no further discussion. Buck dived at Billy Joe's knees, and soon the two men were rolling about in the yard like a couple of alley-cats.

They fought until they were exhausted and the shadows had lengthened around them. Few of their punches made contact, though Buck did hit the back of Billy Joe's head, bruising his knuckles in the process, and then Billy Joe, missing Buck completely, butted the water-pump and slit his cheek. Most of the time they wrestled clumsily, rolling and grunting in the sand, the grit adhering to their glistening skin. Neither man was quite certain what he was trying to do. Certainly they did not want to kill or even seriously to hurt the other. Rather, the fight was simply the culmination of years of envy and petty squabbles. It had to be done, simply because when it was over, like a boil that had been lanced, all would be well.

It lasted less than a quarter of an hour, and even then they were forced to wrestle in spurts, sitting half-exhausted, surveying each other for some time before launching themselves into another ferocious bout of ineffectual grapples and swings. The battle had no aim, no purpose, save that of exhausting in one violent flurry all the resentment of thousands of miles. In the end, they lay on their fronts, their sweating, bleeding faces only inches away from each other. Then Buck wobbled uncertainly to his feet and, stooping, pulled Billy Joe up to join him.

'I think we've done all we had a mind to do,' he said, moving to the pump.

They sat in the twilight by the pump, gasping and bleeding, side by side. There was not an ounce of fight left in them.

Billy Joe gingerly explored the cut on his left cheek.

'How's my face?' he said, flexing his jaw. 'Feels like you cut it clean to the bone.'

Buck peered at Billy Joe in the gloom. 'It's nothing,' he said. 'It'll heal up good — be sort of like a German duelling wound. Mandy will love it.'

Billy Joe stood up and took hold of the pump handle.

'You really think so?' he said, pushing on the pump.

Water gushed forth, splattering Buck, who was sitting directly below it. Undisturbed, he allowed the water to pour over his head and trunk, wiping the blood and grit from his face as Billy Joe cupped his hands and did the same.

'You got in some good ones,' said Buck, fingering his jaw.

'No hard feelings,' said Billy Joe, proffering his hand.

Buck smiled. 'No hard feelings,' he replied.

16

STADE, DIAULOS, DOLICHOS

'*Stade, diaulos, dolichos*,' recited Moriarty, as they wended their way back from the cockpit through the shadowy alleyways of Chihuahua.Moriarty had, like Buck and Billy Joe, left the rail-head at Albuquerque, but had not followed their route south-west into Mexico, choosing instead a route to the south-east. He had picked up Wagstaffe's trail in Presidio Del Monte, where the banker had lost twenty-five thousand dollars at the gambling tables of the El Presidente Hotel. Since leaving New York in March, Moriarty had been out of touch with Eleanor, and knew nothing of his impending fatherhood.

On his arrival in Chihuahua he had been told of the gunfight and had located Buck and Billy Joe at the cockpit, both of them considerably the worse for tequila.

'*Stade, diaulos, dolichos*,' repeated Moriarty. 'That's how we're going to make our way back into the money.'

'Say that again,' mumbled Billy Joe, kicking at an alleycat and missing.

'I've already said it twice,' growled Moriarty.

'It would help,' said Buck.

'You two, you never had the benefits of a Scottish education.'

'Never felt the lack of it,' said Billy Joe.

'*Stade*,' said Moriarty, as they approached the El Grande Hotel. 'What does that word suggest to you?'

Buck and Billy Joe remained silent as they walked together

out of the shadows into the pool of light cast by the torches burning on the adobe walls of the hotel.

'Got it,' said Buck. '*Stadt*, German for town.'

'Good guess,' said Moriarty. 'But wrong.'

'Anything to do with poker?' said Billy Joe, screwing up his face. '*Stade* poker.'

Moriarty mock-grimaced. 'Jesus Christ. All the time I thought I'd been travelling with cultured people. If you two had brains enough to spit. . .'

'Come on, Moriarty. We give up,' said Buck.

'*Stade*, the length of the stadium,' said Moriarty.

They mounted the steps of the hotel onto the balcony in front of the crowded cantina, pausing as they came upon a noisy group of Mexicans. There a smiling Montes sat, surrounded by friends. The Mexican rose, slightly unsteadily, brandishing a bottle of tequila.

'Your Mr Hogg and Mr Taggart,' he said, 'I have arranged a proper Christian burial for these gentlemen, and for your Mr Wagstaffe.'

He raised a fat hand as if they had asked a question, then shook his head.

'No cost, senors. Their horses and saddles are with the undertaker — my friend Mr Valdez here.' A scrawny, cadaverous Mexican at Montes' table stood. He smiled and bowed, revealing a row of black, rotten teeth. 'The rest of their goods I have kept, for necessary expenses. Part of the service. You understand.'

'What about the law?' asked Billy Joe.

'The *policia*?' responded Montes. 'Their costs have been met.'

Buck looked at Billy Joe. His face was expressionless. As one they nodded and again, shook Montes' hand before passing on into the cantina.

'. . . then there was *diaulos* and *dolichos*", continued Moriarty impatiently. 'They were races back in ancient times at the old Olympic Games.'

325

'Where was all this, these Olympic Games?' asked Billy Joe as they made their way through the cantina to a corner table. 'Up Boston way?'

'Olympia, Greece,' said Moriarty, sitting down. 'Two thousand years ago. They held the games every four years, to honour the God Zeus.'

'Sort of like the Highland Games,' put in Billy Joe.

'Sort of,' said Moriarty, looking around him for a waiter. 'The sprint race was about a furlong, the length of the ground — that was the *stade*.'

'So that's how we get the word stadium,' said Buck.

'Top of the class, Buck,' responded Moriarty, smiling. 'Stadium, the *stade* area enclosed by the bleachers.'

'Okay,' said Billy Joe. 'So where's all this taking us?'

'Right back into the money,' said Moriarty.

'I'm not with you,' said Buck. 'What about the other two . . .?'

'The *diaulos* and the *dolichos*?'

'Yes.'

Moriarty at last caught a waiter's eye and ordered a bottle of tequila. '*Diaulos*, that was the quarter-mile: twice the length of the *stade*.'

'Round a track?'

'Not exactly. They all ran up the two hundred yards straight, round the pillar at the end of the stadium then back to the finish.'

'Left to right or right to left?' asked Buck.

'There was no rule,' said Moriarty. 'These Greeks just took it as it came.'

'No rules,' said Billy Joe. 'Then all those runners must've made a lot of friends there, at that pillar. But that was the *diaulos* race, a quarter-mile?'

Moriarty nodded.

'And what about the last one?'

'The *dolichos*? That was about three miles,' replied Moriarty.

'Round and round that same goddam pillar for three miles?' exclaimed Billy Joe.

'Two pillars, one at each end. A four hundred yard lap.'

The tequila arrived. Buck poured out three measures. 'Not exactly my idea of an afternoon's sport,' he said.

Moriarty placed some salt from a plate in the centre of the table on his hand, licked it, then put the tequila down in one, grimacing. Buck and Billy Joe did the same.

Billy Joe was the first to speak. 'This stade, dollos, dolleyecos – what the hell does it have to do with us? You want us to go run against Greeks in these Olympics? Just count me out.'

Moriarty was silent as he refilled his glass.

'Come on,' said Buck. 'You've given us your history lesson. This Greek stuff, what's it got to do with us?'

Moriarty smiled. He had teased them long enough. 'It means,' he said, speaking slowly, 'that we've got ourselves the biggest race of our lives, the biggest foot-race in the history of the world. That's what it means.'

'Where?' said Buck.

'Yuta City, Arizona,' replied Moriarty. 'Just come from there.'

Judge Haynes was the perfect choice to resolve the Big Wet dispute. He had settled the Colson County Land War of 1870, acted as adviser to government in the negotiations with the Sioux on the Black Hills (for which he had been made blood-brother to Sitting Bull in the early 1870s), and had served as arbitrator in the chaotic Lima County Land Rush of 1871. But his biggest popular success had been in sport, back in 1869, when he had refereed the heavyweight fist fight between Bill Noonan and Tom King on a barge moored on the Mississippi, thirty miles west of St Louis.

It was now common knowledge that Judge Haynes had been on to a certain ten grand to give the fight to the challenger King (The Talahassee Tiger), but the portly little judge had played it straight down the line in refereeing a murderous battle lasting seventy-eight rounds, one which had ended in a blinded King unable to totter back to scratch within the prescribed time. Everyone in attendance (saving King's handler) had agreed that it had been as fair and manly a show of fisticuffs as they had witnessed; and that this was as much to the credit of Haynes as to the two men themselves.

But the good judge's role in the Noonan-King fracas had not ended there. After the fight King had been abandoned by his managers in St Louis, half-crippled and virtually sightless. The judge had paid the prizefighter's hospital bills and set him up in a hotel till he was healed up good. Then, when Tom King was fully recovered, Haynes had made him swear to give up fist-fighting and abjure strong liquor, and had secured him a post as barman in the Fighting Chance.

Haynes, now sixty-one, had been brought into the Big Wet dispute as a result of taking up his retirement in Yuta City, Arizona, in late '75. The Big Wet was a lush, wide watering place which divided the spreads of 'Buzz' Brennan, a fiery, red-haired Irishman whose grandfather had fought at the Alamo, and an Australian, Pat Boyle. Boyle, like many Australians, was the son of an ex-convict who had settled in San Francisco in the 1840s. His father, a member of the murderous gang known as the 'Sydney Ducks', had narrowly escaped hanging when the Vigilantes had cleaned up San Francisco in 1850, and had quickly made his way to Arizona. After cowboying for five years he eventually bought himself a spread in Yuta County. Originally the Brennans' and the Boyles' spreads had been separated by the land of another rancher, a Dutchman, Elf Kamerbeck, but Kamerbeck had been driven out by the Apaches in 1865 and his land had been gradually taken up on each side of the Big Wet, without dispute, by his two more powerful neighbours.

In the late 1860s the Irishman and the Australian had joined forces to wipe out the Apaches and make the area safe for

328

ranching, and by Buzz Brennan's death, of smallpox, in 1874, the Indians were no longer the menace they had been. Then, in 1875, Pat Boyle had been accidentally shot, caught in the cross-fire of a gunfight in Sonora, and it had been left to their two sons to run the respective spreads.

If anything, the Brennan and Boyle boys had been even faster friends than their fathers. Indeed, young Pete Boyle had in early 1877 married Sally Brennan, and there were already twins, a boy and a girl, as a result of the union. But in the hot summer of 1877 things turned sour. As the result of a prolonged drought the water in both spreads had dropped to a thin trickle, and on 23 June both parties had large herds watering beside the shallow — but still flowing — Big Wet.

No one would ever be able to say with certainty how the fight over the Big Wet began that torrid, baking afternoon. Suffice it to say that there was an argument between the two foremen, Roy Bass of the Brennan spread and Jake Wood of the Boyle, and that Wood came back with a bullet through a broken right arm that would never be the same again.

Then the following month there was a fist-fight in Yuta City between members of the opposing factions; two days later a dozen Brennan beeves were found shot dead. But it was Roy Bass's death in November that year that brought the feud to a head. On the afternoon of 6 November 1877 Bass and a young cowboy, Danny Malloy, had been out rounding up some mavericks near the Big Wet. Malloy would never be certain where the shot had come from, but Bass had gone down, shot through the head. To his credit, young Malloy stood his ground, but the killer had clean melted away. Two weeks later, on 20 November, the Boyle cowboy, Jimmy Clark, was shot in the back in Yuta City, and the Yuta County War had started in earnest.

By the time Judge Haynes was brought in, in the spring of '78, there were five dead and eight wounded between the spreads, and there was even some talk of bringing in hired guns from up north.

It was Sally Brennan who had been the catalyst. She and Pete Boyle had been hitched by Judge Haynes in January 1877, and during the reception, lubricated by liquor, the judge had regaled her with tales of his past judgements. Surely, reasoned the new Mrs Boyle as Christmas 1877 approached, this was the ideal man to arbitrate on the dispute over the rights to the Big Wet?

It had taken three months to bring the Brennans and the Boyles together with Haynes on neutral ground in the court-house of Yuta City. The judge found that the opposite claims were evenly balanced. Both sides had used the Big Wet inter-mittently for years without argument, and there had always been plenty of water. Only the drought of 1877 and a now-forgotten argument between two dead men had brought the matter into serious question in the first place. However, there was no doubt that the dispute had to be settled one way or another, if more death and disability were not to result.

The judge was both a sportsman and a classical scholar. In his youth he had been a fancy rassler, Cumberland style, and a better than average footracer. He was steeped in Plato, Sophocles and Ovid and other classical writings, the works of thinkers who had been the bedrock of Western philosophy. Haynes knew that the Romans and Greeks, and particularly the latter, had also been the first societies to pursue organised sports competitions. Indeed, the Greek Crown Games, headed by the Olympics, had been a much more fully-developed sports culture than existed in the sand-lot baseball leagues, street-races and impromptu fist-fights that had up till now constituted sport in the United States.

So, thought Haynes, how better to settle the Brennan-Boyle dispute than to mix ancient and modern, bringing the foot-racing of the Olympics together with a little horse-riding — and settle the matter of the Big Wet once and for all?

Albert Haynes knew that if Yuta County was ever going to

develop beyond a dusty, Godforsaken backwater its leaders would have to think beyond their guns. True, the Brennan-Boyle dispute would eventually end — all feuds did — but it was essential that it do so with the minimum of bitterness, and in a civilised fashion.

When Pete Boyle and Bill Brennan, dour and glowering, met Judge Haynes in the adobe courthouse in Yuta on the afternoon of 20 April 1878, they were both convinced that the judge would attempt an immediate and summary arbitration. And, although neither said so, each felt that this would only be acceptable if the decision went his way.

Haynes, the perspiration running down his ruddy face, had poured out ample glasses of the best redeye, as outside the heat hit the white adobe walls like a hammer.

'Ain't nothing new under the sun, gentlemen,' he had begun. 'Way back in olden times when them kings had some dispute — over women, over land, you name it — they had their own ways of settling it, all without blood.'

He again drew on his redeye, took out a white handkerchief and mopped his sweat-pearled brow. 'Blood is a big expense. Is now, always was. So them kings, they said to themselves, why kill good men? Let's find some other way to sort this out.'

Boyle and Brennan continued their glowering, but let Haynes have his say.

'Them kings, they said let the gods decide, in ritual combat.'

'Ritual what?' said Pete Boyle.

'Ritual combat, Pete. Competition,' replied Haynes. 'Sometimes they used rasslers, most often they used runners.'

'You mean footracers?' said Brennan.

Haynes nodded and poured them all out another long bit. 'They reckoned to have their chosen representatives run 'gainst each other. Whoever won, they got the land or the woman or whatever.'

'Is that what you're suggesting now -— for the Big Wet?' said Brennan.

Haynes nodded. 'Here's the way I see it,' he said. 'Each team has three men and one horse. The team is composed of a furlong runner, a quarter-miler and a distance man, just like the Greeks. It's a sort of man and horse relay race, three laps in all. Each lap starts here at Yuta City out across the Big Wet, over El Diablo Mountain, across the Big Wet again at the bridge, then back to town, for one lap. The distance-runners are the only ones to cover the full three laps, either on foot or on horseback.'

'So how does it start off?' asked Boyle.

'With two men from each team, the distance—runner and the sprinter, each team with a horse,' replied Haynes. 'Each team can cover that first stage any way they like — at least until the final furlong into town to end the first lap.'

'What happens then?' said Brennan.

'We have a flag a furlong out from town. That final furlong has to be run by the sprinters. Then they're finished, and it's either one-up to Boyle or one-up to Brennan.'

Brennan nodded. 'Then it's the distance man and the quarter-miler setting off for the second lap?'

Haynes nodded, pouring each man out another large measure. 'Same thing on the second lap,' he said. 'We have a flag a quarter-mile out from the finish. The quarter-milers must dismount and run that final section. Then it's either two-nothing, in which case we don't run the final leg, or it's one-all and everything to play for.'

'And say it's one-all, the final lap — that's just the two distance boys and their horses?' asked Boyle, sipping his whiskey. Both he and Brennan were now totally absorbed.

'Yes,' nodded Haynes. 'But they got to come off their horses one English mile from the finish and fight it out running, so we got a distance race for the final part.'

'Let's get this clear,' said Brennan. 'We both got three men running and riding. Say my distance man beats his man . . . and my quarter-man loses but my sprinter wins?'

'Then you win two to one,' said the judge.

'What happens if a horse goes lame or something?' asked Boyle.

'Too bad,' replied Haynes. 'The will of the gods.'

'What would be the length of the course?' asked Brennan.

'Mutual agreement,' replied Haynes. 'My guess is that a good test would be three laps of five miles round the Big Wet, just like I said. Plenty of variety — scrub, desert, hills. But it's up to you.'

'And the runners could run or ride, except for the final part of each lap?' asked Boyle.

'Tactics,' said Haynes, nodding. 'If someone's hurting bad then he may have to take a rest on horseback for a whiles. That means that his team-mate has to go on foot. It's brain as well as brawn.'

'And these footracers, where would we find them?'

'You would have five, maybe six months to get your teams together,' replied Haynes. 'St Louis, New York, San Francisco — there's plenty of fancy footracers up in them parts. Even all the way from England. You've both got the time.'

There was silence.

'Just think of it, boys. A way to end it all, clean and fair, and have one heck of a time into the bargain. Hell, they'll come from all over just to get a peek — the richest footrace in the history of man.'

Thus it was that, on 20 April 1878, the articles of the Yuta County Foot Race were signed.

Articles of Agreement

1. The competition to take place over three five-mile laps starting at noon on 20 October 1878, a circular course encompassing the Big Wet, El Diablo Mountain and the town of Yuta City itself, the start to be the Buena Vista Hotel.

2. Each team will consist of three men and one horse.

3. The competition will be a relay over three separate laps, two men from each team and a horse competing over each lap, with only the distance-runners completing the full fifteen-mile course, the other runners completing one lap only. Thus, the sprinter and distance-runner from each team will cover the first lap, the quarter-milers and distance-runners the second, with the final lap covered by the distance-runners alone.

4. The two-man teams will be allowed to run or ride at their discretion on each lap, the only proviso being that on the first lap the sprinters must run the final furlong to the finish, on the second lap the quarter-milers must run the final quarter-mile and on the last lap the distance-runners the final mile, these distances being marked by Union flags and being scrutinised by officials appointed by Judge Haynes. The distance-runners are required to cover all three laps, the other two runners competing against each other only on one lap.

5. The winner of the competition is the team which has won the most lap victories, i.e. 2-0 — 2-1, the final arbiter on all competitions being Judge Haynes. Should the first two runs result in victory for any one team, then the final lap by the distance-runners will not be run.

6. The two horses are to be selected by Judge Haynes, and the parties in dispute (Peter Boyle and William Brennan) will throw dice for choice of mounts.

7. The ownership and watering rights of the area known as The Big Wet will be assigned to the sponsor of the victorious team.

Bill Brennan had signed up Moriarty, Buck and Billy Joe in Yuta on their return from Mexico in early May. He offered one hundred thousand dollars between them for a win, nothing if they lost, but with all training expenses paid till the day of the race. Moriarty reckoned that they could pick up at least another twenty-five thousand dollars or more in bets (so long as Eleanor and the girls were willing to pawn their jewels), and a victory would then make the Theatre of the West a going concern again.

After telling Bill Brennan he had a team, they decided to set up training quarters in San Rafael, New Mexico, as the town had a good hotel, baths and sweat-box, and terrain similar to that which they would later face in Yuta County.

But first, they would stay till June in the seclusion of Brennan's ranch, checking out the country and in particular the problems involved in the mountain stretch across El Diablo. At Brennan's they would take time for gentle purges and sweats, the latter from a sweat-box which the rancher had brought in from San Francisco.

This time there would be no short, brutal month of the English Method; they would condition themselves slowly and gradually till the end of September, then taper off into the last three weeks of the race.

It was not long before they knew their rivals.

Moriarty had known for months that William M. Bunn was in the United States. The Englishman had arrived with two top athletes, Josiah Headley and the Scottish miler, Alec Tulloch, in mid-March, and just three weeks later, on 7 April, Headley had shocked the world of American pedestrianism by moving up a distance to run a half-mile in an amazing one minute and fifty-five seconds, the fastest ever run. Two days later Tulloch was to grab the headlines, becoming the first man on American soil to beat four minutes twenty seconds for the mile, running a second inside that time at Hoboken Racetrack. A week after that, at Saratoga Racecourse, he failed by a mere two seconds to break fourteen and a half minutes for three miles.

It was thus entirely predictable that in early May Pete Boyle had travelled east to sign up both Tulloch and Headley, who were on thirty thousand dollars a man to win, with Bunn as their manager on twenty-five thousand dollars. It took only a further week for Boyle's team to be completed, when he signed contracts with the Indian, who had four days before become the first American to run a genuine sub-ten second hundred yards, in St Paul's, Missouri.

For two of Boyle's men the Yuta County race would have a special significance. The Indian had never forgotten that he had been defeated by Billy Joe in Virginia City, even if the judges had handed the race to him. He had been beaten then, but now he was by general judgement at least two yards faster, and, as he told an early eager reporter, with no kangaroo start to help him Billy Joe Speed was going to have to run out of his skin to take him. He felt no malice for the Texan; but he was out to put the record straight.

Josiah Headley's motives were altogether different. The financial consequences of his defeat at the hands of Buck Miller had forced Headley to accept his mentor, William Bunn's suggestion to tour America, where he would find easy pickings. At first he demurred. Headley hated travel; but to his surprise he soon found the United States greatly to his taste. The Americans liked winners, even Limeys who whipped their own boys, and in his first races on the eastern seaboard Headley had thrashed the best men the Yanks had put to him, his opening series of races culminating with his world record over the half-mile. After just two months campaigning he was a star of American pedestrianism.

So too was his colleague, the Scot, Tulloch. He had been kept under wraps by Bunn since 1873, when he had appeared as a sprinter off a long handicap at Sheffield, over three hundred yards, winning his backer five thousand pounds in a finish in which only a yard had separated the six runners. Bunn had raced him only once in 1874, moving him up to half a mile to defeat the Australian, Clowrey, at Newcastle. Then, the following year, in an attempt to break 4 minutes 30 seconds for the mile, the Scot, finishing apparently exhausted, had timed it perfectly, running half a second inside the old record. A series of planned races against the Kent runner, Jackson, early the following spring had come to nothing because of Jackson's illness; Bunn had therefore been able to get long odds on Tulloch when his man made his debut over three miles in December of 1876, against the unbeaten Powe of Hereford. The race was held on the frosty flint-hard surface of the Victoria Grounds, Wigan, before 30,000 spectators. Tulloch, running from the front, had roasted Powe, clocking nine and a half minutes for the first two miles, a record for the distance, the Hereford man retiring from the race half a mile later. In Tulloch Moriarty was facing a runner at the peak of his powers — and one who had been raced sparingly. Most important of all, Tulloch was a man who had never seen another runner's back.

28 June 1878, San Rafael, New Mexico
Training for the Brennan trio was going well. Their bowels had been thoroughly purged, the sweats taken regularly, and Moriarty had been pleased to see that all their stools were now floating, always a good sign. Then on 28 June he had come down with a mild bout of flu and had gone to San Rafael's only medic, the redoubtable Doc Halliwell. The Doc — like everyone in the area — was well aware of the Yuta County challenge and, in the half-light of his gloomy little surgery, had given Moriarty a thorough examination as well as a good dose of physic.

When he had finished he had sat his patient down in a chair in front of him.

'Moriarty,' he said. 'I've got to give it to you straight. You ever had any trouble with your heart?'

The Scot felt his throat go dry. 'Back as a boy,' he said and he told his questioner of the race in the snow against Latour in New York back in 1859.

'Well,' said Halliwell. 'You've got yourself a murmur.'

'What does that mean?'

Halliwell poured himself a short whiskey and offered Moriarty a glass. The Scotsman shook his head.

'We medical men don't know much, Moriarty, no matter what we say or what most folks think. Sometimes I think we're kinda like plumbers trying to fix fancy Swiss watches.' Halliwell paused and sipped his drink. 'But a murmur is a murmur. You want to hear what I reckon you've got?'

Moriarty nodded, his pulse racing.

'A colleague of mine, up Boston way, had to perform an autopsy, must be six years back. It was on a man of thirty-five. This man, I can't recall his name, he had been a great athlete all his life, had been a match-racer in rowing in his youth, had rowed every day God gave him, rain, sun or snow.'

Halliwell took another sip of his drink.

'Then, one day, he just keeled over in the boat, stone dead.

This feller, he had left his body to science in his will, so my colleague performed the autopsy. Know what he found?'

He paused.

'What we in the profession call "athlete's heart". A heart as big as a pumpkin. All loose and weak and stretched.'

He shook his head.

'The way I see it, the human body can only take so much, you see. My friend, he reckoned the ol' heart's like a piece of elastic. Stretch it too far, it's gone, can't pump no more. Know what I mean? Gone, overstretched, no power left.'

'Now I'm not saying that's happened to you. Not yet, leastways. What I *am* saying is this Yuta County race, this could be the last straw that breaks the camel's back. You got to face it, you're no spring chicken. You're thirty-nine years of age. Just how long is the race?'

'You know, Doc.'

'Fifteen miles for you, most of it on foot. Okay, so some of it will be on horseback, but most of it won't be, 'cos you'll have to keep your sprinters fresh. Then there's the heat, and those goddam hills. Moriarty, that kind of race would cripple most young men, men in the full bloom of youth. You, you're well into middle-age.'

338

Moriarty scowled and shook his head.

'Doc,' he said, 'twenty years ago, a doctor just like you told me I had Athlete's Heart. Since then I must have run a thousand races and never had a day's trouble.'

Halliwell shook his head, folded his stethoscope and put it in his pocket.

'You know what my advice would be?' he said.

Moriarty did not reply, his face sullen.

Halliwell drew in a deep breath. 'Pull out. Buy yourself a younger man, someone hungry, someone with some sap in his legs. It's the money you want, ain't it, not the glory?'

Moriarty nodded, but he knew in his heart that he was lying. He stood up and shook Halliwell's hand. For the first time in his life he felt middle-aged. Of course he wanted the money, for the cash took him to his only future. But as he walked from the gloom of Doc Halliwell's office out into the harsh New Mexico sunshine, Moriarty knew that he would run. For he had felt from the moment that he had first met Bill Brennan that this was his race, one which, whatever the outcome, would complete his years of Western wanderings. This would be the one great final contest, the race that would place his name forever in the annals of footracing. In his dreams he had seen himself charging up Main Street, Tulloch nowhere in sight, all the years of running fused into one marvellous moment of victory. But Doc Halliwell might be right. Perhaps the Big Wet race would stretch the heart's elastic to its limits, to the point where there would be no recoil.

Moriarty returned to his lodgings and penned a letter. It was not a long letter, but it took him some time to compose. It was written in a more formal style than Moriarty was accustomed to use, and four drafts were angrily launched towards the waste-paper basket before the final version was despatched to Edwin Booth at Niblo's Theatre, New York:

Dear Edwin,

It now appears that your 'training regime' of two bottles of wine a day may have as much to commend it as my daily programme of running and Jahn callisthenics. I say this because, ironically, a recent medical examination raises the possibility that I may have the condition known as 'athlete's heart', probably the result of that race in the snow against Latour all those long years ago. If memory

serves me well, it was your shout to me of the words 'The moment!' at a critical point in the match that was the difference between victory and defeat. The Yuta City race is my moment, Edwin, more important to me than all the contests of the past twenty years put together, as important as your Richelieu was to you back in England in 1862 when all seemed lost.

Everything rests upon the outcome, but I confess to you that for each of us it goes beyond mere dollars and cents, for in Headley, Tulloch and the Indian we meet the best runners of our era in a contest which will stretch all of us to our limits.

It is in this knowledge, that reaching to my limits may bring me close to death, that I ask from you a favour. It is that you take out for me an insurance policy on my life for a maximum of fifty thousand dollars, a sum which should provide Eleanor with the necessary comforts in the event of my demise. I would ask too that you should mention nothing of this to anyone.

Look forward to seeing you in Yuta City on the day of the race.

Yours,
Moriarty

News of the Big Wet race had now gone far beyond the borders of Arizona, and had appeared in newspapers in New York and Los Angeles as early as mid-June. The first odds had been laid only a fortnight later in both cities, and in London only days later in the leading sporting paper, *Bell's Life*. The finest of Europe's sporting fraternity had set out from Liverpool in late July, a motley mix of English nobility, hard-headed Scots, northern bookmakers, and French and Italian gamblers.

It had taken till early August for the first spies to locate the Brennan group in San Rafael, for Moriarty and his men could have sought training quarters almost anywhere in Arizona or New Mexico. They had therefore pursued the bulk of their preparation free from prying eyes. The Boyle group had been located by Brennan a week earlier, three hundred miles west, in Bitter Springs, just north of Yuta. The first news from Bitter Springs was that Headley, who had ridden as a youth in Yorkshire as a groom to the Marquis of Leeds, was a fine horseman, so there would be little gap in riding skills between Headley and Buck.

There was little that observers in San Rafael could report back to their masters, for Moriarty and his team took care to vary their training times. In any case, any spies could be easily seen in the vastness of the prairie separating the cluster of shops and bars that was San Rafael from the Puentes, a barren, five-thousand-foot range of hills where Moriarty's group pursued their daily training.

At first the odds fluctuated, with most of the big money going on the Boyle team. After all, these were three of the fastest men in the world at their distances. Then in May, when the terms of agreement became public knowledge, disputes arose on the quality of the horsemanship of the Boyle team relative to Brennan's group. It was known that Billy Joe was a fine rider and that Moriarty had done some trick riding in his youth. Buck Miller was an unknown quantity, but nevertheless the odds against Moriarty's group dropped to three to one, for horsemanship rather than running might well decide the contest.

Next it was discovered that Tulloch had, as a young man, been a jockey in the employ of the Duke of Buccleuch. The odds against Moriarty and the Brennan team rose again to four to one.

The afficionados of foot-racing were faced with a problem. True, there had been man and horse races before, but never between top-class athletes. It was clear that over the first two laps the fast men would be kept on horseback till the last possible moment to keep their legs fresh. The big questions related to the ability of these sprinters and the quarter-milers to negotiate the steep incline of El Diablo and their condition at the end of the climb and descent, which was less than a mile from the point of their final sprints.

From all this speculation Moriarty and his men remained aloof, varying their venues from one day to the next to deter the clockers.

For speculation Moriarty substituted strategy. The Big Wet was easily fordable by horse, being mostly two feet deep though a couple of feet deeper in the middle; but the difficulty on each stage would be on the one-mile climb up El Diablo. There was no way of riding up the mountain for any appreciable distance — it was too steep and rocky for that — so the animal would have to be led up. After that the way down would be no problem, particularly for expert horsemen like Billy Joe and Moriarty, and would indeed be a useful point at which to gain further advantage. From then on it was across the bridge and a mile of flat, fast road to the finish, with flags at the various points at which obligatory running had to begin.

Moriarty therefore arranged to have water-bags placed on the course, one just before the Big Wet, another at the base of El Diablo and a third two miles later at its foot, just a mile short of Yuta City. He had broken down the distance as follows: from Yuta City to the Big Wet 11/2 miles of cart track, then 1/2 mile scrub to the base of El Diablo followed by one mile up the mountain and the same down. Finally, one mile on good road into Yuta City.

Central to their preparation were the hill sessions. Their daily repetitions up in the Puente Hills were agony for Buck and Billy Joe — particularly for the latter, for Buck had at least the memory of Norfolk's Cromer Sands to remind him of the pain, and how it could be contained and conquered. For Billy Joe, however, the Puentes held nothing but unconscionable agony. On the first day, after only a furlong on their steep, rocky slopes, he was gasping for breath in the thin air, and although he and Buck soon began to adapt to the specific requirements of the hills, in Billy Joe's case adaptation was only marginal. The Texan was a sprinting animal, and no amount of endurance training could make him into much else. Moriarty knew that the moment of truth for Billy Joe would be on that one mile uphill stretch on El Diablo. If the Indian gained too much there it would take all of Billy Joe's riding skills on the downhill stretch to close the gap before the final furlong of sprinting into Yuta City.

The ladies had been told to stay in New York, if not upon pain of death then on something close enough to deter them from disobeying. For Eleanor there was the general worry over how Moriarty would stand up to the training, as well as the risk of the whole venture. But it was the work of a zealous young reporter called Martin Sykes which brought her most alarm. Sykes had burrowed back into the *Police Gazette* files of the 1850s to locate details of Moriarty's early matches and had unearthed the accounts of his 1859 race in the snow against Latour and the subsequent report that Moriarty had been banned, on doctor's orders, from further competition. Dr. Sutherland, now 75, was duly located in retirement in Hartford, Connecticut, and confirmed that Moriarty had indeed been advised not to run again competitively. He confirmed, too, that in middle age and with a record of athlete's heart Moriarty should long ago have exchanged running spikes for soft slippers, and that the proposed fifteen-mile Yuta City run might indeed prove to be a fatal one.

Eleanor, seven months pregnant, could have done without such speculation and recorded her feelings in her normal style:

26 July 1878
The Big Wet race has now become, because of Dr. Sutherland, in the pages of the popular press, 'The Death Race'. A new set of odds has been created, albeit not openly. These are on Moriarty's expiring, and lie at four to one against, having been as high as eight to one — clear evidence that some 'sportsmen' have been willing to lay good sums on such a melancholy outcome.

29 July 1878
Hettie and Mandy have been immensely supportive since certain knowledge of my pregnancy in March. Buck and Billy Joe are fortunate to have found women of such worth. Both Hettie and Mandy feel that Moriarty should know nothing of my situation until l arrive in Yuta City (when my condition will be all too obvious to him), as such knowledge could only distract him. Edwin feels the same, but I have observed that he himself has been of late moody and depressed. This surprises me, for the reviews of *Hamlet* have been excellent from the start.

My feeling is that Moriarty should know that he is to be a father, and so be allowed the choice of whether to risk running or not, in the full knowledge of the circumstances. I have therefore decided to write to him in San Rafael, giving him a full two months to find and train a substitute, should he choose to withdraw from the race.

1 August 1878
The letter written, I walked with it in my handbag to the Post Office and was within yards of its despatch when, on impulse, l tore it to shreds. Why did l do this?

Most of our life together, I surmise, has been a gamble. Edwin gambled when he came with Moriarty to England to try his luck in 1862, and it was as a result of this gamble that I first came to meet Moriarty. We both gambled in coming west, and every day since in this freezing, blistering, disease-ridden country has trembled on the razor-edge of chance.

And, whatever else it has been, our life has always contained an element of excitement, a note of drama, independent of our theatrical productions. The Big Wet race is simply the biggest gamble we have taken. If we lose, we will be little the worse off, for we have each other, with the sweet prospect of a child to cheer us.

And if there is such a condition as 'athlete's heart' (and there is little evidence that there is) Moriarty seems to have survived it well enough for over twenty years. My guess is that he is now in the finest condition of his life, and that to put any pressure on him at this fragile moment would be a betrayal. Let things run their course.

18 October 1878, Yuta City

Eleanor and the girls had arrived two days before the race, with Edwin Booth and Barnum. From England had come such notables as Lord Astley, Sir Philip Boothroyd, Lord Hardcastle and Ashley Blythe, the editor of *Bell 's Life*; from France Count Philippe de la Salle and Baron Prost; from Canada a former Governor General, Sir Augustus Mackay, and from Mexico Generals de Montoya and de Christobal. From the world of acting, supplementing Booth and the ladies, had come Gregor McGregor and Eammon Grogarty, plus Edwin Forrest and Mrs Charlotte Cushman and a host of minor thespians. Leland Stanford had travelled all the way from San Francisco and was encamped in the style of an Indian rajah in marquees three miles north of town, dispensing largesse on an Olympian scale. From Canyon City had come Mayor Halsey and Judge Perry, and down from Oregon Billy Joe Speed's old trail-boss Cal Frenn. Much of Moriarty's team's past and most of their present were now in Yuta City; and all of their future

It seemed to the natives of the city itself that the whole world was pouring into their home town, and three hotels were hastily built to accommodate two hundred guests at a hundred dollars a night. These new hospices covered their construction costs in the first week, as guests slept in baths, on billiard-tables, in the livery stables, even on the floor and on the bar itself.

But the three extra hotels could not contain the thousands threatening to engulf the little town, and two other townships began to take shape on the outskirts of Yuta. One, to the north, was called Boyle City, and consisted of Boyle team devotees and their fans; the other to the south was called Brennanville, suitably patronised by Brennan team supporters. Both were crazy, haphazard collections of tents and lean-tos, but were microcosms of Yuta City, containing bars, beds, brothels and the equally essential privies.

The Boyle group were lodging at the Yuta Hotel. Moriarty and his team, at the Excelsior, studiously avoided meeting them. Instead, they confined themselves to their course-inspections and to the dark confines of their rooms, playing endless games of poker, dominoes and black-jack for imaginary bets.

But Moriarty was fast running out of ploys to keep his men amused. The physical time was over; the race now lay in their minds, for that was where it would be won or lost. Moriarty, usually voluble, seemed reduced to only one phrase: 'Them that don't give up are never beat.' He kept saying it again and again until it became a litany, almost a hymn to the three men.

As Moriarty, Buck and Billy Joe saw it, their tactics would be simple and flexible. On the first lap the aim would be to have Billy Joe ride against the Indian for almost the whole five miles, across the Big Wet, over El Diablo and back to the sprint-marker, set at a furlong from the finish. There he would dismount and make his final dash.

346

Behind Billy Joe and the Indian, Moriarty and Tulloch would slog it out on foot, only picking up their mounts for short rests at the sprint-markers.

Then, when Moriarty arrived back in town on horseback, ideally with a few yards' lead on Tulloch, Buck would take to the saddle and ride against Headley, again for most of the course, up to the quarter-mile marker. There he would dismount and run all the way to the finish, to complete his lap.

With any luck, there would then be no need for Moriarty and Tulloch to battle it out over the final lap, for they would by then have established a 2-0 lead. If, however, the contest was level, then Moriarty and Tulloch would in the final lap ride four miles to the mile marker, where they would dismount and fight it out on foot.

But that was to paint a simple and optimistic scenario. For if things were going badly with Moriarty it might be necessary for Buck or Billy Joe, if they had established a decent lead on horseback, to dismount early to allow Moriarty more time on horseback to catch an opponent on foot. Buck and Billy Joe would therefore carry binoculars with them, to check on the progress of the race behind them and to make any necessary tactical adjustments.

19 October, Yuta City

Judge Haynes cleared his throat and looked at Pete Boyle and Bill Brennan sitting across the table.

'You two boys seen the horses?'

The men nodded.

'Now, we got ourselves one black, one grey. Both big in the haunch. They'll last the course, no question.'

He reached into a fob pocket and withdrew a dice. 'The contract states that you throw for choice of horses. You gentlemen ready?'

The men nodded once more.

Bill Brennan threw a five and smiled. Then Pete Boyle threw a six.

'I'll take the grey,' he said.

'Don't matter much,' said Brennan, scowling. 'I reckon it's the men that counts.'

'Then that's settled,' said Haynes, his hands flat on the table. 'Now we got what in law we would call a more contentious question. And I freely admit that the fact that it ain't in the contract is my responsibility and mine alone.'

He pulled on his nose. 'Let's say, gentlemen — let's just say for the sake of argument — that we get three dead heats, or one win each and a dead heat. Let's just say that, for argument's sake, tho' it's an unlikely possibility.'

Neither of the other two men responded. Haynes looked at each in turn, took a spotless white handkerchief from an inside pocket, withdrew his glasses and started to polish them.

'Now that would mean that we had a tie.'

'What are you suggesting, Judge?' said Brennan.

'I respectfully suggest that you throw now, here, for the Big Wet in the event of such a tie. That means we get rid of all arguments, all debate, should such an unlikely situation occur.'

'All right with me,' said Brennan.

'Me too,' said Boyle, shrugging.

'Okay,' said Haynes. 'Throw.'

This time Boyle rolled a two and could not suppress a groan. But Bill Brennan rolled a one. The advantage was with Boyle.

17

THE BIG RACE

11.20 a.m., the day of the big race. Main Street was no more than a tunnel — a tunnel of four thousand shouting, gesticulating men, women and children, extending through the town then thinning all the way out into the country, past Brennanville towards the Big Wet and back through Boyle City for a mile towards the base of El Diablo. Judge Haynes' officials were already posted at quarter-mile intervals all the way along the course.

It was a hard, cloudless seventy-eight degrees, perfect for sprinting but bad for distance-running. Moriarty's water-bags would be worth their weight in gold.

All that morning both teams had stayed in the cool of their hotel rooms, behind shuttered blinds, while below them on the hot streets a turmoil of dog-fights, freak-shows, cock-fights, wrestling and medicine shows competed for public attention. For once the 'Theatre of the West' was not on offer.

At 11.30 a.m. Moriarty stood up, stretched, went to the window and pulled up the blinds. The harsh glare of morning hit Buck and Billy Joe, lying eyes closed, but not asleep, on their beds.

The two younger men stretched like contented cats and sat up, yawning. Moriarty looked at them, half-naked in their long-johns. Not a pound of spare flesh between them: old Judge Haynes' Greeks would have recognised Buck and Billy

349

Joe for what they were — runners, Fast Men. For a moment he wondered what the Greeks would have made of him.

And yet he knew that he was in the best condition he had been for a long time, in some ways the best shape of his life. As he slipped on his brown moccasins he felt a cold spot at the pit of his stomach. He had not felt it for years, not since his last big races in St Louis four years back, and he was glad.

11.45 a.m: there was a sustained roar as the two teams walked through the crowds to the start, a white banner proclaiming 'Big Wet Challenge Race'. Boyle's team was led by Pete Boyle himself. They were all dressed English style, in white long-sleeved silk vests. The Indian and Josiah Headley were clad in white long-johns over their undershorts, with leather on the inner thigh because of the chafing involved in the riding, but Tulloch wore tartan knee-length shorts, with similar thigh-protection. All wore brown moccasins.

Moriarty's team, headed by Bill Brennan, had also gone for white silk vests, but with two differences. First, they bore across their chests a thick blue band; second, the surface of the silk had been perforated with holes — Moriarty's idea — in order to let cooling air to the skin. Buck and Billy Joe had greased the insides of their thighs underneath their riding long-johns, while their brown moccasins had also been greased inside, to reduce friction. Finally, each man wore a sweat band, something Moriarty had noted in his past races with Mexican distance runners.

For himself, he wore white silk shorts, wide at the thigh. Like Tulloch, he would not be riding for long stretches, but unlike the Scot he had decided against thigh-leathers. He had instead like Buck and Billy Joe greased his inner thighs with lard in preparation for the final lap, when there would be four miles of riding before the final one-mile run to the finish.

On the balcony of the Excelsior Hotel, directly above the start, Eleanor, Hettie and Mandy stood with Edwin Booth and Phineas T. Barnum and a white-haired Alan Cameron, Moriarty's father. Edwin Booth was troubled. All the New York insurance companies, mindful of Dr. Sutherland's words in the local press, had refused to cover Moriarty. If he died, there would be nothing for his dependants. He had not told Moriarty.

Eleanor's demure, smiling exterior belied her feelings. She had seen Moriarty only for a few moments the day before, when they had arrived in Yuta City. She had still not told him of her pregnancy, and the combination of a judicious wardrobe on her part and Moriarty's intense preoccupation with minute details had avoided any questions from him. It had been an easy pregnancy, and by all calculations there was a good fortnight to go before the birth, by which time they would all be safely back in New York.

But her plans had gone astray. Only an hour before, she had felt the first contractions, and now they were coming at ten-minute intervals.

She scanned the crowd below and the balconies on each side for Doctor Halliwell. She had met Halliwell, who had travelled up from San Rafael for the race the day before, and had confided in him about her condition. He had agreed to position himself nearby throughout the race, in case he was required. But he was nowhere to be seen. He couldn't have forgotten?

Judge Haynes, standing on a dais at the start, rang a bell for silence. The crowd of six thousand was soon hushed and for a moment all that could be heard was the light flapping of the banners above the starting-line.

'My Lords, Ladies and Gentlemen,' Haynes shouted. 'Today we see what may be the beginning of a new era. All of us, we've seen bad things in our time. Injun massacres, back-shootings, we've seen it all here in Yuta County. Now we have a dispute between two leading citizens, Bill Brennan and Pete Boyle, over a stretch of water, the Big Wet. They could've seen

351

it settled in violent fashion, guns brought in from outside, good men killed, good women widowed long before their time. But they didn't. They decided to settle it not with guns but with a foot-race. Only what we're about to see here ain't just a foot-race — no, I truly believe it's the start of modern times. And that's because Bill Brennan and Pete Boyle here' — he gestured to the men on either side of him — 'have agreed to have it settled in civilised fashion like the ancient Greeks did back in olden times, by a race man against man, on equal terms.'

He pointed down to Moriarty and Tulloch with Billy Joe and the Indian, already mounted, and paused.

'Now,' he said. 'So that the rules are the same for both teams, each team is allowed to carry a set of glasses with its horse so that they can see how the runner behind is faring. And each group of contestants can carry as much water as they want and pick up extra water-bottles from my officials at the base of El Diablo.'

Judge Haynes paused again.

'Gentlemen, it is a minute to midday on 20 October, 1878. Are you ready?'

Below him Moriarty, Tulloch, Billy Joe and the Indian nodded.

'Three laps of five miles, horse and man, two men from each team in the first two laps, only one in the final lap. The final furlong of the first lap *must* be run by the sprinters, as must the final quarter of the second by the quarter-milers, and the last mile of the third lap by the last two runners.'

He picked up a pistol from a small table at his side, cocked the gun and raised it above his head.

'Gentlemen, take your marks.'

Moriarty looked at Tulloch for the first time: lean and brown, with mutton-chop whiskers — the fastest miler on earth. Billy Joe and the Indian, poised on their mounts, looked sideways at each other without smiling.

'Get set. . .'

Again, only the flapping of flags could be heard.

The gun and the roar of the crowd were simultaneous. Standing alongside the Indian and Billy Joe, Headley and Buck slapped the rumps of their colleagues' mounts. The race was on.

Billy Joe went into an immediate lead, pushing his black mount through the corridor of noise along the street out towards Brennanville on the edge of town. Behind them, Moriarty and Tulloch ran easily side by side as if in another world. There was a long way to go. By the edge of the tent camp of Brennanville Billy Joe was all of fifty yards ahead, cutting through yelling supporters, while a furlong behind them Moriarty and Tulloch still plodded side by side.

Judge Haynes had been nothing if not thorough. All along the route he had posted Apaches equipped with mirrors; they would flash back mirror-messages to each other and so on to find the Apache chief, Grey Horse, standing on the roof of the Buena Vista, and from there to the street by megaphone. Thus the waiting crowd in Yuta City would never be out of touch with the progress of the race. Grey Horse's first report as the riders approached the Big Wet, with a mile completed, was that Billy Joe was a hundred yards ahead of the Indian, with the runners still trotting side by side about half a mile behind. The implications were clear: if he could retain that lead to the other side of El Diablo, then the final furlong of running into Yuta City would be irrelevant, for he would be too far ahead for the Indian to catch him.

Billy Joe's steed plunged into the waters of the Big Wet, now lying about two feet deep, and the black took the water clean, hardly interrupting its stride. Man and horse charged across the gap, churning up mud and pebbles, and Billy Joe grinned widely as the cooling spray thrown up by his mount fell over him. As they reached half-way he ventured a glance over his shoulder.

353

The Indian was just entering the water, over a hundred yards behind. When Billy Joe made the bank on the other side and galloped up across the shingle the Apache on duty was able to signal that the Texan was a clear one hundred and fifty yards up.

Half a mile back, Moriarty and Tulloch were hardly breathing, padding, flat-footed, side by side at six-minute mile pace along the grass centre of the cart-track. Their time had not yet come.

Billy Joe forced the black along the curving desert path, parallel to the river, seeing up ahead of him, in the heat-haze, the brown steepness of El Diablo. He needed to put as many yards as he could between himself and the Indian before the mile-long ascent, for he feared the climb.

Back at Yuta City, the mirrors told Brennan and Boyle, now standing together on the balcony of the Buena Vista, that Billy Joe had reached the base of El Diablo, with two miles covered, with a lead of close on 400 yards and was beginning to climb. The contest between Billy Joe and the Indian looked a foregone conclusion. There would be no sprint battle over the final furlong because of Billy Joe's superior horsemanship. A mile behind, Moriarty and Tulloch still stolidly plodded, locked together.

At the base of the mountain, Billy Joe made his only mistake. For instead of pacing himself up the rocky incline he immediately began to sprint up it, dragging behind him the lightly sweating black.

After three hundred yards his legs had gone, his thighs heavy and weak. He looked behind him down the mountain, gasping. The Indian was running up the slope at an easy, steady pace. Billy Joe resumed his running but each stride was an agony. Two hundred yards later his breathing went completely and he was reduced to a lurching stagger. There was over three-quarters of a mile of steep, uneven moun-tainside still to cover. The only hope was if his horse could cover more ground He hauled himself up on to the black and dug in his heels, forcing the beast up the mountain. Two hundred yards later the horse, faced with so steep an incline, could move no further. Billy Joe, cursing, dismounted and resumed his painful struggle towards the peak, holding on to the black's tail. Behind him, the Indian was gaining foot by foot, his resolve strengthening as he viewed his opponent's faltering progress.

Billy Joe's body screamed for release as he staggered and stumbled up the final furlong of mountain path, to the summit.

He hardly dared venture to look back, but at the peak he did. The Indian was only a couple of hundred yards behind, perhaps less, advancing remorselessly towards him. Billy Joe remounted, took a swig from his water-bottle, unwound his binoculars from the pommel and looked down the mountain on to the plain. Moriarty and Tulloch were now across the Big Wet. And Tulloch was leading — by about a hundred yards. So Billy Joe knew that he might have to leave the horse early, forty or fifty yards before the furlong marker, to give Moriarty an opportunity to catch up. He took another swig from the water-bottle on his saddle, took the reins and re-mounted, before zig-zagging down the mountain.

Moriarty knew that he had met his match in Alec Tulloch. The Scot was a perfect example of an animal made for distance-running; he covered the ground easily, lightly, as if its rough, uneven contours had been made for his feet and his alone. Even so, Moriarty was feeling good; at this point a hundred-yard lead was nothing.

Billy Joe hit the bottom of El Diablo fast, galloping past the judges and a tiny knot of whooping spectators assembled there.

He slapped the black's rump: just over a mile to the furlong flag where he was obliged to dismount.

He re-crossed the Big Wet at a shaky wooden bridge, walking the black across it. Then he re-mounted and made towards the mile flag, only a hundred yards beyond the bridge. He looked back as he passed the flag; the Indian was over three hundred yards behind. He would take the chance and dismount early, to give Moriarty more time on horseback. In any case, the extra few yards of running would help loosen his legs.

A hundred yards beyond the quarter-mile flag he forced his mount to a halt, dismounted and tied the black to a yucca tree. He pulled off his long-johns and trotted in his undershorts towards the furlong flag, now only about a hundred yards away, trying to loosen the riding stiffness from his legs. He could hear the Indian thundering behind him on the grey.

Billy Joe and the Indian came abreast of each other for the first time twenty yards short of the furlong marker. The Indian dismounted ahead of Billy Joe but did not tether his mount. He pulled off his long-johns as Billy Joe caught up with him, ten yards short of the furlong flag.

'Okay, Fast Man,' he said. 'Hit it!'

Fifty yards short of the tents of Boyle City, the Indian ran as if pursued by demons. Billy Joe Fixed himself on his right shoulder, a yard behind, as they raced through the tented corridor, with the Boyle followers screaming their support. The young Texan glued himself to his man. He had never run at such speed, his legs moving underneath him in a flowing blur. But the yard between them would not shorten. Behind them, Moriarty was still lagging Tulloch by a hundred yards as he approached the top of El Diablo. He was breathing hard from the climb, but was still feeling good. He hoped that Billy Joe had noted his position and left the black early to give him more riding time into Yuta City. Even a hundred yards of riding would suffice. Soon he was zig-zagging down the mountain, his feet finding a natural rhythm: below him lay Tulloch, the mile flag and a little knot of officials and supporters.

Billy Joe and the Indian now ran through a sea of noise, for them a corridor of effort, the disciplined reflexes of their years of running focused into the few square feet between the raging, desperate crowds on each side of the street. With fifty yards to go Billy Joe had closed to within a foot of the Indian: he had him, he could taste it

But the Indian was no talented amateur, running for saloon money. He was class; he held form and drilled on remorse-lessly, with not the slightest flicker of tension in his tawny frame. Billy Joe had pulled back another six inches at thirty yards to go; at twenty-five yards he was level. And still the Indian held. He held, and the two men were fused, their strides in perfect balance and rhythm.

As they hit the tape together, Billy Joe was certain he had got it. But beside him the Indian, too, thought that he had taken his man.

Moriarty, eighty yards behind Tulloch, found the horse where he had hoped it would be, tethered between the quarter-mile and furlong markers. The black was sweating heavily. Moriarty patted its muzzle, withdrew a cube of sugar from a pocket in the saddle and pressed it into the black's mouth. He mounted quickly and had ridden past Tulloch by the furlong marker, just as the Scot was about to mount. By the time he had reached the chaotic start at the Buena Vista, where Buck and Headley stood poised, Moriarty was into a sixty-yard lead.

'Billy Joe and the Indian, how'd it go?' he gasped as Buck began to mount. Buck shook his head as he straddled the sweating black.

'No one knows,' he shouted. 'The judge is sorting it out now.' He pointed above him to the dais where Billy Joe and the Indian stood with Haynes and his officials.

Moriarty looked up at Buck and nodded, then slapped the black's withers and Buck galloped off. As he did so Tulloch rode in behind him to a waiting Josiah Headley, through crowds that were threatening to engulf the central corridor. Buck rode out towards the tents of Brennanville, sixty yards in the lead, as above them sudden, dark storm clouds blotted out the sun, casting Main Street into shadow.

Somehow Eleanor, on the balcony of the Excelsior, had managed to stay erect at the start of the race, but when Moriarty had set off the pains became more frequent and she had to ask Edwin Booth to fetch her a chair, and Mandy to locate Halliwell. Then, as Moriarty set off on the second lap, she knew that it was no false alarm. Her waters broke. Eleanor stood stiffly and, beckoning to Hettie, made her way painfully back into the Excelsior to the bedroom behind her.

The rains came fast and sudden, just as they always did, lashing down in thick warm streams, turning to a pulp the thin grass of the cart-track, streaming across Moriarty's body, making his vest and shorts cling to his skin. Behind him he heard the steady inexorable slap of Tulloch's feet, the Scot now only thirty yards behind as they came within a quarter of a mile of the Big Wet.

The rainwater poured into his mouth and eyes, but somehow, reflexly, he kept the necessary breathing rhythm, slogging flat-footed, his feet splattering on the slippery grass. He was not tired, because the pace was slow. The real pain was still to come: both he and the man plodding behind him knew that.

Ahead, Buck galloped through the torrents of rain and by the Big Wet had added close on three hundred yards to the lead. But the Big Wet was no longer the tranquil stream Billy Joe and the Indian had faced; swollen by the rains, it was a foaming,

358

swirling rush of water which at its centre was over five feet deep. And still the rain poured down, while above there was a rumble of thunder, and lightning gashed the grey clouds. Buck pressed the black into the Big Wet and soon they had lost contact with the gravel base of the river and were swimming, borne downriver by the force of the current. Half-way across Buck felt the animal weaken, and its head twisted and turned as it swallowed water. He slithered off, still holding the reins, and swimming with one arm and using a side-stroke leg-kick, painfully half-swam, half-drifted through the choppy foam as they were pulled downstream. Then, suddenly, Buck's feet touched gravel. He wallowed through the final twenty yards on to the gravel bank, dragging the black behind him, and sat, gasping, on the bank.

He stood for a moment and checked his mount. The waters of the Big Wet actually seemed to have done the horse good, for it had been sweating heavily.

He took the field glasses which had been tied to the pommel and looked back across the Big Wet. Headley was over a hundred yards short of the river, riding strongly. Buck decided to give the black a breather, for he had a big lead, and a rested horse would serve Moriarty well on the final lap. He unwound his water-bottle, took a swig, then seized the reins and ran up on to a mound beyond the bank. As he did so the thunder cracked above, and soon it was impossible to see Moriarty and his opponent, the rain and mist blurring the lenses of his glasses. Buck decided to check again from the top of El Diablo, then make a decision on when to leave his horse. Certainly, as things stood, he could afford to give Moriarty a fair amount of leeway.

He slipped back on to his mount and galloped back upstream to pick up the path to El Diablo. It was looking good, but all now depended on how the decision had gone with Billy Joe.

Doc Halliwell had finally been located by Mandy in the El Dorado saloon, blind drunk. She had explained the emergency to Sweeney, the barman, and six cups of black coffee later Mandy and Sweeney had dragged a semi-conscious Halliwell to Eleanor's bedroom.

Halliwell sat propped in a chair in a corner of the room. He peered blearily around him.

Hettie looked desperately across the room at him from the bed, where Eleanor lay, the sweat beading her forehead.

'Tell us what to do,' she said. 'For God's sake, just tell us what to do."

Judge Haynes looked at the result slips.

All around him was anarchy, as the Mexicans in the crowd made finger-bets on the results while others simply hollered back and forth across the street. In all this chaos Haynes felt himself an oasis of justice and reason. At least the rain had stopped – ceasing as suddenly and dramatically as it had begun.

Finally, he was ready. He stepped forward to the front of the dais, but even before he had placed his hand on his bell to summon silence a hush moved like a wave up Main Street, all the way to Boyle City in the north and Brennanville in the south.

The Judge cleared his throat, then spoke into his megaphone. 'Final decision on the first stage,' he said. 'The judges score it one for Billy Joe Speed, one for the Indian, one for a dead heat.'

He paused, and only the dripping of rain from the roofs could now he heard.

'I rule it, and this is a final and irrevocable decision . . . a dead heat.'

Bill Brennan looked at Pete Boyle. Both his men would now have to win if the Big Wet was to be his.

Moriarty and Tulloch hit the Big Wet together, immediately drifting downstream, carried by the force of the current. The rain might have stopped, but the Big Wet, still swollen

360

with water, ran heavy and fast. The men swam side by side, occasionally touching bottom on the uneven surface of the river bed. Moriarty used a slow, strong breast-stroke, while Tulloch swam on his back, using a short, sculling stroke. To the Apache White Fox, viewing the runners from the top of El Diablo, the two men looked like insects drifting down river. The Indian flashed his message back to Yuta City. The runners were level.

Buck was approaching to the base of El Diablo, taking it easy on the horse and over a quarter of a mile up. He dismounted and started to run gently from the base of the mountain up its rapidly-drying clay and grit surface. He took the mountain as if it had been made for him, his stride and his breathing in perfect unison. It was hurting, true enough, but somehow he preserved that fine balance that enabled him to tolerate the pain, and somehow too this feeling transferred itself to the black, which trotted easily behind him up the mile of winding rocky incline.

As soon as he had reached the top Buck turned back and again took the glasses from the pommel. He looked down towards the Big Wet, and was immediately able to pick out Moriarty and Tulloch making their way across the river. But what he saw amazed him — for Moriarty appeared to be *pulling* Tulloch through the water. Buck shook his head and refocused the glasses. No, it was true: Moriarty was dragging Tulloch out of the river and up the bank.

Eleanor, sweat pouring down her face in streams, lay in her bedroom with Mandy and Hettie on either side of her. The contractions were coming ever faster. Doc Halliwell now stood above her, reeling, held up by Sweeney.

'Not long now,' said Hettie. 'Take it easy.'

Eleanor's breathing came in deep gulps. 'How's it going?' she gasped.

361

Mandy and Hettie, uncertain, looked at each other.

'The race,' groaned Eleanor.

Mandy swiftly picked up the field-glasses from the bedside table, walked to the verandah and pushed open the curtains.

She peered up the crowded street. There was no sign of the runners. She looked down at the crowd below, just as Billy Joe prepared to mount his horse and ride out towards El Diablo. He glanced up.

'Buck's ahead of his man,' he shouted. 'Moriarty twenty yards back.'

Mandy turned and re-entered the bedroom, closing the curtains behind her. She looked at Eleanor, lying on the bed.

The room was in disorder. Halliwell had again collapsed and was being dragged by Sweeney back to the chair in the corner. Hettie, holding back her tears, was desperately struggling with Eleanor's underclothes, while behind her a maid had entered, carrying towels and a bowl of hot water.

'Buck and Moriarty, they're both ahead,' Mandy lied.

Buck checked below him on Headley's position. The English runner was only a hundred yards or so away and coming up the mountain like an antelope. Buck quickly remounted and rode hard down the slope towards the foot of the mountain, where an Apache was relaying messages from another Indian above him on the mountain top.

As Buck approached the base of the mountain he saw that Billy Joe was there, mounted on a pinto, talking with an Apache.

Billy Joe saw him and waved. 'I got a dead heat,' he shouted, riding beside him. 'Me and the Indian.'

'What about Moriarty?' asked Buck.

'This Apache here says he's fifty yards or more down, so give him some time. Come off early.'

Buck nodded and the two men rode together towards the quarter-mile flag. Buck took a glance back. Headley was now at the base of the mountain, only a hundred and fifty yards away and coming fast. Buck slapped the black's rump and sped for the bridge across the Big Wet, Billy Joe alongside him He was still uncertain how much time he needed to give Moriarty.

Billy Joe pointed ahead to a flashing mirror, as they approached to within a furlong of the quarter-mile marker, where an Apache was relaying a signal on into town. The Indian shouted something to him as they passed. The Texan's response was immediate.

'*Now,*' he bellowed. 'They say Moriarty's a hundred yards or more back. Come off *now!*'

Buck dismounted, and started to run towards the quarter-mile marker where an official and some mounted supporters from both camps stood. He resisted the temptation to push hard; if he did, Headley would take him with ease. Behind him, the Yorkshireman saw what had happened and sucked in the yards between them, his grey foaming at the mouth.

Headley dismounted some fifty yards before the quarter-mile mark, ten yards behind Buck, who had jogged a furlong. The Yank had clearly made his first mistake, because the extra running must have sapped his legs, taken his breath. Barnsley would be avenged — and on the cowboy's own cabbage-patch, to boot. Josiah Headley tucked in behind Buck on the centre of the cart-track as on each side of the quarter-mile marker supporters shouted them on. This time he would have his man.

Moriarty did not regret what he had done, for Tulloch would have drowned if he had not pulled him through the Big Wet. It had been no great decision to take, for no race was that important, and every life undoubtedly was. They had said nothing when they had regained the opposite bank, but Tulloch had gravely shaken his hand. Then they had started up and begun to race again. By the base of the mountain

Tulloch was a hundred yards ahead and running up the slope like a stag.

From the balcony, Hettie Carr, using her glasses, peered down the crowded tunnel of Main Street. She knew by the roar of the crowd that Buck and Headley were closing in on the finish. Then she saw them just beyond the tents of Boyle City — Buck leading, but with Headley poised menacingly on his shoulder.

Josiah Headley made his hit with a furlong to go, taking an immediate two-yard lead. But Buck let him get away, keeping his steady, relaxed rhythm, holding his flow. Then, with a hundred yards to run, came that strange sound in his head telling him that it was now time. The only time.

'*Boomp*,' it said in his head, and Buck smiled.

'*Boomp*,' he said aloud, to Headley's back.

Buck went past Josiah Headley in a rush of legs, wiping out his lead and going into a five-yard advantage with fifty yards still to cover. But Headley had nothing in him left to offer. Buck did not simply take the tape, he smashed through it, and above him Bill Brennan danced a jig of joy, while Hertie Carr wept and wept again. She ran in to Eleanor with the news.

But Eleanor was well beyond listening. Halliwell had gained sufficient coherence to mumble advice to the girls, and Mandy now stood above Eleanor, who lay on the bed, legs spread, knees bent, groaning. Mandy dabbed the older woman's forehead with a wet towel, murmuring to her as she did so, 'Push, push.' As Hettie reached her the baby's head had begun to show.

A mile from the line, the horses were at best only trotting. Tulloch's grey was foaming at the mouth and Moriarty's black was also beginning to show signs of strain. The riders heard the roars ahead of them, but it was only at the end of the rapidly-narrowing corridor, almost blocked by hysterical crowds, that Moriarty was told by an hysterical Billy Joe that Buck had won — that there was all to play for.

As they passed the finish almost in line Judge Haynes fired the shotgun that signalled the final lap. There was little left in the horses. Their necks sweat-lashed and foam-specked, they slowly pushed themselves past the start line. Moriarty leaned forward, slipped another cube of sugar into the black's mouth and whispered into the animal's ear. It would now be down to running rather than horsemanship. Behind Moriarty and Tulloch, Buck and Billy Joe made their way back to the base of El Diablo, then started to walk up towards the summit. Moriarty was going to need all the moral support they could provide.

Judge Haynes was in his element. His marshals cleared a passage in the street as the Apache on the hotel roof told him that Moriarty and Tulloch had reached the Big Wet for the last time, Moriarty in a clear hundred-yard lead. He was pleased that there had been no questioning of his decision on the first stage by Brennan and Boyle; indeed, the two men had evinced no hostility to each other throughout. Somehow the foot-racing seemed to have totally dissipated the tension between them.

Billy Joe took the glasses from Buck.

'You saw 'em?' he said.

'Yup,' said Buck. 'Just crossed the Big Wet. Did I tell you what I saw Moriarty do last time round?'

'Yup,' said Billy Joe, peering through the glasses. 'It must be three times you've told me.'

He continued to look down into the scorched plain below the mountain.

'Moriarty's got it in the bag. A two-hundred-yard lead and going away. His horse is in much better shape too. If he picks up another couple of hundred yards on horseback between now and the mile flag, there's no way that Scotchman's ever going to catch him over the final mile, no matter how fast he runs.'

Billy Joe handed back the glasses, just as Moriarty reached the base of the mountain. Billy Joe put his hands to his mouth and shouted down the hill.

'Come on, Moriarty,' he roared. 'You ole has-been! Eyeballs out.'

'He can't hear you,' said Buck.

'I know,' said Billy Joe

The baby came easily, as if it were desperate to get into the world. It slipped out in a rush, grey and slimy. It had been only moments before a fully conscious Halliwell had cut the cord and Eleanor had her baby in her arms.

She kissed the baby's cheek, then looked up.

'How's he doing?' she asked.

Hettie rushed to the window and out on to the verandah.

She knew that the worst had happened when she saw Bill Brennan's face. Below them there was a hubbub in the crowd as the information also reached them. Brennan looked at her, his face a mask of disappointment and concern.

'The base of El Diablo, at the bridge,' he said. 'News is Moriarty's stopped. I'm sorry, ma'am. He must be clean run out.'

But at El Diablo Moriarty was far from finished.

He dismounted and inspected the black. Above him on El Diablo, just over a quarter of a mile away, Tulloch rode slowly down on the grey. Moriarty knew that his own horse was spent. It had been limping for the past half mile, and its sweat-lashed neck was white with foam. Moriarty slipped one last sugar-cube into the black's mouth as, at his side, an Apache flashed messages back to Yuta City. But Moriarty was unconcerned about either the Indian or the small knot of spectators crowded at the base of the mountain.

The black would undoubtedly make it to the mile post, just over half a mile away, for there was not an ounce of give-up in the beast. But enough was enough: the animal had given all he could ask of it, and more. Moriarty decided that he would run the rest of the route.

He patted the black's neck, and beckoned to the spectators to tend to the animal. Then he padded off, across the shaky wooden bridge bestriding the river, towards the mile post which he could already see, its vertical form distorted by the heat-haze.

He resisted the temptation to run hard. It would take over two minutes for Tulloch, on a tired horse, to catch up, and it would be foolish to panic. And the trot to the mile post would loosen him up, he reasoned, and would be the perfect platform for the final mile of hard running into Yuta City.

As he approached to within a furlong of the mile post, Moriarty could hear the hoofbeats behind him. He did not need to look back. The cadence of the hoofbeats told him that Tulloch's grey was not moving much faster than he was himself. The beast was done. All that was now left was the two men, as he had always hoped it would be.

Within fifty yards of the mile flag, at which stood two sombreroed officials, Moriarty could feel Tulloch almost on top of him, hear the wheezing and snorting of the exhausted grey. Tulloch dismounted twenty yards short of the flag, in line with Moriarty. Behind him, the grey collapsed in the brown dust, whinnying plaintively.

Tulloch said nothing as he took up his position on Moriarty's right, running with a fluid, springy stride. There was no perceptible increase in pace as they passed the mile marker — to the whoops of the two officials. Rather, there was a steady increase in tempo, as if the two men were running as one.

It took a quarter of a mile before Moriarty and Tulloch had run the stiffness engendered by the ride out of their limbs. Then they began to move free and fast, at the relaxed, loping pace of the miler, Tulloch, on Moriarty's right, ran with the spring and range of youth. He had been bewildered by Moriarty's decision not to stay on his horse at the base of the hill, almost as surprised as he had been when Moriarty had dragged him through the Big Wet on the second stage. But Tulloch came from the hard school of Scottish pedestrianism. He believed that Moriarty had blundered in running rather than riding, and with $30,000 at stake there was no way that the older man was going to be allowed to win.

Moriarty knew that he was gambling — not only with his own future but with everyone's future. But at the centre of his soul was a feeling that they had come to Yuta City to run, not to ride in a damn horse-race. This was a footrace, and it was on the running-path that it should be settled. He knew that there was little logic in his argument, but felt in his gut that he was right.

Moriarty had thought about it for months. There was only one way to beat Tulloch, and that was to lead from the start, pushing the pace, taking the finishing sting from the younger man's legs, for he knew that he could never match him in a sprint finish.

Beside him, on his left, he felt Buck and Billy Joe riding in a light canter, pacing him as he had required. He looked to Billy Joe and nodded. This was it: time to go.

Billy Joe and Buck broke their mounts into a trot and Moriarty upped the pace slowly, drawing away from Tulloch. At the half-mile stage he was five yards up, running through a thin corridor of spectators into the heat-haze towards the quarter-mile flag, his breathing now deep and harsh. A furlong from the quarter flag, at the fringe of Boyle City, they hit the first big crowds, with Moriarty still in a six-yard lead.

Eleanor had known that it was a boy even before she heard the baby's first cries. She had felt it as she gave the final, painful, immensely satisfying push that brought young Alan

Cameron into the world. The words of Hettie and Mandy had merely been confirmation of what she already knew. She held the slippery little bundle in her arms; its tiny cries somehow blocked out the noises from outside.

Tulloch had been disconcerted by the strength of the older man's commitment to run from the front. Moriarty was pushing hard, not perhaps at record pace, but well inside five minutes for a mile, fancy running after ten miles on foot and four on horseback.

Then, just before the quarter-mile marker, Tulloch made his hit. It was not a sudden, conclusive hit — his legs did not have the snap for that. Rather, it was a gradual opening of the stride, as both runners entered the human tunnel that led to Yuta City. With three hundred and fifty yards to go Tulloch passed Moriarty, and there was an 'Ole!' from the crowd.

Moriarty hung in. Tulloch was some two yards up and Moriarty's eyes bored into a sweat-stain on the Scot's back. That was all he could see, as his breath raged in his throat, and he felt his hips begin to drop. Moriarty sensed that he was losing his man, sensed the umbilical cord which linked them start to stretch as fatigue reached ever deeper into him. The sweat-stain on Tulloch's back had become a grey-white blur, and for the first time he felt old and weary, and his legs began to buckle as the accumulated hurt of fifteen miles of running and riding bit deep into his core. His breathing came in deep, rasping gulps as he struggled to find the reflexes that would enable him, not to win, but simply to finish with pride.

He glued his eyes to Tulloch's vest, straining to retain that thread of contact essential if there were to be the faintest hope of victory, desperately trying to prevent Tulloch's lead moving from the possible to the impossible. Through his fatigue something told him that he had never run so well, never dug so deep; but Tulloch remained there, now eight yards ahead, his lead appearing to grow longer with every stride.

But Alec Tulloch was also feeling the pace. It was not the running but the riding and the hills that had taken their toll. It was strange: his breathing was still strong and solid, but he could feel himself sink, his legs slowly bow as if he were bearing some massive weight. Tulloch was where he had never been before, and was struggling to find his bearings.

Eight yards behind, with less than a furlong to go, Moriarty was holding firm, but there was nothing more left, only the reflexes of quarter of a century of footracing. He ran flat-footed and bow-legged, his stride a parody of the fluent movement of a few minutes before.

Tulloch went suddenly. With one hundred and twenty yards to go and ten yards up he fell, his right foot reaching for a surface that was no longer there, landing flat on his face in the soft brown dirt of Main Street. He lay spreadeagled, his diaphragm working desperately against the ground in its efforts to maintain his breathing. Tulloch was not fatigued: it went beyond that, into a world where fatigue was merely a stepping-stone to a great, dark, endless pain.

Moriarty did not see the fall. Tulloch, a white blur in front of him, simply vanished from his sight. Then he himself was on the ground, the brown gravel of the street mixed with blood from broken lips. He had fallen over the prostrate Tulloch and the two men lay side by side.

Immediately, William Bunn was above Tulloch. Careful not to lay hands upon his man, he bellowed, begged and pleaded with him. Tulloch slowly turned on to his front and, as in a dream, got up on to one knee, then the other, facing in the direction of the finish, his eyes unfocused, sweat streaming in channels over his dust-covered face.

Alongside Moriarty, Buck and Billy Joe dismounted. Buck bent down and hissed his name into his ear. Moriarty did not respond, his breath throwing up little puffs of dust on the surface of the street.

'Them that don't give up is never beat,' said Buck. Moriarty looked sideways at him, a tear trickling down his right cheek.

Billy Joe did not bend down but stood above Moriarty. He too was in tears. For he could see, as could Buck, Moriarty's condition — arms and legs raw and bloody, ripped by yucca and cactus, a body out of which sweat streamed from every pore. Perhaps, for the first time, Moriarty was no longer a foot-racer, no longer even an athlete.

Billy Joe did not notice, as he stood above Moriarty, the silence that now fell on Main Street, did not see that the three of them were somehow suspended in time, as in some faded daguerreotype.

'Them that don't give up is *never* beat,' he roared, pointing up the street.

Moriarty lifted his head, his face a mask of dust. Slowly he levered himself to his knees. He looked sideways at Tulloch, who rested on hands and knees, impervious to the ravings of Bunn above him.

Moriarty staggered to his feet, advanced a few steps then fell on all fours. He shook his head, as if trying to free it of all losing thoughts, then again got to his feet, speaking to himself.

'Never beat,' he mumbled, wobbling towards the tape in a pathetic parody of a running action.

He looked towards the finish, only a hundred yards away. Surprisingly, all was now clear, the tape thick and white, the way it had always been. Somehow, burrowing into a memory of running, the reflexes of a quarter of a century of compe-tition, Moriarty started to sprint, talking to himself all the while. True, it was not the sprint of a Fast Man, but somehow it was running, class running, the running of a master of his craft.

Moriarty pushed on through and beyond his pain, ignoring it as if it were happening to someone else. He ran with legs that he had no right to expect to run, against the dictates of a body chemistry which no longer made sense, against every-thing in him which told him to stop. Moriarty ran the final hundred yards of his athletic career up the narrow corridor of Yuta City, above and beyond himself. As he hit the tape, Buck and Billy Joe were there to catch him as he fell.

'The Theatre of the West, boys,' he mumbled through split lips. 'You just saw it.'

EPILOGUE

Bill Brennan ignored the result of the race. He agreed with Boyle that the water rights of the Big Wet would always be shared, both by them and their heirs, and signed a document to that effect, witnessed and notarised by Judge Haynes, on the morning of 21 October, 1878.

Moriarty showed no ill-effects from his great run and lived to the age of 82, though he never again raced in competition. With Eleanor Cameron he duly set up the Theatre of the West in January 1879 at the Jenny Lind Theatre, San Francisco. Buck Miller and Billy Joe Speed, prompted by Mandy and Hettie, resisted attempts by P. T. Barnum to hold a world-wide series of match-races against Headley and the Indian and instead joined Moriarty and Eleanor in their professional venture.

In 1892, Billy Joe Speed set up his own theatre, the Olympic, in Denver, and the following year Buck Miller the Coliseum in Albuquerque. In 1908 their Olympia Productions was one of the first modern movie production companies.

In 1893, Moriarty met a visiting Frenchman, the Baron Pierre de Coubertin, in New York, and advised him on the creation of a new sports festival, the Olympic Games. Four years later, in 1896, Moriarty and Eleanor and their son Ian, Buck and Billy Joe and their wives, attended the first modern Olympic Games in Athens.